"*The Clan would almost be better* off if something happened to Breezepelt," Gorsetail meowed. "Like a badger took care of him or something."

Crowfeather couldn't suppress a gasp of shock.

The four gossiping cats halted, turning to look at him with expressions of horror on their faces.

"Uh . . . Crowfeather . . . ," Gorsetail began.

Crowfeather stalked past them with his head down. His pelt grew hot with anger as he felt the gazes of his Clanmates piercing him like wasp stings.

It was horrible to hear them talking about his son like that. But the worst of it was . . . he couldn't disagree with them.

WARRIORS

SUPER EDITIONS

WARRIORS
SUPER EDITION

CROWFEATHER'S TRIAL

ERIN HUNTER

HARPER

An Imprint of HarperCollinsPublishers

Special thanks to Cherith Baldry

Crowfeather's Trial

Copyright © 2018 by Working Partners Limited

Series created by Working Partners Limited

Map art © 2018 by Dave Stevenson

Interior art © 2018 by Owen Richardson

All rights reserved. Printed in the United States of America.

No part of this book may be used or reproduced in any manner whatsoever without written permission except in the case of brief quotations embodied in critical articles and reviews. For information address HarperCollins Children's Books, a division of HarperCollins Publishers, 195 Broadway, New York, NY 10007.

www.harpercollinschildrens.com

Library of Congress Control Number: 2018945995

ISBN 978-0-06-269878-0

20 21 22 23   PC/BRR   10 9 8 7 6 5 4 3

❖

First paperback edition, 2019

ALLEGIANCES

WINDCLAN

LEADER

ONESTAR—brown tabby tom

DEPUTY

HARESPRING—brown-and-white tom
APPRENTICE, SLIGHTPAW (black tom with flash of white on his chest)

MEDICINE CAT

KESTRELFLIGHT—mottled gray tom

WARRIORS

(toms and she-cats without kits)

CROWFEATHER—dark gray tom
APPRENTICE, FEATHERPAW (gray tabby she-cat)

NIGHTCLOUD—black she-cat
APPRENTICE, HOOTPAW (dark gray tom)

GORSETAIL—very pale gray-and-white she-cat with blue eyes

WEASELFUR—ginger tom with white paws

LEAFTAIL—dark tabby tom with amber eyes
APPRENTICE, OATPAW (pale brown tabby tom)

EMBERFOOT—gray tom with two dark paws

HEATHERTAIL—light brown tabby she-cat with blue eyes

BREEZEPELT—black tom with amber eyes

FURZEPELT—gray-and-white she-cat

CROUCHFOOT—ginger tom

LARKWING—pale brown tabby she-cat

SEDGEWHISKER—light brown tabby she-cat

BERRYNOSE—cream-colored tom

MOUSEWHISKER—gray-and-white tom

CINDERHEART—gray tabby she-cat

IVYPOOL—silver-and-white tabby she-cat with dark blue eyes

LIONBLAZE—golden tabby tom with amber eyes

DOVEWING—pale gray she-cat with green eyes

ROSEPETAL—dark cream she-cat
APPRENTICE, MOLEPAW (brown-and-cream tom)

POPPYFROST—tortoiseshell-and-white she-cat
APPRENTICE, LILYPAW (tabby she-cat with white patches)

BRIARLIGHT—dark brown she-cat, paralyzed in her hindquarters

BLOSSOMFALL—tortoiseshell-and-white she-cat

BUMBLESTRIPE—very pale gray tom with black stripes
APPRENTICE, SEEDPAW (golden-brown she-cat)

QUEENS

BRIGHTHEART—white she-cat with ginger patches (mother to Snowkit, a fluffy white tom-kit; Amberkit, a pale ginger she-kit; and Dewkit, a gray-and-white tom-kit)

DAISY—cream, long-furred cat from the horseplace

ELDERS   **PURDY**—plump tabby, former loner with a gray muzzle

SHADOWCLAN

LEADER   **BLACKSTAR**—large white tom with jet-black forepaws

DEPUTY   **ROWANCLAW**—ginger tom

MEDICINE CAT   **LITTLECLOUD**—very small brown tabby tom

WARRIORS   **CROWFROST**—black-and-white tom

TAWNYPELT—tortoiseshell she-cat with green eyes
APPRENTICE, GRASSPAW (pale brown tabby she-cat)

OWLCLAW—light brown tabby tom

SCORCHFUR—dark gray tom

TIGERHEART—dark brown tabby tom

FERRETCLAW—cream-and-gray tom
APPRENTICE, SPIKEPAW (dark brown tom)

PINENOSE—black she-cat

STOATFUR—skinny ginger tom

POUNCETAIL—brown tabby tom

QUEENS   **SNOWBIRD**—pure-white she-cat

DAWNPELT—cream-furred she-cat

ELDERS   **SNAKETAIL**—dark brown tom with tabby-striped tail

WHITEWATER—white she-cat with long fur, blind in one eye

RATSCAR—brown tom with long scar across his back

OAKFUR—small brown tom

SMOKEFOOT—black tom

KINKFUR—dark gray tabby she-cat with long fur that sticks out at all angles

IVYTAIL—black, white, and tortoiseshell she-cat

RIVERCLAN

LEADER

MISTYSTAR—gray she-cat with blue eyes

DEPUTY

REEDWHISKER—black tom
APPRENTICE, LIZARDPAW (light brown tom)

MEDICINE CATS

MOTHWING—dappled golden she-cat

WILLOWSHINE—gray tabby she-cat

WARRIORS

MINTFUR—light gray tabby tom

MINNOWTAIL—dark gray-and-white she-cat

MALLOWNOSE—light brown tabby tom
APPRENTICE, HAVENPAW (black-and-white she-cat)

GRASSPELT—light brown tom

DUSKFUR—brown tabby she-cat

MOSSPELT—tortoiseshell-and-white she-cat with blue eyes
APPRENTICE, PERCHPAW (gray-and-white she-cat)

SHIMMERPELT—silver she-cat

LAKEHEART—gray tabby she-cat

HERONWING—dark gray-and-black tom

ICEWING—white she-cat with blue eyes

QUEENS

PETALFUR—gray-and-white she-cat

ELDERS

POUNCETAIL—ginger-and-white tabby tom

PEBBLEFOOT—mottled gray tom

RUSHTAIL—light brown tabby she-cat

CROWFEATHER'S
TRIAL

GREENLEAF
TWOLEGPLACE

TWOLEG NEST

TWOLEG PATH

TWOLEG PATH

CLEARING

SHADOWCLAN
CAMP

SMALL
THUNDERPATH

HALFBRIDGE

GREENLEAF
TWOLEGPLACE

HALFBRIDGE

CAT VIEW

ISLAND

STREAM

RIVERCLAN
CAMP

HORSEPLACE

ABANDONED
TWOLEG NEST

MOONPOOL

OLD THUNDERPATH

THUNDERCLAN
CAMP

ANCIENT OAK

LAKE

WINDCLAN
CAMP

BROKEN
HALFBRIDGE

TWOLEGPLACE

THUNDERPATH

KEY
To The
CLANS

THUNDERCLAN

RIVERCLAN

SHADOWCLAN

WINDCLAN

STARCLAN

NORTH

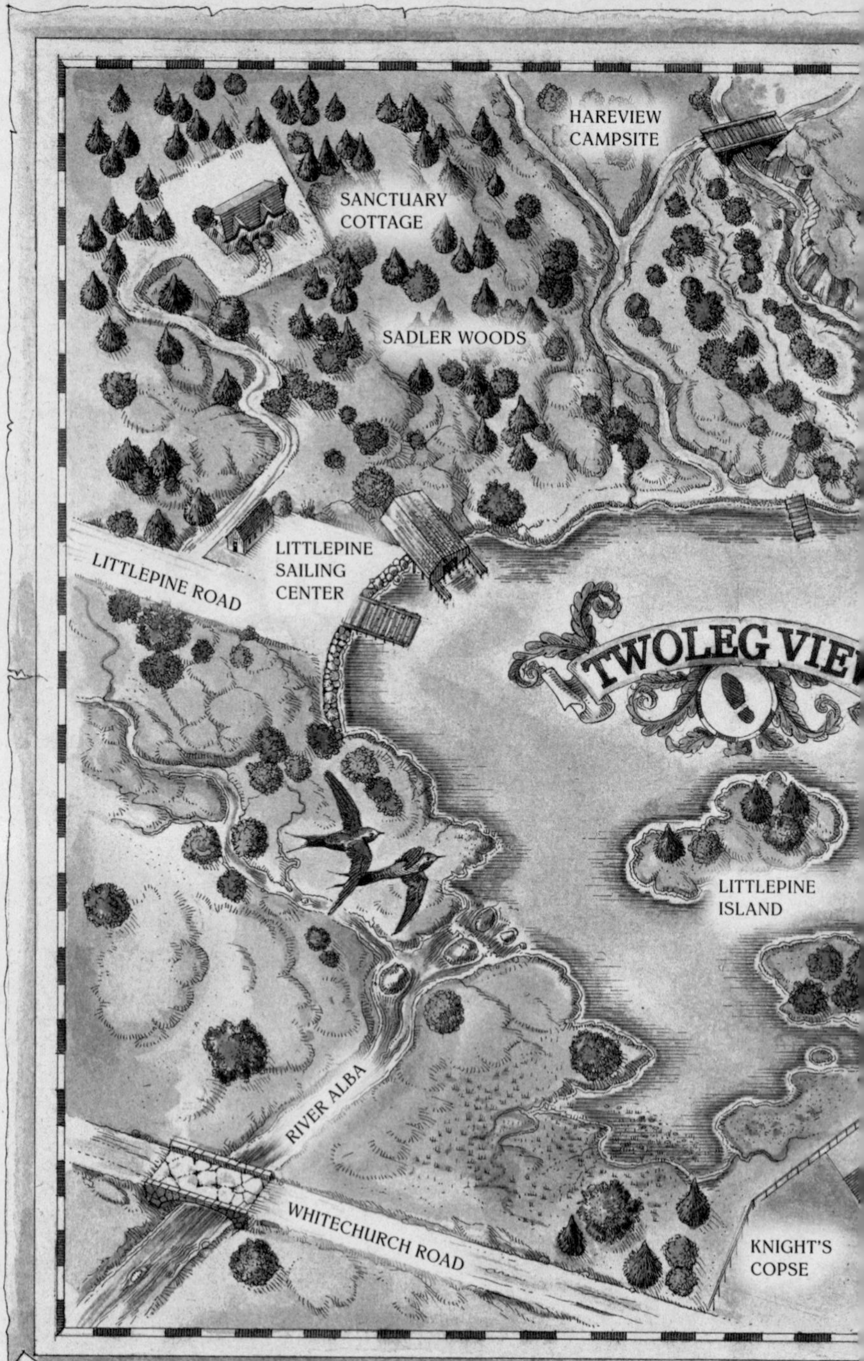
HAREVIEW CAMPSITE
SANCTUARY COTTAGE
SADLER WOODS
LITTLEPINE SAILING CENTER
LITTLEPINE ROAD
TWOLEG VIE
LITTLEPINE ISLAND
RIVER ALBA
WHITECHURCH ROAD
KNIGHT'S COPSE

PROLOGUE

Crowpaw pressed himself back into the crevice. He winced at the sharp points of rock jabbing into his fur; they told him the space was too shallow to shelter him. He let out a cry of terror as he gazed up at the looming head and shoulders of Sharptooth, the huge lion-cat. Sharptooth stooped over him, scraping at the rock with one paw's massive talons. Moonlight filtering through the waterfall cast a glow on his face, showing Crowpaw lips drawn back in a cruel snarl, curved fangs, and jaws dripping with drool. Sharptooth's rancid breath swept over Crowpaw, and his eyes glared down, savage with hunger.

I can't believe I'm going to die like this! Crowpaw thought desperately. Not after all we've been through! We've left our homes, traveled so far, and faced so many dangers. We met the badger Midnight and discovered a new destiny for our Clans. I want to be part of that. . . . I want to be part of our future! But now it's over. . . .

Crowpaw could hear the wailing of the Tribe cats and see skinny forms perched on ledges high above the cave floor in shades of gray and brown. His panicked gaze sought out Feathertail, and his heart warmed when he spotted her gray pelt. She was crouching beside her brother, Stormfur, on a ledge just under the roof.

She is so beautiful! I don't want to die before I have the chance to. . . .

Then, somehow, above the terrified cries of the other cats and the snarling of Sharptooth, Crowpaw heard Feathertail.

"I can hear the voices clearly now," she meowed. "This is for me to do."

For a moment Crowpaw's fear was banished by confusion. What voices?

Silver flashed in the moonlight as Feathertail launched herself from the ledge, hurling herself at one of the pointed stones that hung down from the roof. For a few heartbeats she clung there, digging her claws into the rock.

Crowpaw heard Stormfur yowl, "No!"

He watched in horror, forgetting his own danger, as the stone began to split away from the roof with a sickening crack. It couldn't support Feathertail's weight and was about to collapse. "Feathertail!" he yowled. "No! Get down from there!"

But it was impossible for Feathertail to escape. With a dull grinding noise, the stone broke away and plummeted down. Feathertail was still clinging to it, falling straight toward Sharptooth. Crowpaw could hardly bear to watch, yet he couldn't tear his gaze from the scene.

The lion-cat looked up; his snarl changed to a scream of pain as the spike thrust its way into his neck. He fell to the ground, writhing in agony, as Feathertail tumbled from the spike, hitting the cave floor beside him. For a moment Crowpaw was frozen with shock as he gazed at the gentle she-cat. Her eyes were closed. Crowpaw couldn't tell whether she was breathing. Is she alive?

Stormfur hurtled down the rock toward his sister's side. Beside them the lion-cat twitched for a few heartbeats, then gave a massive shudder and was still.

Sharptooth was dead.

"Feathertail?" Stormfur whispered.

Crowpaw stumbled out of his crevice, still shaking, and crouched beside the two RiverClan cats. "Feathertail?" he rasped, hardly able to keep his voice steady. "Feathertail, are you okay?"

Though Feathertail did not respond, Crowpaw could now see the faint rise and fall of her chest. "She's alive!" he mewed, his pads prickling with hope.

"She'll be fine." Stormfur's voice cracked, as if he didn't believe what he was saying. "She's got to be. She . . . she has a prophecy to fulfill."

But a terrible fear was growing inside Crowpaw. What if Feathertail just did fulfill the prophecy? It had spoken of a silver cat who would save them from a terrible lion-cat. Crowpaw had never imagined that it would actually come true—or that the silver cat would be Feathertail. But did that mean her story ended here?

What if she never goes home to help lead her Clan to its new territory?

He crept forward until his nose touched Feathertail's shoulder. Breathing deeply, he let her sweet scent flow through him, and gently began to lick her ruffled pelt. He thought about the future he had dreamed of, where they found a way to be together even though they were from different Clans. "Wake up, Feathertail," he mewed. "Please wake up."

He let out a gasp as Feathertail's eyes fluttered open. She looked warmly at Crowpaw, then turned her head slightly to look up at Stormfur.

"You'll have to go home without me, brother," she murmured. "Save the Clan!"

"Feathertail," he croaked through a painful lump in his throat. Then her head shifted again, her gaze focusing once more on Crowpaw. He trembled at the intense love he saw in her blue eyes. *I don't deserve her,* he thought. *I never deserved her.*

"Think you have nine lives, do you?" Feathertail whispered. *"I saved you once. . . . Don't make me save you again."*

"Feathertail . . . Feathertail, no!" As she weakened before him, Crowpaw felt as if a huge weight were crushing his chest, so that he could hardly speak. *"Don't leave me."*

"I won't." The words were breathed out so faintly that Crowpaw could scarcely hear them. *"I'll always be with you. I promise."*

Then Feathertail's eyes closed, and she did not move or speak again.

Crowpaw turned to look at Sharptooth's body, bloody and growing cold. Feathertail had killed the lion-cat, fulfilling the Tribe's prophecy, but nothing about it felt right. What good was saving Crowpaw and the Tribe if Feathertail had to give her life to do it? He flung his head back and let out a wordless wail, which echoed off the cave walls, an outpouring of all his love and anguish. Then darkness swirled around him and he crouched beside Feathertail in a tight knot of grief. He felt as if all the light in the world had been snuffed out. How could he live with this loss?

Voices drifted past him in the dark: He heard Stormfur, blaming himself for bringing Feathertail back to the Tribe. He turned his head to look up at the RiverClan cat. *"It's my fault."* Crowpaw's voice was a hoarse whisper. *"If I'd refused to come back to the cave, she would have stayed with me."*

"No . . . ," Stormfur said softly, reaching out to Crowpaw, who could only bow his head.

He could hear Brook and Stoneteller trying to comfort Stormfur, but there would be no comfort for Crowpaw now—maybe not ever.

"The Tribe of Endless Hunting spoke truly," said Stoneteller. *"A silver cat has saved us all."*

Yes, *thought Crowpaw,* but no cat saved her, and now the Clans will never be the same. *Never. The word echoed around Crowpaw until he felt his heart would break.* We'll never be mates or have kits together. I'll never see her again. Never . . .

Crowfeather woke, shivering. His pelt was soaked with early-morning dew, but that wasn't the reason for the chill that struck deep within him. It had been countless moons since Feathertail had died killing Sharptooth, but in his dream it had felt as if it were happening all over again. The pain of losing Feathertail felt like a fresh wound.

I thought I would never love another cat, he thought. *And yet now . . .*

He glanced down at the small tabby-and-white she-cat who was curled up beside him underneath the thornbush. His grief for Feathertail had consumed him, and it had taken him many moons to find the path that would lead him out of darkness. Now he could not understand how Leafpool had made her way into his heart, filling him with more joy than he had ever hoped to feel again.

Like Feathertail, she was a cat from another Clan. But unlike Feathertail, Leafpool was a medicine cat, and had vowed never to take a mate. This made their love even more impossible than his first. *I certainly know how to make things complicated,* Crowfeather thought with a wry twitch of his whiskers. The only way he and Leafpool could be together was to make a huge sacrifice—to leave the Clans and everything they had ever known.

But they had decided to take the risk. *Amazingly,* Crowfeather thought, watching Leafpool's chest rise and fall, *we could have had a future together.*

Leafpool had come with him willingly, heading out into unknown territory. But then, the night before, they had met the wise badger Midnight, who had told them that savage badgers were gathering to attack the Clans. The battle would be fierce and bloodstained; cats would die. Leafpool had said nothing about returning, and neither had he, but as he watched her sleeping form, Crowfeather knew what she would say to him when she woke. Her dedication and her loyalty to ThunderClan were part of why he loved her.

And that meant their dream of being together would soon come to an end.

"Oh, Leafpool," he sighed aloud. "I would have taken care of you until my last breath."

As if his words had disturbed her, Leafpool awoke, leaping to her paws, her eyes wild and distraught. "Crowfeather!" she gasped. "I can't stay here. We have to go back." She looked at him, her wide eyes full of regret.

Crowfeather raised his head. "I know," he mewed, sadness rising inside him like a flooding stream. "I feel the same way. We have to go and help our Clans."

He could see the relief in her eyes as she pressed her muzzle against his. He wished they could stay that way forever, but much too soon she let out a purr and meowed, "Let's go."

As they trekked across the moorland toward home, though neither one of them said it, Crowfeather realized that he was losing another mate—not as terribly as he had lost Feathertail, but just as finally. Leafpool was choosing to return to her Clan because they needed her, needed their medicine cat, and that meant that Crowfeather's only option was to reunite with WindClan. He imagined what it would feel like, walking back into a camp he'd never expected to see again. Everything would seem foreign to his eyes; he himself would feel like a stranger.

If they'll even have me, he thought bitterly. *They all know where I went, and why, and they'll blame me for leaving. There'll be questions about my loyalty, that's for sure.*

"I'll never forget what we shared," Leafpool murmured as they approached the stepping stones that led across the stream into ThunderClan territory. There was grief in her face, but a set determination that was stronger.

"Nor will I," Crowfeather responded. Halting at the edge of the stream, he pressed himself against Leafpool's side, and parted his jaws to taste her scent for the last time. *I'll miss her so much,* he thought. *Her softness, and her strength and courage. And how we could play together as if we were no older than kits again. . . .*

Leafpool pushed her nose into his shoulder fur. Her amber eyes were full of love for him.

But it's not enough. She doesn't love me enough. Her heart lies here, with her Clan. She's so loyal. . . . I just wish that she could be as loyal to me.

"Good-bye, Crowfeather," Leafpool whispered. "I'll see you again when all this is over."

"What do you mean, 'good-bye'?" Crowfeather made his voice harsh. Otherwise he would have started wailing like a lost kit. "I'm not leaving you when there are hostile badgers around."

"But you need to warn WindClan," Leafpool protested.

"I know, and I will. But I'll see you to your camp first. It won't take long."

Leafpool didn't argue with him. But as he followed her across the stepping stones and into the trees, Crowfeather knew that he was only prolonging their anguish.

That's it, he thought as he raced along. As Leafpool disappeared into the thick undergrowth, he knew that he would never be with her this way again. They would cross paths during Gatherings and other Clan business, but they'd have to keep their distance, as if they'd never loved each other at all. He couldn't bear to imagine how much that would hurt. He couldn't think of anything worse. If he was lucky, maybe a badger would tear him apart.

If I do survive, he thought, *I'm finished with love.* It only ended in pain and loss, an ache in his belly as if he'd swallowed jagged stones. *From now on,* he vowed as he forced himself to follow Leafpool, *I'll only worry about my duty to my Clan. No more love—not ever again.*

CHAPTER 1

❧

Wind swept across the moor, ruffling Crowfeather's gray-black fur as he stood among the rest of his Clanmates at the crest of the hill. They were gathered in a ragged circle around their Clan leader, Onestar, who stood beside a small pile of stones. Crowfeather remembered what hard work it had been to find the right number of smoothly rounded stones and push them up the slope to the place they had chosen. His paws still ached from the effort, and he raised one forepaw to lick a scrape on his pad.

But it was worth it, to do this.

"We will honor our Clanmates who fell in the Great Battle," Onestar meowed. "Each of these stones stands for a fallen warrior, so that we will never forget their sacrifice. From now on, a patrol will visit this place every day, to repeat the names of those who died and to give thanks."

Yes, Crowfeather thought. *That way we'll never forget their courage. They saved us from the Dark Forest.*

The Clan leader paused for a heartbeat, then dipped his head toward the brown-and-white tom standing next to him. "As our new deputy, Harespring," he continued, "you should put the last stone in place."

9

Crowfeather stiffened, making a conscious effort not to let his shoulder fur bristle as he watched Harespring thrust the final stone across the springy moorland grass and slide it neatly into the gap left for it.

"This stone is for Ashfoot," Harespring mewed solemnly. "She served her Clan well."

Crowfeather felt a fresh pang of grief for his dead mother, whose throat had been ripped out by the claws of a Dark Forest warrior, and realized that his pain was mingled with disappointment that he hadn't been chosen as the Clan's new deputy. He was aware of some of his Clanmates casting sidelong glances at him, as if they had expected it, too. After all, he was a senior warrior, and one of the chosen cats who had traveled to the sun-drown-place to meet with Midnight. *Both my parents were deputies,* he thought, *and I've given up more for my Clan than any cat . . . but I suppose I never will be deputy. Well, Onestar wanted to send a message by choosing a Dark Forest cat, and however mouse-brained that message may be—it's sent.*

He suppressed a sigh, admitting to himself that this was a strange time for the Clans, as they tried to come together after the Great Battle, almost a moon ago. *It's like Kestrelflight trying to heal a wound just by slapping cobweb on it, without cleaning it out or using any herbs.*

Crowfeather narrowed his eyes as he gazed at his Clan leader. Onestar looked relaxed, content, his amber eyes gleaming—as if he truly believed that WindClan was united again. But Crowfeather knew it didn't always work like that. And maybe that was another reason why he hadn't been chosen.

He was incapable of pretending that life could ever be that simple.

When the last stone was in position, Kestrelflight, the WindClan medicine cat, padded up to stand beside the pile, looking out over the horizon. The wind ruffled his mottled gray pelt, but his voice rang out clearly across the moor. "We feel the loss of all our dead Clanmates, but we know that they have been made welcome in StarClan. May they have good hunting, swift running, and shelter when they sleep."

He dipped his head in deepest respect, then moved back into the crowd of his Clanmates. A ripple of agreement passed through the Clan, voices hushed with the solemnity of the moment.

Onestar began to speak again, but it was hard for Crowfeather to concentrate when he spotted his son Breezepelt hovering on the fringe, his expression angry and uncomfortable. *Like he always looks,* Crowfeather thought bitterly. His mind drifted inexorably back to the Great Battle, especially how he'd had to sink his claws into Breezepelt's shoulders and haul him back to keep him from killing his half brother Lionblaze.

He knew that Onestar had forgiven Breezepelt, as well as all the other cats who had trained in the Dark Forest. They had each taken a new oath of loyalty to WindClan. But Crowfeather knew that the rest of the Clan wasn't as eager to forgive as their Clan leader, and the cat they were finding it hardest to forgive was Breezepelt. Even now he could see suspicious looks directed toward his son and knew that he would hear whispers once they had returned to camp.

All the other Dark Forest warriors had come to their senses and fought beside their Clan—all except Breezepelt. He had actually stood *with* the Dark Forest; he had fought on their side.

It would be many moons before *that* was forgotten.

As Crowfeather watched his son, Breezepelt turned his head, and for a heartbeat their gazes locked. Breezepelt's gaze was dark with anger and confusion. Then Crowfeather glanced away, not wanting Breezepelt to see the mixture of guilt and disgust he could feel in his eyes.

How did I fail so badly as a father? How did I raise a flea-brain who grew up to become a traitor to WindClan? He's as much use as a dead fox.

Onestar drew his speech to an end, and with the ceremony over, the Clan began breaking up into smaller groups, making their way down the hill toward the camp. Crowfeather noticed that the other Dark Forest cats—Harespring, Larkwing, Furzepelt, and Whiskernose—were heading down together, as if they still felt that they didn't belong with the rest of their Clanmates.

I was afraid of that, Crowfeather thought. Onestar had made Larkwing a warrior because of her bravery in the Great Battle, and given the injuries Whiskernose had suffered in that same battle, Onestar had let him retire with honor to the elders' den. And Harespring was the new deputy. But none of that mattered if the rest of their Clan wouldn't accept them. *Why can't Onestar see that? Does he have bees in his brain?*

Crowfeather made his way back alone, padding along just

behind a cluster of his Clanmates.

"I can't believe it!" Gorsetail exclaimed. "Onestar tells us all to remember the fallen warriors, but he's fine with the traitors who killed them staying in the Clan."

"Hey, that's not fair," Crouchfoot protested, his ginger pelt bristling as the new warrior turned to his former mentor. "WindClan cats didn't kill their Clanmates. Most of the cats who trained with the Dark Forest turned against them when they found out what was really going on."

"*Most*," Leaftail repeated with a lash of his tabby tail. "Not all."

Moving as one, the cats turned to stare at Breezepelt, who was padding past them with Heathertail at his side.

"I know what you mean," murmured Gorsetail. "It doesn't seem right that Breezepelt is still here. I know Onestar thinks he isn't a traitor because he didn't try to kill a *WindClan* cat, but isn't fighting on the side of the Dark Forest just as bad? How can we ever trust him again?"

"I never will," Leaftail asserted confidently.

"The Clan would almost be better off if something happened to Breezepelt," Gorsetail meowed. "Like a badger took care of him or something."

Crowfeather couldn't suppress a gasp of shock. *Great StarClan, are they featherbrained?* He wasn't sure that he trusted Breezepelt, but he couldn't believe he had heard a cat wishing death upon a warrior from her own Clan.

The four gossiping cats halted, turning to look at him with expressions of horror on their faces. Clearly they'd had no idea that he could overhear what they were saying.

"Uh . . . Crowfeather . . . ," Gorsetail began.

Crowfeather ignored her, not in the mood to give them the rebuke they were obviously expecting. *I don't give a mousetail what these flea-brains think . . . they don't deserve the effort it would take to insult them.* Instead he stalked past them with his head down, making for the camp. His pelt grew hot with anger as he felt the gazes of his Clanmates piercing him like wasp stings.

It was horrible to hear them talking about his son like that. But the worst of it was . . . he couldn't disagree with them.

Back in camp, Crowfeather looked for his apprentice, Featherpaw, and found her near the fresh-kill pile, sharing a vole with Slightpaw and Hootpaw. He noticed with approval how she kept her gray tabby pelt neatly groomed, and her alert look as she spotted him approaching. He jerked his head to summon her.

"Come on. We're going hunting."

Featherpaw hastily swallowed the last mouthful of prey and swiped her tongue around her jaws. Then she stood up. "Great! Hootpaw and Slightpaw are going out, too. Can we all hunt together?"

Crowfeather was about to refuse when Harespring, Slightpaw's mentor, strolled up to join them. Hootpaw's mentor, Nightcloud, was walking just behind him.

"That's a great idea," Harespring mewed warmly. "The more hunting styles the apprentices get to see, the better."

Crowfeather groaned inwardly. The last cats he wanted to

spend time with were the new deputy and Nightcloud, who was his former mate and the mother of his WindClan son. *I should never have mated with her,* he thought. *It was a mouse-hearted attempt to make a family in my own Clan.* He had been angry and bitter over losing Leafpool. He'd never loved Nightcloud, and she'd never forgiven him for it.

Nightcloud didn't look too pleased about this idea, either, but the three apprentices were exchanging delighted glances at the thought of training together. Crowfeather didn't feel he had much choice; besides, he didn't want to disappoint Featherpaw.

"Okay," he muttered.

"Onestar wants us to go and hunt down near the Thunder-Clan border," Harespring announced, gathering the patrol together with a sweep of his tail. "There have been reports of weird scents in that area, and for some reason prey is scarce."

Crowfeather nodded. "Good idea. I tried hunting over there the other day and came back empty-pawed."

Harespring took the lead as the patrol left the camp and headed downhill toward the border with ThunderClan. The apprentices scampered along together, jostling one another and boasting about how much prey they were going to catch.

The chilly wind had faded to a faint breeze, and wide patches of pale blue sky showed between the clouds. Crowfeather sniffed the air and picked up the scent of rabbit.

"I've got a good feeling about today," Harespring announced. "I think the prey will be running well." He sounded cheerful, though Crowfeather thought he had to be aware of the tension between him and Nightcloud, who was stalking along beside Hootpaw as if she was trying to pretend Crowfeather wasn't there.

What's her problem? Well, I'm not going to beg for her attention, if that's what she expects.

The deputy had hardly finished speaking when a rabbit started up unexpectedly from a tussock of long grass and fled across the moor. Nightcloud raced after it; Crowfeather could not help admiring her strong, graceful bounds and the way her muscles rippled under her black pelt.

But she's not my mate anymore, and that's just fine by me. Life is easier now.

Suppressing a snort of annoyance, he turned to Featherpaw. "Watch Nightcloud," he instructed her. "See how quickly she reacted? And when the rabbit changes direction, she doesn't lose a step. Why is that?"

Featherpaw's head tilted as she searched for the answer. After a moment she looked back at him with wide, questioning eyes. "I don't know . . ."

"Because a good hunter is always thinking," Crowfeather told her. "Always alert to a prey's best route of escape. You can't just follow it. You have to work out where it's going to run. That's what Nightcloud is doing now."

Featherpaw nodded, her gaze fixed on the black she-cat. "She's great!"

As she spoke, the rabbit vanished behind an outcrop of rocks, with Nightcloud hard on its paws. A shrill squeal of terror was abruptly cut off, and a moment later Nightcloud emerged from the rocks with the limp body of the rabbit dangling from her jaws.

"She got it!" Hootpaw exclaimed.

"Brilliant catch!" Harespring meowed heartily as Nightcloud padded back to the rest of the patrol.

"Yeah, good job," Crowfeather added when her eyes briefly met his.

Nightcloud swiftly looked away from him. "Thanks, Harespring," she mewed.

Crowfeather swallowed a rumble of annoyance, not wanting to look angry in front of the apprentices. *How petty! She can't even accept my praise.*

When Nightcloud had finished scraping earth over her rabbit to collect it later, the patrol continued farther down the hill. Crowfeather was the first to spot the black-tipped ears of a hare poking up from where the creature was crouching in a shallow dip in the ground.

"Who can tell me what the problem is here?" Harespring asked the apprentices in a low voice.

Featherpaw waved her tail excitedly but had the sense to speak in a quiet murmur as she answered. "The breeze is blowing from us to the hare."

"Right," Harespring mewed, while Crowfeather felt proud that his apprentice had spoken first. "So it's going to scent us long before we can get up close enough to pounce. What do you think we should do about that?"

This time it was Hootpaw who replied. "Move around so we're in a better place?"

"Good," Harespring praised him. "And this is one of the times when it can be better to hunt in a team, rather than alone. Crowfeather, I'm going to work my way around until I'm on the far side of the hare. When I give the signal, I want you to chase the hare over to me."

Crowfeather nodded, thinking that if he had been leading the patrol, he would have given that task to one of the apprentices. *But I must be mouse-brained, because Harespring's the deputy. What do I know?* "Okay."

Harespring set off at once, creeping along with his belly fur brushing the ground, taking advantage of every scrap of cover. Crowfeather could barely make out his brown-and-white pelt among the tussocks of wiry grass. The apprentices watched, their claws flexing in anticipation.

But before Harespring was in position, a stronger puff of wind passed over the ground. The hare's head lifted from its cover, its nose twitching.

Then it sprang, fleeing back up the hill, forcing itself along with powerful strokes of its hind legs. Harespring rose to his paws, his tail lashing in frustration. "Fox dung!" he exclaimed.

Crowfeather hurled himself after the hare, quickly noticing that a black shape was streaking alongside him. *Nightcloud.*

"I'll try to overtake it," she gasped. "Drive it back to you."

She put on an extra burst of speed, flashing past the hare and turning to confront it with teeth bared and claws extended. The hare almost tripped over its paws as it doubled back, skidding downhill. Crowfeather bunched his hind legs, launching into a leap, then landed on top of it and sank his fangs into its throat.

Once the hare was dead, Crowfeather stood back, panting, and waited for Nightcloud to rejoin him. He wanted to share the triumph of a successful kill, just as he would with any of his Clanmates, but Nightcloud padded past him toward the others as if she were hardly aware that he existed. *Who made dirt in her fresh-kill?* Crowfeather gave a shrug, picked up the hare, and followed her. If that was how she wanted things to be between them, he was not going to give her the satisfaction of showing her that he cared.

"Wow, it's huge!" Slightpaw exclaimed as Crowfeather dropped his prey at Harespring's paws.

Crowfeather gave the deputy a nod. "Like you said, teamwork," he mewed dryly.

Harespring looked slightly discomfited. "Let's go farther down," he suggested. "We might find some smaller prey nearer the stream, and the apprentices can have a try."

"That will take us past the place Onestar asked us to check out, too," Nightcloud added.

When they had buried the prey, Harespring took the lead again, making for the stretch of woodland on the WindClan side of the border stream. Before they reached the trees, the deputy drew to a halt at the edge of a gorse thicket that straggled over the hillside. At the foot of the slope a stretch of flat ground led to a steep bank riddled with holes.

"Onestar thinks there's something odd going on here," he meowed. "Let's see if we can find out what it is."

Hootpaw's tail shot straight up into the air. "Are we going to explore the tunnels?" he asked. "Cool!"

"*You* aren't going to explore anywhere," Nightcloud informed him sternly, flicking his shoulder with her tail. "All the apprentices, keep back."

"We never get to do *anything*," Hootpaw grumbled, his tail drooping.

"If you're not careful, you'll get to do the elders' ticks," his mentor warned him. "Now, let's all see what we can scent."

Crowfeather opened his jaws to taste the air, and at once an unfamiliar scent trickled past them. "Can you smell that?" he asked.

"Weird . . . ," Harespring murmured. "I feel like I should recognize it, but . . . I'm not sure."

"It might be coming from the tunnels," Nightcloud pointed out.

Crowfeather turned a slow circle, looking about them. The tunnels that gaped in the bank stretched for countless fox-lengths underneath the territory, joining WindClan to ThunderClan. The nearest hole in the side of the steep bank gaped open only a few tail-lengths away. It was quite possible that some kind of animal had made its den inside there.

"There's nowhere else it *can* be coming from," he responded to Nightcloud. "Maybe we ought to take a look."

Even though Crowfeather had made the suggestion, his pelt prickled with apprehension at the thought of padding down into the darkness under the earth. So few cats used the tunnels now that he had no idea what condition they were in these days. "Featherpaw, you were told to stay back," he added, as his apprentice craned her neck to peer into the gaping hole.

Harespring paused thoughtfully, jaws open, then shook his head. "The scent is pretty stale," he meowed. "Whatever left it might be long gone."

Or maybe they're just camped out very deep inside the tunnel. Crowfeather didn't speak this thought aloud, though. The Clan's new deputy had obviously decided not to investigate, and Crowfeather admitted to himself that he was relieved to stay out in the open air.

"So are we hunting or not?" Nightcloud asked irritably.

"Sure we are," Harespring responded. "Why don't we see what we can find around here? If the scent is stale, the prey might be coming back."

"Good luck with that," Nightcloud muttered. "It's been scarce on this side of the territory since just after the Great Battle."

Harespring shrugged. "We can still give it a try. And we may find out something useful."

The three warriors split up, each taking their own apprentice. Crowfeather caught no prey-scents on the ground, and only faint traces in the air, but eventually he spotted a sparrow perched on a jutting spike of rock. Perfect for an apprentice's practice.

Just as he was beginning to advise Featherpaw on how to pounce on it, a loud yowl split the air from farther along the bank.

"Great StarClan!" he exclaimed. "What's that?"

He whipped around and raced alongside the bank toward Hootpaw, who was standing rigid, his gaze fixed on another of the dark tunnel entrances. His fur was so bushed up, he looked twice his size.

Crowfeather's pelt prickled with apprehension as he wondered what could have spooked the apprentice like that. Hootpaw wasn't easily frightened; he was usually a bold and adventurous young cat.

"Hang on, I'm coming!" Crowfeather called out as he charged up, half expecting to see a fox or a badger emerging from the tunnel. *Except that wasn't fox or badger scent.*

As Crowfeather halted beside Hootpaw, he thought that he spotted something white and shining at the mouth of the tunnel, whisking out of sight into the blackness.

That looked like a tail . . . , he thought. *Or am I seeing things?*

Featherpaw joined him, panting, while Nightcloud hurried up with a vole in her jaws. Harespring and Slightpaw ran up shortly after.

"What happened?" Nightcloud asked, dropping her prey. "Hootpaw, tell me you didn't go into the tunnel, after what I told you!"

"I didn't!" Hootpaw protested. "But I . . . I saw something in there. An animal I've never seen before, like a glowing, pure white cat! It looked right at me, like it wanted to tell me something."

"Oh, for StarClan's sake, don't be so mouse-brained," Nightcloud snapped. "There's no such thing as glowing white cats—only StarClan, and they glitter like *stars.* Honestly, you made such a noise, I thought a badger must be ripping your fur off!"

"I know what I saw," Hootpaw mewed stubbornly. "I've never seen anything like it. It was scary!"

Harespring looked thoughtful. "Smoky from the horse-place told me once that kittypets sometimes came back after they died, all shining white, to visit their Twolegs. He said he'd seen ghosts with his own eyes."

"That's the most flea-brained thing I've ever heard!" Crowfeather exclaimed, glaring at Harespring. It was bad enough that Hootpaw was scared out of his fur. They didn't need Harespring encouraging him. "Maybe kittypets *believe* that, but they don't even commune with StarClan." Harespring returned his glare for a moment but finally looked away as if he was embarrassed. *He should be,* Crowfeather thought, annoyed. *This is who Onestar chose over me? A warrior who can barely catch a rabbit and now believes in ghosts? Some deputy.*

"I saw a glowing white cat," Hootpaw insisted. His fur was lying flat again, but his eyes were still wide and frightened, and Crowfeather could see that Featherpaw and Slightpaw were beginning to look apprehensive as well, casting nervous glances at the tunnel entrance as if, at any moment, whatever the apprentice had seen was going to come charging out of the shadows.

Crowfeather knew it was nonsense, but all the same, something was niggling at the back of his mind. *If there were ghost cats,* he thought, *this would be the right time for them to show up. We lost so many of our Clanmates in the Great Battle.* But he quickly dismissed the thought. Clearly, he was letting the apprentices—and their mouse-brained deputy—get to him. There had to be a perfectly reasonable explanation for whatever Hootpaw had seen, but now wasn't the time to find it.

"I think we've done enough hunting for one day," he meowed decisively. "Let's carry our prey back to camp."

Harespring opened his mouth as if to argue, but he quickly snapped it shut and nodded his head. Crowfeather knew the deputy was probably irritated that he was calling the shots, but since he was eager to leave the area, he went along with him. Without any further discussion, the patrol set off, collecting their prey as they went. The deputy loaded up the apprentices and sent them on ahead, while he padded along behind with Crowfeather and Nightcloud. Crowfeather couldn't help noticing how subdued the apprentices seemed now, so different from their earlier playfulness.

"I have no idea what got into Hootpaw." Nightcloud still sounded cross. "He's usually so sensible."

"I know," Harespring responded. "That's why I believe him." At Nightcloud's annoyed expression, he continued. "Look, I'm not saying they were glowing white cats, but he must have seen *something*."

"He did," Crowfeather mewed thoughtfully. "I know because I saw something, too."

"Oh, really, you 'saw something'?" Nightcloud turned an incredulous gaze on him. "Not a glowing white cat, by any chance?"

"No." *Featherbrain.* Crowfeather swallowed his anger, not

wanting to get into an argument with Nightcloud. "But something white . . . like maybe a tail vanishing down the tunnel. There could have been another animal there."

"But there aren't any white animals on the moor," Harespring objected. "Still . . . perhaps we should report it to Onestar."

"What can he do about it?" Nightcloud asked.

"I'm not sure," Harespring replied. "But we were told to check out this area, and that's what we've found. Besides, suppose this is the start of some kind of trouble, and we *didn't* report it. The Clan would be unprepared, and if anything terrible were to happen, it would be our fault. Onestar needs to know what's going on in his own territory."

Crowfeather was surprised to find himself murmuring in agreement. Harespring might not have been the deputy he would have chosen, but he had to admit that everything he'd just said was true. He gave Harespring a sideways glance. Maybe the tom wasn't the worst deputy Onestar could have appointed after all.

Crowfeather picked up his pace until he caught up with the apprentices. Featherpaw was trudging along, carrying the rabbit Nightcloud had caught earlier; as she glanced up at Crowfeather, he could see the worry in her eyes.

"It'll be okay, you know," Crowfeather reassured her. "If there is anything in the tunnels, Onestar will help us figure out what to do about it."

Featherpaw blinked at him. "I know," she mumbled around her prey. "I just wish we could be sure what Hootpaw saw."

"We will be soon," Crowfeather responded. "And then, whatever it is, WindClan will deal with the problem."

Featherpaw's tail shot up in the air and her gaze cleared. "Yeah! WindClan can deal with anything."

Crowfeather gave her an approving nod, reflecting on what a bright young cat she was. She would make a great warrior. He imagined how proud he would be if he were her father. But the thought made his gut twist, and he suddenly felt guilty, thinking of Breezepelt, and how he had a better relationship with his apprentice than his son.

Returning to the camp, Crowfeather spotted Onestar outside his den, stretched out in the pale sun of leaf-bare. He sat up alertly as Harespring led his patrol across the camp toward him. "Did you find anything down there?" he asked.

Harespring began to explain about the weird scent they had picked up near the tunnels, and how Hootpaw—and maybe Crowfeather—had seen something at one of the entrances.

"It was a ghost!" Hootpaw interrupted. "A shining white ghost cat!"

Onestar looked befuddled. "A ghost?" he echoed, twitching his whiskers in confusion.

Harespring explained what he had learned from Smoky at the horseplace about how he claimed he'd seen dead kittypets returning as shining white "ghosts." Crowfeather could see that Onestar was listening carefully, but also that he didn't believe a word of it.

"I can see you were all very brave," the Clan leader told the apprentices when Harespring had finished. "But I don't think there's any such thing as a 'ghost cat.' Only StarClan. What you saw must have been a trick of the light, or your imagination."

Hootpaw still looked mutinous, but he had enough sense not to argue with his Clan leader.

"It's that weird scent that's bothering me," Onestar went on. "It seems like there must be *something* around the tunnels, and I don't like the sound of that. I think we should organize another patrol to take a look inside and check it out."

"I'll take one now, if you like," Harespring offered.

Onestar shook his head. "The sun will have gone down before you get there," he responded. "It will have to be tomorrow. I expect some kind of animal has made its home in the tunnels," he continued. "It wouldn't be the first time that has happened, especially in the cold of leaf-bare. But if there is something living there, we need to drive it out. Those tunnels are *ours*." Looking down reassuringly at the apprentices, he added, "Hootpaw, you did well to spot potential danger, but I don't want any of you to go spreading wild stories around the camp. I want every cat to keep calm. There's really nothing to worry about."

Crowfeather was impressed by his leader's authority and the way he comforted the apprentices, though he doubted that Hootpaw would be able to keep his mouth shut about what he had seen. Once the first shock was over, he would be too excited to keep quiet. *And too fuzz-brained.*

"Okay," Onestar meowed, "go and get yourselves something

to eat. No, not you, Crowfeather," he added, as the patrol began to move away. "I want a word with you."

Crowfeather halted. *What now?* he wondered.

Onestar waited until the rest of the patrol was gone. "Tell me again what you saw. Give me as much detail as you can."

"I ran up to the tunnel entrance when I heard Hootpaw yowl," Crowfeather explained. "And I caught a glimpse of something white disappearing into the darkness. I thought it looked like a tail, but I can't be sure. Maybe it was as you said—just a trick of the light . . . or my imagination making me see danger."

Onestar listened intently, saying nothing until Crowfeather had finished. Then he shook his head sadly. "If there *were* a time for WindClan cats to be seeing ghosts, it would be now," he mewed, echoing Crowfeather's earlier thought. "We lost so many Clanmates in the Great Battle."

Crowfeather nodded, his throat suddenly dry. It hurt to think of all the cats they would never see again.

"The loss of Ashfoot must weigh heavily on you," Onestar went on, his eyes full of sympathy. "I know you miss her every day."

Crowfeather met Onestar's gaze, surprised to hear the leader mention his mother. Even the sound of her name made his chest tighten with sorrow. Talking about his grief for his mother was still too painful. He had to struggle to respond without breaking down. "Yes, it has been . . . difficult," Crowfeather admitted finally, almost having to push the words out of his mouth.

"Perhaps you can find comfort in the rest of your family," Onestar suggested. "Nightcloud and Breezepelt."

Crowfeather felt his muscles tense and said nothing. *Does he have bees in his brain? Onestar knows very well there's no comfort for me there.*

"But that's just it, isn't it?" Onestar went on. "Breezepelt tells me you haven't so much as looked in his direction since the Great Battle. Is that true?"

Fury began to build up in Crowfeather's belly. *I don't want to talk about this!* "I suppose so," he muttered.

"Then tell me why," Onestar persisted. "I've made it clear, as Clan leader, that *I've* forgiven Breezepelt for his part in the battle. And he has sworn a new oath of loyalty to WindClan. So why, as Breezepelt's father, do you refuse to accept that?"

"I know that what you say is true," Crowfeather replied, struggling not to unleash his pent-up frustrations on his Clan leader. "But . . . well, you know that I caught Breezepelt about to kill Lionblaze."

"Lionblaze may be your son, but he is a ThunderClan cat," Onestar responded in a level voice. "Breezepelt is a *WindClan* cat. It seems clear to me where your loyalty should lie."

Crowfeather drew his lips back in the beginning of a snarl, but he could find nothing to say in answer to his leader's arguments. He knew that what Onestar said made sense. He just found it hard to pretend that his time with Leafpool, and the kits they'd had together as a result, meant nothing to him.

But no cat would understand that but me.

For a few heartbeats, Onestar was silent. "Crowfeather," he

began again at last, "are you aware that many cats thought I would choose you as my deputy after Ashfoot's death?"

Now Crowfeather felt even more uncomfortable. Whatever other cats had thought, the choice of a deputy was for the Clan leader to decide, and Crowfeather had never thought of objecting to Onestar's choice of Harespring. Even if he did think it was mouse-brained.

"Yes, I knew that," he admitted. "But—"

"Do you know *why* I made the choice that I did?"

Crowfeather took a deep, calming breath, wishing he could see the point of these questions. *Because you're mouse-brained?* "I suppose that by choosing Harespring, you were sending a message that the Dark Forest cats can be trusted."

"That's true," Onestar agreed. "But there is also a reason that I *didn't* choose you."

Crowfeather's ears pricked in surprise. "There is?"

"Yes," Onestar meowed sternly. "Because you care about your own anger and prejudices more than you care about WindClan."

"That's not true!" *Is it?*

"Wouldn't you have accepted Breezepelt if it weren't?" Onestar challenged him. "He is your Clanmate, not to mention your own son. Accepting him would clearly be the best thing for your Clan."

Crowfeather had no answer to this. He felt his whiskers twitch with irritation as he looked away.

"I am your leader," Onestar went on, "and I have said we *will* trust him. But you choose not to follow my lead. Instead of trusting your own son, you cling to your anger and disappointment."

Crowfeather was silent, his claws flexing in and out as he struggled to calm himself. Part of him felt as if he should leap onto Onestar and rake his claws through his leader's tabby fur. But he knew that attacking his leader would be crazy. If he lifted a claw to Onestar, he would be driven out of WindClan forever. Even thinking about doing it surprised and confused him. Why was he so angry all the time?

"I expect more from you, Crowfeather," Onestar continued. "You are a brave and talented warrior. But you need to get to the bottom of your own problems and become a true WindClan warrior once again."

"Do you know what I've given up to be loyal to WindClan?" Crowfeather demanded, his anger spilling over at last. "I've sacrificed so much, and you don't give a mousetail about that!" Yet even as he said these words, guilt began to seep into his mind. There had been a time when he would have left WindClan to be with Leafpool; it was her decision that had led them back to the hunting grounds by the lake. From the way Onestar was looking at him, Crowfeather could tell that he suspected as much.

Onestar inclined his head. "I do know what you have sacrificed—or what you think you have," he meowed. "But if you were sincerely a WindClan cat above all else, you wouldn't have gotten yourself into that situation. And once you had, you would have accepted why it needed to end. You would not still be bitter about it."

Full of rage and confusion, Crowfeather let his claws slide out and dig hard into the ground; he felt as if his blood were bubbling and his fur prickling. He didn't know how to respond.

"You can go now," Onestar told him with a dismissive wave of his tail. "Tonight, Kestrelflight will go to the half-moon meeting," he added. "Perhaps StarClan will give him some guidance. And tomorrow I will send another patrol to see if we can find out what's going on in the tunnels."

Crowfeather waited until his fur had stopped prickling. Then he dipped his head respectfully to his Clan leader and stalked away. As he headed for the fresh-kill pile, he spotted Nightcloud and Breezepelt talking together. They broke off and raised their heads to watch him as he padded past, their eyes narrowed mistrustfully. Crowfeather thought of what Onestar had just said, about letting his anger go.

But I'm not ready to do that. Not yet.

Even more annoyed, Crowfeather seized a thrush from the pile and carried it away to the edge of the camp, far away from any other cat. He ate alone, in swift, angry bites.

I've given everything to my Clan, he thought resentfully. *What more does Onestar want from me?*

CHAPTER 2

Crowfeather chased a rabbit across the moor, reveling in the feeling of cold wind flowing through his fur, and the strength of his own muscles as they bunched and stretched to propel him effortlessly after his prey. He raced along so fast it felt as if his paws hardly touched the tough moorland grass.

A hole in a bank loomed up ahead, the entrance to one of the tunnels. The rabbit plunged into it, and without hesitating Crowfeather followed. He chased the rabbit down tunnels that twisted far more than he remembered, growing narrower and narrower until he could feel his fur brushing both sides in the blackness.

At last Crowfeather halted, his flanks heaving. He couldn't scent the rabbit anymore, or hear the scrabble of its paws on the stone floor of the tunnel. Damp cold struck up through his pads, and he realized with the first stirring of panic that the passage was too narrow for him to turn around. He had no idea where he was.

Slowly now, Crowfeather began to pad forward, his heart pounding as he felt water flowing around his paws, growing deeper as he struggled onward.

Cats have drowned down here, he thought.

His belly fur was brushing the water when he spotted a feeble, flickering light ahead of him. Hoping he had found a way out, he waded on more rapidly, until he came to a place where the tunnel wall was scooped out at one side to form a kind of den. Crowfeather's jaws dropped open with shock and disbelief as he recognized the cat who was sitting there.

"Ashfoot!" he choked out.

His mother sat with her head erect and her tail wrapped around her paws. Crowfeather couldn't tell where the pale light was coming from. It seemed to radiate from Ashfoot, yet she didn't have the frosty glitter to her fur that was the mark of a StarClan cat.

As Ashfoot spotted her son, she stood up and fled down the tunnel, her paws seeming to skim the surface of the water.

"Wait!" Crowfeather yowled, splashing clumsily after her. "Don't leave me! Ashfoot!"

But she was gone, and the light gone with her. Crowfeather was alone in the darkness, with water lapping around his shoulders. "Ashfoot, why are you here?" he asked, as if his mother could still hear him. "Why are you not in StarClan?"

No answer came back, only Ashfoot's voice raised in a screech that echoed around the tunnel like a roll of thunder. Terror shook Crowfeather from ears to tail-tip, and he startled awake to find himself in the warriors' den under the stars. He lay panting and trembling as his horrific vision receded.

What was that? Just a dream? Or was what Hootpaw saw in the tunnel entrance truly a ghost . . . the ghost of Ashfoot? Is she trying to send me a message? As soon as the idea occurred to Crowfeather, he gave his head an angry shake, annoyed with himself for thinking something so mouse-brained. But he couldn't let go of the idea. *If Ashfoot was trying to tell me something, what could it be?*

Once more, Crowfeather tried to shrug off the feeling, telling himself not to be a fool. In his dream, Ashfoot's fur had been gray, just as it was when she was alive, not the shining white Hootpaw had described, and that he had glimpsed for himself at the tunnel.

Besides, it can't be ghosts, he told himself. *Smoky was probably just being stupid.*

All the same, Crowfeather still felt shaken to the depths of his belly, and he caught only troubled snatches of sleep before the sky began to pale toward dawn.

The sun had not yet risen when Onestar's voice rang out commandingly across the camp. "Let all cats old enough to catch their own prey join here beneath the Tallrock for a Clan meeting!"

Crowfeather struggled to his paws to see Onestar perched on top of the Tallrock, his figure outlined against the brightening sky. Harespring and Kestrelflight were standing at the base of the rock.

Is all this really necessary, just to announce who will be going out on the patrol today? Crowfeather wondered, stretching his jaws in a massive yawn. Or was there more the leader needed to say?

Around Crowfeather, more of the warriors were rising from their nests, shaking scraps of moss from their pelts and shivering in the early-morning chill. Crowfeather spotted Nightcloud and Breezepelt padding out into the open to sit side by side near the Tallrock. One of Crowfeather's forelegs twitched, as if to walk over and sit with them, but then he turned away and took his position on the other side of the group of gathered cats.

They wouldn't want me to sit with them anyway, he thought, surprised to feel a heaviness in his chest.

Whitetail and Whiskernose emerged from the elders' den in the disused badger set. "What's gotten into his fur now?" Whiskernose muttered, pausing to scratch himself vigorously behind one ear. "Whatever it is, couldn't it wait until the sun's up?"

All four apprentices scrambled out of their den and plopped themselves down in a furry heap at the edge of the gathering crowd. Crowfeather guessed from their wide eyes and excited looks that they were expecting momentous news, and Oatpaw—Leaftail's apprentice, who hadn't been with the hunting patrol on the previous day—looked just as thrilled as the rest.

So much for telling Hootpaw not to talk about it, Crowfeather thought wryly. *That featherbrain has probably told all of the apprentices by now.*

Sedgewhisker padded to the edge of the warriors' den and sat down to groom herself, while Emberfoot bounded over to sit beside her. Larkwing was heading over to join them when the other two cats turned a chilling look on her. Crowfeather saw Larkwing veer away and crouch down next to Whiskernose.

I don't like the look of that, Crowfeather thought. *We shouldn't treat the Dark Forest cats badly—not anymore.* It reminded him uncomfortably of the time when he had returned to Wind-Clan after leaving with Leafpool. He had often been on the receiving end of cold looks like that; it had been many moons before all his Clanmates had accepted him again. *If they ever did. Maybe it will take just as long for the Dark Forest cats to be considered true Clanmates.*

But the meeting was about to start, and Crowfeather had no time to give any more thought to what he had seen.

Onestar's gaze swept around the camp, checking that all the cats had assembled. "Kestrelflight visited the Moonpool last night, for the half-moon meeting," he began eventually. "He had a vision there—a vision that both he and I find troubling. Kestrelflight, please tell the Clan what you told me."

Crowfeather felt a stirring of anticipation as the young medicine cat drew himself up to address the crowd. "Barkface came to me last night in StarClan," he announced, "and he gave me a vision about the tunnels that lie between our territory and ThunderClan's."

Crowfeather was instantly alert, feeling his pads prickle with apprehension. This couldn't be a coincidence! It had to have something to do with what he and Hootpaw had seen the day before.

Or maybe it's to do with my dream.

"Barkface showed me the tunnel entrances," Kestrelflight went on, "and as I watched, I saw dark water gushing out of them in huge torrents, the kind of deluge that could sweep cats away and completely drown a camp."

As he spoke, anxious murmurs rose from the cats around him. Crowfeather saw many of them exchanging fearful looks. It sounded as if a terrible fate was creeping up on WindClan—as if they were being stalked by some huge predator. Crowfeather was just thankful that Barkface, the former WindClan medicine cat, was watching over them. *At least StarClan is giving us a warning.*

"At first," Kestrelflight continued, "a wild wind kicked up and drove the water back. But eventually the wind dropped, and the water kept on rushing and gushing out into a second huge wave until it swallowed up everything." The mottled gray tom winced at the memory. "The sound of it was unbearably loud."

Crowfeather suppressed a shiver as he remembered the horrible moment in his dream when he had stood alone in the dark tunnel with water up to his shoulders.

"But what does it mean?" Emberfoot called out from where he sat beside Sedgewhisker.

Kestrelflight hesitated a moment before replying. "I think it means something dangerous is lurking in the tunnels," he mewed eventually. "The way the wind controlled the water suggests that WindClan can win this conflict. But the wind also dropped suddenly. Perhaps that means it will be a tough battle."

For a moment the WindClan cats gazed at one another in silence. Then a sudden clamor broke out, cats calling out ideas of what the vision might mean and then arguing with one another's suggestions. Onestar yowled for silence, but no cat was listening.

"The tunnels *did* flood before." Weaselfur's voice rose above the rest. "Maybe it's going to happen again."

Now the Clan was silent, pondering his words. After a moment Harespring meowed, "You could be right. But I—and the rest of the patrol who were with me yesterday—scented something weird at the tunnel entrances. And Hootpaw saw—"

"Ghost cats!" Hootpaw interrupted, leaping to his paws with his shoulder fur bristling. "I saw ghost cats!"

The apprentice stood tall, his chest puffed out. Crowfeather guessed that even though he was scared, Hootpaw was enjoying the attention and the feeling of importance his announcement gave him. Nightcloud was giving him an annoyed glance, as if she didn't like to see her apprentice showing off in a Clan meeting.

I'm not a medicine cat, but I can see tick duty in Hootpaw's future, Crowfeather thought with a wry snort of amusement.

Yowls of disbelief and confusion greeted Hootpaw's words, while Onestar flicked his tail in irritation. "Very well," he snapped. "Hootpaw, tell the Clan what you think you saw."

"A ghost cat!" Hootpaw responded, his eyes round with awe. "It was all white and glowing, and it stared at me like it wanted to give me a message."

"A message for you?" Whiskernose sniffed dismissively. "Why would it give a message to an apprentice?"

"And what was the message?" Gorsetail asked.

Hootpaw gave his chest fur an embarrassed lick. "It didn't say. It just vanished into the tunnel again."

Heathertail let out a *mrrow* of amusement. "Or maybe it sprouted wings and flew away?"

"It did *not!*" Hootpaw exclaimed indignantly. "I know what I saw. And Crowfeather saw it, too."

Crowfeather tensed so as not to shrink backward as every cat turned their gaze toward him. "I caught a glimpse of *something*," he admitted. "But it wasn't a ghost cat. There's no such thing as ghost cats."

To his dismay, many of his Clanmates were looking scared, as if they believed what Hootpaw had told them. They didn't seem to share his denial of ghosts. Instead they were exchanging nervous glances, their eyes wide with dismay as they murmured doubtfully to one another.

Do they all have bees in their brain? Crowfeather wondered.

"Do you think it could be the Dark Forest cats?" Crouchfoot asked, his voice quivering. "Could they have come back, to get revenge?"

"Of course not," Whiskernose asserted with a contemptuous flick of his tail. "Dark Forest cats wouldn't come back as *white*, would they? *White* is sort of like StarClan. These must be cats who fought on our side! Kestrelflight, not every cat who died in the Great Battle has been seen in StarClan yet, right?"

Though Kestrelflight was looking definitely uneasy with all these suggestions, he shook his head. "No, they haven't," he replied.

"So maybe there's a way to bring them back!" Larkwing suggested excitedly.

Annoyance prickled Crowfeather's pelt as if a whole Clan of ants were crawling through it. "Dead cats don't come back," he snapped. "Except for leaders who have lives left. For StarClan's sake, Larkwing, don't you understand death?"

The pale brown tabby drew back her lips and hissed at him, but then looked away, saying nothing more. Crowfeather instantly felt guilty; the young she-cat was obviously having a tough time in the Clan, and he hadn't meant to make it worse. *Great StarClan, she was only an apprentice at the time of the Great Battle. She hardly knew how to groom her own fur!*

"In any case," Onestar meowed, raising his tail to draw his Clan's attention to him, "it wasn't a ghost cat! But there *are* animals who might have gone to live in the tunnels and could be threats to us. Prey has been scarce for a while in that part of the territory, and that suggests we're dealing with something real."

"Good point," Crouchfoot murmured, looking slightly happier.

"So I've decided to send a patrol to explore the tunnels and see what they find," Onestar went on. "Meanwhile, we all need to be careful. If there are hostile creatures living there, we must be ready to fight."

"Of course we are!" Heathertail called. "We're warriors!"

Onestar nodded. "Harespring will lead the patrol," he announced. "Are there any volunteers to go with him?"

For a moment no cat answered; they only murmured among themselves and exchanged doubtful glances.

"If we might be fighting Dark Forest ghost cats,"

Crouchfoot muttered, "then we should send Breezepelt."

Crowfeather glanced across at his son and saw that his face wore the wounded, angry look that was so familiar now. Clearly Crouchfoot's words had hurt him.

But Crowfeather also knew that this was a challenge Breezepelt would not want to meet. As a young cat, he had been caught in a flood that had raged in the tunnels, and he had been terrified of them ever since.

Crowfeather felt a pang of sympathy for him and was about to open his jaws to defend his son when, to his surprise, Breezepelt stepped forward, his chest puffed out proudly. "Yes," he meowed. "I *will* go."

Onestar looked impressed, dipping his head toward Breezepelt. "There speaks a true WindClan warrior," he announced to the others.

How about that. Crowfeather was surprised to see Breezepelt volunteering for such a dangerous task—and a little bit impressed. But from elsewhere around the Tallrock came murmurs of disapproval; clearly not all the cats agreed with their leader's praise.

The murmurs were silenced as Nightcloud stepped forward beside her son. "I'll go too," she stated.

Crowfeather caught a glance exchanged between his former mate and their son: hers protective and motherly, his thankful. He huffed out his breath, trying to ignore the pain like a piercing thorn at the sight of the love and trust between them. *Neither one of them ever felt that way about me.*

When Breezepelt was a kit, Nightcloud had been so

overprotective. Maybe because he'd been the only one of their litter to survive. But Crowfeather couldn't do anything right. He was too rough when he tried to play with him, or he was too strict. *And now look how Breezepelt has turned out!* Crowfeather thought sadly. *Irritable, defensive, angry . . .*

Crowfeather suddenly realized that Onestar was speaking to him. "Is that all right with you, Crowfeather?"

Mouse-dung. Now what have I missed? "I'm sorry?" he mewed, trying to look attentive.

"I said, I want you to join the patrol," Onestar responded. "After all, you saw this strange animal as well. Furzepelt and Heathertail will go, too."

Stifling a growl, Crowfeather nodded agreement. It made sense that he would be chosen to join the patrol, as he was the only cat besides Hootpaw who had seen anything. But from the look Onestar was giving him, he sensed there was more to it than that.

That mouse-brain wants to force me to spend more time with Breezepelt.

Glancing at Nightcloud and Breezepelt, Crowfeather could see they both looked distinctly unimpressed at the idea of his joining them. The memory of his horrific dream of Ashfoot came surging back into his mind, and he admitted to himself that he wasn't exactly thrilled to be going back into the tunnels, either.

This is going to be just great.

When the meeting was over, Harespring sent out the dawn patrol and the usual hunting patrols, though he left out the six cats who had been chosen to go to the tunnels. At sunhigh they gathered with their Clanmates around the fresh-kill pile to eat before they set out. Crowfeather crouched to gulp down a mouse, half turned away from his son and his former mate.

"I think there may be rats in the tunnels," Gorsetail mewed between mouthfuls of vole. "And maybe what Hootpaw saw was a snow-white cat—a kittypet—going in after them."

"So you don't think the cat was a ghost, then?" Leaftail asked.

Gorsetail's gray-and-white tail curled up in amusement. "Well, if it wasn't a ghost then, it may be one now! Only a kittypet would be mouse-brained enough to try fighting a whole colony of rats by without backup."

"But isn't that sort of what we're doing?" Slightpaw asked; Crowfeather noticed how confident the young cat seemed among a group of warriors. "We're only sending six cats, and who knows how many . . . whatever . . . there are down there."

"We're sending six of our *best* cats," Onestar pointed out. "I trust WindClan warriors to defeat anything that might be in the tunnels!"

Slightpaw nodded, accepting what his Clan leader told him, though Crowfeather spotted some of the others exchanging dubious glances.

They're probably suspicious of Breezepelt, he thought. He had to admit to himself that he wasn't sure how his son would react when he had to go down deep into the tunnels. If the darkness stirred up Breezepelt's old fears, Crowfeather hoped that he wouldn't give in to panic. *That would embarrass both of us.*

"I sort of hope we do see ghost cats," Heathertail mewed wistfully. "I'd like to see the cats we lost in the battle—it's usually only medicine cats who get to talk with the warriors of StarClan."

"But it *wasn't* ghost cats," Onestar reminded her gently.

"That's true," Kestrelflight added. "Don't you think that if there were, the medicine cats would know about it?"

"But just suppose our Clanmates *did* return as ghosts," Larkwing murmured. "What would we say to them, do you think?"

"I'd say we were sorry," Whitetail responded. "Sorry that they never got to live out their lives as members of their Clan."

"I'd tell them we loved them," Leaftail added softly.

The other cats' eyes were filled with sorrow, and their heads and tails were drooping. Crowfeather became aware of a great tide of grief and loss surging through his Clanmates. His own lost ones came back into his mind, with pain sharper than a badger's claws.

Ashfoot . . . and Feathertail . . . and Leafpool. She isn't dead, but she's lost to me, just as if she were.

"That's enough," Onestar meowed as the murmurs of regret continued. "We must not look back, or we could drown in our grief. Perhaps *that* is what Kestrelflight's vision is about."

"But how do we avoid grief?" Whitetail asked. "Our loss is all around us."

"We look forward," Onestar responded, his voice full of determination. Glancing across at Crowfeather, he added, "First we figure out what is really in the tunnels."

Crowfeather looked back at his Clan leader and gave him a single nod. Even though they both shared doubts over Hootpaw's claims of seeing ghost cats, Crowfeather knew that Onestar was happy to have a clear task. A patrol to establish the safety of their borders after the Great Battle might be just the thing that would restore calm to WindClan.

CHAPTER 3

❧

"*I think we should stick together* in the tunnels," Breezepelt announced as the patrol headed down the hill. "Who knows what might be lurking in there?"

How stupid! Crowfeather's neck fur rose with his annoyance. "Do you have bees in your brain?" he asked harshly. "How can we possibly expect to search the whole tunnel system if we stick together? No, we'll have to split up into smaller groups."

Breezepelt glared at him, seeming about to defend himself, then turned away abruptly and bounded off down the hill, leaving the rest of the patrol behind. Too late, Crowfeather felt a twinge of regret, realizing that his son had probably suggested that they should stay together because he was afraid. *But it was still mouse-brained.*

"Did you have to be so brutal?" Nightcloud asked, echoing his thoughts as she came to pad alongside Crowfeather.

"Oh, who's that? You're speaking to me now, are you, Nightcloud?" Crowfeather retorted, not sure whether he was pleased or annoyed. "I didn't realize. You've barely said a word to me since the Great Battle."

Nightcloud let out an irritated sigh. "I didn't have anything to say before. I do now."

Crowfeather rolled his eyes. "Well, this should be good. Go on, then. I'm listening."

"Surely you've seen how the other warriors behave toward Breezepelt?" Nightcloud continued, slowing her pace so that they dropped behind the rest of the patrol. "You need to set an example for the others, and start being kinder to him. How is the rest of the Clan going to accept him again if even his own father treats him like rotten prey?"

"It's kind of hard to bond with a cat who only thinks of himself," Crowfeather told Nightcloud, suppressing a sigh. "One who's so quick to think that every cat is against him. One who is so stubborn he can't even *pretend* he feels bad about the mistakes he's made."

"Really?" Nightcloud murmured. "That sounds awfully like another tom I know."

That's a load of badger droppings. Crowfeather's pelt prickled with resentment at the comparison, though he knew that just as a cat could inherit the color of their parents' eyes or fur, they were also likely to inherit parts of their personality and character.

Even so, neither Crowfeather nor Nightcloud was an angry, hateful cat. So how had their son turned out to be so angry all the time, always ready to fight? Where had Breezepelt's hatred come from?

A chill ran through Crowfeather from ears to tail-tip. *What if Breezepelt is simply an evil cat?*

"Don't you see how desperately Breezepelt wants approval from his Clanmates?" Nightcloud went on in a low and furious voice. "That must be because he feels so distant from his own father—a cat who is supposed to love him!"

Crowfeather glanced away, fearing that Nightcloud might see revealed on his face the thought that was running through his mind.

I'm not sure I can love Breezepelt like a son. I'm not sure if I ever did.

"I understand why it was no good between you and me," Nightcloud continued. "You never loved me, and I couldn't bind us together as a family." Her voice caught, and she looked away for a moment. Then she turned back to him. "But that's not important now. Breezepelt is what matters, and if his own father is so dismissive of him, so quick to bicker with him—well, it might give the rest of our Clanmates the impression that he can't be trusted. And if that happens, and he still hasn't been properly accepted back into the Clan, it might push him away again." Her voice grew lower still, her fury fading into anxiety. "I couldn't bear that. Could *you*?"

Crowfeather didn't know how to respond. Nightcloud was right: Crowfeather hated to think that his son might even leave the Clan—or, worse, commit some act of treachery that would get him banished. But he couldn't find the right words to respond to his former mate.

Nightcloud waited for a couple of heartbeats, then huffed out an exasperated breath and picked up her pace until she caught up with the others. Crowfeather trudged along at the rear of the patrol, wondering whether any cat would allow him to forgive Breezepelt on his own terms, and in his own time.

If I ever can forgive him.

At the foot of the hill Breezepelt waited beside the nearest tunnel entrance. Harespring led the rest of the patrol to join him, halted a tail-length away from the dark, gaping hole.

"We'll stick together until we reach that cave where several passages lead off," Harespring announced. "After that, we'll split up. Crowfeather, you go with Heathertail. Nightcloud with Breezepelt. And Furzepelt, you're with me."

"What then?" Crowfeather asked.

"That depends on what we find," the Clan deputy replied. "But we'll meet back here at the entrance in . . . oh, in about the time it takes to do a dawn patrol. And may StarClan watch over us all."

He turned and led the way with Furzepelt into the tunnels. Nightcloud and Breezepelt followed, leaving Crowfeather and Heathertail to bring up the rear.

Crowfeather padded along warily in the dimness. The tunnel stretched in front of them, wide and straight and lit by thin shafts of light that penetrated through chinks in the tunnel roof. His paws quickly started sticking to the damp and sandy floor, and he shivered as the raw cold probed into his pelt.

Opening his jaws to taste the air, Crowfeather couldn't pick up any scents except for his own and his Clanmates', and of moist moss and the occasional clump of fern growing from cracks in the rock. All he could hear was the sound of their own paw steps and their soft breath. But even though there seemed to be no danger, Crowfeather couldn't stop his shoulder fur from rising. Uncomfortably, he remembered his glimpse of something white, and his dream of Ashfoot.

It seems quiet and safe, but I know there's something down here. . . .

The patrol did not take long to reach the cave Harespring had mentioned, its roof a mesh of interlacing tree roots. From here, several passages led off into darkness. Crowfeather knew that each of the tunnels sloped steeply downward, farther into the ground, and stifled a shiver at the thought of the weight of all that soil and rock above his head.

"This is where we split up," Harespring announced. "Be careful, all of you."

Breezepelt's back was arched and his eyes were wide as Nightcloud began walking into one of the passages, but he held his head high and padded purposefully after her. Crowfeather thought that he was handling his fear well.

Heathertail beckoned Crowfeather with a jerk of her head. "Let's go this way."

Who died and made you Heatherstar? Crowfeather almost objected to being ordered around by a younger warrior who had once been his apprentice, but he decided it wasn't worth it. He followed the tabby she-cat without comment.

Almost at once the light died away behind them and they padded along in complete darkness. Crowfeather pricked his ears, straining to hear the slightest sound from the passage ahead, and kept his jaws parted, tasting the air for the weird scent they had picked up outside on the day before. But at first there was nothing.

A flow of colder air told Crowfeather that they were passing a side tunnel, and from that direction he picked up the faint sound of lapping water.

"Is that the underground river we can hear?" he asked Heathertail, trying not to sound as nervous as he felt.

"Oh, no, we're not nearly deep enough for that." Heathertail's voice was cheerful and confident. "Water often collects down there. It's nothing to worry about."

"You know your way around these tunnels very well," Crowfeather remarked, impressed in spite of himself.

"Well . . ." There was a trace of guilt in Heathertail's voice as she replied. "I often used to explore down here when I was an apprentice."

"I never knew that!" Crowfeather's pelt bristled with outrage. Back then he had felt Heathertail was a model apprentice, and now she was admitting she had done something that would have earned her tick duty for a whole moon if he had found out.

Heathertail let out a *mrrow* of laughter. "You weren't supposed to know! You would have clawed my ears off."

"You're right. I would have. Now let's get going."

Crowfeather padded onward in the black night of the tunnels, his anxiety rising with every paw step. *No star will ever shine here. Does that mean we are hidden from StarClan's eyes?* Once again he remembered his dream of Ashfoot, and how she hadn't shone with the frosty glimmer of a StarClan warrior. *Why hasn't she gone to StarClan, where she belongs?*

Farther and farther down they went, until Crowfeather

began to pick up a new scent drifting on the dank air.

"What's *that*?" he muttered.

He realized that Heathertail had halted when he blundered into her and felt her tail swipe across his face.

"It's foul . . . like crow-food," she mewed.

"It *is* crow-food," Crowfeather decided after another sniff. "Something must be bringing prey into the tunnels and then leaving it to rot."

"That's mouse-brained!" Heathertail exclaimed. "What does that?"

"Not ghost cats, that's for sure," Crowfeather muttered. He wished he could take the lead, but the passage was too narrow for him to push past Heathertail, so he added, "Keep going. But be *very* careful."

A few fox-lengths farther on, Crowfeather could tell from the echoing of their paw steps that they had emerged from the tunnel into a larger space. The stench of crow-food had grown and grown until it was almost overwhelming.

"Yuck!" Heathertail's voice sounded as if she was going to be sick. "I've just stepped in something. It's all slimy and horrible."

"Something has been stockpiling prey here," Crowfeather remarked. "So at least we know that there *are* animals in these tunnels. And whatever they are, they're obviously not planning to move on anytime soon. There's masses of prey."

"And they're going to *eat* it?" Even in the darkness Crowfeather could imagine the disgust on Heathertail's face. "What sort of creature eats spoiled prey?" she asked again.

"I don't know, and I'm not sure I want to know," Crowfeather responded grimly. "Let's get back and report."

But before they could do more than turn toward the tunnel they had entered by, Crowfeather heard a fierce snarling and a rush of pattering paw steps. The sounds were followed by a jolt of pressure on his pelt. Something barreled into him; his paws skidded on the slick surface of the rock, and he landed on his side with a thump that drove the breath out of his body. He felt his attacker's weight pin him down before he could get to his paws, and then a burst of pain in his shoulder where sharp teeth sank into his fur and flesh.

Letting out a yowl, Crowfeather desperately lashed out with his hind legs. One paw hit something solid and he raked his claws, feeling them slash across a furry body. He heard a high-pitched screech from the creature that was attacking him, and it released its grip on his shoulder.

A growl sounded beside Crowfeather's ear and he realized it was Heathertail, flinging herself into the battle.

"Got it!" she gasped. "It—" She broke off with a shriek of pain.

Crowfeather hurled himself in the direction of the sounds. His outstretched paws clamped down on a long, thin body, pinning it to the ground. It writhed under his claws, but for a moment he managed to hold it.

"Heathertail, are you okay?" he asked.

"Fine." The answer came out of the darkness. "The fox dungeating mange-pelt bit my tail!"

As Heathertail spoke, the creature under Crowfeather's

paws gave a massive heave, throwing him off. For a moment he tottered, his paws sliding on something sticky and rank-smelling.

"Crowfeather, this way!" Heathertail's voice was urgent. "We have to get out of here."

"I'm with you." Crowfeather stumbled after the sound of her paw steps and realized they had reentered the tunnel. For a few heartbeats he heard the skitter of claws on the tunnel floor as the animal followed them, and then the sound died away behind.

"Thank StarClan!" he panted.

He was thankful too for Heathertail's knowledge of the tunnels; he would never have found his way out if he had been alone. Sooner than he would have thought possible he saw a faint light filtering down the passage, and he burst out after Heathertail into the first cave. Heartbeats later they emerged into the open air, to see the sun casting long shadows across the moor, and Harespring and Furzepelt waiting for them.

"What happened to you?" Furzepelt asked, her eyes stretching wide with amazement as Crowfeather and Heathertail padded up. Her nose wrinkled. "Great StarClan, you stink!"

"Thank you for that insight," Crowfeather mewed dryly. "You would stink too if you'd been where we've been."

"There was a cave full of crow-food," Heathertail explained, and went on to describe the pile of rotting prey and the vicious creature they had encountered in the tunnels.

"What was it?" Harespring asked.

"Your guess is as good as mine," Crowfeather replied sourly.

"We couldn't see it, and we couldn't smell anything but that disgusting prey-pile. But I can tell you one thing: It wasn't a ghost cat. Not unless ghosts have teeth and claws."

"You're both hurt," Harespring meowed, sniffing at the bite on Crowfeather's shoulder. "Kestrelflight should have a look at that. You might need some burdock root."

"I'll see him as soon as we get back to camp," Crowfeather agreed. "Did you find anything?" he asked Harespring.

The Clan deputy looked slightly embarrassed. "We got lost in the tunnels," he admitted. "It took us a long time to find our way back to the entrance, and to be honest, once we did, we weren't too keen on going back in. But we didn't come across any animals—not even any ghost cats."

"I wonder what Nightcloud and Breezepelt found," Furzepelt mewed. "They should be back soon."

The cats waited as the sun went down and twilight fell over the moor. They were too alert to sleep, but they remained in watchful silence as the wind swept through the trees and stars burned brightly against the darkening sky. It was a long time before Harespring shifted his paws uneasily. "They should be back by now. Maybe they got lost like we did."

Anxiety prickled Crowfeather like a thorn as he remembered Breezepelt's fear of the tunnels. *I hope he didn't panic and do something stupid.*

Finally it was Heathertail who spoke, her blue eyes worried. "What if something *has* happened to them? What if they met the same creature that we did?"

"They're both experienced warriors." Harespring was

trying to reassure her, although it was obvious that he felt just as uneasy. "They should be able to cope."

"But they might—" Heathertail began, then broke off, flexing her claws and tearing at the springy moorland grass.

Each moment seemed to drag out like a moon. When he looked up, Crowfeather saw that all eyes were on him. He could not tell, though, if his Clanmates were waiting for him to suggest they should go after his son and former mate, or whether they expected him to go in by himself.

"Maybe . . . ," Crowfeather suggested at last, "maybe we should go and look for them. Heathertail, you could lead us—"

A loud, terrified yowling interrupted him. Every cat spun around to stare at the tunnel entrance. A heartbeat later the yowl sounded again, and Breezepelt exploded into the open from another entrance a few tail-lengths farther along the bank. His eyes were wide with fear, and every hair on his pelt was bristling.

Behind him Crowfeather saw what looked like some kind of white cloud surging from the tunnel entrance. But in the next heartbeat he realized the cloud was actually a pack of furious animals, snarling and hissing as they chased the fleeing Breezepelt. Their eyes glittered with malice as they poured out of the tunnel and up the slope after him. They weren't ghosts or wayward kittypets. He'd never seen white ones before, but there was no mistaking the creatures that were about to overtake his son.

"Stoats!" Crowfeather gasped. *Snow-white stoats!*

CHAPTER 4

❧

Briefly Crowfeather stood frozen in confusion. He'd never seen a white stoat before. But a moment later he had to push his astonishment aside. The crowd of stoats split in two, like a river breaking on a rock in midstream. Some of them still raced after Breezepelt, while the rest flung themselves at Crowfeather and his Clanmates, who remained still, stupefied by what they were seeing.

"Keep together!" Harespring's yowl focused Crowfeather's mind, and he tensed his body, ready to fight.

The stoats were smaller than the cats, but they were fast and nimble, their long, wiry bodies easily dodging the blows the cats aimed at them. Crowfeather found himself fighting beside Harespring, trying to drive the brutes back into the tunnels. But there were too many of them; when Crowfeather lashed out at one stoat, two or three others would hurl themselves at him, trying to climb onto his back or knock him off his paws. He knew that if he lost his balance and fell, he would not get up ever again. He shuddered inwardly at the thought of those thorn-sharp teeth meeting in his throat.

Now I know what it was that Heathertail and I fought in the tunnel!

After a few moments, Crowfeather lost sight of Hare-spring, and he had no idea where the rest of his Clanmates were. Occasionally a screech rose above the snarling and chittering of the stoats, but he couldn't tell if they were cries of pain or of defiance. Blood was dripping from a scratch on his forehead, so he could hardly see.

At last he heard Harespring's voice raised high above the clamor. "Retreat! Retreat!"

At first Crowfeather thought he wouldn't be able to obey. Too many stoats were pressing around him, the air now so full of their scent that it made him choke. He struck out with his forepaws at the white bodies that gleamed eerily in the gathering darkness, trying to force his way up the slope.

What if we fail to escape them?

Dazed with pain and exhaustion, Crowfeather thought it would be better to go down fighting than show these ferocious enemies the way to WindClan's camp.

Then he heard Heathertail's voice, calling to him from close by. "Crowfeather! This way!"

Blinking the blood from his eyes, Crowfeather turned his head to see Heathertail peering out from the bottom of a gorse thicket. He stumbled over to her, thrusting himself in among the thorns, clenching his jaws at the pain of the sharp points tearing at his pelt.

At first he thought the stoats would simply follow him into the thicket. Relief surged through him as he realized they were drawing back. He crouched among the thorns, listening to the pattering paw steps and vicious snarling of the stoats outside the thicket, until gradually the sounds died away.

Following Heathertail, Crowfeather wormed his way through the bushes until they emerged on the far side. He was even more relieved to see that his Clanmates had pushed their way through the thorns, too. They all looked battered, with clumps of fur missing and blood trickling from scratches along their sides, but they were alive and on their paws.

"Well," Heathertail mewed, "I guess we know what's in the tunnels now. Stoats! I'm glad you brought enough for every cat, Breezepelt."

"It was horrible!" Breezepelt still looked terribly shaken, hardly able to stand upright. "Nightcloud and I were surrounded by the disgusting things. I thought we'd go to StarClan for sure. And then we found a way out, and just ran. . . ."

A murmur of apprehension greeted his words, but Crowfeather was silent, alarm striking him like lightning from a clear sky. He looked around.

"Wait," he meowed. "Where *is* Nightcloud?"

"What happened, exactly?" Onestar asked.

Back on WindClan territory, the battered survivors of the patrol stood in the middle of the camp, surrounded by a crowd of their Clanmates. Crowfeather could hardly bear to meet their anxious gazes or see the urgency in Onestar's face as he repeated his question.

By now night had fallen, and an icy wind was sweeping over the moor, driving ragged clouds across the moon and probing deep into the cats' fur. But no cats thought of returning to their den or settling into their nest. They were all too worried about the discovery of the white stoats in the tunnels, and the disappearance of Nightcloud.

Breezepelt stood with his head lowered, staring at his paws, and seemed unable to look up at his Clan leader, much less answer his question. Crowfeather guessed that he was afraid of having to explain the disaster to a Clan that already didn't trust him.

"Breezepelt?" Onestar prompted him. "You have to tell us what happened. Where is Nightcloud?"

"I don't know!" Breezepelt flashed back at him, desperation in his voice. "It was more . . . more complicated than we expected. Once we got down the tunnel, there was a fresh scent—it was very strong, and different from anything I'd scented before. Then those . . . those creatures attacked us. It was too dark to see what they were, or even how many of them were there."

"What did you do?" Gorsetail asked, her blue eyes fixed intently on Breezepelt.

"What *could* we do?" Breezepelt retorted. "We fought. One of the creatures injured Nightcloud, and I tried to help her and get her out. Finally we managed to escape, but the creatures followed us."

"*Stoats,*" Crowfeather put in. "We know now that they are stoats."

Breezepelt nodded, looking utterly wretched. "Nightcloud told me to run," he continued, "so I did. I thought she was right behind me. But when I finally got out, she wasn't there. We looked, but we couldn't find her."

"And we couldn't go back into the tunnels to search for her," Harespring added, "because the stoats were guarding the entrances."

Breezepelt lowered his head again, his claws extended, digging into the ground. "Oh, StarClan!" he choked out miserably. "Please don't let those things have killed her. They were so vicious . . . and she was so brave. . . ."

Watching Breezepelt as he struggled with his grief, Crowfeather felt warm sympathy flow over him, like sunlight striking down through a gap in dark clouds. He hadn't felt like that toward his son in a long time. Pangs of compassion and anxiety gripped him like two sets of claws.

A dark pit seemed to open up in front of Crowfeather as a chilling thought went through his mind.

Nightcloud is a tough warrior. If she thought the stoats were a threat to Breezepelt, she would have fought to defend him—to her last breath if she had to. And maybe she did.

Crowfeather's chest felt as if he had swallowed a thorny rose stem. It made sense that Nightcloud would have chosen to give her life to save her son's, but the idea that she might have died alone in the dark made him ache with grief and regret.

"I don't like to say this," Leaftail began, breaking the silence that had followed Breezepelt's last words, "but, Breezepelt—why didn't you make certain that Nightcloud was with you when you were fleeing from the stoats?"

Breezepelt didn't meet the tabby tom's gaze. "I told you . . . I thought she *was* with me."

Leaftail let out a contemptuous snort. "You 'thought.' I see . . ."

The rest of the Clan exchanged uncomfortable glances as Leaftail's voice died away. Crowfeather realized that every cat was wondering whether Breezepelt hadn't fought for his mother as valiantly as he should have. He felt his shoulder fur bristling in unexpected defense of his son.

Breezepelt and Nightcloud have always had such a strong bond. I know Breezepelt would never have let any other animal hurt her. But a worm of doubt stirred and writhed within Crowfeather's belly. *Or would he . . . ?*

Breezepelt's gaze slowly drifted over his staring Clanmates. Finally he glared at Leaftail. "What are you suggesting?" he asked. "That I would abandon my mother like that?"

No cat answered.

Breezepelt dug his claws into the earth. "I was *convinced* Nightcloud was behind me when we left the tunnels!" he protested, clearly desperate to be believed. "There was nothing I could have done."

Leaftail gave his whiskers a dubious twitch but said nothing more.

Crowfeather was opening his jaws to speak up on Breezepelt's behalf when Onestar forestalled him.

"You needn't defend yourself, Breezepelt," the Clan leader meowed. "*I* believe you, because you're an honorable WindClan warrior." His gaze raked commandingly over the assembled cats. "And I expect every one of you to believe him, too. We must unite, because we are in grave danger. There's an infestation of stoats in the tunnels, which means they are closer to camp than I'm comfortable with."

Anxious murmurs broke out among the Clan as their leader spoke. Their attention momentarily shifted away from Breezepelt, who stood silently in their midst, head and tail drooping. It didn't look as if Onestar's faith in his loyalty had encouraged him in the slightest.

"Onestar, do you think we should warn ThunderClan?" Harespring asked. "After all, they share the tunnels. The stoats could cause trouble in their territory, too."

"No," Onestar responded, every cat's gaze turning to him at the brusqueness of his tone. "We'll keep this to ourselves for now. WindClan can solve this problem without involving ThunderClan, or their inexperienced new leader."

Harespring dipped his head in agreement, though Crowfeather thought that he still looked doubtful. Crowfeather understood his doubts—but he understood Onestar's hesitation, too. Onestar had always bristled at Firestar's attempts to involve himself in other Clans' business. Maybe he was hoping for a new relationship with ThunderClan, now that Bramblestar was leader.

"It's possible Nightcloud is trapped or being held prisoner by the stoats," Onestar continued. "If so, we have to concentrate on rescuing her."

"Yes!" Hope suddenly sprang up in Crowfeather, like an unexpected sunrise. *We're acting as if Nightcloud is dead, but she could still be alive. If only we can get back there in time. . . .* "We have to send a patrol out tomorrow—and I'll lead it this time."

Even if we can only make sure that she's not left alone out there, prey for scavengers, he thought but did not say aloud. *Or thrown on that pile of rotting crow-food.* The idea almost made him retch, and he struggled for self-control.

"Good," Onestar responded with a nod of approval for Crowfeather.

After a moment's hesitation Crowfeather suggested: "Maybe Heathertail should come, too."

Onestar tilted his head, as if wondering why Crowfeather was asking specifically for Heathertail. Crowfeather wondered how he would explain it without giving away Heathertail's history with the tunnels, but his leader just shrugged. "Sure. And I'll need two or three more cats to volunteer as well."

Crowfeather saw relief on Heathertail's face, as Crouch-foot spoke up. "I'd like to go," he mewed, determination in his face.

"And me," Larkwing added eagerly. Crowfeather guessed she was trying to shake off her reputation as a Dark Forest cat.

Many more cats raised their voices then, volunteering to help rescue their Clanmate. Crowfeather saw Onestar's chest puff with pride at the courage of his warriors; then he shook his head as he called quickly for quiet.

"We should keep the search party small," he meowed. "A small group will have a better chance of going unnoticed by the stoats. And if our enemies somehow leave the tunnels and find their way to our camp, WindClan will be better defended if we have strong fighters here, ready to meet an attack."

"If any stoat tries to invade WindClan territory," yowled

Emberfoot, "it'll be the last thing it ever does."

As the gathered cats spoke their agreement, warmth began to spread inside Crowfeather at the way the Clan was coming together. After the terrible battle against the Dark Forest, he knew that all the Clan cats felt protective of their Clanmates and their territory, ready to defend them from every threat.

Especially if that threat is not a cat!

Breezepelt raised his head, the light of resolve in his eyes. "I'm going too," he stated, with a glare at Crowfeather as if daring him to tell him he couldn't.

But it was Crouchfoot who objected. "You don't have to."

"I *am* going." Breezepelt spat out each word. "Nightcloud is *my* mother."

"Of course you can go," Onestar agreed before Crowfeather could respond. "You're more familiar with these creatures' scent than the rest of us."

Crowfeather gave his son a nod, and was rewarded by seeing a flicker of surprise in Breezepelt's eyes, as if he had expected a refusal from his father. "We'll leave at dawn," he meowed.

That night, Crowfeather found it hard to sleep. The moss and bracken in his nest felt as if they were full of thorns and spikes, the sharp prickles reminding him all too clearly of the claws of the stoats they had fought. If he closed his eyes, he could see their sinuous white bodies glowing in the dusk and their cold, malevolent eyes, and hear their chittering cries. Once or twice he half started up, convinced that the evil creatures were invading the camp, only to realize that the attack was all in his mind.

At the same time, Crowfeather couldn't stop worrying

about Nightcloud. Making her his mate had been a huge mistake, and things were so bad between them now that they could hardly go out on the same patrol without snapping at each other—but that didn't mean he no longer cared about her. He felt heaviness like a stone in his belly at the thought that he might never see her again, realizing that, despite everything, he would miss her. And he wasn't the only one.

WindClan needed her! Crowfeather might not have loved her the way he should have, but he knew she was an amazing cat: courageous, intelligent, and loyal.

And what about Breezepelt? he added to himself. *He needs Nightcloud . . . now more than ever, when there are so many questions about his loyalty. And if she were to die in the tunnels, would those questions ever really go away?*

There were so many other concerns, too. *If his mother is no longer in the Clan, who will be the one to encourage Breezepelt and defend him to the others?*

As soon as Crowfeather asked himself the question, the answer came back, in the sharp tones of the black she-cat.

Who do you think, flea-brain? You're his father—you do it!

Crowfeather was so shamed by the chiding he imagined she'd give him that he turned his face away as if avoiding her. Because this thought brought a question: Yes, he was Breezepelt's father, but . . . how long would it take him to really *feel* as if that was true?

Then he let out a long sigh, and waited impatiently for the dawn.

I hope it's soon. . . .

CHAPTER 5

✿

Crowfeather drew his patrol to a halt outside the tunnel entrance where the stoats had appeared the day before. They had traveled across the hills in a gray, reluctant dawn, the moorland grass spiky with frost beneath their pads. A cold wind gusted down from the ridge, but the ice Crowfeather could feel inside himself, spreading from his ears to the tips of his claws, had nothing to do with the bitter weather of leaf-bare.

"Listen, all of you," he meowed, turning to his Clanmates. "This isn't going to be easy. We're going to face the stoats on their own territory, and—"

"What do you mean?" Larkwing interrupted. "The tunnels are *our* territory!"

Crouchfoot let out a snort. "ThunderClan might not agree with you there."

"Well, it's our territory up to the underground river," Larkwing retorted. "And one thing's for sure—it doesn't belong to these crow-food-eating stoats!"

"That's enough," Crowfeather snapped, raising his tail to put an end to the wrangling. He knew that his Clanmates were only arguing because they didn't want to think about the danger they would soon be facing. Working themselves up into a rage would distract them from the dread they felt. "The point is, the *stoats* think it's their territory. Remember that they didn't follow us very far when they chased Breezepelt out of the tunnels last night. But inside the tunnels, they'll be a lot more confident."

"Encourage us, why don't you?" Crouchfoot muttered.

Crowfeather ignored the comment. "Every cat needs to be very careful," he continued. "We have to stick together, avoid the stoats if we can, and do whatever it takes to find Nightcloud."

But where is Nightcloud? he wondered *Trapped in a stoat's den? Or lying on one of those piles of rotting crow-food?* He shuddered. Then another thought occurred to him, terrifying in its own way. *What will we do if we can't find her?*

The tunnel gaped in front of them, seeming darker and eerier than ever before. Glancing at Breezepelt, Crowfeather could see fear in his son's amber eyes, but instead of worrying he might panic, he felt a renewed pang of sympathy for him.

It would be a weird cat who wasn't *unnerved,* he thought. He couldn't help but admire Breezepelt for his determination to be part of the patrol, even after his earlier encounter with the stoats.

Impulsively he turned to his son, meaning to tell him this, but Heathertail, who had padded right up to the entrance and stuck her head inside, interrupted before he could speak.

"I think I can scent Nightcloud!" she exclaimed.

Crowfeather hurried to join her, sniffing carefully at the

air just inside the tunnel. The stench of stoat was overwhelming, and he could distinguish Breezepelt's scent, reeking of his fear when he fled. But there was a faint trace of Nightcloud, too.

Turning to the rest of the patrol, Crowfeather was about to discuss with them what the best approach would be, when he realized that Heathertail was simply walking into the tunnel. He caught a glimpse of her tail disappearing into the darkness.

"Wait for us!" he called out with an exasperated lash of his tail. Just because the tabby she-cat knew the tunnels well didn't mean that she should just stroll in there unprotected. *What happened to "stick together" and "be careful"?* he asked himself. *Does she think she's a kit exploring her own camp?*

"Come on," he added to the others. His muscles tensed with urgency as he imagined Heathertail pulled down by a crowd of bloodthirsty stoats.

Just as the patrol was about to enter the tunnel, Crowfeather heard a strange scrabbling sound and stopped to listen. *That doesn't sound like a cat's paw steps.*

A faint gust of air floated out of the tunnel, making his nose and whiskers twitch. It was the scent of stoat—and it was fresh.

"Heathertail!" Breezepelt exclaimed hoarsely. "She's in danger!" He sprang forward, but Crowfeather was faster, leading the way into the passage. Breezepelt pressed up close behind him, with Crouchfoot and Larkwing following.

Soon the last of the light died away, and the cats padded

forward in darkness. Crowfeather kept his ears pricked, straining to hear what was ahead. He could still taste stoat scent in the air, mingled with Heathertail's. Every instinct was telling him to call out to her, but he kept silent, in case his voice would draw more stoats toward them.

Now we have two missing cats, he thought. *And we have no idea where either of them might be.*

Crowfeather's heart pounded harder with every paw step. He could hardly bear to think what Breezepelt must be feeling. But Crowfeather could detect no signs that his son was panicking; he could hear Breezepelt's paw steps following steadily behind. If he had any impulse to bolt, he was doing a good job fighting it.

Then a faint shimmer from somewhere above showed Crowfeather that the tunnel was widening out into a cavern. Looking up, he saw a thin ray of light striking down from a hole in the roof. The scrabbling sound came again, claws scraping on the stone floor of the tunnel. At the same moment Crowfeather heard a chittering cry and saw a flash of white in the dimness. Briefly he halted.

They're taunting us, trying to draw us farther in, he thought. *Then they can pick us off at their leisure.*

"This is mouse-brained," Crouchfoot meowed, padding up to stand beside Crowfeather. "We could be heading right into an ambush."

"But we *have* to go on," Breezepelt protested. "We have to do whatever we can to save Nightcloud and Heathertail."

Crowfeather gave his son a nod of approval, pleased at how

he was overcoming his fear. "Breezepelt is right," he declared, noticing his son sharply turning his head toward him, surprise in his eyes. "What choice do we have? Go back to camp with another cat missing when none of us has even seen a stoat yet?" But still an inner voice warned him: *Cats might get hurt, or even killed, trying to save their Clanmates. . . . Oh, StarClan, help us. . . . Help us all make it back to camp today!*

Crowfeather shuddered. He wondered how StarClan could give them any help at all, down here in the earth where no stars had ever shone.

"We keep going," he mewed.

Determinedly he padded on across the cavern with his Clanmates behind him, aware of flickering white shapes ahead of them and on either side. Their high-pitched cries came from all directions, as if the creatures were calling out to one another. *Or taunting us,* Crowfeather thought.

Then one of the stoats darted out less than a fox-length in front of Crowfeather, appearing so quickly that he had no time to warn the others. It was almost a relief, after the long tension of waiting—the attack they had been expecting was finally about to start.

Instinctively Crowfeather drew backward, only to collide with Breezepelt, feeling his son's body rigid with tension and anger. For a moment neither of them could move, and in that brief hesitation the small, long-bodied creature leaped forward and fastened its teeth in Crowfeather's side.

Crow-food-eating mange-pelt! Crowfeather let out a screech of pain and batted the creature away with a fierce swipe of his paw. The stoat fell back, tearing out a chunk of Crowfeather's fur as it went.

Why are you such a pain in the tail? Normally, Crowfeather knew, an infestation of stoats would be easy for WindClan to deal with. But these stoats were so destructive! Peering through the weak light, Crowfeather saw that it was pure white, except for a black tip on its tail—exactly like the stoats that had come pouring out of the tunnels on the previous evening. A shiver of fear passed through him at the sight of it.

They're so eerie. . . . I'd rather face a fox or a badger.

The stoat leaped at Crowfeather again, and Crouchfoot and Larkwing thrust their way forward, dragging it off as it sank its claws into Crowfeather's shoulders. Crouchfoot raked his claws down its side and the stoat fled, whimpering, into the darkness. But as it vanished, more and more of the white shapes came skittering into the cavern, converging on the group of cats. The stoats' malignant eyes glinted in the pale light, and their lips were drawn back to reveal their spiny fangs.

So they're showing themselves at last, Crowfeather thought grimly. *That first one was just to get us in the mood for a battle!*

Breezepelt charged ahead with an earsplitting caterwaul, obviously ready to fight every single one of them. Crowfeather's belly lurched with fear, and he sprang forward to put his own body between his son and their enemies. Larkwing helped him drag Breezepelt back down the passage, with Crouchfoot in the rear, slashing and raking his claws to drive the stoats back until they all burst out into the open.

"But what about Heathertail?" Larkwing gasped. "I didn't see her in there."

"I'll find her!" Breezepelt yowled.

Before Crowfeather could stop him, he whipped around and barreled back into the tunnel, slamming into the stoats and knocking them aside to force his way through them.

"Breezepelt, no!" Crowfeather screeched after him. But his son paid no attention. The lithe, white-furred stoats closed around him as he fought his way through and vanished into the darkness. Soon the sound of skittering claws and pounding paw steps died away.

For a heartbeat Crowfeather stood frozen, stunned by the speed of Breezepelt's attack. Then, with a massive effort, he pulled himself together. "We have to go after him," he meowed.

Larkwing and Crouchfoot exchanged an anxious glance, then nodded and stood a little taller—as if, by pretending, they could make themselves feel more confident than they actually were. "We're with you," Crouchfoot responded.

Crowfeather braced himself to plunge back into the tunnel, into the deadly crowd of stoats, but before he could move, Larkwing yowled, "Wait!"

Turning toward her, Crowfeather saw that she was pointing with her tail. Looking in that direction, Crowfeather spotted a light brown tabby she-cat stumbling out of another tunnel opening farther along the bank, with a black tom hard on her paws. *Heathertail and Breezepelt . . . they're alive!* As soon as they emerged, Breezepelt spun around and dropped into a crouch, baring his teeth and sliding out his claws.

"Come out if you dare, you filthy stoats!" he snarled.

Crowfeather raced along the bank; he could hear the paw steps of Crouchfoot and Larkwing as they pounded along behind him.

A few stoats were jostling one another in the entrance, snarling in response to Breezepelt's challenge, but before any cat could attack, they crept backward and vanished into the darkness.

As Crowfeather and the others reached him, Breezepelt rose to his paws, blinking in surprise. Crowfeather knew that Breezepelt had nearly drowned once in these tunnels. He guessed his son had never seen himself as brave enough to charge into them again like that, in search of Heathertail.

He must really have wanted to prove himself.

With the danger over for the time being, Crowfeather whirled around to confront Heathertail. "Are you completely mouse-brained?" he demanded. "If you don't care about your own safety, what about your Clanmates'? We could have lost you *and* Breezepelt because you were such a stupid furball!"

He got the impression that Heathertail was hardly listening. She was staring past him, and he realized that her blue gaze was fixed on his son.

"Thanks, Breezepelt," she murmured. "You were really brave."

Oh, for StarClan's sake. Breezepelt had an admirer. *I suppose there's a she-cat out there for every tom,* Crowfeather reflected. *No matter what a fuzz-brain he may be.*

Breezepelt gave the ground a couple of awkward scrapes with one forepaw. "It was nothing," he mumbled.

Breezepelt didn't just do that to prove himself, Crowfeather realized with a tingle of shock in his whiskers. *He must really care about her. And it might not be one-sided. . . .*

He knew that Breezepelt had been padding after Heathertail ever since they were both apprentices. But back then, she had seemed more interested in Lionblaze, the ThunderClan tom. Crowfeather had been vastly relieved when that friendship fizzled out.

No good can come out of relationships outside your own Clan. He suppressed a sigh. *No cat knows that better than I do.*

Now Crowfeather blinked at his son with approval of the choice he had made. Even though he had just clawed Heathertail with his tongue, he couldn't think of any she-cat he would rather see as his son's mate.

His anger fading, he turned back to Heathertail. "Are you all right?" he asked.

"I'm fine," Heathertail replied. "And I'm sorry for dashing off like that. I thought you would be right behind me."

"Sorry" catches no prey, Crowfeather thought, acknowledging her apology with a curt nod. "As long as you're okay."

Larkwing was already giving a careful sniff at Heathertail's hindquarters. "No, she's not okay," she meowed. "Those StarClan-cursed mange-pelts have torn out all her fur!"

Crowfeather padded over to take a look. Huge clumps of Heathertail's pelt had been wrenched out, and blood was trickling from so many wounds he couldn't count them. He could also see two claws missing from one of her hind paws, and he remembered how she'd been stumbling as she came out of the tunnel. None of her injuries looked life-threatening, but the loss of blood alone was going to weaken her badly.

Crowfeather realized that shock, or relief at being rescued, must have been keeping Heathertail on her paws. But pretty soon the rush would wear off and the worst of the pain would hit her, and then she would need poppy seed to help her sleep.

Taking another look at the tabby she-cat's injuries, he was surprised that she was still standing. *Heathertail is one tough cat!*

"She really ought to go back to camp and see Kestrelflight," Larkwing pointed out. "We should all go, and come back another day with more warriors—enough of us to deal with those stoats."

"Are we sure they were stoats?" Crouchfoot asked. "They were all white!"

"I've never seen white stoats before," Larkwing added. "Do you think they're ghosts after all?"

Crowfeather rolled his eyes. "Great StarClan, is every cat bee-brained?" he asked. "If they were ghosts—which they're not—how could they touch us?"

Larkwing and Crouchfoot just looked at each other; they didn't argue, but Crowfeather didn't think he had managed to convince them. But at least Crouchfoot was treating Larkwing just like any of his other Clanmates, as if she had never set paw in the Dark Forest.

"Humph." Crowfeather let out an annoyed grumble. *I suppose we don't know what ghosts could do, but since our enemies aren't ghosts, there's no point in worrying about it.*

"I think I know why they're white," Heathertail meowed. "Because we're in leaf-bare, and once there's snow on the ground the stoats will be practically invisible. Their white pelts will make it easier for them to stalk their prey. I don't know why they have a dark tail, though," she added as an afterthought.

Crowfeather blinked at her, struck by the cleverness of her explanation. "I think you're probably right," he responded. "Thank StarClan one cat has a bit of common sense. The rest of you go back to camp with Heathertail," he added to the others. "Report to Onestar. But I can't go with you. Not until I've found Nightcloud." *Dead or alive,* he added silently to himself.

With a pang of guilt, he remembered their argument about the way he treated Breezepelt, on the way to the tunnels the day before. Right after that, Nightcloud had disappeared. He couldn't help wondering whether their argument had driven her into the paws of these strange stoats. *She might have been so angry, or upset, that it made her reckless. . . .*

His thoughts were interrupted by Breezepelt. "I'll stay, too," he meowed.

Heathertail cast him a worried glance, and Crowfeather thought she was about to protest. Then she gave her pelt a quick shake. "Just be careful when you go in there," she warned them. "I scented water up ahead, which means some of the tunnels will be flooded."

Her gaze rested on Breezepelt, deeply serious now, and

Crowfeather wondered if she was thinking the same as he was. *Will Breezepelt panic if we go too deep into the tunnels?*

Crowfeather stood still, watching as Heathertail limped away, with Crouchfoot and Larkwing on either side of her, giving her a helping paw over the rough places.

"Are you ready to go back in?" he asked Breezepelt, when the others had disappeared over the ridge.

Breezepelt glanced at him, his amber eyes widening with nervous anticipation. For a moment he hesitated; then he gave a nod. "Let's go," he muttered.

Crowfeather turned to face the dark holes gaping in the bank. "We'll go this way," he decided, heading for the entrance at the far end, the one the patrol had used the day before. "At least we won't be walking straight back into the stoats' paws."

In the first part of the tunnel, wider than most and lit from above, there was only a faint scent of stoat, and even that was stale. Crowfeather could pick up the scents of the first patrol, too, including Nightcloud, though that wasn't going to help them to find her now.

"Which tunnel did you and Nightcloud take yesterday?" Crowfeather asked Breezepelt when they reached the cave where the tunnels branched off.

"That one," Breezepelt replied, pointing with his tail.

"Lead on, then," Crowfeather meowed.

Breezepelt gave a start of surprise at his father's order, then padded cautiously into the tunnel he had indicated. Crowfeather watched him for a moment, to be sure that his courage would hold, that his nerves would not get the better of him.

When he was sure that Breezepelt was not going to flee the tunnel, Crowfeather followed. He could sense fear in his son's scent, but determination too, and his paw steps were steady.

Within moments they were plunged into complete darkness, and Crowfeather could detect damp air rising from somewhere ahead of them. "Don't forget that Heathertail warned us about flooding," he reminded Breezepelt.

He could sense his son shivering, and remembered once again the time Breezepelt had nearly drowned in the tunnels when he was an apprentice.

"It's best not to think about the past," he advised Breezepelt. Somehow it was easier to talk to him in the thick darkness than when they could face each other in the searching light of day. "But if you must think about it, remember how you survived. The memory of the terrible thing that happened here should remind you of how strong and brave you are."

His son was silent for several heartbeats, just padding on steadily down the tunnel. It had been moons since Crowfeather had paid Breezepelt a compliment, and he wasn't sure how he would take it. *Maybe I should have kept my mouth shut.*

"I'm not afraid anymore," Breezepelt responded at last. "I take after my mother, and she's the bravest cat I've ever met. That's how I know that Nightcloud is still alive."

Crowfeather had known plenty of brave cats who had met terrible ends, but he wasn't about to say that to Breezepelt. He wondered, though, if he should advise his son not to get his hopes up too high.

What if Nightcloud has drowned? Or maybe the stoats killed her.

What if we're looking for her body?

Crowfeather tried his best to push those thoughts away as he and Breezepelt moved on through the tunnels, the passages leading them farther and farther downward. Now and again Crowfeather picked up the scent of water, but they were able to avoid the flooded tunnels Heathertail had warned them about. By now the last traces of Nightcloud's scent had faded—swamped, Crowfeather guessed, by the dampness in the air and on the slick stone floor.

Finally Crowfeather became aware of a faint light filtering up from below. The scent of water grew stronger still, until the cats emerged into a huge cavern lit by a jagged hole in the roof, high above their heads. The floor was rippled stone, and across the center a river flowed, appearing from a dark hole at one side of the cave and disappearing again into another hole opposite.

Crowfeather breathed in fresher air from the other side of the river, and with it another familiar scent. He exchanged a glance with Breezepelt. *Oh, fox dung.*

"ThunderClan!"

We don't want to get any closer to them, Crowfeather thought. *After the Great Battle, it's not going to take much to create new tension among the Clans.*

"Maybe we should turn back," he told his son.

Breezepelt glared at him. "Without finding Nightcloud?"

Crowfeather flexed his claws uncomfortably on the damp stone of the cavern floor. "We haven't picked up her scent since just after we entered the tunnels. "There's no evidence that she ever came this way."

"But we have to try!" Breezepelt protested. "If she's lying injured somewhere, time could be running out for her. She could bleed to death . . . or she could be defenseless against more stoats."

Crowfeather grimaced, unsure what to do. The last thing he wanted was to put his son in danger for no reason. But what if Breezepelt was right? Staying on good terms with ThunderClan was important, but would he ever be able to forgive himself if he gave up now and later discovered that he could have saved Nightcloud if they'd kept searching just a little bit longer?

He nodded slowly. "Okay, we'll keep going."

Padding alongside the river, Crowfeather came to a narrower place where the water roared along in a deeper gully. "We can cross here," he murmured.

Drawing back a few fox-lengths, he took a run up to the bank and pushed off in a massive leap. As he took off, he felt his paws slip on the wet rock, and for a moment he was afraid that he would fall short of the opposite bank. Then he felt his paws strike the rock, but so close to the edge that he stumbled and barely managed to stop himself from falling back into the current. Regaining his balance, he turned back in time to see Breezepelt make the leap and land neatly beside him with a smug twitch of his whiskers.

"Follow me," Crowfeather murmured, ignoring his son's triumphant look. "And step quietly. There might be Thunder-Clan cats lurking."

He chose a tunnel that led upward from the far side of the cave. Light died away behind them, and the tunnel rapidly grew narrower, until he could feel his pelt brushing the walls on either side. Now and again they passed tunnels leading off to the side, but the air down there smelled musty, and there was never any doubt about which tunnel led out into the open.

Crowfeather kept on tasting the air, but there was still no sign of Nightcloud. However, the ThunderClan scent grew stronger and stronger: not just the Clan scent that clung to any territory, but fresh and complex, the mingled scent of several cats.

There are three or four different cats up there, he thought. *They must be a patrol. I hope they're just passing, and not meaning to explore the tunnels.*

"Don't make a sound," he warned Breezepelt in a low murmur.

A green light grew ahead of them, and soon Crowfeather could see the end of the tunnel, covered by an overhanging growth of fern. He could make out the shapes of cats moving around just outside. Crowfeather halted, crouching down to the tunnel floor. Glancing back at Breezepelt, he raised his tail to remind him to be silent.

"I'm talking about the safety of *all* the Clans." The voice came down the tunnel to where Crowfeather crouched concealed, the tone loud and argumentative.

Crowfeather recognized the voice. *It's that waste of fresh-kill Berrynose.*

"We should be making sure that the other Clans have been

testing the cats who fought on behalf of the Dark Forest," Berrynose went on. "As long as there are doubts about those cats' loyalties, the forest might never be peaceful."

"But we—" Another voice, which Crowfeather couldn't identify, tried to interrupt.

"Yes, we have asked stern questions of *our* warriors." Berrynose ignored the interruption. "But how do we know that the Dark Forest warriors in other Clans can really be trusted? If they can't, they should be driven out."

Crowfeather could feel the roiling anger wafting off Breezepelt, as strong as the reek of fox scent. Glancing back, he saw his son's shoulder fur bristling and his amber eyes glittering with fury. He was sure that in a couple of heartbeats Breezepelt would launch himself out of the tunnel and fling himself on Berrynose.

And it's not just Breezepelt, he told himself, thinking about the Clan deputy, Harespring; Whiskernose, who should be allowed to retire with honor to the elders' den; and Furzepelt and Larkwing, both struggling as hard as they could to be seen as loyal WindClan cats. *What right has that flea-brain Berrynose to talk about driving out any cat?*

Crowfeather began to ease his way carefully back down the tunnel, signaling to Breezepelt to do the same.

"Let's get back to looking for Nightcloud," he murmured when they had put several fox-lengths between themselves and the ThunderClan cats. "Nothing good will come of you listening to anything more that stupid furball has to say."

"I'd like to claw his pelt off," Breezepelt growled. But to

Crowfeather's relief he didn't try to argue. He simply rose to his paws and began to pad back the way they had come.

But before he and Breezepelt had traveled more than a few fox-lengths, they heard the sound they had come to dread: the scratching of innumerable claws on the stone floor of the tunnel.

"Run!" Crowfeather yowled.

The word had hardly left his jaws before the scuttling noises were all around them, and glittering, malevolent eyes reflected the dim light of the tunnel. He choked on the reek of the scent that had become horribly familiar by now. Chittering calls broke out on all sides, and before the cats could flee, they were engulfed in a rising tide of white stoats.

CHAPTER 6

Thrusting the stoats aside, Crowfeather struggled down the passage, casting a glance over his shoulder to make sure that Breezepelt was following. As he lashed out with his foreclaws, the stoats drew back, so he was able to run. With Breezepelt hard on his paws he raced down the passage toward the cavern where the river flowed, all the while hearing the scrabbling of the stoats' paws as they gave chase.

What if we meet more of them coming up?

As the thought went through his mind, a stoat sprang at Crowfeather out of the darkness, fastening its teeth in his shoulder. Letting out a screech of pain, Crowfeather shook it off and veered away down a side passage. Too late he realized how stale the air was and how the tunnel floor suddenly became uneven, littered with loose stones and soil. The passage narrowed rapidly until the walls pressed in on him on either side, almost crushing his ribs, and his ears brushed the roof.

This is a dead end!

Crowfeather stumbled to a halt and felt Breezepelt crash into him from behind, driving him even farther into the tiny space. He could taste soil in his mouth, and the air was heavy with stoat scent; he could hardly breathe.

"Go back!" he choked out.

"Can't—stoats!" Breezepelt gasped in reply.

Crowfeather could feel Breezepelt's weight on his hindquarters as he strained against the narrow walls, and could hear the chittering of the stoats as they approached, but he was too tightly stuck to get free and help his son. He braced himself, digging his claws into the ground, and felt with a shudder of horror the light trickle of earth falling from the roof onto his pelt like a dry rain.

Oh, StarClan, get us out of this!

Suddenly the pressure of Breezepelt's body on his hindquarters eased and Crowfeather was able to start moving backward. At the same moment, the stoats' shrill calls of defiance changed to sounds of alarm, and the scrabbling of their claws died away.

What happened? Crowfeather asked himself, stunned.

The stoat scent began to fade, too, and another, stronger scent rose up to take its place. A familiar voice spoke from somewhere behind him.

"You can come out now. The stoats are gone."

That's that mouse-brain Berrynose's voice, Crowfeather realized. *So much for not alerting ThunderClan that we're here!*

Paw step by paw step Crowfeather backed out of the tight tunnel until he reached the main passage again. Breezepelt was waiting for him, along with four ThunderClan warriors.

Every hair on Crowfeather's pelt grew hot with shame at

the thought of being rescued by another Clan. *Could we have been any more undignified, creeping out with our tails and hindquarters in the lead?* He was grateful that it was too dark to make out the ThunderClan cats; he was embarrassed enough without having to see the satisfied look in their eyes.

"Thank you," he meowed, the two words needing a massive effort.

Berrynose spoke again, his tone brusque. "Follow us up the tunnel."

Crowfeather and Breezepelt had no choice but to comply; Berrynose took the lead with another ThunderClan cat behind him and the remaining two ThunderClan warriors bringing up the rear. Crowfeather almost felt as if he had been taken prisoner, and had to fight to stop a growl escaping his throat. The last thing he and Breezepelt needed was to start a fight when they were not only on another Clan's territory, but also outnumbered.

As they brushed past the hanging ferns into the open, Crowfeather recognized Spiderleg following Berrynose; Rosepetal and Cinderheart made up the rest of the patrol.

No problem. Nothing to worry about here. Crowfeather gave his pelt a shake, raising his head and tail, and tried to look like a seasoned, competent warrior as he faced the ThunderClan cats. But when he caught sight of Breezepelt, his fur torn and clotted with earth, his eyes wide with the memory of terror, he realized that he probably didn't look much better himself.

"You're on ThunderClan territory," Berrynose snapped. "What are you doing at our end of the tunnels?"

"That's none of your—" Breezepelt began defensively, but Berrynose paid no attention.

"Don't you know how it looks, WindClan cats lurking up here?" he demanded. "We haven't forgotten the last time you tried launching an attack from the tunnels."

"We're not here to fight," Crowfeather mewed, trying to sound peaceable.

"Even so, you should know better," Spiderleg pointed out, the tip of his tail twitching to and fro. "Suppose we'd been a group of more hotheaded cats? There could have been trouble."

Who are you to lecture me, you bee-brain? But before Crowfeather could respond, Breezepelt let out a furious hiss. "It sounds like ThunderClan is planning for trouble—trying to tell other Clans what to do about their Dark Forest warriors. Saying they should be driven out. We're not the cats who are causing problems!"

Crowfeather winced as a tense silence followed his son's words. *Breezepelt, I may be angry too, but that was a really bad idea.* The two ThunderClan she-cats exchanged an alarmed glance, while Spiderleg's tail lashed even more furiously, and Berrynose slid out his claws and flattened his ears.

"Were you eavesdropping?" he challenged Breezepelt. "Is that what you were up to? Is WindClan *spying* on us now?"

Crowfeather could see Breezepelt's muscles bunching beneath his pelt, and stepped forward quickly before his son could leap at Berrynose. Crowfeather realized he was in the strange position of trying to temper another cat's anger.

Usually *he* was the angry cat. But as much as he would have liked to claw Berrynose's mangy pelt off and use it to line his nest . . . they were outnumbered here. And Onestar probably wouldn't like it if they accidentally started a war with ThunderClan.

"Breezepelt wasn't up to anything," Crowfeather assured them. "We were just in the tunnels . . ." He paused, wondering whether he ought to tell them about Nightcloud. *If they know stoats possibly killed one of our warriors, they might try to interfere, because that's what ThunderClan does. . . .* "We weren't spying, or trying to cause trouble," he went on rapidly, before the ThunderClan warriors could get annoyed at his hesitation. "The stoats took us by surprise, and we didn't realize we'd ended up close to ThunderClan until it was too late."

Spiderleg's gaze flicked from Crowfeather to Breezepelt and back again. "I suppose you might have had your reasons," he admitted grudgingly. "But given everything that's happened, we really should take you to Bramblestar."

"Yes, just to make sure he knows *exactly* what's going on," Berrynose agreed.

"You can try," Breezepelt growled.

Crowfeather fixed him with a glare. He sympathized with his son's anger, but if he started a fight with the ThunderClan cats, there was no guarantee either one of them would come out of it alive. He urged him silently to keep quiet.

"Hang on, Spiderleg," Cinderheart meowed. "Aren't you making too much of this? It's not like we caught Crowfeather and Breezepelt stealing prey. Wouldn't it be better just to escort them off our territory?"

Finally, Crowfeather thought, *A ThunderClan cat speaks reason.*

"And we can report this to Bramblestar without them," Rosepetal added.

"You bet we will," Berrynose muttered.

Flea-brain.

He and Spiderleg exchanged a glance; then Berrynose shrugged. "I suppose they might be right."

At a nod from Spiderleg, Crowfeather stalked away from the tunnel entrance and headed for the stream that formed the border with ThunderClan. Breezepelt followed him, with the ThunderClan cats following in a ragged half circle.

At first Crowfeather was relieved that the tension has passed and that he and Breezepelt were not going to be dragged into the fight that he was fearing. But then he remembered why they'd stepped into the tunnels, and his relief was replaced with a twinge of bitterness, a sick feeling in his throat, as if he had eaten crow-food.

That went about as badly as it could have, he thought. *And we still haven't found Nightcloud.*

"Don't come back," Berrynose snarled as Crowfeather and Breezepelt padded across the stepping stones to the Wind-Clan side of the stream. "And stay out of the tunnels. Next time you get into danger, ThunderClan might not be around to save your tails."

Breezepelt opened his jaws to retort, but he closed them again when Crowfeather slapped him on the shoulder with his tail. Both WindClan cats watched in silence as the Thunder-Clan warriors turned and vanished into the undergrowth.

Crowfeather's fur was tingling with anger—partly at the arrogance of the ThunderClan cats, but mostly at his own son.

"If you had just kept your jaws shut, we wouldn't have had that argument. Whatever tension remains between Thunder-Clan and WindClan after the Great Battle, you've just made it worse."

"But they were talking about driving cats out," Breezepelt responded. Crowfeather could see his own anger reflected in his son's eyes. "It might start with the cats who fought for the Dark Forest, but who's to say it will stop there? What if they decide it will make their whole Clan safer if they just drive the whole of WindClan away?"

"Oh, be quiet!" Crowfeather snapped. "That's ridiculous." Inwardly, though, he conceded that Breezepelt might have a point. Bramblestar hadn't been leader of ThunderClan for very long. How *would* he react if he felt WindClan was a threat? *He might be quicker to start trouble than Firestar used to be.*

Crowfeather had lost track of time while he and Breezepelt had been searching the tunnels. Now he saw that the sun was going down, the short leaf-bare day drawing to a close.

"We can worry about ThunderClan later," he meowed to Breezepelt. "Right now, our main problem is that we haven't found Nightcloud, and we can't go on looking for her in the dark. We'll have to try again in the morning. And I'm going to have to speak to Onestar about looking on the Thunder-Clan side of the tunnels. I think those are the only tunnels we haven't checked yet."

Breezepelt's only response was a grunt. Sadness rose up

in Crowfeather like rain filling a pool. What he wasn't saying—what he dreaded saying—was that if Nightcloud was alive, there had to be a reason she wasn't coming home on her own. And if she was injured or confused, it would be easier to understand her staying lost on ThunderClan territory than being unable to find her way home from WindClan's side of the tunnels.

He glanced at Breezepelt, who stared at the ground as they walked. Down in the tunnels, he and his son had briefly grown closer to each other, but now that seemed to be over. For a moment he tried to find something to say, something that might help to heal the breach—but the words eluded him like wily prey.

And now isn't the time to worry about that, he told himself. *Not with Nightcloud still missing. It's been more than a day since the stoats' attack. Do we still have time to help her, if she's injured? Or are we now just looking for a body?*

CHAPTER 7

"*We're going to need a patrol,*" Crowfeather told Onestar confidently the next morning, "but this time we should confine our search to the ThunderClan side of the tunnels. If Nightcloud made it out, that must be where she is. We've checked all the entrances on the WindClan side; we know she's not here."

Onestar, who was resting outside his den, let out a sound that landed somewhere between a growl and a purr. He didn't look pleased by this idea. "And you think ThunderClan will cooperate with this search?" he asked.

If we ask the right cat, Crowfeather thought. He hadn't forgotten Berrynose's snarl when he'd dropped them off at the edge of WindClan territory. And he'd purposely approached Onestar without Breezepelt, so that the conversation wouldn't shift to the confrontation with the ThunderClan warriors. "I think Bramblestar would," he replied.

Onestar twitched his whiskers. "Do you?" he asked. His expression was curious, and not entirely pleased.

Crowfeather hesitated before replying. He remembered his comradeship with Bramblestar on the journey to the sundrown-place. The young leader had worked hard to throw off the dark shadow Tigerstar had cast over all his kin. Long before he became leader he had proved himself to be a brave and loyal warrior. *I feel I can trust him,* Crowfeather mused, *whatever Onestar believes of him.*

"I haven't spent much time with Bramblestar lately," he meowed honestly, "but what I have seen makes me think that he is an honorable cat."

Onestar snorted and got to his feet. "Honorable cat or no, I don't want him involved in WindClan business." He avoided Crowfeather's eyes, casting his gaze across the camp to where Oatpaw was cleaning out Whiskernose's nest.

But is it just WindClan business? Crowfeather wondered, remembering Kestrelflight's vision. *Whatever's coming for us—the wind wasn't enough to drive it back alone.*

"Onestar," he said, carefully choosing his words. *Don't say "flea-brained"; don't say "flea-brained."* "It would be . . . foolish . . . of us to give up on finding Nightcloud just because we don't want to involve ThunderClan."

"Who said we're giving up?" Onestar retorted, turning back with an irritated expression. "No, I don't want to look on ThunderClan territory. But if you want to look *elsewhere* . . ."

"But what if she's *on* ThunderClan territory?" Crowfeather asked, struggling to hide his frustration. *If you make Onestar mad, he'll dismiss the patrol idea for sure.* "It isn't a matter of where we want to go. It's a matter of where she is. We know there's something wrong. Nightcloud must be injured, or confused. If she'd come up on the WindClan side of the tunnels, she would be home by now."

"It hasn't been that long," Onestar mewed calmly. "Don't give up on her so easily. Nightcloud is a strong warrior. If she's alive, she'll find her way home."

"I'm not *giving up* on her," Crowfeather retorted, gritting his teeth. *Why will no cat listen to reason in this bee-brained Clan?* "Badgering you to find her is the opposite of giving up."

Onestar turned away now, in the direction of the fresh-kill pile. "No," he said shortly. "I've heard you, but I won't involve ThunderClan. Just be patient, Crowfeather. She'll come home . . . if she's alive."

As the leader strolled away, Crowfeather felt frustration gripping his heart like a rabbit in a trap. *What if she's alive and can't come to us?* he thought miserably.

And how am I going to explain this to Breezepelt?

Later that morning, Breezepelt returned from the dawn patrol and strolled immediately up to Crowfeather. "When do we leave?" he asked.

"Leave?" Crowfeather asked, caught off guard. He was finishing up a vole and preparing to take Hootpaw and Featherpaw on a hunt. With Nightcloud missing, Hootpaw was temporarily his second apprentice. The two apprentices tousled with each other in the grass, laughing and taunting each other. It reminded Crowfeather how close they were to still being kits. *And how little sense they have.*

"To find Nightcloud," Breezepelt explained. The irritated tone in his voice seemed to add "obviously." "I was thinking of her when we passed the memorial stones this morning. Wind-Clan lost so many warriors in the Great Battle. . . . Nightcloud must know we need her more than ever. If she were able to come back on her own, I know she'd be here." He looked at Crowfeather urgently.

"Ah." Crowfeather swallowed the last of his vole and took a deep breath. "Well . . . I spoke to Onestar this morning."

"And?" Breezepelt asked.

And he proved himself to be a furball, Crowfeather thought. *But I shouldn't think that of our leader.* "He's . . . reluctant to involve ThunderClan."

Breezepelt looked confused. "Okay. So?"

"Like I said, we've already looked at all the WindClan entrances," Crowfeather explained. "And really, Nightcloud could find her way home from any of them, even if she were injured. Now I think—if she survived—she must have come out on ThunderClan territory."

Breezepelt looked blank for a moment, but then his eyes lit with understanding. "You think ThunderClan has her?"

No, no, no! Crowfeather shook his head hard. *The last thing we need is Breezepelt charging into ThunderClan, demanding his mother. . . .* "No, but I think she may have come out on their territory and evaded their patrols. Or else she came out on their territory and wandered elsewhere, off any Clan's territory."

Breezepelt nodded. "That makes sense. So what does Onestar want to do? Talk to Bramblestar? Sneak onto their territory?"

Crowfeather looked away. He wasn't sure how to tell Breezepelt the truth: that Onestar seemed to want to do nothing.

"Crowfeather?" Breezepelt asked.

Crowfeather's eyes lit on Hootpaw and Featherpaw, whose roughhousing had gotten more intense. "You two there, cut it out! You're not flea-brained kits anymore!" he yelled.

The two apprentices disentangled, looking at Crowfeather with mingled embarrassment and amusement.

"Sorry, Crowfeather," Featherpaw said. "Will we be leaving soon?"

"Very," Crowfeather replied. "Get ready."

"Leaving for where?" Breezepelt asked. When Crowfeather turned back to his son, he could read the disappointment in his eyes. And then his expression turned hard. "We're not going on any patrol, are we?"

Crowfeather flicked his ear awkwardly. "Not today . . ."

"When, then?" Breezepelt asked, taking a step toward Crowfeather, his expression challenging. "When exactly are we finding my mother? What did you and *Onestar* decide?"

The tom's voice was rising, attracting attention from the other warriors who were collected around the fresh-kill pile, chatting and relaxing as they ate their morning meal. Crowfeather saw Harespring look over at the two of them with dread in his eyes. Even Emberfoot, who'd defended Breezepelt in the past, looked concerned about the anger in his voice.

They're staring. Embarrassment prickled beneath Crowfeather's pelt. And—as it often did—he felt that embarrassment turn into annoyance with Breezepelt.

"We can't just go traipsing over into ThunderClan's territory," he meowed scornfully. "You know that, Breezepelt." He lowered his voice. "Especially not when you practically start a battle with ThunderClan warriors the moment you catch sight of them! Don't you think your spat with Berrynose and the others will come up the minute we ask for ThunderClan's help?"

"You think this is *my* fault?" Breezepelt exclaimed incredulously—and *loudly*. "I trusted you! I trusted you to speak with Onestar without me, and you bungled it all up! We're losing time!"

"I know," Crowfeather hissed, his throat hot. "But we have—"

Have to be careful, he'd meant to say. Or *have to think of a way to convince Onestar.*

But it didn't matter, because Breezepelt whirled away and stomped off before he even got past the first word.

Watching him go, Crowfeather felt his embarrassment and anger fade into disappointment. He saw the other warriors watching Breezepelt too, disapproval in their eyes.

But he's not wrong, Crowfeather thought, turning back to collect the apprentices. *We have to figure out a way to find Nightcloud—before it's too late.*

The sun's light was pure, blinding white, but the air was frigid, and Crowfeather's, Featherpaw's, and Hootpaw's paws crunched against the hardened snow that clung to some parts of the moor. The sky was pure blue, dotted with silver-gray clouds.

"I can't wait for newleaf," Hootpaw mewed as he and Featherpaw trailed Crowfeather. "Leaf-bare is the hardest season."

This *leaf-bare certainly is,* Crowfeather thought. *And it has nothing to do with the cold or lack of prey.* "Hard or not, a cat must know how to survive in all seasons," Crowfeather replied. "So today we'll focus on working together to catch prey."

He explained how changes in the terrain presented new challenges in leaf-bare. Snow that crunched beneath paws could serve as an alert system for the prey they chased—or, cats could use it to their advantage.

"Let's try a new technique," Crowfeather went on. "Hootpaw, I want you to wait behind this bush, where the snow is piled. When prey approaches the bush, you move your paws to crunch the snow—that will startle the prey, and it'll run toward us. Then Featherpaw—it's your job to surprise it and make the killing blow."

The apprentices eagerly agreed, and Hootpaw settled down, hidden behind the bush in the hardened snow. Crowfeather crawled into a small indentation in the ground to watch. All three cats grew silent.

It seemed like a long time before a tiny brown mouse, fluffed up in the cold, darted into the bush from a nearby hole. Crowfeather watched, not making a sound, as Hootpaw's eyes widened and then he scrambled to his paws, scrabbling them on the ground to make a satisfying crunch. Unfortunately, Hootpaw was so excited, or so cold, that he stood awkwardly and slid on the snow. As his paws went out from under him, Hootpaw fell on his back in the snow, making the expected crunch—but not in the intended way at all.

The mouse was still startled, though, and began to dart back to the hole. Crowfeather turned expectantly to Featherpaw, only to find her doubled over with amusement, her eyes dancing as she stared at Hootpaw.

As the mouse passed near Featherpaw, she made a half-hearted attempt to grab it, but her attention was still clearly on Hootpaw.

"Pay attention!" Crowfeather snapped.

The mouse slipped easily back into its hole. When it was gone, both Featherpaw and Hootpaw dissolved into laughter.

"I'm sorry!" Featherpaw mewed. "It's just . . . Hootpaw looked so ridiculous!"

Hootpaw, who was still lying on his back, shook his head. "It was an accident! The snow was so slippery. . . ."

Crowfeather got to his feet and stalked toward them, his neck fur ruffled with annoyance. "Do you think this is a *game*?" he asked.

Both apprentices abruptly stopped laughing, looking up at him with regret.

"No . . . ," mewed Hootpaw. "It's just . . ."

Crowfeather turned his attention to Featherpaw. "Do you think your Clanmates' bellies will be filled with your amusement? Do you think a good warrior turns away from a hunt to entertain her friends?"

Now Featherpaw really looked ashamed. "No, Crowfeather." She cast her eyes at the ground.

Crowfeather strode to a stop just in front of her. "You're usually a good apprentice," he murmured. When he sensed Hootpaw shifting uncomfortably from where he stood, Crowfeather turned to him and added, "You usually are, too,

Hootpaw. At least, I have every reason to believe that from Nightcloud."

Hootpaw swallowed and nodded, his eyes on the ground.

Crowfeather let out a sigh. *Am I being too hard on them? Hootpaw lost Nightcloud, too.*

He nodded. "Right, then. Let's try that again. Maybe we're all just a little off today."

Or maybe it's going to be hard to handle two apprentices at once, Crowfeather mused as he stalked back to the indentation in the ground, settling in and focusing his attention on the bush Hootpaw hid behind.

Just one more reason we need Nightcloud back as soon as possible. . . .

CHAPTER 8
❧

Crowfeather limped through the tunnels, lost in the darkness with no idea of where he was going. He couldn't remember fighting against the stoats, but one of his paws was bleeding from a bite and several of his claws had been ripped out. He felt so exhausted that he could hardly force himself to put one paw in front of another.

But I have to keep going. I have to find Nightcloud.

Then Crowfeather saw movement ahead, though how he could see anything in this thick darkness was a mystery to him. At first he thought it must be more stoats, but after a moment he recognized that it was a cat's tail, whisking around the bends in the tunnel, always just ahead of him.

Nightcloud!

But then he noticed that this cat's tail was gray, not black. *Then who . . . ?* At last Crowfeather realized who the cat must be. "Ashfoot!" he called out, warmth spreading through his pelt in anticipation of seeing his mother again. "Ashfoot!"

Summoning all his strength, Crowfeather put on a burst of speed and rounded the next corner. *There she is!* Ashfoot was sitting beside the tunnel wall where the passage widened out into a small cave. Her gray fur glimmered with a pale light, and her eyes shone as she gazed at Crowfeather.

"Oh, Ashfoot," Crowfeather whispered. Here in the tunnels, under his mother's gentle gaze, he didn't have to be the fierce, unapproachable warrior that his Clan knew. "I miss you so much. . . . But why are you here? Why aren't you in StarClan?"

"I can't leave you yet," his mother replied. "There are tasks you must do. You could lose everything."

Crowfeather scowled. "Do you mean Breezepelt?" he asked with a sigh. "Are you yet another cat telling me I have to work things out with him?"

Ashfoot shook her head sadly and gestured with her tail toward the other side of the cave. Crowfeather turned and saw a pool of blood spreading out on the cave floor from a mound of black fur beside the wall. He glanced at Ashfoot, confused, but his mother said nothing. He turned and padded toward the black shape, carefully skirting the dark, sticky pool. His heart slammed into his throat as he realized he was looking at a dead cat.

"Nightcloud!"

Crowfeather woke with a gasp. He was lying in his own nest under the stars, his breathing fast and shallow and his heart pounding so hard he thought it would burst out of his chest.

It was a dream . . . , he told himself. *Just a dream . . . It doesn't mean Nightcloud is really dead. It doesn't.*

He lay still until his breathing settled and his heartbeat calmed, but he didn't think he would get any more sleep that night. He felt too tense: He was worrying about Nightcloud, afraid that if she was dead they would never have the chance to settle their unfinished business. He wondered whether Kestrelflight's vision of the flood could be related to Nightcloud's disappearance. The clash with the ThunderClan warriors came back into his mind, too, and he imagined the whole of the Clan pouring out of the tunnels, just as Breezepelt had suggested, ready to attack WindClan.

Across the den, he could hear a cat tossing and thrashing around. Breezepelt. His son hadn't slept quietly in the short amount of time since they'd lost Nightcloud. Slowly, Crowfeather rose to his paws and gave his pelt a shake.

The truth was, he couldn't ignore the dream he'd just had. He was no medicine cat, but he knew it meant something. He also realized knew that Onestar was unlikely to approve another patrol for what he already felt was a lost cause—certainly not on ThunderClan territory, which was where Crowfeather meant to go. If any cat saw him leave, they'd likely stop him and tell him as much. Still, he couldn't just lie around until morning, worrying himself into a froth. He had to *do* something. *I have to go look for Nightcloud.* And if he left now, he could survey the ThunderClan territory before the dawn patrol arrived.

Crowfeather padded over to Breezepelt, avoiding the sleeping bodies of his Clanmates, keeping his head turned away from the empty nest of moss and bracken where Nightcloud used to sleep. His son wanted to find Nightcloud even more than he did. He'd want to go. But by the time Crowfeather reached his son's nest, Breezepelt had settled down a little, and Crowfeather changed his mind.

It would be unkind to wake him now. Besides, there will be less chance of getting caught if I go alone.

Hesitantly he stretched out a paw and held it just above his son's shoulder, not quite touching. He almost drew it back, but then he laid it on Breezepelt's fur, murmuring, "It will be all right."

He was rewarded by seeing Breezepelt sink into a deeper sleep, though his ears twitched now and again, and he let out faint whimpers. Crowfeather left him and slipped away to the edge of the camp, waiting for the first light of dawn to touch the moor.

As soon as he could make out the line of the ridge above the camp, and the memorial pile of stones, Crowfeather rose to his paws and slid silently out of the camp, stepping as lightly as if he were stalking a mouse. As soon as he was well clear, where no cat was likely to hear him, he picked up his pace and raced down the hill toward the tunnels.

A strong drive to find Nightcloud gave strength and energy to Crowfeather's limbs. He pushed away any thought of the risks he was taking, except to feel glad that he hadn't taken Breezepelt with him. He didn't want to expose his son to any more danger. He'd already been through enough.

Am I worrying about finding Nightcloud because I want to protect Breezepelt? he asked himself. *Nightcloud and I weren't on the best* terms when she disappeared, but his life will surely be easier if I bring her back. . . . If nothing else, he won't have to beat himself up over losing her.

He considered the question for a long time, but he wasn't sure of his own intentions. He knew he owed Nightcloud a great debt, too. . . . Perhaps I need to repay her for the way things ended between us. Either way, he couldn't leave her out here. He had to find her—dead or alive. At least then they'd know what happened to her.

Crowfeather didn't enter the tunnels on the WindClan side. Instead he skirted the steep bank and the dark, gaping holes as he followed his own scent trail back to the border stream. With every paw step he kept his ears pricked and his jaws parted to pick up the faintest sound or scent of the white stoats, but nothing disturbed the silence of the night.

Every hair on his pelt prickled with apprehension as he bounded lightly across the stepping stones and onto ThunderClan territory.

If the ThunderClan cats find me here, after what happened yesterday, he thought, then I'll really be in trouble. Still, it would be worth it, if he could bring Nightcloud home.

It was too early for the dawn patrol, but Crowfeather stayed alert in case there was a cat or two out for some night hunting. He slid furtively through the undergrowth, shivering as the frosty grass scraped along his pelt. He reached the tunnel entrance where he and Breezepelt had met the ThunderClan cats, but he couldn't pick up even the faintest trace of Nightcloud there.

His belly was churning as he moved on to where he thought

he could find another entrance. He didn't know this territory well, and every heartbeat that passed made him fear that an unexpected ThunderClan patrol would find him.

The first birds were beginning to twitter as Crowfeather approached the next tunnel entrance, low down between a couple of rocks that jutted out of the forest floor. There he stopped, quivering. A tail-length from the nearest boulder he picked up a scent: faded and stale, but unmistakably Nightcloud's.

She was here.

Hope sprang up inside Crowfeather at finding proof that Nightcloud had left the tunnels alive, that the stoats hadn't killed her. *Breezepelt was right. She is a fierce warrior....*

Then he saw a smear of blood on the rock. *No!*

She was wounded, then... but how badly? If she escaped from the tunnels, why didn't she come home? For a moment Crowfeather wondered whether it had something to do with the way he and Nightcloud had argued, then gave his head a dismissive shake.

It's not always about you, mouse-brain! he chided himself. *Nightcloud is far too loyal to leave her Clan over an argument with you—she doesn't even like you.*

Forgetting all about possible ThunderClan patrols, Crowfeather put his nose to the ground and began to follow Nightcloud's scent. It veered in the direction of the WindClan border, but from here she had a long way to go. With every paw step Crowfeather was afraid that he would find her body, but although he spotted more traces of blood, the scent trail did not disappear.

Then Crowfeather came to a shallow dip in the ground, with a pool of water at the bottom surrounded by ferns. Nightcloud's scent led down toward the water; flattened and broken grass stems suggested that she had fallen or slid down. He traced her path through the ferns, guessing that she must have been desperate for a drink of water. Maybe she was still there, waiting for her Clan to come find her!

But as Crowfeather reached the water's edge, his remaining hope vanished. A flattened patch among the plants that overhung the pool told him where Nightcloud must have lain down. Blood had soaked into the ground and was clotted on the fern fronds. And Nightcloud's scent was almost drowned by the mingled smells around the pool: the faint, stale tang of dog and Twolegs, and the overwhelming *reek* of fox.

Crowfeather shivered. *Did the fox get her? That's most likely. She would have already been injured, perhaps too exhausted to fight it off.* He pictured the black she-cat, weak and wounded, her glossy fur matted with blood, turning on the fox with her teeth bared and her claws out, using the last of her strength in a desperate attempt to escape its cruel fangs.

She was so brave. . . . She wouldn't be easy prey.

Crowfeather bent his head to the flattened patch of plants and breathed in Nightcloud's scent. He felt a sharp pain in his chest, as if every thorn in the forest were digging into him. *She was a loyal WindClan warrior. We're not too far into ThunderClan territory . . . she would have known where she was. If she were alive, she would have done whatever it took to get back to camp. Oh, Nightcloud . . .*

He realized that while he and Nightcloud had never loved

each other as mates were meant to, he cared about her more than he had ever admitted. He admired her strength and her loyalty, and the way she had always protected Breezepelt. Crowfeather knew now that he had never appreciated what a good mother she had been.

I wish I'd told her that . . . but now it's too late. She's gone.

CHAPTER 9

Crowfeather sat at the edge of the warriors' den, forcing himself to choke down a vole. Memories of his terrible discovery earlier that morning—the blood-soaked nest in the ferns, and the stink of fox that tainted the air around the pool—took away the last traces of his appetite. But he made himself eat because he knew he would need all his strength for what he had to do now.

Nightcloud is surely dead. . . . How am I going to tell Breezepelt?

On his way back to camp, Crowfeather, still stunned by his discovery, had almost forgotten that he was trespassing on a rival Clan's territory. Heading for the border stream, he had thrust his way through a bank of ferns and emerged into the open to see a ThunderClan patrol padding through the undergrowth a couple of fox-lengths away from him. *Fox dung!*

Quickly he withdrew into the ferns and crouched there, peering out, convinced that at any moment his scent would give him away, and that this time he *would* be brought to Bramblestar. *And Onestar will have my head.* Then, to his relief, he noticed that all four cats were loaded with prey. Hardly daring to breathe, he prayed to StarClan that the scent of the fresh-kill would mask his own, just long enough for the patrol to pass him without realizing he was there.

He was in luck—they walked by close enough that they ruffled the fern fronds where he was hiding, but didn't spot him, didn't scent him. Crowfeather had stayed there for many heartbeats, shaking from ears to tail-tip, until he felt fit to go on.

When Crowfeather returned to camp, he was almost relieved that Breezepelt was nowhere to be found. For a few moments, at least, he could delay the inevitable. *How am I going to tell him his mother is dead?* Now Crowfeather spotted him stalking back into camp with a rabbit dangling from his jaws. Heathertail and Harespring were with him, also laden with prey.

Crowfeather's gaze followed Breezepelt as he padded across the camp and deposited his prey on the fresh-kill pile. His belly churned as he tried to decide what he would say to his son.

I can't put it off any longer. . . .

When Breezepelt had dropped his prey, he turned immediately to Heathertail. Crowfeather was close enough to overhear their conversation.

"You have to help me," Breezepelt meowed urgently. "I'm not asking you to go back into the tunnels, just show me how to figure out the layout. I'm going down there again to find Nightcloud, and no cat is going to stop me!"

"But, Breezepelt—" Heathertail began.

While Breezepelt was speaking, Crowfeather had bounded

over to join the two younger cats, and now he interrupted whatever Heathertail had been about to say.

"That won't be necessary," he mewed gently in response to Breezepelt.

Pain tore at him like a badger's claw as he saw the hope flaring in his son's eyes.

"You mean you went? You found her?" Breezepelt asked.

Crowfeather sought the right words, but for a moment all he could do was let his head droop, shaking it sadly. "I couldn't sleep last night," he began at last, "so I went out and looked for Nightcloud again at the ThunderClan end of the tunnels. But I didn't find her. I caught her scent and followed it to a clearing with a pool. Her blood was on the ground, and there was a terrible reek of fox. I think . . . Breezepelt, I think a fox may have taken her."

Crowfeather had expected a furious denial, or perhaps a wail of despair from his son. Instead, as the hope died in Breezepelt's eyes, the black tom seemed to shrink, drawing into himself. Crowfeather's heart was wrenched at the change in him.

"I don't want you to blame yourself," he meowed. "It wasn't your fault."

Several heartbeats passed before Breezepelt responded. "No, I don't blame myself. It's *their* fault." His voice was deadly quiet. "*They* killed her."

"Who?" Crowfeather asked, bewildered, unsure what Breezepelt was talking about. *ThunderClan? Onestar?*

"The stoats. Those vicious mange-pelts in the tunnels."

There was a savage glare in Breezepelt's eyes, and he tensed his muscles as if he could see his enemy in front of him. "Nightcloud was a great fighter, and so brave. The stoats must have hurt her badly, or she could have fought the fox, or run away."

"Breezepelt, I'm so sorry," Heathertail mewed, stroking the tip of her tail down his flank.

Breezepelt seemed hardly aware of her. "We can't put it off any longer," he told Crowfeather. "We *must* kill every last stoat. After what they did to Nightcloud, they have to pay! I don't care what it takes."

"Calm down," Crowfeather told him sternly. "Yes, it's terrible what the stoats have done, but they're stupid, crow-food-eating creatures—hardly cold-blooded killers. We'll get the stoats out, and prevent that horrible scene in Kestrelflight's vision, but you mustn't do anything rash."

His son gave him a glare as cold as the wind that swept across the moor in leaf-bare. "I don't care about Kestrelflight's vision," he hissed, "and I don't care what you call them. I just want the stoats dead. Nightcloud was the only cat who really cared about me, and they murdered her. I'm going to make them regret ever laying their filthy paws on my mother."

For a moment Crowfeather was frozen into silence, stunned by the force of Breezepelt's anger. He knew that he should reassure Breezepelt, tell him that he had a father who cared for him, too—but for some reason the words were stuck in his throat.

Breezepelt was *scaring* him a little bit. *Is this how the rest of the Clan sees him? Angry and unpredictable?*

Before he could find what he needed to tell his son, Leaftail sidled up to them, a suspicious look in his amber eyes. "Did you just say you don't care about Kestrelflight's vision?" he asked.

Oh, StarClan.

Crowfeather wanted to tell Leaftail to leave Breezepelt alone, because he had just learned of his mother's death. But before he could speak, Breezepelt turned on the tabby tom with a snarl of anger.

"I *don't* care! I need to kill the animals in the tunnels. That's the only thing that matters." With a lash of his tail he strode off into the warriors' den.

By now more cats were gathering around, listening to the exchange in curious silence.

"That proves it, then," Leaftail announced, his gaze raking across the crowd. "If Breezepelt were truly loyal to Wind-Clan, he would respect his medicine cat. Every cat knows how important Kestrelflight's vision was! How can we prevent the flood if we don't work together?"

A murmur of agreement rose from some of the other warriors, while the rest exchanged doubtful glances. Irritated, Crowfeather let his voice rise above the sound.

"Don't be such a sanctimonious cleanpaw. Of course Breezepelt cares about the vision," he snarled. "But he just learned that Nightcloud is dead—that's why he's angry. How would any of you flea-brains feel if those animals had killed *your* mother? You think you're so much better than him? Please! Give him time to deal with his grief."

For a moment the cats around were silent, exchanging shocked, incredulous glances. "Wait, Nightcloud is dead? How do you know?" Leaftail challenged Crowfeather.

"I found signs she was gravely injured in the tunnels, and then she was attacked by a fox," Crowfeather replied. "If she'd been healthy, the fox would have been no match for Nightcloud, but with her wounds . . . She must have been too weak. I just told Breezepelt, and he's not taking it very well. You should all understand that."

Crouchfoot twitched his whiskers into a sneer. "Maybe Breezepelt is taking it so badly because he knows he could have done more to save his mother. After all, he was the only one with her in the tunnels."

Again Crowfeather could see that many of his Clanmates agreed with Crouchfoot, as they gazed after Breezepelt with unsympathetic eyes. But Heathertail's shoulder fur bristled with indignation as she faced them.

"I can't believe you said that!" she spat at Crouchfoot. "Breezepelt is just as loyal to WindClan as any of you—maybe more. Like you said, he was with her in the tunnels, putting his life on the line for all of us—and where were *you*?"

"I was on the second patrol!" Crouchfoot began indignantly, but Heathertail ignored him.

Spinning around, she headed after Breezepelt, only to halt as Crowfeather stepped into her path. He felt a warm glow of appreciation at the way she had defended his son, but he knew Breezepelt well enough to see that he wouldn't welcome any cat right now, not even Heathertail. "Give him some space," he advised her. "He's angry now. Don't give him the opportunity to say things he doesn't mean."

"Yeah, don't bother," Leaftail put in. "We're all sorry Nightcloud's dead, but Breezepelt can't be trusted. There's something dark inside him. He fought on the side of the Dark Forest, after all. Maybe he deserves all this bad stuff that's happening to him."

Heathertail's eyes widened in fury and disbelief. "You . . . you heartless flea-pelt!" she snarled. "How could you say that? He just lost his mother!" She gave a single lash of her tail, then turned and ran up the side of the hollow and out of the camp.

The rest of the cats watched her go, then turned to look at Crowfeather. Clearly, they were waiting to see what he would do.

Crowfeather wanted to join Heathertail in speaking up for his son, but his Clanmates' hatred of the Dark Forest cats hung in the air like the reek of fox beside the pool where Nightcloud died. He felt burning in the depths of his belly, and a lump in his throat that stopped him from speaking.

Fighting on the side of the Dark Forest was wrong, but Breezepelt is still my son, even if we have never been close. How long can he be expected to go on paying for his past mistakes?

He stood gazing at his paws, then gave his head a helpless shake. He knew that Breezepelt had been loyal to WindClan ever since the Great Battle, but it hadn't done him any good. His Clanmates would always look at him with suspicion. *Maybe he's doomed to always be an outsider.*

Worry about Breezepelt threatened to overwhelm

Crowfeather. His son had suffered more than any cat could be expected to take: the loss of his reputation, the attack by the stoats, and now the death of his mother. *I don't want him to turn out even more angry and wounded than he already is.*

But Crowfeather had no idea how he could reach Breezepelt or comfort him. He realized that what he wanted was to go and discuss their son with Nightcloud. She would be able to comfort Breezepelt. *But she's gone now. Breezepelt only has me . . . his father.*

A huge weight seemed to descend on Crowfeather's shoulders as he admitted that he had no answers to offer Breezepelt, only more questions and doubt. And he had no answers to give his Clanmates, either. They were determined to distrust Breezepelt, and he wasn't sure they entirely trusted *him*, either. Nothing he could say would change that.

Slowly he turned and padded away in the opposite direction from Breezepelt. It was time to talk to Onestar, and tell him that Nightcloud was dead.

CHAPTER 10

❧

"Tonight, we will sit vigil for Nightcloud," Onestar announced. "We will honor her as a brave warrior and a valued member of our Clan."

As soon as the sun had risen on the day after Crowfeather's discovery of the place where Nightcloud had died, Onestar had called a Clan meeting. He hadn't been thrilled to learn that Crowfeather had sneaked onto ThunderClan territory, but his anger had softened when he'd learned of Nightcloud's death. She was a beloved WindClan warrior, and the leader was clearly sad to lose her. The loss felt even worse coming on the paws of so many Great Battle deaths.

Every cat was subdued as they gathered around, and Crowfeather's paws itched with restlessness.

I want to be out there doing something, not standing here listening to our Clan leader.

As saddened as he was by Nightcloud's death, knowing that the stoats were still in the tunnels was worrying Crowfeather. He couldn't forget Kestrelflight's vision of the storm, suggesting that WindClan might almost be destroyed if they failed to deal with the threat. And he couldn't stop thinking about how the wind hadn't been enough to stop the flood. *Does that mean we'll have to involve other Clans? Is Onestar going about this all wrong?*

At dawn that morning, Breezepelt had tried to leave the camp, intent on taking revenge by entering the tunnels alone and killing every stoat he found there. It had taken five cats to hold him back, and finally Heathertail had convinced him to wait. She'd told him they would take on the stoats, but to do that, they needed him at his full strength. He needed rest. He argued for a while, but eventually he gave in, and now Heathertail watched over him as he slept.

But what happens when he wakes up? Crowfeather asked himself gloomily. *How do I help him deal with his grief, without running foolishly into an ambush of stoats?* He had no idea. He hadn't even spoken to Breezepelt since he announced that Nightcloud was dead, and he doubted that his son wanted his support.

"Now there's one more task for me to do," Onestar continued. "Hootpaw, Nightcloud was a good mentor to you, but she is gone, and you will need another cat to guide you through the rest of your apprenticeship. Gorsetail, you are a loyal and intelligent cat. I know you will pass these qualities on to Hootpaw."

A look of pleased surprise spread over Gorsetail's face. "I'll do my best, Onestar," she responded.

Crowfeather blinked at the gray-and-white she-cat, not sure how he felt about this. On the one paw, he was relieved to be back to one apprentice—training Featherpaw would be easier now. But on the other, Crowfeather couldn't forget that Gorsetail had openly mocked Breezepelt and said he couldn't be trusted. It seemed wrong, in a way, for her to take over Nightcloud's apprentice.

Hootpaw was standing in the circle of cats, his head and tail drooping in dejection. Crowfeather knew he was grieving for his lost mentor. But when Onestar mentioned his name he looked up and gave his pelt a shake. As he padded over to Gorsetail and touched noses with her, he was clearly determined to do his best.

Even though training two apprentices had been a challenge, Crowfeather liked the sturdy, enthusiastic young apprentice. *Gorsetail isn't my favorite cat, but I'm sure she'll try to be a good mentor for Hootpaw. And I'll keep an eye on him, too—it's the least I can do for Nightcloud.*

"Harespring, it's time to send out hunting patrols," Onestar meowed, angling his ears toward his deputy. "But no cat is to hunt near the tunnels for the time being."

A murmur of disapproval greeted the Clan leader's announcement. Crouchfoot called out, "Are we just leaving that part of our territory to the stoats?"

"Certainly not," Onestar responded with an irritated flick of his tail. "But we've lost Nightcloud, and some of our warriors are still bearing wounds from the last skirmish. I intend to wait until every cat is healed and strong again and we've had time to figure out what to do next. Meanwhile, I don't want the creatures provoked. If they think that cats aren't coming back to fight them, they might get lazy and careless—which means they will be easier for us to deal with."

Crouchfoot shrugged and muttered something inaudible but didn't protest again.

Onestar declared that the meeting was over, and Harespring began to organize the hunting patrols.

"Please, Harespring, can Hootpaw and I hunt together?" Featherpaw asked as the deputy padded over toward her and Crowfeather, who gave his apprentice a stern look. "That's not for you to decide," he scolded.

Featherpaw didn't seem bothered by his rebuke; she kept a hopeful gaze fixed on Harespring.

"I don't see why not," Harespring mewed kindly. "I'll go and tell Gorsetail, and find a couple of other cats to go with you."

Crowfeather was just about to tell Featherpaw that an apprentice's job was to do as she was told and keep her mouth shut, but he heard a low-voiced murmur from behind him.

"I still think it's really suspicious, how Nightcloud went missing in the tunnels. I mean, no cat was there to see what happened. . . . Well, no cat except Breezepelt."

Crowfeather felt his muscles tense and every hair on his pelt start to rise. He had recognized Weaselfur's voice, and he flicked an ear back to hear more clearly.

"Yeah, all that yowling and wailing this morning." That was Leaftail's voice. "It felt like he was just pretending. That's suspicious, all right!"

Shifting slightly, Crowfeather managed to steal a glance at the two cats without letting them see that he could overhear them. Weaselfur and Leaftail were standing with their heads together, surrounded by a few of their Clanmates, who were waiting to be assigned to a patrol.

"Why is Breezepelt so sure Nightcloud is even dead?" Weaselfur continued. "After all, we only have Breezepelt's word for it, and he was one of the cats who fought for the Dark Forest. Maybe he's sure because he killed her, and he's beside himself with guilt. How much can we trust him, or any of the Dark Forest cats?"

Is he serious? How many times do I have to say it—Breezepelt would never hurt Nightcloud! It was all Crowfeather could do not to leap out at Weaselfur and confront him, but he forced himself to stand still and listen to what else the ginger tom might have to say.

"Oh, come on, now," Emberfoot protested loudly at Weaselfur's accusation.

"Ridiculous," Sedgewhisker agreed. "Hasn't Breezepelt been punished enough, losing his mother? Must you now make these silly accusations?" When the other cats ignored them, the two of them turned away and padded off.

Leaftail watched them go, then nodded in agreement with Weaselfur. "I don't know why Onestar doesn't just drive out the cats who trained with the Dark Forest. Wouldn't that be the wise thing to do? Better safe than sorry."

Crowfeather slid out his claws, digging them into the ground. *Why are these cats turning against Breezepelt? He's just lost his mother! And they must know that he would never have hurt her. Whatever problems Breezepelt has had with his Clanmates, he has always loved Nightcloud.*

Guilt gripped deep inside Crowfeather when he thought about his own recent distrust of his son. It seemed as mousebrained now as these theories that Breezepelt had hurt Nightcloud. He foresaw, too, that more cats turning against

Breezepelt could mean trouble for the entire Clan. If Onestar defended him, as Crowfeather expected, cats would end up taking sides, which meant that soon there would be a split in the Clan that would be almost impossible to repair.

"I agree. Onestar should just exile the Dark Forest cats. I mean, I know they swore an oath of loyalty, but they've broken oaths before. Why take the chance and keep them around?"

Crowfeather started at the sound of Featherpaw's voice just behind him. He hadn't realized that she had been close enough to overhear what Weaselfur and Leaftail had been saying. He was shocked that the rumors were spreading among the impressionable apprentices; it was bad enough that the warriors were saying such things.

Before Crowfeather could speak, the reply came from Gorsetail, who padded up with Hootpaw at her side. "Because we are one Clan," she growled, "and we forgive our Clan-mates—even when they've made terrible mistakes. Now let's get on with this hunt. Larkwing is going to join us, too."

Crowfeather shot a grateful look at Gorsetail as together they chivvied the apprentices away from Weaselfur and Leaftail and up the slope to the edge of the camp, where Larkwing was waiting. He was glad to see that Gorsetail had chosen her; it seemed as if the gray-and-white she-cat had changed her mind about the Dark Forest cats—or most of them, at least. Maybe the responsibility of being a mentor again would do her good.

Hootpaw and Featherpaw were padding along side by side. Crowfeather could see their fur bristling with excitement at the thought of hunting, and was glad that Hootpaw had something to distract him from missing his mentor.

But it won't last long, for either of us, he thought sadly. Tonight they would sit vigil for Nightcloud, and there would be nothing left to do but face their grief.

The sun had gone down, though a few streaks of daylight still stained the sky. Above the moor the first warriors of StarClan had begun to appear. Crowfeather raised his head and gazed up at them.

Are you looking down at us, Nightcloud? Or are you still searching for the path that leads to StarClan?

Cats padded past him where he stood at the edge of the warriors' den, making for the center of the camp. Onestar was already there, waiting to begin the vigil for Nightcloud.

Crowfeather glanced toward the dark shape of Breezepelt curled up in his nest. To Crowfeather's relief he hadn't made another attempt to head for the tunnels to attack the stoats. Crowfeather felt that he should try to talk to him, but he didn't know how.

Hesitantly, Crowfeather slipped between the empty nests of other warriors until he reached Breezepelt's side. His son was awake, but he didn't get up as Crowfeather approached, only looked up at him with dull, incurious eyes.

"Do you want to walk over to the vigil with me?" Crowfeather asked, half expecting Breezepelt to snap at him and say he didn't need an escort as if he was an apprentice.

But Breezepelt's actual response surprised his father even

more. "No. I don't need an escort, because I'm not going."

"Why not?"

Breezepelt's claws extended briefly, and he growled through clenched teeth. "None of these cats trust me." His voice was bitter. "I've heard them whispering about what I might have done to Nightcloud."

So the rumors have *reached Breezepelt,* Crowfeather thought, swallowing his fury as if it were a tough piece of fresh-kill.

"Not every cat," he meowed, remembering that several of his Clanmates had protested at Weaselfur's accusations. "Heathertail stood up for you."

A pleased, grateful expression flickered across Breezepelt's face. "She did? Really?"

"Really. And I know it's hard to hear your Clanmates spread rumors, Breezepelt, but the best thing you can do is hold your head high. You and I both know you haven't done anything wrong."

Breezepelt blinked up at him, as if he was surprised at his father's sympathy and support. For a moment Crowfeather thought he might rise to his paws and accompany him to the vigil. Then Breezepelt let out a long sigh. "I'm still not going. I just . . . can't."

"Okay. I understand," Crowfeather responded, though he wasn't sure he really did. And a small part of him worried that Breezepelt's absence would give more fuel for gossip. Cats like Weaselfur would assume the worst: that Breezepelt wouldn't go to Nightcloud's vigil because of guilt over her death.

Well, so be it. Those flea-pelts can think what they want. I won't force Breezepelt if he doesn't feel ready to face the Clan and the vigil. The Clan will just have to get over it.

"I'll speak for you," Crowfeather continued to Breezepelt. "I'll tell every cat how much you loved her—and what a good mother she was to you."

"Thank you," Breezepelt mewed. He closed his eyes, laid his head on his paws, and wrapped his tail over his nose as if he was trying to shut out the world.

Crowfeather briefly touched his nose to Breezepelt's forehead, then turned and headed for the center of the camp, where his Clanmates were already gathered in a ragged circle around Onestar. The empty space beside the Clan leader, where Nightcloud's body should have lain, was like a yawning gap at the heart of the Clan.

Onestar dipped his head solemnly to Crowfeather as he took his place, acknowledging his arrival. Crowfeather caught some furtive looks from the other cats, and he could hear them whispering among themselves. Some of them seemed angry, while others simply looked wary, as if they found it hard to meet his gaze. He realized they had been waiting for him to arrive before they could begin.

Well, tough. Checking on Breezepelt was important.

For a moment Onestar still hesitated, perhaps expecting Breezepelt to arrive. He shot a questioning look at Crowfeather, as if asking whether they should wait. Crowfeather shook his head, trying not to let his frustration and disappointment show.

Onestar took a breath and began to speak. "Nightcloud was a strong warrior, and an important part of WindClan," he meowed. "She will be truly missed by every cat."

That's true, Crowfeather thought. He knew he missed Nightcloud as the mother of his son, and he was worried about how her death was affecting Breezepelt. But now he realized that he felt more than that. He would miss Nightcloud as a friend, too. He knew he hadn't treated her well when she was alive, but he had always thought he would have the chance to work it out later.

I guess it's too late for that now.

Crowfeather listened in silence while other cats spoke about Nightcloud and how much she meant to them all.

"She's one of the bravest cats in the Clan."

"And a great hunter. No rabbit can—I mean could—outrun her!"

Crowfeather noticed that some of them were finding it hard to refer to her as if she was really gone. *They're having trouble paying tribute to her heroic death when no cat knows exactly how she died.*

"She showed her courage when she went into the tunnels to attack the stoats," Crouchfoot declared. "And when she was abandoned there—"

Abandoned?

"Hold on. Stop," Crowfeather interrupted. Were some of his Clanmates really about to use the vigil to attack Breezepelt? He wouldn't have it. He hadn't planned to challenge any cat at Nightcloud's vigil, but now that Crouchfoot had brought it up, he couldn't just keep silent. That would make it seem as if he agreed. *It's time to bring this into the open—especially now, while Breezepelt isn't here.*

"Are you accusing Breezepelt of something?" he demanded.

"If we are, we have good reason," Crouchfoot replied. "Why would Breezepelt leave the tunnel without his mother? How could he have left her behind?"

"Yes, no warrior would do that," Leaftail added. "Unless Breezepelt had something to do with her disappearance."

"That's enough!" Onestar's voice rang out commandingly and his eyes were glittering with anger. "I have told all of you, many times, that I trust Breezepelt, but you choose to question my decision—and at a vigil, of all places?"

Murmurs of disagreement rose from some of the warriors. Crowfeather felt a prickle of uneasiness beneath his pelt. He appreciated that his leader was supporting Breezepelt, but would Onestar's trust end in splitting the Clan?

He remembered, again, how the wind in the medicine cat's vision hadn't been enough to drive back the flood. *Maybe Kestrelflight's vision was a sign of a threat from* within *the Clan.*

But Crowfeather had no time to think that through now. "All of you flea-brains are wrong!" he meowed, turning on his accusing Clanmates. "Breezepelt can be prickly, and I've had my problems with him, too, but I've never questioned his love for his mother. When she and I argued, Breezepelt always took her side. He supported her in any way he could. The two of them always took care of each other. He would never hurt Nightcloud," he asserted.

As he spoke, he realized that Onestar was staring at him

with a mixture of surprise and approval. *Fine*, he thought. *You told me to support Breezepelt, and now you've got what you wanted.*

"Then why isn't Breezepelt here?" Weaselfur challenged him.

"Because he's grieving, you mouse-brain!" Crowfeather snapped. "Think about it. Because he thinks he has no support from the cats in this Clan, and he's right—you're all accusing him of things he would never do."

"Not all of us!" Heathertail called out. "I agree that Breezepelt would never hurt his mother—or any WindClan cat. He's a protector—he saved me when the stoats attacked me in the tunnels. I've seen how hurt he is about what happened to Nightcloud. You should all be ashamed of yourselves for spreading these rabbit-brained ideas!"

She glared at Crouchfoot as she spoke, and Crouchfoot let out a snarl in return, his shoulder fur bristling up. "You only say that because you like him!" he cried. "And Crowfeather is his father. Of course you don't want to see him as a bad cat—but that doesn't mean he isn't bad!" Several other cats let out yowls of agreement.

Onestar raised his tail for silence. "*Enough!* We need to remember," he began, "that whatever happened in the past, we are all WindClan cats now. Our unity is more important than anything else. I have forgiven Breezepelt for his part in the Great Battle, and I don't want to hear another word of accusation against him. This is a vigil, and we are here to honor one of our own. It is not a time for arguing."

Every cat—even Weaselfur and Leaftail—seemed chastened

by their leader's words. An awkward silence followed, most cats staring at the ground or their own paws. Gradually the outward signs of hostility faded, but Crowfeather could see that beneath the surface the tension was still there.

Suddenly he was glad that Breezepelt hadn't attended the vigil. Even if the cats hadn't accused him to his face, he would have felt their distrust and ill will in every hair on his pelt. *He's right to feel as though he doesn't belong,* Crowfeather thought. *I don't know what it would take to prove his loyalty to some of these cats. Maybe it isn't even possible.*

As the time for him to speak drew closer, Crowfeather struggled to find the right words. *How do I honor Nightcloud? Perhaps these cats suspect my motives as well,* he thought. *They're all watching to see if I'll mourn the death of a mate I never truly loved, or defend a son I barely know.*

But when Crowfeather's turn came, the words were there. "We will miss Nightcloud," he mewed simply, "and Breezepelt will always love her."

CHAPTER 11

It was a few days after Nightcloud's vigil, and every one of Crow-feather's muscles ached with tension as he padded across the tree-bridge to the Gathering island. He swore he could hear hostile voices in the lapping of the black water a tail-length beneath his paws, and the silver glitter of moonlight on the lake seemed to mock the darkness in his heart.

This is far worse than going to Nightcloud's vigil.

He wished that Onestar hadn't chosen him to attend the Gathering, and even more that he hadn't chosen Breezepelt to come with him. *He isn't ready.* Breezepelt had stopped using his every waking breath to declare war on the stoats, but he was still clearly grieving. He barely ate anything, and he seemed morose, unable to talk much to any cat—even Heathertail. Now Crowfeather's son was trailing along behind his Clan-mates, enveloped in a fog of misery. When they thrust their way through the bushes into the central clearing, he stayed at the back in the shadow of a holly bush, looking down at his paws with a sullen expression on his face. Crowfeather wondered whether he should go and stand beside him, but then he remembered that Onestar would be announcing the

132

circumstances of Nightcloud's death at the Gathering.

I shouldn't draw more attention to Breezepelt right now. I just hope he understands why. I don't want him to feel any more rejected.

Besides, Crowfeather was still mulling over his dream of the night before, when he had met Ashfoot again, then followed her pale gray shape through the tunnels until he'd caught up with her on the banks of the dark underground river.

"Are you . . . a ghost?" he had asked her.

"I never thought you were a stupid cat, Crowfeather," his mother mewed, dismissing his question with an irritated flick of her tail. "I'm what you see in front of you, and I can't continue to StarClan until I've given you a message."

Crowfeather's heart raced with anticipation. *Can she really tell me something that will put this whole mess right? Can she tell us what to do about the stoats, or how to settle our differences with ThunderClan?* Then he remembered what he really wanted—more than peace within the Clan, more than peace with the stoats, more than anything.

Can she tell me how to help Breezepelt?

"What message?" he asked urgently.

But his mother's response was only a single word. "Love."

"Love what?" Crowfeather spat out, hugely disappointed. *Has death made her mouse-brained? How can she possibly think that love can help me?* "Love is no friend of mine. I loved you; I loved Feathertail; I loved Leafpool. Do you see a pattern here? Every cat I've loved, I lost."

Ashfoot blinked at him, undaunted. There was tenderness and understanding in her gaze. "That shouldn't have made you close your heart," she murmured. "I wish I'd said more to you while I was alive, but this is my last chance. . . . Love."

"Love who?" Crowfeather yowled in desperation, but already the dream was fading, Ashfoot's form blurring until all he could see was her gaze fixed on him, bright with affection. "Nightcloud is dead, and Breezepelt—"

The brilliant light of a sunny leaf-bare morning had pulled Crowfeather out of his slumber, and once awake he'd wondered what he had meant to say in his dream. *Breezepelt is beyond my love? Breezepelt won't be helped by my love?*

He'd closed his eyes again and tried to concentrate, to cling to the last remnants of his dream, but they'd slipped away from him like mist through his claws. His pelt was bristling with frustration as he gave up at last and rose from his nest.

Now, sitting with his Clanmates beneath the branches of the Great Oak, Crowfeather felt his pelt grew hot with embarrassment at the memory of his dream. *I'm glad no cat can see into my mind. They'd think I'm going soft. I'm not a medicine cat— that means my dreams are just fluff and nonsense, like any cat's.* But at the same time, Crowfeather couldn't entirely dismiss what his mother had told him in the dream. It had to be significant, that he kept dreaming of her, when she hadn't been seen in StarClan. . . . *Could it be a vision? Could it mean something?*

As Onestar headed toward the Great Oak to take his place with the rest of the Clan leaders, Crowfeather glanced around at the other Clans. RiverClan and ShadowClan still looked wary after the tensions that had followed the Great Battle, while the ThunderClan cats were stiff and bristling, glaring across the clearing at the WindClan warriors. It made Crowfeather glad of the Gathering truce: StarClan had forbidden fighting under the full moon.

When all four Clan leaders had taken their places in the branches of the Great Oak, Mistystar's voice rang out across the clearing. "Cats of all Clans, welcome to the Gathering!" As the voices of gossiping cats faded into silence, she added to the leaders, "Which of you will speak first?"

Blackstar shifted on his branch, and then announced, "Before we begin, let us remember the fallen."

Crowfeather caught Larkwing's eye and could see the pale brown tabby she-cat was thinking the same thing as he was. Was any warrior keen to dwell on the terrible battle with the Dark Forest cats?

But as the ShadowClan leader reeled off names—"From ShadowClan: Redwillow, Shredtail, Toadfoot"—Crowfeather could not deny he felt a strange sense of calm fall over the Gathering. It suddenly felt right that all the fallen Clanmates were remembered, their shared sacrifice honored.

It took a horribly long time for Blackstar to get through all the names, but when he had finished, Onestar rose to his paws. "Thank you, Blackstar. I'm afraid I must continue this Gathering by sharing some sad news with the Clans." He paused before continuing, meeting Crowfeather's gaze for a heartbeat and casting a sympathetic glance toward Breezepelt. "Nightcloud is dead."

Yowls of shock rose from the crowd of cats in the clearing. Another twinge of grief for his former mate pierced

Crowfeather; then his tension eased slightly as he realized that the other Clans felt grief for her too. Nightcloud's prickly nature meant that she had never exactly been popular, but every cat was aware of her courage and loyalty.

"How did it happen?" Mistystar asked gently, concern in her blue eyes.

"She fought so well in the Great Battle." Blackstar spoke before Onestar could reply. "It's hard to lose her now, after she survived that."

"Stoats have come to live in the tunnels between Wind-Clan and ThunderClan," Onestar explained, dipping his head in acknowledgement of the ShadowClan leader's words. "Nightcloud—"

"And of course it never occurred to you to warn Thunder-Clan about the stoats," Bramblestar interrupted, a sarcastic edge to his voice.

Mouse-brain, Crowfeather thought. *You've known about the stoats at least since Berrynose's patrol caught me and Breezepelt in the tunnels. Are you trying to make trouble?*

"I understood that ThunderClan already knew about them," Onestar responded with a curt dip of his head. "I trust you've been able to cope?"

"We're coping very well," Bramblestar replied, his shoulder fur beginning to rise. "We've doubled the patrols in that area, and—"

"Bramblestar, this isn't the time," Mistystar pointed out with a whisk of her plumy tail. "Onestar was speaking."

Crowfeather saw with satisfaction that the ThunderClan

leader looked discomfited as he subsided, digging his claws into his branch. *It's challenging to be a leader, isn't it, Bramblestar?*

"As I said," Onestar continued, "stoats are living in the tunnels, and Nightcloud was part of a patrol that tried to clear them out. She never came home."

Very clever, Crowfeather thought. Onestar had told the exact truth, and yet he had managed not to mention any possible involvement by Breezepelt. That was something that Wind-Clan would keep to itself.

At least that was what would have happened if Weasel-fur hadn't sprung to his paws and meowed loudly, "Yeah, ask Breezepelt why not!"

Crowfeather's belly cramped with renewed tension. *Must we do this at the Gathering?* Murmurs of confusion arose from the other Clans. Harespring, sitting on the roots of the Great Oak with the other deputies, called out, "Weaselfur, keep your mouth shut!"

"Why should I?" Weaselfur challenged him. "We all know that Breezepelt was with Nightcloud in the tunnels when the stoats attacked. Why was *he* the only one who got out alive?"

Up in the branches of the Great Oak, Onestar was looking furious. Crowfeather knew how unhappy his leader would be at WindClan business being tossed around like a piece of prey in front of all the other Clans. They were at a Gathering! WindClan's warriors needed to show that their Clan was united, not start spitting accusations at each other.

Weaselfur, I wouldn't want to be you when we get back to camp!

But it was too late for Onestar to do anything now. Cats of

all the other Clans were turning their heads to shoot accusing looks at Breezepelt. Berrynose gave him a particularly intense stare, and Lionblaze was eyeing him with suspicion in his gaze.

Spiderleg leaned over to talk to Graystripe, who was sitting beside him, and Crowfeather was close enough to hear his whisper. "So she was left behind while her son ran to safety. So much for loyalty . . ."

Graystripe gave Spiderleg an irritated shove. "Shh, that's enough. We don't want to make more trouble."

Too late. Crowfeather craned his neck to find his son, hoping that Breezepelt hadn't overheard that or anything like it from where he sat at the back of the crowd. But when he saw that Breezepelt had raised his head and was glowering at the cats sitting near him, Crowfeather felt as if he had been drenched in icy water.

Of course he heard them. . . . He wished Breezepelt weren't here. He knew it must be hard enough for him to put up with the scorn of his own Clanmates while he was grieving for his mother. What would it be like to suffer the scorn of all four Clans?

Spiderleg exchanged a glance with Berrynose before rising to his paws. Crowfeather noticed that flecks of gray had appeared around his muzzle, making him look like a cranky elder, though he was still a relatively young cat. He raised his voice to carry beyond his first sneering whisper.

"Our wounds from the Great Battle are still healing," he began, "and not all of those wounds are in our flesh. It's not unreasonable for cats to wonder about those who were treacherous. Some reparations have been made, but . . ." He shrugged.

If I were Spiderleg's Clan leader, I would shut him up, Crowfeather thought. Ordinary warriors didn't have the right to make speeches at a Gathering without permission. Had the Great Battle changed things so much, that even Gatherings were chaotic these days?

But whether Bramblestar was too inexperienced to know what to do, or whether he wanted to hear what Spiderleg had to say, he didn't interrupt, only listening from his branch of the Great Oak with an unreadable expression on his face.

"After all," Spiderleg went on, "I think most cats would agree that before the battle they wouldn't have believed that any cat could betray the Clans as they did. But it happened. Who's to say it won't happen again?"

"That's right," Berrynose put in. "After we suffered so much betrayal from Dark Forest cats, *nothing at all* would surprise me."

While Berrynose was speaking, Crowfeather spotted Larkwing sitting alone in the crowd with her gaze fixed firmly on her forepaws. He felt another twinge of compassion for her; she must be finding it hard, too, to listen to these warriors who refused to trust the cats who had trained in the Dark Forest.

Then Crowfeather became aware of movement behind him, distracting him from Larkwing, and glanced over his shoulder to see Breezepelt rising to his paws. Other cats were turning their heads to look at him as he leaped forward and charged straight at Spiderleg. Some of the cats instinctively darted aside, and those who stayed in Breezepelt's way were thrust aside with powerful strokes of his paws. Crowfeather sprang up to intercept him, terrified that he was going to attack Spiderleg and break the Gathering truce.

But instead Breezepelt halted in the middle of the crowd, a tail-length away from the black ThunderClan tom. The cats nearby turned around to stare, shaking their ruffled pelts.

"If so many cats have a problem with me," Breezepelt snarled, "they should say so directly, not prowl around it like little mouse-hearts!"

Onestar gazed down at him from the Great Oak, lashing his tail in frustration and anger. "Breezepelt, stop now!" he commanded.

But Crowfeather could see that his son wasn't looking at their leader, either unaware that he had spoken or determined to ignore him.

"I know very well what you might think about me," Breezepelt continued. "But in *my* opinion, some warriors in other Clans are just looking for a reason to fight. Doesn't that make them just as much of a threat to our day-to-day lives as the cats who once trained with—or even fought for—the Dark Forest?"

"Oh, you'd like to pass the blame on elsewhere?" Berrynose sneered. He paused to lick one cream-colored paw and draw it over his ear. "The difference is, Breezepelt, that even after you found out what the Dark Forest was up to, you stayed with them. You were prepared to kill Lionblaze—prepared to kill your own kin! How can we just accept your word if you tell us that you'd never hurt Nightcloud?"

"Because Nightcloud was the only cat who ever cared about me!" Breezepelt flashed back at him.

Crowfeather knew his son's answer was too honest and came too quickly to be a lie. He could see the hurt in his eyes, and his instant regret at revealing such a vulnerable part of himself to hostile cats without meaning to.

At Breezepelt's pain, Crowfeather felt a piercing within his own heart. *I should have cared,* he thought helplessly. *I should have tried to understand earlier. Instead I let Nightcloud handle it all. . . .*

"There's no way I'd ever want my mother to come to harm," Breezepelt continued. "I was there, you weren't, and I *know* what really happened. It wasn't my fault that Nightcloud disappeared. It was the fault of the StarClan-cursed stoats that have taken over the tunnels! Why is no cat doing anything about them? Because it's easier to sit here and accuse me? Well, fox dung to that!"

He began to back away, then turned and headed for the bushes that surrounded the clearing.

"Breezepelt! Where are you going?" Crowfeather asked.

Breezepelt halted and glanced over his shoulder, giving his father one scathing look. "Back into the tunnels to kill stoats," he snapped. "Since no other cat is doing it!"

Spiderleg twitched his whiskers. "Is that so? Or are you going to eavesdrop on ThunderClan some more?" he mewed.

Breezepelt whirled to face the ThunderClan warrior, his muscles tensed and his claws extending. "How dare you, you mangy—"

Crowfeather's belly lurched as he saw that once again the Gathering truce was within heartbeats of being broken. Quickly he stepped between the two hostile warriors, breaking their furious glare.

"Calm down," he began. "This isn't—"

Berrynose interrupted him, his voice ringing out clearly. "No, that's a good idea. Why not let Breezepelt go into the tunnels and take on the stoats by himself? If he succeeds, he'll have helped us all and proven his loyalty. And if he doesn't, the stoats will make him pay for his treachery. Maybe StarClan is nudging us that way."

Crowfeather remembered hearing the cream-colored tom suggest that all the Dark Forest cats should be tested, to prove that their loyalties lay with the Clans. *I used to think he might have a point. . . . But could that really be what StarClan wants? For the Dark Forest cats to risk their lives to show their loyalty?*

"Are you still meowing on about testing the Dark Forest cats?" he growled, reluctant to agree, even partly, with Berrynose in public.

Berrynose faced him, undeterred by his aggressive tone. "That could be the only way to make sure of their loyalty," he responded. "I haven't changed my mind since the day we caught you WindClan cats spying."

"Great StarClan!" Crowfeather wished they weren't having this confrontation at a Gathering. *If we were anywhere else, I could claw that smug look off his silly face! But I'd start a war if I did that here.* "You dense furball! How many more times do I have to say this?" he meowed, twitching his whiskers irritably. "We were not *spying* on ThunderClan! We were looking for Nightcloud."

Berrynose shrugged, disbelief evident in every hair on his pelt. "WindClan promises don't mean much to me." Mutterings of suspicion came from many of the other cats around, while yet others remained silent, merely looking bewildered.

Jayfeather, the blind ThunderClan medicine cat, was one of those who looked unconvinced by Crowfeather's claim. Crowfeather wondered whether he really believed they had been spying, or whether it was all part of his usual hostility toward his father and his half brother in another Clan. As Crowfeather understood it, Jayfeather could even be hostile to the cats he liked, so it was hard to tease out what he was actually feeling.

Where does he get that from?

Now Jayfeather spoke up. "Spying or not, why did Nightcloud and Breezepelt go into the tunnels in the first place?"

"I can answer that," Onestar replied, to Crowfeather's relief.

Glancing across the clearing, he could see Leafpool standing beside Jayfeather, and for a moment Crowfeather's gaze locked with hers. It was clear from the look in her eyes that she too was concerned about the rising tension between their two Clans.

Even though it's been moons and moons since we were together, I can still tell what Leafpool is thinking.

"It was because of the stoats," Onestar continued. "And because Kestrelflight had a vision. Kestrelflight, tell them about it."

The gaze of every cat turned toward the young WindClan medicine cat. Kestrelflight rose to his paws, looking slightly nervous at the prospect of addressing the whole Gathering. "I saw . . . ," he began. His voice croaked as if he had a piece of fresh-kill lodged in his throat, and he cleared it before he continued. "I saw a great wave of water," he mewed. "It swept out of the tunnels and drowned WindClan's territory. Clearly it was a warning."

For a moment an uneasy silence fell on all the Clans, the cats exchanging dismayed glances. From the surprise apparent in their eyes, Crowfeather could tell that Kestrelflight hadn't even shared his vision with the other medicine cats. *Perhaps that's good,* he considered. *Onestar is so suspicious of the other Clans and their motives right now.*

Then Bramblestar rose to his paws and padded along his branch until he was visible to every cat in the clearing. His amber gaze was fixed on Onestar. "Does WindClan intend to share *any* information with ThunderClan?" he demanded. "This vision wasn't just a warning for you. It affects Thunder-Clan, too, because some of the tunnels lead into our territory. Why wasn't I told about this?"

Onestar drew his lips back in the beginning of a snarl. "It was a WindClan vision to warn WindClan," he snapped. "Does ThunderClan need to stick its nose into everything?"

"I'm not trying to meddle," Bramblestar responded, obviously struggling hard to hold on to his patience. "But we need to work together to take care of the threat before any more cats get hurt. It seems to me that the vision referred to the stoats that killed Nightcloud," he added. "Is that what you believe?"

Onestar responded with no more than an annoyed lash of his tail, but Kestrelflight spoke up, with a respectful dip of his head to the ThunderClan leader. "Yes, that's what we think."

"And you needn't worry, Bramblestar," Onestar meowed, contempt in his voice. "WindClan is putting together a plan to drive the stoats out."

"I *am* worried," Bramblestar retorted. "We'd noticed that prey had been getting scarce around the tunnel entrances, but we knew nothing about the stoats until Berrynose's patrol rescued *your* cats from them. Sharing information would have been friendly, don't you think?" When Onestar didn't reply to his provocation, he went on, "I believe ThunderClan and WindClan should work together. Two Clans are stronger than one."

Crowfeather remembered his thoughts about the vision . . . how he, too, had wondered whether it implied that the Clans should be working together. It felt strange to agree with the ThunderClan leader over his own, but he couldn't help it. He spotted Leafpool nodding in agreement, but a moment later Lionblaze rose to his paws. "How can we work with WindClan when I was nearly killed in the Dark Forest by a WindClan cat?" he demanded.

Onestar gazed down at the golden-furred warrior. "Wind-Clan has received Breezepelt back as a loyal WindClan warrior," he told Lionblaze. "I understand that you might have trouble accepting that."

"He's only loyal to *WindClan*," Lionblaze snorted, turning to glare at Breezepelt. "That doesn't mean he follows the rest of the warrior code. If we work together, what's to stop him attacking me again—or any other Clan cat who gets under his fur? He's a menace!"

Crowfeather had to admit to himself that not long ago he would have agreed with Lionblaze. But now he was beginning to see things from Breezepelt's point of view. He felt as if claws inside him were trying to rip their way out through his belly fur. Sorrow weighed on his heart to see his sons facing each other with hostile glares, and he surprised himself by feeling a protectiveness toward Lionblaze, the son he never saw grow up.

He had always told himself that Lionblaze and Jayfeather— and their sister, Hollyleaf, who died in the Great Battle—were not his kits, because he never raised them. But now . . . he just knew that he didn't want to see Breezepelt and Lionblaze in conflict like this.

Every hair on Crowfeather's pelt was rising, telling him that this was *wrong*. Even though the two toms were not Clan- mates, Crowfeather reflected, they were kin. *Yet fate has made them enemies.*

Breezepelt's eyes narrowed with fury as he stared at Lionblaze. "You're right, but I'm not the cat I was then," he responded to his half brother's accusation. Turning to address the rest of the Clans, he continued, "You can all believe whatever you want. I don't need any cat's help. As soon as I get the chance, I'm going back into the tunnels to kill all the stoats and avenge my mother—even if I have to do it alone."

Spinning around, he stalked back to the edge of the clearing and slid through the bushes. Crowfeather called after him, but Breezepelt ignored him. He left an uncomfortable silence behind him.

Mistystar was the first cat to speak, giving RiverClan's news in an attempt to continue the Gathering in the usual way, as if a skirmish hadn't almost broken out.

"Twolegs came tramping over our territory with a dog," she informed the assembled warriors. "Reedwhisker and Mintfur tracked them, and they went away without causing any trouble."

But no cat was paying much attention, their heads together as they gossiped eagerly about Breezepelt's declaration, and after quick reports from Blackstar and Bramblestar, the Gathering broke up. The air still vibrated with tension as each Clan in turn crossed the tree-bridge and headed off separately into the darkness.

Crowfeather padded along the edge of the lake with Onestar and the rest of his Clanmates. Every time he thought about Breezepelt and Nightcloud, his anxiety swelled. He knew that if Nightcloud had been here, she would have been able to calm Breezepelt down. *But now it's up to me, and I have no idea what to do.* His chest felt so tight that he could hardly breathe.

Will this feeling ever go away?

Back in the WindClan camp, Crowfeather was heading for the warriors' den when he spotted Heathertail talking to Breezepelt, clearly trying to comfort him. His son's claws were tearing at the ground in a fit of anger, as though Heathertail's efforts weren't having much effect.

Crowfeather veered aside to talk to them, when he heard Onestar calling to Breezepelt from just outside his den.

"I need a word with you," the Clan leader meowed, beckoning Breezepelt with his tail. "Come here for a moment."

Breezepelt hesitated, obviously reluctant. *Come on,* Crowfeather urged him silently. *Don't make this any worse.* To his relief, Breezepelt headed toward Onestar after a couple of heartbeats, and Heathertail padded after him. Crowfeather followed, too, not joining the others but halting a few tail-lengths away so that he could hear their conversation where they clustered together outside the leader's den.

"I don't think going into the tunnels alone is a good idea, Breezepelt," Onestar began. "I told you, we'll mount a proper attack once every warrior is recovered from the last skirmish."

Breezepelt, looking mutinous, was about to retort, but Heathertail stepped forward before he could speak. "He won't be alone. I'll be with him."

Breezepelt's head whipped around and he gazed at the brown tabby she-cat with a mixture of surprise and gratitude. "But your wounds from last time aren't healed yet," he protested.

"They're healed enough," Heathertail told him. "And if I can't talk you out of going, then you're not going without me."

"But I need to do this alone," Breezepelt protested. "If you go in with me and something happens to you . . . I'll never forgive myself. And neither will the Clan. I want you to be safe."

At his words, Crowfeather felt his paws tingle with a mixture of pity and affection. It was an unfamiliar emotion, and it made him feel that he wanted to go back into the tunnels and fight on Breezepelt's behalf.

"Neither of you is going unless I say you can," Onestar pointed out. His voice was sharp, but his gaze was sympathetic as he looked at Breezepelt. "I can't approve one—or even two—of my warriors charging into those dark tunnels by themselves. I won't send you there to fight, but—"

"I need to do this!" Breezepelt interrupted.

"Listen." Onestar gave his tail-tip a single twitch. "I won't send you to fight, but going to check on the stoats and find out where they're living—and what their weaknesses might be— wouldn't be a bad idea. It would help both WindClan and ThunderClan."

"I'd be good at that," Heathertail mewed eagerly.

But Onestar had no idea how much time Heathertail had spent underground. "No, I don't mean for you to go inside the tunnels," he told her. "That will only provoke the stoats, and we're not ready for that yet. Keep watch from outside, and see what you can learn."

Heathertail's tail-tip twitched, but she didn't object aloud.

"You could go when it's dark," Onestar continued. "Tonight, in fact, if you have the energy."

Crowfeather gazed at his son, wondering if Breezepelt would accept Onestar's suggestion, when back at the Gathering he had been so eager to slaughter stoats. He wasn't sure that the black tom would be able to control his emotions. *And how will Onestar react if he can't?*

Breezepelt and Heathertail exchanged a glance, then nodded. "We can do it," Breezepelt replied.

"The stoats should be out hunting," Onestar continued. "But if there are any remaining near the tunnel entrances, you must *not* attack them on your own. It's too dangerous."

Crowfeather wondered again whether Breezepelt would object, but now his son just seemed relieved to have something active he could do. "Okay, we won't," he promised.

Onestar nodded approvingly. "I'm not sure you two should go by yourselves, though," he mused. "Perhaps you need one more cat. . . . Hey, Weaselfur!"

The ginger tom, who had been heading for the warriors' den, halted and turned toward his Clan leader.

Once again, Onestar beckoned him over with his tail.

Weaselfur padded up and dipped his head respectfully to his Clan leader. "Is everything all right, Onestar?" he asked, with an unfriendly glance at Breezepelt.

"Breezepelt and Heathertail are going to keep watch outside the tunnels to find out what they can about the stoats," Onestar replied. There was a gleam in his eyes as he spoke to Weaselfur, and Crowfeather realized that he was enjoying himself. "You can go with them."

Weaselfur gaped. "What? Go with *him*?"

"Do you have a problem with obeying your Clan leader?" Onestar asked, his eyes narrowing.

"No, but—"

"Perhaps this will make you change your mind about

making unkind comments during a vigil," Onestar interrupted. "Not to mention blurting out information at a Gathering that should have been kept within this Clan. I had thought about giving you a moon of dawn patrols, but this will be better. And by the time you return to camp, I expect you to have learned that there are times when you should keep your mouth shut."

Weaselfur hung his head, his tail drooping. "Yes, Onestar," he mumbled.

"And since you seem to have a problem with Breezepelt," Onestar went on, "perhaps it will help you to spend time with him, and work together on a WindClan task. In fact, Weaselfur, *it had better.*"

Weaselfur nodded, looking completely crushed.

"Don't worry, Weaselfur," Heathertail meowed cheerfully. "We won't let the nasty stoats get you."

"It's not the *stoats* I'm worried about," Weaselfur retorted in a low hiss. Fortunately for him, it didn't reach Onestar's ears as the Clan leader turned away and entered his den.

Breezepelt didn't look particularly pleased at having Weaselfur as a companion, but Crowfeather was glad to see that he had the sense to say nothing. *He also needs to learn that there are times when a cat should hold his tongue.*

Crowfeather watched as the three cats turned and headed out of the camp. He could feel nervous flutterings in his belly, as if a nestful of blackbirds were trying out their wings inside him. His paws itched to join his Clanmates, but then he reflected that he couldn't look after Breezepelt all the time.

He had accused Nightcloud of being overprotective, and now it was important for Breezepelt to take responsibility for himself.

Whatever they find at the tunnels, he thought, *I just hope it brings Breezepelt a little peace.*

CHAPTER 12

❧

The yowls and screeches of battle rose all around Crowfeather. The air was thick with the stench of blood. As far as he could see in all directions, the ground was covered in tussling cats, and beside Crowfeather lay the body of his daughter, Hollyleaf, her black fur soaked in her own blood. Recognition tingled through his pads.

This is the Great Battle! Crowfeather thought, realizing that he was dreaming. *It's exactly as I remember it.*

The memory grew sharper, even more painful, as he saw Breezepelt leap onto Lionblaze, catching him off-balance and taking him to the ground and raking his claws along his cheek. "You're not as strong as I expected," Breezepelt gloated.

Crowfeather charged forward, hearing Ivypool pleading with Breezepelt not to destroy the Clans.

"Lionblaze should never have been born," Breezepelt told her. "None of them should . . ."

Then his tail flicked triumphantly, spitefully, toward Hollyleaf's body. "She's dead; now it's your turn, Lionblaze." And then he bit into Lionblaze's neck.

Finally reaching his sons, Crowfeather gripped Breezepelt's

shoulders with his claws. "This has to stop!" he yowled as he dragged him off his other son.

But then the dream changed. As Crowfeather released Breezepelt, and Lionblaze dived back into the battle, Breezepelt took a step forward, then turned to face Crowfeather, whose neck fur rose at the look in his son's eyes. Before he could react, Breezepelt raised a paw and slashed his claws down Crowfeather's face.

Dazzling light, unimaginable pain, exploded inside Crowfeather's head and faded, leaving him in darkness. *I'm blind! Breezepelt blinded me. . . . Does he hate me that much?*

For a moment Crowfeather was too stunned to do more than crouch close to the ground, feeling a pelt sticky with blood pressing against his side. *That must be Hollyleaf's body,* he thought. He knew this wasn't what had happened in the waking world.

"Now you've got what you deserve!" Breezepelt taunted him. His voice sounded unnaturally loud, as if it was echoing inside Crowfeather's mind. "For never loving your WindClan mate, and for choosing your ThunderClan kits over me. Why did you do that, Crowfeather?"

Feeling blood trickle from his ruined eyes, Crowfeather couldn't answer his son's challenge. *I hardly know Lionblaze and Jayfeather . . . but I couldn't let Breezepelt kill my other son. Could I? There would have been no way back for Breezepelt if he had killed Lionblaze. But if Breezepelt can't see that, can there ever be any help for him?*

Dizziness swept over Crowfeather, and he felt the scene shift around him. The shrieks of battle faded, though he could sense that some cat was still close by. *Maybe more than one,* he thought, peering around uselessly through the black fog of his blindness.

Then, gradually, the darkness Breezepelt's claws had created began to lift. The forest swam into Crowfeather's vision, lit by a gray, weak dawn. Standing in front of him was a muscular dark tabby tom. Even before his sight had cleared completely, Crowfeather recognized him by his powerful shape and brown tabby pelt, and at last by his piercing ice-blue eyes.

Hawkfrost!

This was the treacherous cat from RiverClan, the cat who had supported Mudclaw when the former WindClan deputy had tried to oust Onestar from the leadership of his Clan. The cat who had given Hollyleaf her fatal wounds.

Rage surged through Crowfeather, driving out the pain in his eyes. *It's because of you, you piece of fox dung, that I'll never know my daughter!*

Summoning every scrap of his strength, Crowfeather launched himself at Hawkfrost, but the sleek tabby tom simply darted aside, his scarred muzzle curling in contempt.

Crowfeather charged again, and again Hawkfrost nimbly stepped aside. "I'm too quick for you, rabbit-chaser," he sneered. "Give it up, before you make me angry."

Crowfeather knew his vision was still too blurred for him to fight effectively. *It's a dream,* he told himself. *I can't really take vengeance for Hollyleaf's death.* But his grief and fury propelled him forward to attack Hawkfrost one more time.

Hawkfrost slipped aside with a disdainful twitch of his tail-tip. As Crowfeather landed from his leap, he felt his body slam into another cat. He lost his balance and fell, paws flailing, and looked up into the face of his son Breezepelt.

Breezepelt stood over him, fixing him with an amber glare, pinning him down with his forepaws. "Why are you fighting for your ThunderClan kin?" he hissed. "What about your WindClan son?"

Crowfeather tried to reply, but no sound came out of his mouth. Breezepelt drew back, raising one paw as if he was about to strike again.

Crowfeather jerked awake. Darkness surrounded him; the moon had set, though he could see the top of the moor and the pile of memorial stones outlined against a sky that showed the first pale traces of dawn. Around him he could make out the curled-up bodies of his sleeping Clanmates and hear their faint snores and snuffles.

After his terrible dream, Crowfeather's mind felt heavy and yet restless. He was sure that he wouldn't sleep again, and he couldn't bear to go on lying still in his nest. His whole body demanded movement, but if he paced up and down in camp he would just wake his Clanmates. Instead he crept out of the warriors' den and up the slope to the edge of the camp, with a nod to Larkwing, who was on watch.

Outside the camp, padding to and fro on the frosty grass, Crowfeather could at last be alone with his troubling thoughts.

He was missing Nightcloud more than he'd ever thought

he could. And he couldn't work out what he felt about Breezepelt. *Sometimes he annoys me out of my fur, but at other times it's as if—almost as if—I'm starting to love him.*

Crowfeather remembered too the curious sadness he had felt at the Gathering when he'd seen the animosity between Lionblaze and Breezepelt. *They're both my sons, even though neither of them probably wants me for a father. And I don't even know what's going on with Jayfeather.*

He sent his thoughts out across the moor to the tunnels, where Breezepelt, Heathertail, and Weaselfur would be still investigating the stoats. *I hope they're all okay—even Weaselfur.* Crowfeather wanted to believe that Breezepelt genuinely meant to prove himself, though he couldn't entirely banish the nagging fear that his son wasn't the loyal WindClan cat he pretended to be. That one day his emotions would get the better of him and lead him into reckless behavior—or worse, down a dark path from which there would be no return.

And that's what my dream was about, Crowfeather realized. *Deep down, I still don't trust my own son. I don't trust that he won't fall prey to some snake-tongued cat who can encourage him to give way to his bad instincts. If that happens, what difficulties could it cause for WindClan—or even for all the Clans?*

The thought knotted Crowfeather's muscles and made him dig his claws deep into the earth. *Why does everything have to be so difficult? For StarClan's sake, we fought off the Dark Forest cats. So why do disagreements within the Clan seem to matter so much?*

Crowfeather was beginning to realize that outside threats like the Dark Forest could destroy a Clan, but it was emotion that would destroy a single warrior from within. *I want things to be simpler,* he thought. *All this messy emotion only weakens a cat. I'd rather live my life without it.*

A paw step behind him distracted Crowfeather from his musing. He whirled, his claws at the ready, then relaxed as he saw that the newcomer was Kestrelflight.

"Are you okay?" the medicine cat asked.

"Fine," Crowfeather responded, retracting his claws. "You startled me, that's all. I'm sorry if I woke you up."

"No, it wasn't your fault," Kestrelflight told him. "I've been awake for a while—and it looks like you have, too."

Crowfeather nodded. "I had a dream . . . ," he began. He was reluctant to reveal the details, but a heartbeat later he found himself pouring out the story of how he had found himself back in the Great Battle, how Breezepelt had blinded him, and how he had tried in vain to fight with Hawkfrost.

"I'm pretty sure it wasn't an actual prophecy," he finished. "But I can't help feeling it means something. Maybe my mind is dwelling on cats like Hawkfrost, and that horror Mapleshade, because it's . . . warning me?"

"Warning you about what?" Kestrelflight asked.

Crowfeather was reluctant to answer. He knew that many of his Clanmates didn't trust Breezepelt, and if he—Breezepelt's own father—expressed his doubts, he might make everything worse.

But if I can't trust our own medicine cat, who can I trust?

"About Breezepelt," Crowfeather confessed at last. "I've been feeling better about him lately, and at the Gathering he vowed to get rid of the stoats, but I still can't shake off the worry that he can't be trusted."

Kestrelflight let out an amused purr. "*I'm* the medicine cat," he pointed out. "It's usually me who gets the visions."

His words reminded Crowfeather of Kestrelflight's latest vision: water pouring out of the tunnels, the wind driving it back, then fading away, allowing the surge of water to engulf everything.

"When you had your vision at the medicine cats' meeting," he meowed thoughtfully, "StarClan must have been warning us about the stoats in the tunnels, but . . . surely the vision seems more complicated than that? Do you think there could be more to it? That the stoats are just the first problem we'll face?"

Kestrelflight let out a weary sigh. "I've been wondering the same thing, ever since it happened," he replied. "The stoats could have crept onto our territory at any time while we were recovering after the Great Battle, but even so, they're the sort of enemy that the Clan should have been able to deal with easily."

Crowfeather nodded. "That's true. That skirmish shouldn't have gone so badly. We should never have lost Nightcloud."

"That's what makes me wonder what the vision of water means," Kestrelflight continued. "At first I thought that the way the wind drove back the water meant that WindClan would win a victory, but there was a second surge, and no wind to defeat that. Does that mean WindClan will be defeated? And what will that mean for the other Clans? Will we have to face the teeth and claws of another enemy, whether that's the stoats or some other hostile force lurking in the darkness?"

"I've wondered the same," Crowfeather admitted. "Well, what the second surge means—and if it implies we should be working with the other Clans." A chill ran through Crowfeather from ears to tail-tip as he considered the medicine cat's words. He asked himself whether this hostile force in the darkness could be Breezepelt's rage and bitterness, lurking within him.

But the wind in Kestrelflight's dream *did* have an effect on the first flood that threatened to drown their camp. Maybe that meant there was a chance of victory.

And a breeze is a type of wind. . . . Hope and excitement warred with disbelief inside Crowfeather, swelling just as the dawn light grew in the sky above the moor. *What if the wind in Kestrelflight's vision didn't mean the whole of WindClan, but just referred to Breezepelt? A breeze is a soft, weak wind, for sure, but . . . what if Breezepelt is to play a role in saving us?*

Could there be a better redemption?

CHAPTER 13

❧

"Rear up on your hind paws," Crowfeather instructed, demonstrating the move as he spoke. "Then you can get in two blows at your enemy—one with each forepaw—before you land and dart away."

"That's cool!" Hootpaw exclaimed.

The sun was rising over the moor, though the grass was still white-furred with frost, and the air was crisp and cold. Crowfeather found the heaviness of the night before vanishing as he focused on the training session. He had agreed to take Hootpaw along with his own apprentice, Featherpaw, since Hootpaw's mentor, Gorsetail, was leading the patrol that climbed the moor daily to visit the pile of memorial stones. So far, the session was going much better than the last time Crowfeather had tried to train the apprentices together.

"Both of you try it," Crowfeather meowed after he had demonstrated the move for a second time. "For now, just imagine your opponent."

While he watched the two apprentices trying to copy what he had shown them, Crowfeather reflected that a major onslaught against the stoats couldn't be far off. Breezepelt and

Heathertail were still checking on the tunnels. *I hope they're all right.* But Crowfeather knew that the rest of the Clan must be prepared for the next step. The apprentices wouldn't be chosen for the first attack, but no cat knew what might happen after that.

I want them to be ready.

"That's very good, Hootpaw," Crowfeather meowed, pleasantly surprised at how quickly the young cat had picked up the new move. He balanced well on his hind paws, and there was real strength behind his blows. "Go on like that, and you'll scare the fur off the stoats!"

Hootpaw ducked his head in embarrassment. "I had a great mentor," he reminded Crowfeather. "Nightcloud was smart and strong, and she taught me a lot about strategy."

Crowfeather hadn't expected to hear such praise of his former mate, though of course Hootpaw, as her apprentice, would have been closer to her than almost any other cat, except for Breezepelt. Crowfeather had always known that Nightcloud was a capable warrior, but he wondered whether he had ever given her the due she deserved. *There was probably a lot about her that I never knew.* He stifled a sigh. *And now I never will.*

"You're doing well too, Featherpaw," Crowfeather continued to his own apprentice. "Just remember that—"

He broke off at the sound of distressed yowling from the edge of the camp, and recognized Heathertail's voice. Turning swiftly, he saw Heathertail and Weaselfur at the top of the slope, carrying the limp, black-furred body of a cat between them.

Breezepelt! No!

Why wasn't Breezepelt moving? Crowfeather's belly lurched in terror.

Why would he be hurt? Onestar made clear they weren't supposed to engage the stoats. . . . But seeing Breezepelt's limp form, Crowfeather knew that there would be plenty of time for explanations later. *Great StarClan,* he begged, *please tell me he isn't dead. . . . I don't think I could bear it.* His mind flashed back to seeing Hollyleaf's bloodstained body in his dream. *Is that why I had the dream? Was something trying to prepare me for this?*

Crowfeather raced up the slope toward the returning warriors, spotting as he did that Weaselfur's white paws were stained red with blood.

Shock pulsed through Crowfeather's body from his ears to his claws. *Where did that come from? Did Weaselfur kill my son?*

Crowfeather stormed to a halt in front of the group of cats, his pelt bristling all along his spine. Breezepelt hung motionless between them, supported on their shoulders, a wound gaping open all along his side.

"What happened?" Crowfeather demanded. Turning on Weaselfur, he added, "Did you do this to him?"

For the first time Crowfeather noticed that Weaselfur was carrying something limp and bloody in his jaws. As he dropped it, Crowfeather could see that it was the body of a stoat, its white fur completely covered in drying blood.

"Of course I didn't!" Weaselfur snapped, his eyes narrowed in fury. "I don't think I could cause this much damage if I tried."

"Please, Crowfeather," Heathertail meowed, "leave Weaselfur alone and help us get Breezepelt to Kestrelflight's den."

He's not dead!

Relief flooded so strongly through Crowfeather that he had nothing more to say. He rushed to support Breezepelt's hindquarters, and he and the others struggled across the camp to the medicine-cat den.

"We were doing as Onestar said and watching the tunnels from outside," Weaselfur explained on the way, "but when we saw so many of them leave to go hunting, we thought it would be a good chance to explore. We found the stoats' dens and their prey-piles, and the entrances and exits they're using. Everything was quiet in there, and we were on our way out before we scented stoats. We worked out they were in a den off the main tunnel."

"We wanted to sneak past, avoiding danger like Onestar told us to," Heathertail continued. "But Breezepelt . . ." Her voice choked.

"Breezepelt dived in there and *attacked* them," Weaselfur meowed, taking up the story again. "He killed one easily." He jerked his head back to the edge of the camp, where he had left the body of the stoat. "But the other was fiercer, and fought back. It slashed Breezepelt's side. He would have gone on fighting, but Heathertail and I forced him to retreat. He was losing blood, and finally he lost consciousness. So we carried him out and headed back to camp."

Crowfeather glanced at Heathertail, who nodded in confirmation of what Weaselfur had told him. "We both tried to stop Breezepelt," she mewed. "But he was too intent on killing the stoats."

As she spoke, Crowfeather could see the worry in her eyes. Shivers were passing through her pelt, and she kept turning her head to lick Breezepelt's wounded side. *She must really care about him.*

More cats were gathering around as Crowfeather and the others approached Kestrelflight's den. Shock mingled with gleams of interest in their faces. Crowfeather could hear muttering among them, though he couldn't make out the words. *I imagine most of them are hoping Breezepelt is dead. That would solve a lot of their problems! But it's not going to happen yet, flea-pelts.*

Featherpaw had raced over to the medicine-cat den to alert Kestrelflight, and now the mottled gray tom emerged from the cleft in the rock and padded up to meet them.

"Great StarClan!" he breathed out at the sight of Breezepelt's injury.

Crowfeather's pelt prickled with apprehension. *It has to be bad when a medicine cat reacts like that!*

At once Kestrelflight pulled himself together and added more briskly, "Quick—bring him inside."

Crowfeather helped the others carry Breezepelt into the den and lay him down on a nest of springy moss. As he watched Kestrelflight examine his son, Crowfeather felt a new feeling flowing through him, warming him from ears to tail-tip. At first he couldn't identify it, until at last he realized that it was pride.

Breezepelt must have had bees in his brain to go into that stoats' nest, he thought. *But still, that was very brave.* Breezepelt had been afraid of the tunnels since he was an apprentice, and Nightcloud's death couldn't have helped. It would have taken real courage to face his fears and attack the stoats.

Kestrelflight rose from where he had been crouching beside Breezepelt, licking his wound clean, and turned to Crowfeather. "His injuries are serious," he reported, "but you can see that already. He'll need watching carefully."

Crowfeather's belly roiled at the medicine cat's words. *Surely I'm not going to lose my son just as I'm beginning to understand him?*

"I can stay with him," Heathertail offered immediately.

Crowfeather shook his head. "Thanks, Heathertail," he meowed, "but I want to watch over my son—at least for now. Will you go and tell Onestar what happened, and take the stoat to show him?"

Heathertail hesitated, casting an uncertain glance at Breezepelt. Crowfeather could tell that she wanted to stay with him.

"I'll call you when he wakes," he promised the young she-cat. "But for now it's important for Onestar to know what we're up against."

"I understand." Giving her pelt a shake, Heathertail left the den.

While Kestrelflight headed to his herb store at the back of the den, Crowfeather found himself standing beside Weasel-fur. The ginger tom's head was lowered, his expression hard to read. Crowfeather's pelt prickled with the awkwardness of the moment, remembering what he had said when Weaselfur first appeared. "I'm sorry I accused you of attacking Breeze-pelt," he muttered after a moment.

"It's okay," Weaselfur responded, his lack of anger surprising Crowfeather. "You had your reasons, after everything I said about your son. But when I saw how brave he was, going after those stoats, I knew there was no way he could have had anything to do with Nightcloud's death. I'm sorry I said that."

Crowfeather felt even more awkward, giving his shoulder an embarrassed lick. "You should apologize to Breezepelt when he wakes up," he mewed.

Weaselfur nodded. "I'll do that. I'm still not entirely sure Onestar should have let Breezepelt back into the Clan after the Great Battle, but—about this—I can give him the benefit of the doubt. He really did fight for us today."

Crowfeather was disappointed to hear that Weaselfur still did not entirely trust his son. *But at least he's willing to give Breezepelt a chance,* Crowfeather thought. *That's a start.*

"Thanks for bringing him home," he meowed.

"It was the least I could do," Weaselfur responded, then headed off toward the warriors' den with a nod of farewell.

Crowfeather stepped back while Kestrelflight chewed horsetail into a poultice and plastered it over Breezepelt's wound, fastening it in place with a thick wad of cobweb.

"That should help," the medicine cat mewed, gazing thoughtfully down at Breezepelt. "At least the bleeding seems to have stopped. Can you watch him for a while? I need to report to Onestar."

When Kestrelflight was gone, Crowfeather settled down

beside Breezepelt, listening to his labored breathing. He could smell the tang of dried blood still matted in his son's fur. For a few moments he felt as if he were back beside the sun-drown-water and a huge wave was crashing over him, overwhelming him with its power.

But it wasn't a wave that was doing this to Crowfeather. It was seeing Breezepelt injured, and knowing that Nightcloud was already dead.

Crowfeather leaned toward him, but before he could get close enough to whisper in his ear, Breezepelt's eyelids slowly eased open. Crowfeather felt a rush of relief that he had regained consciousness, but when he looked into his son's eyes, all he could see was pain.

Breezepelt blinked a few times, then focused his gaze on Crowfeather. "I killed the stoat, and Nightcloud is still dead," he whispered miserably. Crowfeather's heart almost broke with sadness as his son added, "I should never have left her in the tunnels in the first place."

"Don't talk now," Crowfeather told him gently. "You need to rest. I'm sorry about what you've been through, but we *will* avenge your mother, I promise you." When Breezepelt looked unconvinced, he added, "If there's a battle ahead, WindClan will need a warrior as bold and strong as you."

Breezepelt's eyes widened, and he fixed Crowfeather with an incredulous amber gaze. He remained silent, but that look seemed to be asking, *Is it really my father, Crowfeather, telling me this?*

Crowfeather cleared his throat, embarrassed. "I'll fetch

you some prey to help you regain your strength," he meowed. "I'll be right back."

Outside the medicine-cat den, Crowfeather found Heathertail hovering with Featherpaw and Hootpaw.

"How is Breezepelt?" Heathertail asked anxiously.

"He's awake," Crowfeather replied, seeing Heathertail's blue eyes grow brilliant with relief. "But he needs to rest. In the meantime, all the Clan should get ready."

"Ready for what?" Hootpaw asked, flicking his tail straight up in the air.

"To fight," Crowfeather meowed.

CHAPTER 14

❧

"*Certainly not,*" *Harespring meowed, with a* stern look at all four apprentices. "Onestar has ordered that no apprentices are going to be in the battle with the stoats."

"But WindClan needs every cat!" Hootpaw protested, looking up at the Clan deputy with pleading eyes.

"WindClan needs every *warrior,*" Harespring corrected him.

"Not fair," Slightpaw muttered.

Crowfeather gave an irritated twitch of his whiskers. They were already wasting valuable practice time while the apprentices argued that they should be allowed to take part in the battle.

"We could let them join in the training," he suggested to Harespring. *Maybe that will shut them up.* "After all, it's possible the stoats will attack the camp. The apprentices should be able to defend themselves and the elders, and any cats who might be in the medicine cat den."

Featherpaw bounced gently on her paws with a gleam of excitement in her eyes. "Oh, yes, *please,* Harespring!"

The Clan deputy hesitated for a moment, then nodded.

"I suppose it won't do any harm," he decided. "You can be responsible for them, Crowfeather."

Thanks a bunch.

But Crowfeather had to admit to himself that he didn't mind working with the apprentices. They were all shaping up to be fine warriors. *Especially Hootpaw,* he thought as he paired them up to practice the battle move he had taught Hootpaw and Featherpaw a few days before. *Nightcloud taught him well,* Crowfeather thought, with a renewed pang at how much he missed her, *and now Gorsetail is doing a good job, too. She'll have an easier time because Nightcloud started Hootpaw off so well.*

Thinking about Hootpaw made Crowfeather pay more attention to his own apprentice. Featherpaw had learned the move well; she had good balance while she stood on her hind paws and attacked her opponent with her forepaws. But she was slightly hesitant, as if she was afraid of hurting her Clanmate, while the rest of the apprentices piled in enthusiastically.

"Be bold!" Crowfeather advised her. "And strike out faster. In a real battle, your enemy won't wait for you."

Featherpaw nodded vigorously, then returned to her practice with Oatpaw. Crowfeather watched with approval as she put more speed and strength into her blows, knocking Oatpaw to the ground and then leaping on top of him with a yowl of triumph.

"Well done!" Crowfeather praised her.

Almost the whole of WindClan had assembled on a flat stretch of moorland near the camp, for a training session to prepare for battle. Using the information Breezepelt, Heathertail, and Weaselfur had brought back, Onestar and Harespring had made a plan: Some cats were to go into the tunnels and drive the stoats toward the entrances, while others would wait in ambush to attack when the stoats appeared. Prey would be left near the entrances to lure the stoats into the open.

It should work, Crowfeather thought. *And maybe we'll be able to get rid of these StarClan-cursed creatures for good!*

"Okay," Crowfeather meowed to the apprentices when they had all practiced the move for some time, "you've gotten in a couple of good blows, you've darted back out of range, so what are you going to do now? Sit and sniff the flowers?"

"Attack again!" Hootpaw yowled, while Featherpaw curled her tail up in amusement.

"Right," Crowfeather responded. "But your enemy won't be sniffing the flowers, either. They'll be coming for you, so you need to do something unexpected. Any ideas?"

"Claw their throat out!" Slightpaw snarled, raising one forepaw with claws extended.

"You could try," Crowfeather agreed, privately reflecting that it wasn't as easy as that. "Anything else?"

"Attack from behind?" Featherpaw suggested.

"Good idea," Crowfeather responded, pleased by his apprentice's intelligence. "Let's try that. Practice the first move, then follow it up by attacking your opponent's hind-quarters. And remember, Featherpaw, be bold!"

"But remember too how dangerous your enemy is." Breeze-pelt's voice came from just behind Crowfeather. "You need to be careful."

Crowfeather realized that Breezepelt had padded up beside him. In the few days since his expedition into the tunnels, he had mostly recovered from his injuries, but Crowfeather felt that the fire inside him had gone out. *He's finally realized that his mother is gone forever.*

Seeing the sadness in his son's eyes, Crowfeather firmly stifled his annoyance that Breezepelt had interrupted his training session. He was determined not to start any more arguments with him.

"That's right," he agreed. "In a real battle, no *unnecessary* risks."

Crowfeather was aware of Breezepelt standing beside him as the apprentices began practicing again. He hadn't joined in the training session; instead he had limped along the edge of the practice area, his gait slow and careful, his tail trailing along the ground. Now they were standing so close that they must have seemed comfortable with each other, though Crowfeather knew that wasn't true. He could hardly bring himself to look at his son and see his dull, lifeless eyes.

Crowfeather believed that most of the Clan was feeling sorry for Breezepelt, as he was. Then he spotted Leaftail and Gorsetail with their heads together a couple of tail-lengths away. Leaftail's eyes sparkled with mockery.

"He's supposed to be some scary Dark Forest warrior," he whispered to Gorsetail. Clearly, he had been eavesdropping on Breezepelt's advice to the apprentices to be careful. "Sounds more like a mouse-hearted cat to me."

Crowfeather saw Breezepelt freeze as he overheard the

snarky comment. His eyes lit with fury, as if he would have liked to fight both cats at the same time.

"It's great that you have time to gossip," Crowfeather hissed, glaring at Leaftail. "And that you're not worried about these stoats that were foretold to destroy the whole Clan. Now shut up and get back to work."

Leaftail opened his jaws as if he was going to make a rude retort, but Gorsetail gave him a nudge, and both cats bounded away. Crowfeather kept an eye on them until he saw them beginning to practice the leap-and-roll battle move.

"Ignore what they're saying," he mewed softly to Breezepelt. "They have no idea what you went through. They don't know what a great warrior you can be."

Breezepelt had a grim, determined look on his face. "Well, they're going to find out," he meowed. "I'm going to prove it in the battle today."

Crowfeather was startled. "You're not back to battle fitness yet!" he blurted out.

"Fox dung to that," Breezepelt growled.

Crowfeather wanted to talk Breezepelt out of joining in the attack on the tunnels, but Breezepelt's expression, the intense tone of his voice, told him there would be no point in trying.

At least this time I'll be there to watch his back, Crowfeather thought. *And this time I don't intend to let him down.*

Sunhigh was still some way off when the WindClan cats set out for the tunnels. Harespring was in the lead, with Crowfeather and Weaselfur, while the rest of the warriors streamed across the moor behind them. Breezepelt lagged at the rear, still limping from his injuries, but managing to keep up. Crowfeather had tried keeping an eye on him, until Breezepelt had realized it and fixed him with an irritated glare.

"Are you sure about this?" Crowfeather heard Heathertail asking Breezepelt, padding at his side.

"Yeah, you know how tough the stoats are," Emberfoot added.

"I'm quite sure," Breezepelt retorted through clenched teeth.

Before they set out, Heathertail had talked to the apprentices about what had happened in the tunnels, making it clear that the coming battle was beyond their skills. Crowfeather suspected that Breezepelt had asked her to do it. After her talk, the apprentices seemed to have gained new respect for the enemy their Clan was about to face.

"How big do you think they are?" Hootpaw had asked his denmates, fluffing up his fur to increase his own size. "As big as this?"

"Much bigger!" Slightpaw had responded, wide-eyed.

"And I bet they have really long claws and teeth," Featherpaw had added. "Breezepelt was so brave to fight them all by himself."

Crowfeather, listening with amusement to their speculations, had given a nod of approval: *Finally!*

Now, as the Clan came within sight of the steep bank where the tunnel entrances gaped open, Harespring called a halt and gathered his Clanmates around him.

"I'll just remind you about what we're going to do," he began. "I'll enter the tunnels with Heathertail and Weaselfur."

Crowfeather shifted his paws impatiently. He had volunteered to join the group that was to go underground, but Harespring had assigned him to lead the ambush outside instead. *At least he hasn't chosen Breezepelt to go back in there.* There had been anger in Breezepelt's eyes when he learned he wouldn't be at the forefront of the battle, but he remained beside Crowfeather without complaining.

"Larkwing and Gorsetail will put the rabbits in place," Harespring continued. "We hope the scent of prey will lure the stoats out so we can fight them on our own ground."

Yes, we know all this, Crowfeather thought. His claws tore at the grass in his impatience to sink them into stoats, turning their white fur red. *Stop meowing and let's get started.*

"The rest of you, hide in the bushes." Harespring waved his tail toward the gorse thicket, a few fox-lengths away from the tunnel entrances. "Any questions? No? Then let's go!"

Harespring led the way into the tunnels with Heathertail and Weaselfur padding warily after him. Crowfeather watched while Larkwing and Gorsetail put two rabbits in position outside the entrances, dragging them over the grass to spread their scent. Then the two she-cats headed for the thicket where the rest of the Clan was hiding.

Now there was nothing to do but wait.

Moons seemed to pass before Harespring shot out of the nearest tunnel, with his two companions hard on his paws.

They raced across the open ground and joined their Clanmates in the bushes.

"They're coming," Harespring mewed tensely.

Several heartbeats later a few stoats peeked their heads out of the tunnel, sniffing the air and darting their gazes around as if they expected trouble.

Come on, Crowfeather urged them silently. His legs were aching with the effort of holding back when all his instincts were to leap forward and fight. *Don't you want some of that nice juicy rabbit?*

Then a voice spoke behind him. "*Those* are the dangerous enemies in the tunnel that every cat's warned us about?"

Slightpaw! Crowfeather whirled, tearing his pelt on the gorse spines. "What are you apprentices doing here?" he demanded.

All four apprentices were crouched in front of him, smug looks of satisfaction on their faces. His throat choked on mingled anger and fear, so that for a few heartbeats he couldn't speak.

"You told us to be bold," Featherpaw mewed, "so we've come to help fight."

"Yeah, Harespring isn't going to keep us away from all the excitement," Hootpaw declared, sliding his claws out and scraping them along the ground.

"It doesn't even look as if it'll be that hard," Oatpaw added as he peered out at the stoats. "They're kind of . . . cute!"

"I can't believe we were so scared!" Hootpaw exclaimed. "Come on, let's get them!"

"No!" Crowfeather yowled. "Get back to camp!"

By now the stoats had emerged from the tunnels and were sniffing around the prey. Wild with enthusiasm, the apprentices ignored Crowfeather. With Hootpaw in the lead they thrust their way out of the bushes and hurled themselves at their enemies.

The stoats whipped around to face the four young cats charging at them. As Crowfeather raced to catch up, they let out their weird chittering cries and flung themselves into the attack.

"Get back!" Crowfeather yowled again. Fear shook him like a leaf in the wind as he realized that he was too late.

CHAPTER 15

❧

Stoats poured out of the tunnels in an unending stream. *There are too many of them!* Crowfeather realized, his chest tightening with fear. Soon the four apprentices were surrounded. The stoats were smaller than badgers, but they were fast and wily, and Crowfeather knew from the previous skirmish that their teeth were sharper than eagle talons. And in the bright sunlight, their pure white pelts were unnerving.

It's like being attacked by a blizzard.

Before he could move, the stoats had the apprentices trapped. Oatpaw nervously struck out with one of their battle moves, but the stoats were too fast and too vicious—and there were too many of them.

Crowfeather charged toward the apprentices, with Breezepelt and Gorsetail following. When he was just tail-lengths away, Crowfeather cast one glance over his shoulder to make sure that the rest of his Clanmates were following—they were. Then he hurled himself into the fray.

They disobeyed, and there's no way of getting them out unscathed, he thought desperately. *I hope they're ready to fight!*

"Remember your training!" he yowled. "Be bold and strike out!"

In an effort to obey him, Featherpaw pounced on a stoat at the mouth of the nearest tunnel. Crowfeather batted aside one stoat and had another stoat pinned to the ground, digging his claws into its shoulders, but he caught sight of his apprentice as she rose on her hind paws and gave her opponent two sharp blows around its ears.

The stoat shrieked in pain and fled. Featherpaw let out a screech of triumph, but at the same moment more stoats appeared in the tunnel behind her and leaped on top of her, tearing at her pelt. Featherpaw disappeared under the tide of white bodies.

"No!" Crowfeather yowled. *I've lost too many cats lately!* His heart lurched at the thought of the apprentice he cared for dying under the claws of these filthy invaders.

Tossing his stoat aside, he dived into the tunnel entrance after Featherpaw, lashing out with both forepaws to pull the creatures off her. The young she-cat was crouching on the floor of the tunnel, letting out whimpering cries. Blood was already seeping from her wounds, matting her gray tabby fur.

Crowfeather snarled with fury as he drove the stoats back into the tunnel. He paused, listening, wanting to make sure he had enough time to pull the apprentice to safety. As their chittering cries faded away, he lifted Featherpaw gently by her scruff and dragged her out into the open. Her body was covered with scratches, and there was a particularly deep wound on her back. One of her hind paws was dangling awkwardly.

For a moment Crowfeather's mind flew back to Feathertail's death, the sickening crunch as her body hit the floor of the cave. *I couldn't save her, but I* will *save Featherpaw,* he thought grimly.

Battle raged around him as his fellow WindClan warriors clashed with the stoats. He could see several of the white bodies stretched out on the ground, but his Clanmates were still on their paws.

Glancing around, Crowfeather spotted Breezepelt and Heathertail fighting side by side, with Hootpaw close to them. To his relief, none of them seemed to be badly injured.

"Over here!" he called out to them. "Featherpaw is hurt—we have to protect her!"

Breezepelt and Heathertail dashed across to him, while Hootpaw scurried after them, all three gasping in horror as they saw the blood welling from their young Clanmate's wounds. Together the four cats formed a barrier around Featherpaw, who was feebly trying to rise to her paws.

"Stay still," Crowfeather ordered. "The stoats aren't finished. Let us handle this."

But the tumult of battle was dying down. Crowfeather could hear the scurrying of paws through the tough moorland grass. The fierceness of the stoats' attack had faded, and they were beginning to retreat into the tunnels. The other WindClan warriors drove them back: Gorsetail and Crouchfoot were in the lead, clawing at the stoats' black-tipped tails until the last of the white-pelted creatures had disappeared into the darkness.

"Yeah! We won!" Oatpaw yowled. The pale brown tabby was leaping up and down with excitement. His only wounds,

Crowfeather was grateful to see, were a couple of scratches on one shoulder.

"It's over for *now*," he mewed angrily to Oatpaw. "But the stoats will be regrouping down there, and there may be many more of them. We need to retreat and get Featherpaw to the medicine-cat den."

"I'm okay," Featherpaw murmured. "I can stay and fight. I did well, didn't I?" she added, gazing up at Crowfeather. "I struck out swiftly, just like you said."

Her voice faded and her eyelids fluttered closed as she lost consciousness.

"You have less sense than a newborn rabbit," Crowfeather told her, even though he wasn't sure she could hear him. "But you were so brave—and so reckless."

Breezepelt joined him to help lift Featherpaw. Guilt washed over Crowfeather like a tide of blood as he saw the young she-cat's body hanging limply between them; only her shallow breathing showed that she was still alive.

"That's a bad wound on her back, and if her paw isn't seen to right away, it won't heal right," he mewed miserably. *I'll never forgive myself if she doesn't recover.*

Breezepelt was silent as they began to carry Featherpaw across the moor; Crowfeather was aware of his son's gaze fixed on him, a look that Crowfeather couldn't interpret. But he said nothing, and Crowfeather had too much on his mind to bother challenging him.

The WindClan camp was in sight before Breezepelt spoke. "You don't have to worry about Featherpaw's paw," he meowed abruptly. "As long as Kestrelflight wraps it with a good clump of comfrey leaves and cobweb, it should be fine."

Crowfeather gave his son a curious look. "How do you know that?" he asked. "You never trained as a medicine cat."

"No," Breezepelt responded. "But I had the same injury when I was an apprentice, and that's how Barkface treated me. I was up and walking again in just a few days."

Crowfeather was about to say that he didn't remember Breezepelt being injured back then, but stopped himself. When he thought about it, he did remember the injury—or, more accurately, he remembered Nightcloud's worrying over it. Busy with his duties as Heathertail's mentor, he had just assumed that Nightcloud was being overprotective as usual.

Now Crowfeather understood Breezepelt's strange look. He was envious that his father had praised Featherpaw and was worried about her injuries.

It wasn't just my kits from ThunderClan that I wasn't there for, he realized, shock striking him like a lightning bolt. *I paid so little attention to my WindClan son that I hardly remembered that he suffered a major injury. Have I really cared more for my apprentices than my own son?*

Crowfeather had a horrible feeling that he knew the answer—or what *would* have been the answer, until recently. But Crowfeather hoped that however lacking he had been as a father, he could make up for that now. In fact, he had to, now that Nightcloud was gone. He had to accept that he'd been a different cat back then, just as Breezepelt was no longer the cat whose loyalties lay elsewhere.

Now Crowfeather had become the kind of warrior who could pass his experience on to younger cats. He suppressed a wistful sigh. *If only my kits had been born later . . . I could be a better father now, but is it too late for Breezepelt?*

As he and Breezepelt struggled into Kestrelflight's den with Featherpaw, Crowfeather saw the young medicine cat's eyes stretch wide with alarm. But a moment later he recovered his air of efficiency.

"Bring her over here," he meowed, pointing with his tail to a nest of soft moss. "I've got all the herbs ready to treat injuries from the battle."

But no cat expected the worst-injured cat to be one of the youngest, Crowfeather thought. He could read as much in Kestrelflight's eyes. *It doesn't seem fair.*

The young medicine cat was too kindhearted to scold Crowfeather for not taking better care of his apprentice. In any case, he couldn't have blamed Crowfeather any more than Crowfeather was blaming himself.

Crowfeather and Breezepelt laid Featherpaw down, settling her comfortably in the nest, and Kestrelflight crouched over her, licking the blood from the wound on her back to clean it up.

"What happened out there?" he asked between licks.

"When we left, the stoats had been driven back into the tunnels," Crowfeather replied, a worm of uneasiness stirring in his belly. "I just wonder why none of the other warriors have made it back."

He found the answer to his question a few moments later, when Heathertail stuck her head into the entrance to Kestrelflight's den.

"What's wrong?" Breezepelt asked urgently. "Are you okay?"

"I'm fine," Heathertail replied. To Kestrelflight she added, "We drove the stoats into the tunnels and thought it was all over. But then more of them came pouring out, and we had to retreat. We killed a few of them, but we're still vastly outnumbered."

So what do we do now? Crowfeather asked himself, a dark cloud of disappointment descending on him at the news that they hadn't won even a minor victory. They had already assured ThunderClan that they had the stoat problem under control. But that wasn't true. *What's going to happen if we can't handle this ourselves?*

Then he pushed the thought away. There were more important things to deal with.

"Heathertail, can you fetch Featherpaw's parents?"

Heathertail gave a swift nod. "Emberfoot might not be back yet, but I saw Sedgewhisker just now. I'll go get her." She disappeared, and her hurrying paw steps faded away.

Kestrelflight was chewing up marigold leaves for a poultice when both Emberfoot and Sedgewhisker arrived, their eyes full of anxiety. Crowfeather could taste their fear-scent.

"How did Featherpaw get hurt?" Emberfoot demanded, while Sedgewhisker crouched down beside her unconscious kit and began to lick her ears. "She wasn't supposed to be in the battle!"

"She and the other apprentices followed us and joined in without permission," Crowfeather explained.

Emberfoot and Sedgewhisker exchanged a shocked glance. "It must have been those others, encouraging her!" Sedgewhisker meowed. "Featherpaw would never have done such a thing by herself."

"So what happened?" Emberfoot demanded.

"Featherpaw was ambushed by a group of stoats," Crowfeather replied, "and that's how she was injured."

"She's lost a lot of blood, and her paw is broken," Kestrelflight added.

"But she will be all right?" Sedgewhisker asked, looking up at him with pleading eyes.

Kestrelflight hesitated. "I can't be certain," he admitted at last. "I'll set her paw and treat the wound on her back, but we'll have to wait until she wakes up to know for sure if she'll recover."

Emberfoot and Sedgewhisker exchanged a glance of mingled grief and fury. Crouching down beside her kit, Sedgewhisker began to lick the clotted blood from Featherpaw's fur, while Emberfoot stroked her shoulder with the tip of his tail.

"You're her mentor, Crowfeather," he snarled. "You should have made sure that she didn't end up on such a dangerous mission!"

"The apprentices were ordered not to take part in the battle," Crowfeather insisted, seeing Breezepelt looking at him uncertainly. "But I did tell her to be bold," he admitted, feeling his throat tighten with guilt. "I suppose she took it the wrong way. She's so brave . . . she already has all the makings of a warrior. When I said to be bold, I never meant for her to join in battles far too dangerous for an apprentice."

"So it was *you* who gave her the idea to do this?" Emberfoot's shoulder fur began to bristle, and his voice was a deep, threatening growl. "Why? She's just an apprentice!"

"I wanted to inspire her," Crowfeather replied, "but—"

"What's *wrong* with you lately?" Sedgewhisker interrupted. "Ever since the Great Battle, it's like you're barely here! I know you've suffered some losses, but still . . . if it weren't for you, Featherpaw wouldn't be lying here now, and we don't even know if she'll survive!"

Crowfeather wanted to tell the distraught cats that it was a mentor's job to inspire their apprentice, and that Featherpaw would still be fine if she had done what Harespring had told her and stayed in camp. But he knew what their reaction would be, and it wasn't an outpouring of understanding. Even Hootpaw, who had slipped inside and was sitting next to Featherpaw, couldn't meet Crowfeather's gaze.

Does he blame me as well? Crowfeather asked himself, heat rising beneath his pelt. *If he does, he's right to. They all are. Onestar, too, when he told me why he didn't choose me as deputy. I have been barely here lately. And it's cost WindClan so much.*

"I'm so sorry," he meowed to Sedgewhisker and Emberfoot. "I feel terrible about this. I know I haven't been the greatest of mentors." *Just like I haven't been the best of fathers.*

"I wish I could disagree," Emberfoot meowed coldly. "I used to trust you completely, Crowfeather. I was pleased when

Onestar chose you to mentor Featherpaw. But now—now I wonder if your carelessness contributed to Breezepelt's foolishness. I thought his problems were being overblown by some cats, but now I look at you differently. I'm not sure either of us will ever trust you again. You could've gotten Featherpaw killed!"

Crowfeather met Breezepelt's gaze, unsure of what he was hoping to find there. Support? Maybe sympathy? *Or does he agree with the others? He's never been shy about letting me know how frustrated he is with me.*

But Breezepelt showed nothing of what he was thinking, lowering his head to look at the ground while he scuffled his forepaws on the earth floor of the den.

"My den isn't the right place for this argument," Kestrelflight declared. While the others had been talking, he had poulticed the wound on Featherpaw's back and plastered cobweb all over it to hold the herbs in place. "I want you all to leave and give Featherpaw some peace and quiet."

"No—I want to stay with her!" Sedgewhisker objected.

"But she needs to rest," Kestrelflight pointed out. "If you stay, she'll only try to get up and prove what a brave warrior she is."

"He's right," Emberfoot meowed, padding up to Sedgewhisker and nudging her to her paws. "Come on. Kestrelflight will let us know as soon as Featherpaw wakes up."

"Of course I will," Kestrelflight promised.

Reluctantly Sedgewhisker allowed her mate to coax her out of the den. Breezepelt and Hootpaw followed. Crowfeather brought up the rear after one last long look at Featherpaw's inert form.

Outside the den, Harespring had returned with the rest of the warriors. He was assembling the wounded, picking out the ones with the worst injuries for Kestrelflight to see first.

"How is Featherpaw?" Gorsetail asked.

Crowfeather shook his head. "Not good," he admitted.

"And why was she even there?" Crouchfoot added. "I thought the apprentices were forbidden from taking part in the battle."

"They were. They disobeyed," Crowfeather responded. "But I did tell Featherpaw to be assertive," he added reluctantly.

Shocked exclamations rose from the crowd of warriors; Leaftail's voice rose above the rest. "I can't believe you'd say that to an apprentice right before a battle! You couldn't have encouraged them more if you'd sharpened their claws yourself."

Crowfeather felt the accusing glances of his Clanmates like a whole gorse bush full of thorns driving into his pelt.

They're right. I made the wrong decisions at nearly every turn. But there's one thing I wasn't wrong about. The threat in the tunnels can't be ignored.

"There's something I want to say," he announced, raising his voice to be heard above the murmurs and pain-filled mews of the crowd of cats.

Harespring turned toward him. "Go on, say it, then," he ordered curtly.

"Maybe I expressed it wrong," Crowfeather meowed. "But I wasn't wrong that the apprentices—and all of us—need to be brave and assertive. Have you all forgotten Kestrelflight's vision? The dark water that emerged from the tunnels, whipped by the wind, fierce enough to swamp WindClan and ThunderClan—maybe ShadowClan and RiverClan too? Suppose that we don't manage to deal with this stoat problem, and something else follows them? What if the Clans are so tired and wounded from fighting with the stoats that we don't have the strength to handle another threat?"

Hootpaw's fur bushed out as he stood in front of Crowfeather with alarm in his eyes. "What are you saying?" he demanded, seeming to forget that he was an apprentice talking to a senior warrior. "That there's going to be another battle? That the Dark Forest cats will return?"

"No, I'm not saying that," Crowfeather responded, trying to reassure Hootpaw. "Because I don't know for sure. But there *must* be a reason Kestrelflight had that dream. And what worries me is that a new conflict—maybe a threat from outside, maybe trouble within the Clan—is going to fall over us like the shadows in the tunnels, and maybe wash us away like a great flood."

Some cat in the crowd muttered, "He's got bees in his brain," but Crowfeather ignored the insult.

The idea he needed was in Crowfeather's mind like an elusive piece of prey. So close, but always *just* out of reach . . . "I know there's an answer there," he mewed. "I can feel it."

The cats gathered around Crowfeather were exchanging

dubious glances, as if none of them believed what he was trying to tell them. To Crowfeather's surprise, Breezepelt was the first to speak.

"I think you could be right," he began. It surprised Crowfeather even more that Breezepelt, of all cats, was on his side. "After all, there were two waves in the vision. The wind defeated the first one, but the second one overwhelmed everything. So do you think getting rid of the stoats will ward off this bigger threat?" His tone was thoughtful, as if he was taking his father's worries seriously. "How do you think we can do that? There were so many of them in the battle, and there must be more of them lurking in the tunnels. We'll be outnumbered, and they know the tunnels much better than we do. It's not easy to lure them out into the open."

Crowfeather nodded. "That's true." He paused for a moment, uncertain of how to respond to his son, though the idea he needed to capture was still lurking at the back of his mind. *Maybe I should treat it like cunning prey,* he thought. *Pretend to ignore it, and trick it into overconfidence . . .*

Then, like a stoat peering out of the shadows, the thought emerged into the light. *And like the stoats, what I have to say won't be welcome.* He took a deep breath. "If we're going to succeed in wiping out the stoats and clearing the tunnels," he meowed, "we're going to need help. We're going to need ThunderClan."

Murmurs of dismay arose from the cats clustered around him. One voice rang out above them, from somewhere behind Crowfeather. "Absolutely not!"

Turning, Crowfeather saw that Onestar had padded up

to join his warriors, and was glaring at him with cold disapproval.

"Crowfeather, I can't believe you would even suggest we turn to ThunderClan," he growled. "WindClan can handle itself. What's happened here is none of ThunderClan's business. There's no way I'm going to allow the other Clans to find out that we're vulnerable right now. Firestar was always meddling in our business," he added. "I don't want to set that precedent with Bramblestar, or soon ThunderClan will be sticking their noses into all our problems."

"And especially if we can't even trust all the cats in our own Clan," Leaftail mewed, with a nasty look at Breezepelt.

Even before Leaftail had finished speaking, Heathertail whipped around to glare at her Clanmate. "How *dare* you say that!" she hissed. "Breezepelt was the first to kill one of the stoats. You should be grateful."

Leaftail's only response was a disdainful flick of his tail.

"I don't need you to defend me," Breezepelt informed Heathertail, fur rising all along his spine. "In fact," he added, his cold stare raking across his Clanmates, "I don't need any of you."

Heathertail's eyes widened in shock and hurt at Breezepelt's response. Crowfeather was surprised, too, when Heathertail had done nothing but defend his son. He knew that Breezepelt was just lashing out in anger and frustration, but he guessed that when he calmed down, he would regret snapping at Heathertail. She was one of the only true friends he had in the Clan.

"Traitor!" Crouchfoot yowled as the clamor continued.

More yowls rose from the assembled cats, most of them accusing Breezepelt, though a few tried to make themselves heard in his defense. With bristling pelts and claws sliding out, the cats were heartbeats away from attacking one another. Weaselfur pushed past Crowfeather, almost knocking him off his paws, as he squared up to Leaftail, his lips drawn back in a snarl.

Crowfeather could do nothing but stand in dismay as he watched his beloved Clan falling apart before his eyes.

"That's enough!" Onestar's caterwaul rose above the outcry. "Sheathe your claws!" As the warriors turned toward him, he added, "Don't you think the stoats would enjoy seeing us fight among ourselves?"

Crowfeather crept off into the medicine-cat den. The sounds of argument faded away as Onestar got control of his Clan and, with Harespring's help, sent the uninjured warriors out on hunting patrols. Crowfeather didn't want to be chosen.

I'm sure every cat would rather chew off their own tail than patrol with me.

"Do you mind if I stay in here for a while?" he asked Kestrelflight. "I could help you watch Featherpaw."

To Crowfeather's surprise, Kestrelflight gave him a sympathetic glance. *He must be the only cat who doesn't think I'm a waste of space.*

"That would be a real help," Kestrelflight replied. "I've been sorting out the herbs I need to treat the other injuries, but I don't want to leave Featherpaw alone. Can you stay with her until I get back?"

"Sure."

Kestrelflight padded out of the den with a leaf wrap of herbs in his jaws. Left alone with Featherpaw, Crowfeather settled down beside her nest and lowered his head to give her a sniff. Though she was still unconscious, the clean tang of comfrey and marigold was stronger than the scent of blood, and her breathing seemed to be deeper and steadier than before.

Crowfeather wanted to speak to her, but guilt made the words stick in his throat. *I've failed her, just like I failed Breezepelt.*

"Featherpaw, I'm so sorry I encouraged you to go into danger," he mewed at last. "I should have been more careful with what I said to you, and as soon as I saw you out there by the tunnels, I should have sent you straight back to camp. But I never thought everything would go so wrong, so quickly."

His mind drifted back to his sense that some greater threat was looming over the Clans, and that the only way to deal with the stoats was to involve ThunderClan. *But Onestar won't hear of it,* he thought resentfully. He'd hoped that, after the Great Battle, the Clans would realize they needed one another more than ever. Instead it felt like they were even more divided.

And what about WindClan? he wondered. *There's not only fighting between the Clans . . . there's fighting within, too.* Was WindClan doomed to tear itself apart with arguments? Could they ever work together when so few cats trusted Breezepelt?

"And then there's Breezepelt himself," he murmured aloud. "What's going to happen to him?"

He wondered if Breezepelt could ever get over his anger and hurt at the events of the Great Battle. *Will the Great Battle haunt us always?*

Crouched in the quiet of the medicine-cat den, Crowfeather

felt sleep stealing up on him. The stress of the battle, Feather-paw's injuries, and the quarrels among the Clan had sapped his strength. His own wounds, even though they were minor compared to Featherpaw's, stung as if a whole swarm of bees were attacking him. Crowfeather struggled against sleep for a while, then curled up even closer to Featherpaw so that if she moved she would rouse him, and let himself slip into darkness.

Instantly Crowfeather found himself running through the tunnels, faster and more confidently than he ever had in the waking world. A pale gray light just ahead of him told him that Ashfoot was there, though at first he couldn't see her.

"Wait for me!" he called out to her. "Why do you keep doing this?"

Then an even brighter light shone in front of Crowfeather. He burst out into the open and saw that he had reached a forest clearing. A full moon was overhead, shedding a silver light over the trees and bushes, and stars blazed down through gaps in the branches. A small pool in the center of the clearing looked as if it was made of liquid starlight.

Fear and wonder shivered through Crowfeather until he felt as if his blood were turning to ice. *Where am I?* he asked himself. The full moon alone told him that this wasn't the world he lived in when he was awake. Yet he knew that only medicine cats were allowed to enter StarClan before they died.

"Crowfeather?" His mother's voice startled him out of his thoughts. "Why are you standing there gaping as if you expect prey to come and fly into your jaws?"

Now Crowfeather spotted Ashfoot sitting in the shadow of an arching clump of ferns. He padded over to her, hardly feeling as if his paws were his own.

"What is this place?" he asked hoarsely.

Ashfoot gave an impatient twitch of her whiskers. "It's your dream, mouse-brain," she responded.

"Then why have you brought me here?"

"I'm still trying to make you see sense," Ashfoot told him. "And since you won't listen to me, I've brought a friend."

A rustling came from the bushes behind Crowfeather. He spun around, his pelt prickling with apprehension. He stared as the undergrowth parted and a silver tabby she-cat stepped into the open. Her plumy tail was raised high, and her blue eyes glowed with love for him.

"Greetings, Crowfeather," she mewed.

"Feathertail!" Crowfeather breathed out. Astonishment and disbelief gripped him like giant claws, and the ache of loss awoke again in his heart. "Is it really you?"

The last time he had seen the beautiful RiverClan she-cat had been in the mountains, in the cave where the Tribe lived. There she had leaped to the cave roof and gripped a pointed stone until it had given way and plummeted downward to drive into the heart of Sharptooth, the ferocious lion-cat. But Feathertail had fallen with it; her courageous action had cost her her life.

She saved the Tribe, and she saved me. Oh, Feathertail . . . I loved you so much!

Crowfeather stood still, stunned by shock, while Feathertail padded forward, twined her tail with his, and nuzzled him affectionately. He could feel the warmth of her pelt and taste her sweet scent as it wreathed around him. He could hardly believe that this was only a dream.

"I've missed you," he choked out.

"I've missed you, too." Feathertail took a pace back and looked deeply into Crowfeather's eyes. "But you're not quite the same cat that I knew back then."

"What do you mean?" Crowfeather asked.

"You remember that I'm in both StarClan *and* the Tribe of Endless Hunting," Feathertail meowed. "The Tribe has given me permission to come and speak to you. I've been watching you, and I'm troubled by what I've seen."

"What do you mean?" Crowfeather asked.

"I've seen how you are with Breezepelt," Feathertail replied. "The Crowfeather I knew had so much love to give. Why have you been withholding love from your own son?"

Crowfeather turned his head sharply to gaze at Ashfoot. "Are you ganging up on me now?"

Ashfoot shrugged. "I had to make you see . . . and I knew she was the one cat you would always listen to."

With a long sigh, Crowfeather turned back to Feathertail. "What you say is true," he admitted. "I've tried to set things right with Breezepelt, but I'm worried that it's too late. Everything went wrong between us because of what I did—or didn't do—when Breezepelt was just an apprentice, and I can't go back in time, however much I might want to. Now Breezepelt is still troubled. What more can I do?"

Feathertail blinked at him affectionately. "You can accept Breezepelt for who he is."

"I'll try," Crowfeather promised. "But right now, keeping the Clan safe is the most important task for every cat. I know we need ThunderClan's help to clear the stoats out of the tunnels, but Onestar just won't see that."

Feathertail's blue eyes sparkled with sympathy. "Then there's only one thing you can do," she mewed. "Be true to yourself."

Crowfeather's whiskers twitched in surprise. "If I were being true to myself . . . I suppose I would go to Leafpool," he murmured. But would Feathertail really suggest going to the only cat he had loved after her—and disobeying his Clan leader to do it? "Should I go behind Onestar's back?" he asked.

Feathertail stared at him intensely. "Crowfeather . . . ," she began, but her voice trailed off.

"Leafpool would be able to persuade Bramblestar that it's for the good of ThunderClan to help me," Crowfeather went on as the pieces came together in his mind. "And once I get rid of the threat, Onestar won't care how I did it."

Ashfoot leaned forward. "Crowfeather . . . the Clan is what matters. You must put the good of the Clan above everything else."

Her voice faded on the last few words, and the brilliant moonlight in the clearing began to fade too. Before darkness fell, the last things Crowfeather saw were Feathertail's eyes, as warm and blue as the sky in greenleaf.

Crowfeather blinked awake in the dim light of the

medicine-cat den. Featherpaw was still unconscious beside him, and Feathertail and Ashfoot were gone, but their words remained fresh in his thoughts. He rose to his paws and arched his back in a good long stretch.

Sedgewhisker was right, he thought. *I haven't really been present since the Great Battle, not for my Clan. Even though I'm not deputy, I seem to be the only cat who can see reason. It's time for me to put my Clan first.*

Now Crowfeather knew what he had to do.

CHAPTER 16

Crowfeather slipped through the undergrowth in the wooded area at the edge of WindClan territory. He didn't like the damp sensation of moist earth under his pads, or the feeling of being closed in by branches above his head. He longed for the springy sensation of moorland grass, and the feeling of cold wind in his whiskers as he raced across the hillside.

No wonder ThunderClan cats are so weird, when they live in the forest all the time!

On leaving camp, Crowfeather had considered cutting through the tunnels to reach ThunderClan territory, his paws and fur itching with the urge to kill a few stoats on the way. *But if I tried that, I might never come out on the other side,* he realized.

As he headed for the border stream, Crowfeather seemed to hear Kestrelflight's voice. *A wild wind kicked up and drove the water back. But eventually the wind dropped, and the water kept on rushing and gushing . . . until it swallowed up everything.* The image the medicine cat had spoken of was so vivid that Crowfeather felt that he could see the restless waves for himself, almost as if the vision had been his, a special message sent to him from StarClan.

After everything that had happened since, particularly how Nightcloud and Breezepelt had suffered so much from the stoats in the tunnels where the floodwater came from, Crowfeather couldn't shake off the feeling that somehow the responsibility for fixing this problem rested on *his* shoulders.

Or, if I fail, maybe my kin will feel they have to do it. I can't put that burden on them.

It felt strange for Crowfeather to muse that maybe *not* being deputy was a good thing. If he had been, he would never have dared to go behind Onestar's back like this; as a warrior, he had less to lose. That conviction was all that kept him going, once he could hear the gurgling of the stream that formed WindClan's border with ThunderClan. He couldn't help remembering how forcefully Onestar had refused to ask for help from the rival Clan.

And now here I am, going to do just that. Cats have been banished from their Clans for less.

Approaching the stream, Crowfeather tasted the air, picking up the stench of the ThunderClan scent markers and, beyond that, the fresh scent of ThunderClan cats. A few heartbeats later, Berrynose and Thornclaw emerged from behind a clump of elder bushes that grew on the bank of the stream.

Oh, StarClan! Not Berrynose again!

Crowfeather signaled to them with his tail. The two warriors stiffened at the sight of him, and Crowfeather saw them slide out their claws. He didn't move any closer to the border, waiting while the ThunderClan cats sniffed warily and let their gazes flicker along the bank to either side of him.

After a moment the two cats relaxed, retracting their claws; clearly, they hadn't picked up any other WindClan scent. Even so, Crowfeather stayed where he was, not moving forward to the edge of the stream.

"What do you want?" Berrynose asked.

"I need to speak with Leafpool," Crowfeather replied with a respectful dip of his head. *Like I'll ever respect Berrynose! But for now, I need him to cooperate.* "I have something very important to discuss with her, and it can't wait."

Berrynose and Thornclaw exchanged a dubious glance with a hint of hostility. "What's this all about?" Thornclaw asked. "Clan business? Medicine-cat business?"

"*Private* business," Crowfeather responded.

Berrynose let out a snort of amusement, though Thornclaw remained serious as he glared at Crowfeather with narrowed eyes. "I think you've shared enough *private* business with Leafpool," he growled.

Oh, for StarClan's sake! Crowfeather forced his neck fur to stay flat. "It's nothing like that," he mewed defensively.

The two cats hesitated for a moment. Then Berrynose gave Crowfeather a brusque nod.

"You'll have to stay there, on your own side of the stream," he responded. "I don't think it would be a good idea to escort you into camp just now."

No, not after all the trouble at the Gathering, Crowfeather thought, trying not to feel insulted. *It seems like every cat is feeling extra protective these days.*

"That's fine, thanks," he replied. "I'll wait here."

The two ThunderClan cats disappeared into the undergrowth, heading for their camp. While he waited, Crowfeather found himself staring at the stream as it flowed lazily over the stony bed. There were times when he had seen it running faster, and the thought drew him back once again into Kestrelflight's vision.

I don't think the underground river would ever swell enough to surge out in the kind of flood Kestrelflight saw. The water must mean something else—but what?

Crowfeather pursued the answer as if he were stalking a crafty bit of prey, lying in wait for it to show itself, but for all his efforts he was no closer.

"Best give up," he growled aloud, though no cat was listening. He gave an annoyed flick of his tail as he wondered if he really did need to take on the responsibility for his Clan's survival.

Crowfeather hadn't waited for long before the undergrowth parted and Berrynose and Thornclaw reappeared. Crowfeather felt a tingle of excitement in his pads at the thought of seeing Leafpool again. While his feelings for her had changed over time, he knew he could count on her to understand the urgency of what he had come to say.

Then the ferns parted again. He stifled a hiss of irritation as he saw that the cat who appeared wasn't Leafpool.

It was Jayfeather.

"I said I wanted to see Leafpool," he meowed, gazing at the ThunderClan cats in confusion.

"We weren't too sure about your *private* business,"

Thornclaw explained. "Besides, Leafpool was busy, so we figured Jayfeather would be fine."

A furious retort rose to Crowfeather's lips, but he bit it back. He had experienced enough awkward encounters with one son; he wasn't prepared for another.

The two warriors withdrew, while Jayfeather padded up to the bank of the stream and leaped across as confidently as if he could see the edge. Crowfeather was impressed to see how capable his blind son was. An odd kind of affection swelled inside him, but he knew that he'd played little part in Jayfeather's life. *It's no thanks to me that he turned out so well.*

Jayfeather's ears were pricked, and the fur on his shoulders was beginning to rise. He didn't look any happier than Crowfeather felt.

"What are you doing here?" he asked, a hint of surprise in his voice. "Whatever it is, it had better be good. I've interrupted my duties to come to see you. I don't like being summoned as if I'm a lazy apprentice."

Crowfeather fought against an impulse to turn around and go home. Jayfeather was difficult and gruff at the best of times. With all that had been going on, it wouldn't be easy to ask him for help.

But I'm like that, too, he admitted to himself. *Perhaps I have passed down something to this kit.*

Crowfeather remembered his dream, and the good advice Feathertail had given him. He knew he had no choice but to give it a try.

"I want to talk to you about the stoats," he began. "WindClan hasn't been able to deal with them at our end of the tunnels. In fact, they're a much bigger problem than we thought at first." He hesitated, scraping at the ground with one forepaw. "The truth is, Jayfeather . . . WindClan needs ThunderClan's help."

Just as he had expected, Jayfeather gave an angry lash of his tail. "Then why did Onestar insist on handling it himself? And why didn't he come with you and ask to talk to Bramblestar?" His ears pricked suddenly in a gesture of astonishment. "Does Onestar even know that you're here?"

"Well . . . no," Crowfeather confessed, expecting that Jayfeather would refuse to say any more.

Instead, to Crowfeather's surprise, Jayfeather seemed almost impressed, a rusty *mrrow* of amusement coming from his throat. "You've got some nerve, I'll give you that," he meowed. "So Onestar is still insisting on coping with this alone. . . . Doesn't he realize that if the stoats get bolder and stronger around the tunnels, it'll be a threat to ThunderClan as well?"

"Of course, but—" Crowfeather broke off as Jayfeather interrupted him.

"We've extended our patrols, and we haven't seen much of the stoats on our side lately. I assumed they had gone for good, but obviously they haven't."

"No, and the problem on our side is pretty bad," Crowfeather admitted, with a renewed pang of regret as he thought of Nightcloud's death. "We thought we could handle it on our own, but we underestimated the stoats, and that was a mistake. Besides, I'm getting the feeling that they're more than just a pest."

"Why is that?" Jayfeather asked.

"You were at the Gathering," Crowfeather replied. "You heard what Kestrelflight said, about the vision of water emerging from the tunnels, water that could flood the Clans' territories? I'm beginning to think that the stoats are part of that."

Jayfeather said nothing, but Crowfeather could see from the tilt of his head that he was listening intently.

"What if the stoats are a small problem," he went on, feeling slightly encouraged, "but one that would leave the Clans vulnerable when faced with a bigger challenge?"

Jayfeather rolled his sightless blue eyes. "After everything that happened with the Dark Forest," he mewed, "you think StarClan is going to try to frighten us using *stoats*? You should leave the prophesying to the medicine cats." He half turned away, as if he was about to leave.

Crowfeather did his best to ignore the jibe. "It's the Great Battle that has me worried," he responded, desperate to make Jayfeather listen. "That showed me that all our tussles over territory until then had been minor. I never expected that the Clans could be pulled into a conflict that claimed so many lives. If it happened once, it could happen again."

Jayfeather let out a snort; clearly, he was still unconvinced. "And a bunch of stoats are really going to start the next Great Battle?"

"They could," Crowfeather insisted. "It's not so far-fetched. The stoats have already killed one cat and seriously injured another. And they're getting bolder every day—maybe because we're still gathering our strength. They're fast and spiteful, and that makes them deadly—and there are a lot of them. Even if all the WindClan warriors went up against them at once, we would still be outnumbered. WindClan and ThunderClan need to work together, for the good of both Clans—and maybe ShadowClan and RiverClan too."

"But Onestar hasn't changed his mind?"

"No," Crowfeather admitted. "Onestar still won't hear of cooperating. The idea will have to come from . . . some other cat."

Jayfeather's whiskers arched in surprise. "You *are* sticking your nose into a bees' nest, aren't you?" He hesitated for a moment, then let out a sigh. "Okay, fine. I'll talk to Bramblestar about it. He's reasonable; he'll probably take this seriously."

His confident tone and his obvious respect for Bramblestar reminded Crowfeather of how close Jayfeather was to his Clan leader: At one time, they had believed themselves to be father and son. *And Bramblestar was a great father to him . . . maybe better than I could have been.*

"If you want my advice," Jayfeather continued, "WindClan needs to sort itself out. If you had brought this up right from the start, maybe Nightcloud would still be here."

Crowfeather winced at his son's blunt criticism, but said nothing. *He's not wrong.*

"If nothing else," Jayfeather went on, "the Great Battle should have taught all the Clans the importance of working *together.*"

"You're right, of course," Crowfeather acknowledged.

Jayfeather twitched his ears irritably. "I always am," he meowed.

Crowfeather dipped his head, then felt his pelt bristle with embarrassment—Jayfeather couldn't see his gesture. So he thanked his son sincerely, and watched as Jayfeather leaped neatly across the stream, back to the ThunderClan side.

It's amazing how a blind cat can cross a stream of water without once stopping to feel his way with his forepaws.

As Jayfeather disappeared into the bushes, Crowfeather watched, feeling as though a thorn had pierced his heart. Jayfeather was ornery, it was true . . . but he was also a clever and special cat. *He got the orneriness from me,* Crowfeather reflected. *Of that I'm fairly sure. But what about the rest?*

He couldn't help but wonder how Jayfeather might have turned out, had he raised him instead of Bramblestar. *Would he have become the medicine cat he is now? Or would Jayfeather's paws have led him down a different path?*

He thought of Breezepelt . . . insecure, angry, and struggling. *How much of that was because of me? Would Breezepelt be any different now, if he'd been raised by another cat?*

On his way back to the WindClan camp, Crowfeather felt a weight settling over him, as if his pelt were soaked with muddy water. He tried to shake it off, telling himself that it was too late to have these thoughts about Jayfeather. Jayfeather was grown up, a full medicine cat, a vital part of a different Clan.

But Breezepelt . . .

Crowfeather shook himself, thinking that he didn't have

time to think about the problems of his own making right now.

There were more important matters to be dealt with.

When Crowfeather reached the WindClan camp, he immediately spotted Onestar sitting outside his den. The Clan leader rose to his paws, glaring at Crowfeather as he padded down the slope and crossed the hollow to join him.

"Where have you been all day?" Onestar demanded.

Crowfeather took a breath. He had known when he left that Onestar would want an explanation, and he had decided to tell the truth. "I've spoken to Jayfeather," he replied. "I told him what's been happening at our end of the tunnels. ThunderClan needs to know for their own safety—and ours. I've asked them for their help."

Onestar tilted his head, his eyes widening. He drew his lips back into a snarl, while the fur on his pelt bristled in fury. "How dare you?" he spat. "How could you go behind my back like that and share our private business with ThunderClan? Are you a loyal WindClan warrior or not?" Lashing his tail, he let out a growl deep within his throat, then continued without giving Crowfeather a chance to defend himself. "I can't figure out what's going on with you lately. It's this kind of reckless behavior that kept me from making you deputy. I thought you put your Clan first, but maybe I was wrong."

Anger swelled up inside Crowfeather, but he forced himself to stay calm. "It's *because* I'm a loyal WindClan warrior that I went to ThunderClan for help," he responded. "I know working with ThunderClan isn't ideal, but it feels like the only way to make sure we all survive. I won't stand by and let what happened to Breezepelt and Featherpaw—and Nightcloud—happen to any other cat in camp because we were too stubborn to ask for the help we need. I won't put Hootpaw or Heathertail in harm's way just to protect WindClan's pride!"

Onestar lashed his tail again, his anger clearly mounting. "Who are you to talk about WindClan's pride?" he demanded. "It's your *own* pride that's important to you, Crowfeather. A loyal warrior would have asked his leader's permission before going to ask for help from another Clan. And a disloyal warrior has no place in WindClan!"

Crowfeather was silent, his gaze locked with Onestar's. *Is that a threat? But you wouldn't have given your permission, would you?*

The Clan leader was the first to look away. "What's done is done," he snapped. "Now I'll have to decide what I'll say to Bramblestar."

He rose and turned to enter his den, then paused and looked back at Crowfeather over his shoulder. "Don't think this is over," he snarled. "I'll deal with *you* later."

The sun was starting to go down as Crowfeather returned to camp, a small vole dangling from his jaws. Dropping it on the fresh-kill pile, he glanced up at the sky, judging that there was time to go out again before darkness fell.

But I'll take a few moments to rest first, he thought, padding over to the warriors' den. His pads ached from pounding the hard ground. *I can't wait for leafbare to be over.*

As Crowfeather settled into his nest, he spotted Breeze-pelt and Heathertail returning to camp, deep in conversation, and so close together that their pelts were brushing. Even as he noted Leaftail and Gorsetail huddling nearby, eyeing the couple suspiciously, he felt an unfamiliar emotion swelling in his chest: happiness that his son had a cat who cared about him, but also optimism that one day—maybe soon—Breeze-pelt would be accepted as a Clan cat once again.

After all, if Breezepelt became Heathertail's mate—Heathertail, who was such a respected warrior—and had kits with her, raising a whole litter of new WindClan warriors, which cat would dream of doubting where his loyalties lay?

When Heathertail moved off to the fresh-kill pile, Crow-feather rose to his paws and padded over to Breezepelt. "How's your injury?" he asked.

"Oh, it's fine," Breezepelt responded with a dismissive flick of his tail. "Hurts a bit, but I can deal with it."

"You know, Heathertail isn't listening," Crowfeather mewed, gently teasing. "You don't have to act tough."

Something flashed in Breezepelt's eyes, and for a moment Crowfeather thought it was irritation. He felt panic beating inside him like a trapped bird, worried that Breezepelt wouldn't take his comment in the way he meant it. Then he saw a faint gleam of amusement in his son's eyes.

"Are you trying to tell me you've never done the same?" Breezepelt retorted.

"Well . . . I can't remember a specific time," Crowfeather replied, his pelt beginning to grow hot with embarrassment.

"But I'm sure I must have acted tough to impress a she-cat at *some* point."

Once again, as soon as the words were out of his mouth Crowfeather regretted them. *Breezepelt must be thinking of how many she-cats I've loved.*

But there was no hostility in Breezepelt's expression. "I feel guilty, thinking only of Heathertail and my feelings for her," he meowed, surprising Crowfeather with his honesty. "There's so much else going on in the Clan, and we've lost Nightcloud. . . ."

"Maybe that means you truly love Heathertail," Crowfeather suggested, feeling daring, as if he were about to fight a fox. "There's nothing wrong with that."

Breezepelt said nothing, only giving his chest fur a couple of embarrassed licks.

No wonder he feels embarrassed, Crowfeather thought. *He's young, and it's hard to discuss she-cats with your father—especially when you don't know your father all that well. Come to think of it, my father, Deadfoot, was always busy, since he was Clan deputy. I'd have died if I'd had to talk to him about she-cats!*

"You'll be okay," he mewed, risking a joke to reassure his son, "provided you make less of a mess of things than I did."

He braced himself for a scathing retort, wondering yet again if he had said the wrong thing.

But Breezepelt simply let out a snort of amusement. "That wouldn't be hard!"

The two toms settled down together, gazing across the camp, in the first comfortable silence Crowfeather could remember between them. Even though it was a bad time for the Clan, even though he and Breezepelt were still grieving for Nightcloud, Crowfeather felt a pleasant warmth spreading beneath his pelt. Just for a moment, they were starting to feel like father and son.

I can be a better father, he thought confidently. *And if nothing else is going right . . . at least I'm making progress here.*

CHAPTER 17

The scent of ThunderClan cats drifted into Crowfeather's nose where he lay dozing in his nest in the warriors' den just after sunup the next day. Startling awake, he spotted Gorsetail; her apprentice, Hootpaw; and Furzepelt, who had gone out on the dawn patrol, leading Bramblestar, Jayfeather, and Lionblaze into the camp. The WindClan cats' fur was bristling as they hustled the visitors over to Onestar's den.

Crowfeather rose to his paws and bounded over to the den as Harespring and some of the other WindClan cats began to gather around, gazing at the newcomers with narrowed eyes, the fur on their shoulders beginning to bristle. Lionblaze spotted Crowfeather as he drew to a halt in front of the leader's den, then quickly looked away.

Crowfeather felt his pads tingle with apprehension. His news had brought the ThunderClan cats to this meeting, but he had no idea how Onestar would treat them. He hadn't spoken to his Clan leader since his angry dismissal the day before. He could only hope that Onestar had seen sense and would welcome ThunderClan's help.

"Bramblestar wants to talk to Onestar about Kestrelflight's

vision," Furzepelt explained to Harespring.

"What about Kestrelflight's vision?" Onestar's voice came from his den underneath the Tallrock, and a heartbeat later the Clan leader emerged.

Crowfeather felt a heavy, sinking feeling in his belly. He could see that Onestar felt no friendliness toward the ThunderClan cats. The WindClan leader was looking at Bramblestar with an expression as icy as the leaf-bare wind that swept over the moor.

I don't regret telling Jayfeather the truth . . . but I don't think Onestar sees it my way. He's not going to make this easy for Bramblestar. And Bramblestar hasn't been a leader for very long. He might not know how to handle this.

Crowfeather stared at the ThunderClan leader. He was facing Onestar with a calm confidence that must surely have impressed the older cat.

Crowfeather took a pace or two closer to the Tallrock as Onestar gave the smallest possible dip of his head toward Bramblestar. "Greetings," he mewed coldly.

The ThunderClan leader lowered his head respectfully. "Greetings, Onestar," he began. "I've come to discuss what Jayfeather told me about the vision. I understand that you haven't handled the stoats at your end of the tunnels, as you said you would, and you might need some help."

Onestar twitched his whiskers irritably and exchanged a glance with Harespring. "I'm not sure where you got that idea," he responded. "WindClan is doing just fine. We are coping with the threat ourselves."

Bramblestar blinked in surprise and cast a confused look at Crowfeather. "That's not what I was told."

Crowfeather felt like he'd been dipped in freezing-cold water as he looked from Bramblestar to his own leader. He wished he could tell Bramblestar that he shared his surprise. He had known Onestar wasn't exactly enthusiastic about accepting ThunderClan's help, but he hadn't thought he would outright deny that there was a problem.

That means the Clans won't work together . . . which means the stoats might never be defeated. And that would leave WindClan vulnerable to whatever was being foretold in Kestrelflight's vision.

Crowfeather's neck fur prickled with frustration.

Does Onestar have bees in his brain?

Worse, his Clanmates were about to find out that he had gone behind their leader's back. *If anything could make me more unpopular, it would be that.*

"One of your own warriors asked for a meeting with Jayfeather, to tell him—" Bramblestar began, only to have Onestar interrupt him.

"Of course, Bramblestar, you don't understand this yet," Onestar meowed, giving Bramblestar the kind of haughty look he might have given to a misbehaving apprentice, "because you're a very new leader. But you need to learn that ordinary warriors don't know everything. To get at the truth," he continued with a pointed look at Crowfeather, "one must ask the Clan leader, and I'm telling you quite clearly that we don't need help. Firestar would have understood that, but alas . . . he's gone."

Crowfeather winced at the mention of the previous ThunderClan leader. *That's hardly fair to Bramblestar. What cat could compare to Firestar?*

Bramblestar's amber eyes lit with anger, yet his voice was even as he replied. "If there are still stoats in the tunnels, they'll eventually try to establish territory at our end. The threat must be contained for both our sakes. Arguing about it is just wasting time. There's no reason our Clans can't work together."

Onestar's mouth twisted in mockery. "You're a young cat, but you're already so hard of hearing! So I'll say it again, as clearly as I can: WindClan deals with WindClan's own problems. We don't need ThunderClan's meddling."

"Meddling!" Lionblaze broke in, digging his claws into the ground. "I've heard you were pleased enough to have us *meddle* when Mudclaw led his rebellion."

Bramblestar glared at his warrior. "Be quiet!" he snapped.

Crowfeather suddenly felt some cat's gaze boring into him. He turned to see Jayfeather sitting at the edge of the group of cats, his blind blue eyes fixed on him. As he met that compelling stare, hardly able to believe that Jayfeather couldn't see him, the ThunderClan medicine cat rose to his paws, swishing his tail angrily.

"If WindClan wants to deal with WindClan's problems, fine," he hissed. "We should leave now. We tried."

"But it's not that easy," Bramblestar responded patiently. "If whatever is in the tunnels is a threat, it's a threat to both Clans." Turning to Onestar, he added, "You have the right to make decisions for your Clan, but no right to make decisions that will endanger *mine*."

"That's right!" Lionblaze agreed, his golden tabby fur beginning to bristle.

Crowfeather felt an anxious flutter in his belly at the sight of his son defending the cat who raised him. *And I think they're right,* he mused. *Does that make me a traitor to WindClan?*

When he turned back toward the two Clan leaders, Bramblestar was meowing, "I *insist* that you work with me to deal with this threat."

Briefly Crowfeather closed his eyes, feeling his pelt prickle with anxiety at Bramblestar's obvious inexperience. *If he'd had dealings with Onestar before, he would know that's the* worst *thing to try. Onestar won't let any cat force his paw.*

Onestar's calm air of superiority vanished entirely at Bramblestar's words. His tabby fur bushed up until he looked twice his size, and he laid his ears flat against his head. "You can't *insist* that I do *anything*," he snarled. "I feel sorry for ThunderClan, stuck with you as leader, when every cat knows the bad blood you've inherited."

Crowfeather couldn't repress a gasp. Onestar must have really lost control to let himself mention Bramblestar's evil father, Tigerstar. Glancing at his Clanmates, he saw that they were gazing at their leader with wide, shocked eyes, as if they, too, couldn't believe what they had just heard.

It's not fair to Bramblestar, Crowfeather thought. *He only came here to offer his help.*

"And you're bringing that up now?" Bramblestar asked, dangerously quiet.

Onestar let out a snort of contempt. "Your father killed Firestar in the Dark Forest. You must be so proud of him! If not for his savagery, you might never have become leader. Did you and Tigerstar make that plan together?"

Crowfeather caught his breath as he saw Bramblestar's neck fur begin to rise, and he feared briefly that he might attack the WindClan leader. There was such fury burning in the depths of his amber eyes. His muscles rippled under his dark tabby pelt as he gathered himself for a leap. Just as Crowfeather braced himself to step between the two quarreling cats, Bramblestar made a massive effort to control himself. But the air still sang with tension as the two leaders glared at each other.

"We should just leave," Jayfeather repeated. "This is going nowhere. We tried to help."

Bramblestar relaxed slightly. "Very well. But hear this, Onestar," he growled. "You've made it clear that our two Clans are not allies. Remember that when the threat in the tunnels turns out to be too much for you to handle on your own. Remember that we offered to help, and you turned us away and insulted us."

Onestar let out his breath in a derisive huff. "Why would I remember such a weak, useless Clan?"

Bramblestar ignored him, and after a moment the ThunderClan group headed out of the camp, their anger and frustration obvious in every hair of their pelts. Onestar waved his tail to order Gorsetail and Furzepelt to escort them.

Once they were on their way, Onestar turned to Crowfeather, his eyes narrowing in a gaze of disapproval.

"Was that necessary?" Crowfeather asked. "ThunderClan won't work with us now, and if that's not bad enough, we've got a hostile relationship with them. Who knows what will happen?"

"Unfortunately, it *was* necessary." Onestar spat out each word. "Because one of my warriors gave ThunderClan information they had no right to. Who would have thought that Breezepelt would turn out to be more trustworthy than his father? As for you, Crowfeather, you're getting under my fur. I'm warning you, put one more paw out of line, and you'll be in real trouble!"

He whipped around and stalked back into his den with a single lash of his tail. Crowfeather was left to watch the ThunderClan cats growing smaller as they crossed the camp and climbed the far slope, to vanish at last onto the moor. His heart twisted at the sight of his ThunderClan sons stalking off with their backs to him.

We couldn't be more divided.

Harespring gave Crowfeather an apologetic glance. "It will be all right," he meowed.

"I'm not so sure about that," Crowfeather retorted. "Look, Harespring, you're Onestar's deputy. Can't *you* make him see sense? Can't you tell him that we'll never get rid of the stoats if we don't have ThunderClan's help?"

"I can't do that!" Harespring's eyes stretched wide and his tail bushed out in shock. "I'm loyal to Onestar. It's my duty to see that my Clan leader's orders are carried out."

Even if your Clan leader is being mouse-brained? Crowfeather knew that there was no point in speaking his thought out loud. *This is what comes of making a Dark Forest cat deputy.* Harespring was so desperate to prove his loyalty that he didn't dare put a paw wrong. Instead of making Onestar think about his decisions—even if eventually he had to accept them—he was following where Onestar led without question.

"Just think about what I've said," Crowfeather pleaded.

"There's no need to think," Harespring snapped. "Onestar has got this. I told you, everything will be all right." He stalked off, calling to his apprentice.

Crowfeather felt even more uneasy, his pelt prickling from ears to tail-tip. He wondered whether Harespring was just trying to convince himself. He wondered too whether he had fully understood Ashfoot and Feathertail's advice.

I'm not *a medicine cat,* he told himself. *What if that was just a dream, and not a message from StarClan? Or what if I misinterpreted the message?* He let out a growl of frustration. *Now I have no idea how all this will end.*

But Crowfeather couldn't stifle the feeling that it would not end well.

Night had fallen, and Crowfeather was plumping up the bedding in his nest when Harespring came into the warriors' den and padded over to him.

"Onestar wants you to escort Kestrelflight to the half-moon meeting," he announced.

A jolt of surprise struck Crowfeather like the blow from an outstretched paw. "Onestar's overreacting a little, isn't he?" he asked. "Sending a warrior to escort a medicine cat? That's just making a big deal of *showing* that he doesn't trust Thunder-Clan. Okay, there's some tension between us, but would any cat attack medicine cats?"

Harespring shrugged. "Probably not, but what can you do? That's what Onestar wants."

If you ask me, Crowfeather thought, *Onestar just wants to get under ThunderClan's fur.* But he remembered Onestar's warning. He couldn't risk disobeying his Clan leader again, not after the disaster that had followed last time.

"That's fine," he responded to Harespring. "I'll go find him now."

Part of Crowfeather was pleased at the prospect of trekking up to the Moonpool with Kestrelflight; he and the medicine cat had always gotten along well. And it would be something to take his mind off Breezepelt and the stoats.

When he reached the medicine-cat den, Kestrelflight was waiting outside. He gave Crowfeather a friendly nod as he approached, and the two toms padded side by side up the slope and out of the camp.

"How is Featherpaw?" Crowfeather asked, feeling slightly guilty that he hadn't been to see her since Bramblestar's disastrous visit.

"Doing very well," Kestrelflight replied cheerfully. "She's still sleeping, but her breathing is much stronger, and her wounds are healing nicely. I've left Sedgewhisker with her while I'm at the Moonpool, but I'm not expecting any problems."

"That's good to hear."

But the reassuring news about his apprentice wasn't enough to distract Crowfeather from the hostile reaction he was likely to get from ThunderClan. "There's going to be trouble behind this," he murmured after a while. "You don't need a warrior to escort you as if you were a kit. The other medicine cats won't like it."

"You mean Jayfeather won't like it," Kestrelflight meowed. "I wasn't there when Bramblestar appeared with the other ThunderClan cats, but I heard all about it. I hate to say this about my Clan leader, but I think this time Onestar has it wrong."

"Why?" Crowfeather asked, giving Kestrelflight a sharp look. "Have you had any more visions about the tunnels?"

Kestrelflight shook his head. "I've had some upsetting dreams," he replied, "but I think they're just dreams, not visions. Still, I'll feel better when the stoats are driven from the tunnels."

And that's not going to happen without ThunderClan, Crowfeather thought.

For all his worries, it felt good to be padding across the moor, invigorated by the brisk wind blowing through his fur. The short springy grass was silvered by the light of the half-moon, with the stars blazing overhead in a clear sky. Crowfeather liked the idea that the warriors of StarClan were watching over them, caring for their Clans as they had when they were alive, sending their advice to the medicine cats through dreams and visions.

His pelt warmed as he remembered Feathertail, and the love for him that had shone from her eyes. *Surely that was a true vision, and not just a dream?*

"Tell me about your dreams," he mewed curiously to Kestrelflight. "How do you know when they *mean* something, instead of just being nonsense?"

Kestrelflight's tail curled up in amusement. "I suppose it's part of being a medicine cat," he answered. "But usually I just . . . know. I can *feel* it."

For a moment Crowfeather was silent, thinking that over. Then he continued, "I'm not a medicine cat, so all the dreams I have *are* just nonsense . . . right?"

"Not necessarily," Kestrelflight replied. "Dreams can tell us things, whether they're a message from StarClan or not— perhaps things we're trying to tell ourselves."

Crowfeather shook his head, more confused than ever. For a while the two cats plodded on side by side, reaching the stream and following it up into the hills where the Moonpool lay. To Crowfeather's relief, there was no sign so far of any of the other medicine cats.

"Tell me something, Kestrelflight," he mewed at last. "Have you ever seen Ashfoot in StarClan?"

The medicine cat shook his head apologetically. "No, not yet," he replied. "But we lost so many cats in the Great Battle. It doesn't mean anything. I just haven't seen them all."

You haven't seen her because she isn't there yet, Crowfeather thought, remembering what his mother had told him. *Which means it's true . . . she stayed behind to visit me in dreams.* He swallowed hard. *Doesn't that imply they mean something after all?*

"I'm really sorry about Nightcloud," Kestrelflight went on after a few heartbeats. "It must be terrible, not knowing what happened to her."

Crowfeather nodded. He didn't really want to talk about his former mate, but he was encouraged by Kestrelflight's sympathetic look. He knew that the young medicine cat would listen without judging him. "It wasn't right, our being mates," he meowed hesitantly. "But I always assumed we'd have time to work out our problems and become friends. Now that can never happen."

Kestrelflight let out an understanding murmur. "I hear that some of our Clanmates suspect that Breezepelt had something to do with Nightcloud's death," he mewed hesitantly.

Fury surged through Crowfeather and he lashed his tail. "No way is that true!"

"I don't believe it for a heartbeat," Kestrelflight assured him. "Breezepelt loved Nightcloud."

Crowfeather nodded, his rage dying at Kestrelflight's understanding. "More than any cat," he responded.

A comfortable silence fell as the two cats padded on together, farther into the hills. The slope was growing steeper, and the stream they followed was narrower, its water turned to silver as it leaped from rock to rock. Its gentle gushing was the only sound except for the soft pad of the cats' paw steps.

"I had an idea," Kestrelflight went on after a while. "Do you remember, before the Great Battle, Dawnpelt of Shadow-Clan accused Jayfeather of murdering her brother Flametail?"

"Yes, of course," Crowfeather replied, wondering why Kestrelflight was bringing that up now.

"Jayfeather found Flametail in StarClan," Kestrelflight meowed, "and got him to tell the other medicine cats that Jayfeather was innocent."

Suddenly understanding, Crowfeather halted and gazed wide-eyed at Kestrelflight. "Yes . . . ," he breathed out.

"So tonight, when I dream my way into StarClan, I'm going to look for Nightcloud. If I find her, I'll ask her to tell the others what really happened to her, and that Breezepelt had nothing to do with it."

"Are you sure that will work?" Crowfeather asked. "Some cats are so determined to believe Breezepelt is guilty, Nightcloud herself could appear to all of them to tell them the truth, and they'd still have doubts," he finished harshly, remembering how unfairly some of his Clanmates had treated Breezepelt. *I treated him unfairly, too.*

"Of course." Kestrelflight twitched his whiskers. "The Great Battle has made life hard for all of us, and we all recover in our own way. Different cats make up different stories to explain what happened. But Breezepelt is still among us, and he wants to be a loyal WindClan cat, so his name must be cleared." His eyes narrowed. "No WindClan cat will accuse *me* of lying—or at least they'd better not."

"Thank you," Crowfeather responded, impressed by the discovery of the young medicine cat's more formidable side, and beginning to feel hopeful. It was reassuring, too, that another cat could feel the same way he did, and wanted to help. *Maybe I have one friend, at least. And maybe for once we can take some good news back to our Clan.*

When Crowfeather and Kestrelflight reached the last rocky slope up to the Moonpool, the other medicine cats were just ahead of them. As he scrambled up the rocks, Crowfeather was acutely conscious of the group of them staring down at him.

"What are *you* doing here?" Jayfeather demanded, glaring at Crowfeather as the two WindClan cats reached the row of bushes that edged the hollow of the Moonpool. "This place isn't for warriors."

"I'm not the first warrior to come here," Crowfeather retorted, guessing that Jayfeather was angry with him for convincing him to lead Bramblestar into Onestar's unjustified attack.

"And the others had good reason," Jayfeather snapped. "What's yours?"

Crowfeather felt awkward as he searched for an answer. He didn't want to admit that Onestar had made an error in judgment. "Does it matter?" he asked eventually, wishing he could have a conversation with one of his sons without getting into an argument.

He wondered, too, what was the right way to be a loyal WindClan warrior. *Do I just obey Onestar, as he seems to think, or do I speak up when I think he's wrong?*

"No, it really doesn't," Leafpool murmured in response to Crowfeather's question, resting the tip of her tail lightly on

Jayfeather's shoulder. "Come on, we're wasting moonlight."

"Well, he's not coming down to the pool," Willowshine of RiverClan put in, giving Crowfeather a hostile stare. She was alone, Crowfeather noticed; for some reason Mothwing hadn't come with her. "I'll claw your pelt off if you try."

Huh! Like you could! Crowfeather thought.

Littlecloud of ShadowClan shook his head testily. "We're medicine cats," he told Willowshine. "We don't claw pelts. But she's right," he added to Crowfeather. "You stay here, outside the hollow."

"Fine," Crowfeather snapped. "I have no interest in your little get-together, so you can all relax. I'd rather be home sleeping, believe me."

With a last huff of annoyance, Jayfeather turned and stalked up to the bushes, his scrawny frame slipping easily between the branches. Leafpool gave Crowfeather a sympathetic look as she followed, and Crowfeather dipped his head in return, no longer trying to explain. *Leafpool always understood me.*

Kestrelflight was the last of the cats to push his way through. "I won't forget," he promised Crowfeather before he disappeared.

Left alone, Crowfeather settled himself in the shelter of the bushes, his paws tucked under him while he looked out across the moon-washed landscape. He could see the dips and swells of the moor, and far away in the distance a dark mass that must be the forest. Behind him he could hear the soft splashing of a waterfall, and imagined the starlit cascade falling endlessly into the Moonpool. After a short while, he slept.

Once again he was in the tunnels, following Ashfoot, who whisked around the corners ahead of him in a swirl of pale light.

"What are you trying to tell me *now*?" he called after her. "Are you really here, or am I just dreaming?"

But Ashfoot didn't reply. This time she led him out of the darkness and through a forest filled with translucent dawn mist. Dew-laden grass brushed at Crowfeather's pelt and soaked it as he trod in his mother's paw steps.

"Where are you taking me?" he asked Ashfoot.

His mother did not reply. Instead she halted at the top of a shallow dip in the ground, and waved Crowfeather on with a swish of her tail. Looking down into the hollow, Crowfeather recognized the pool at the bottom, surrounded by ferns, where he had found Nightcloud's blood and her scent, almost overwhelmed by the reek of fox.

Horrified, Crowfeather turned back toward Ashfoot. "Why?"

But his mother had disappeared. Reluctantly, every step an effort, Crowfeather padded down toward the edge of the pool. Before he reached it, the fern fronds stirred slightly, and he saw that a cat was lying among them. A black she-cat, with blood pulsing from a wound in her side . . .

"Nightcloud . . . ," he whispered.

Nightcloud raised her head to look at him, fury glaring from her eyes. "Don't you see me?" she hissed. "Don't you?"

Crowfeather jerked into wakefulness. His legs were shaking and his heart was pounding as if it was going to burst out of his chest. *What does it mean?* he asked himself. He heard an echo of Nightcloud's words in his mind, and desperately tried to hold on to her fading image. Grief stabbed at him as they slipped away from him like water through his paws. *Have I missed something?*

The sound of paw steps and the murmuring voices of cats came from behind the barrier of bushes. Crowfeather sprang to his paws and gave his pelt a shake, desperate not to show how distraught he was. *If I had to explain myself to Jayfeather...*

His ThunderClan son was the first cat to emerge from the bushes. He swept one sightless glance across Crowfeather and then ignored him, leaping sure-pawed down the rocky slope. Leafpool followed, giving a polite dip of her head to Crowfeather, with Willowshine and Littlecloud after her.

Kestrelflight was the last to emerge. As soon as Crowfeather saw him, he knew that something had happened. The medicine cat was bristling with excitement, and his eyes shone like small moons.

"Did you find her?" Crowfeather demanded, stepping up to him.

Kestrelflight paused, checking that the other medicine cats were on their way home, well out of earshot. "Ashfoot or Nightcloud?" he asked.

"Either. Both." *But Ashfoot couldn't be in StarClan,* he reminded himself. *She was just with me, here.*

"Well, I didn't see Ashfoot..." Kestrelflight was drawing

out his news, almost teasingly. "But I found Barkface. And he said that Nightcloud isn't anywhere in StarClan. That means that there must be hope for her!"

Crowfeather stared at him, briefly confused. He wondered, could Nightcloud be with Ashfoot, trapped between here and StarClan? Could she, too, be trying to tell him something? But then he realized that if that were true, Ashfoot would have told him long before. He had given up on Nightcloud too easily. *She asked me, "Don't you see me?" Is this what she meant?*

Crowfeather's grief gave way to a great surge of hope and optimism, like a massive wave carrying him away.

She's alive!

CHAPTER 18

The sun was rising, shining palely through a thin covering of cloud, when Crowfeather staggered back into camp, exhausted after his trek across the moor and the excitement of discovering that Nightcloud might be alive.

Yawning and foggy from lack of sleep, Crowfeather's first instinct was to look for Breezepelt. *At last I have some good news to tell him! And if Nightcloud's alive, we have to figure out why she hasn't come back.*

But as he headed for the warriors' den, Crowfeather spotted a group of cats clustered around the medicine-cat den, and his ears pricked at the sound of their excited chatter. He exchanged a puzzled glance with Kestrelflight.

"That's odd . . . ," the medicine cat murmured. He bounded over to join their Clanmates, and Crowfeather followed.

"What's going on?" he asked Whitetail.

The small white elder turned to him with gleaming eyes. "Featherpaw is awake!" she purred.

A huge wave of relief surged through Crowfeather. "That's great news!" he exclaimed.

Kestrelflight had already vanished into his den. Crowfeather thrust his way through the crowd of cats until he came to the entrance. As he reached it, the medicine cat reappeared in the cleft, looking pleased and harassed at the same time.

"No, you can't come in," he meowed, speaking in general to all his Clanmates. "Featherpaw is going to be fine, but she needs rest and quiet. Go hunt, or kill a few stoats or something, but don't hang around here."

Crowfeather was about to withdraw again, then halted as Kestrelflight spotted him and beckoned him with a wave of his tail. "You can come in, Crowfeather," he mewed. "She wants to see you."

Crowfeather was aware of one or two disapproving hisses as he slipped into the den behind Kestrelflight, but he ignored them. He felt too happy to start a quarrel with any Clanmate. *I got Featherpaw into this mess, and she still wants to see me!*

Sedgewhisker and Emberfoot were crouching beside the apprentice's nest, relief and excitement in their eyes. They rose to their paws as Kestrelflight entered, leading Crowfeather. Sedgewhisker bent her head over her daughter and murmured, "We'll fetch you some fresh-kill and a nice clump of wet moss." She and Emberfoot slipped past Crowfeather; to his relief, they didn't notice him as he drew back into the shadows beside the den wall.

When they had left, Crowfeather padded forward to see Featherpaw lying in her nest of moss and bracken; she raised her head and blinked sleepily at Crowfeather as he approached.

"Featherpaw, I'm so sorry I put you in danger," Crowfeather mewed, crouching down beside her.

His apprentice's eyes stretched wider at his words. "But you didn't!" she protested. "I don't remember much of what happened, but I know it wasn't your fault. Hootpaw and I and the others decided we wanted to be in the battle. *You* didn't force us to do anything."

"But I'm your mentor. I shouldn't have told you to be so aggressive. I put you in danger, and—"

"No," Featherpaw interrupted. "That was just advice, and it was good advice. The other apprentices and I made the choice to join in the battle. We were angry at being left out, and when we got there, we thought the stoats didn't look so threatening—but we were wrong. You're the best mentor in all the Clans!"

I wish that were true, Crowfeather thought. "I'm just glad you're going to be okay," he mewed huskily, touching his nose to hers.

Featherpaw closed her eyes and let out a drowsy sigh. "I'll be fine."

Crowfeather crept quietly away; as he left the den, he came face to face with Sedgewhisker and Emberfoot returning. Sedgewhisker was carrying a plump mouse, while Emberfoot had a bundle of dripping moss.

Feeling awkward, Crowfeather stepped back, but this time there was no avoiding them in the narrow opening. He braced himself for Featherpaw's parents to blame him again for her injuries. Then he realized that they looked just as uncomfortable, clearly finding it hard to meet his gaze.

"I'm sorry, Crowfeather," Sedgewhisker mewed, setting

down her prey. "We were too hard on you before."

"I deserved it," Crowfeather responded with a dip of his head. "Part of it, at least."

"No cat could have deserved what we said to you," Sedge-whisker insisted. "It's just that she's our kit, and we were so worried. . . ."

"I understand," Crowfeather reassured her. "I care about her, and I'm just her mentor. I can only imagine how you felt." As he spoke, he saw the deep concern and caring in the eyes of Featherpaw's parents, and realized again how long he had withheld that from his own son.

A bright image flashed into his mind, of Breezepelt bumbling around the camp as a kit, falling over his own paws and chasing his tail. He had been so lovable, so vulnerable, and Crowfeather remembered how intensely he had wanted to protect him. But he had held back from loving him as a father should. *I was afraid to love any cat.*

Emberfoot's voice drew him out of the memory. "I know you do your best to train Featherpaw," the gray tom was meowing, speaking with difficulty around his mouthful of wet moss. "If you could just . . . in the future . . . be a bit more careful?"

Crowfeather felt a twinge of annoyance. *I tried to be careful! And apprentices have to learn.* But he remembered in time that Emberfoot was a father who had just nearly lost his kit. He could understand that, after his fear for Lionblaze in the Great Battle, or for Breezepelt wounded by the stoats. He responded in a heartfelt tone, "I would never want any more harm to come to Featherpaw. From now on, I'll do everything I can to protect her."

Emberfoot gave him an approving nod, and the two cats headed into the den to see their daughter.

Turning away, Crowfeather spotted Breezepelt with Weaselfur and Larkwing, padding over to the fresh-kill pile, their jaws loaded with prey. *At last!* Crowfeather thought. *I can't wait to see Breezepelt's face when I tell him about Nightcloud!*

He waited until the other two warriors had moved away before joining Breezepelt and beckoning him over to a quiet corner behind the nursery.

"What now?" Breezepelt asked, sounding surprised.

Crowfeather took a deep breath, remembering what Kestrelflight had told him the night before. He hoped Breezepelt wouldn't get his hopes up *too* much, imagining that they would discover where Nightcloud went and bring her home: It would crush him so badly if his mother turned out to be dead after all.

"You know I went with Kestrelflight to the Moonpool last night?" he meowed. Breezepelt nodded. "Kestrelflight said that he would look for Nightcloud in StarClan, and . . . she isn't there. That could mean she's alive!"

Breezepelt took in a sharp, gasping breath, but for a moment he didn't say anything. Crowfeather couldn't tell what he was thinking.

"I truly thought she was gone," he explained, assuming his son would be angry that he hadn't searched harder. "I'm sorry . . . I'm still not entirely sure what it means, but I didn't mean to make you grieve unnecessarily."

Breezepelt shook his head, and Crowfeather realized that he was more confused than angry. "No . . . that's okay." He met his father's gaze, and Crowfeather saw hope begin to creep into his eyes. "I'm just glad we might still find her. This isn't about us, Crowfeather. It's about saving Nightcloud."

Crowfeather nodded, impressed by his son's mature reaction. "I've been thinking about it, and if she's alive," he began, "there has to be some reason she isn't coming back to us. She's the most loyal WindClan cat there ever was. Suppose she's trapped, or in danger? We need to start searching for her again, together."

Breezepelt licked one forepaw thoughtfully and drew it over his ear. "We had a hard enough time looking for her before. Where do you suggest we start?"

"We'll have to go back to the spot on ThunderClan territory where I found her blood," Crowfeather replied.

Breezepelt let out a snort. "That should please Bramblestar!"

"Well, I don't intend to ask for Bramblestar's permission," Crowfeather mewed dryly. "Anyway, if she made it out of the tunnels and we haven't found her—it must have been over there."

"But it's been a half-moon since then. Won't her scent have faded by now?"

"Maybe not." Crowfeather hadn't thought about that before. Afraid that his son was right, he struggled with disappointment, then braced himself, trying hard to sound optimistic. "It hasn't rained since then. Anyway, it's the best chance we have. Let's go talk to Onestar."

Crowfeather led the way across the camp toward Onestar's den and spotted the Clan leader just outside, in conversation with Harespring. As Crowfeather and Breezepelt approached, Harespring gave a brisk nod and bounded away toward the warriors' den.

"Well?" Onestar asked, turning toward Crowfeather. "What mouse-brained idea have you gotten into your head this time?"

Crowfeather was aware that his leader still hadn't forgiven him for going to ask ThunderClan to help. His tone was icy and his eyes narrowed, irritable. *This is the worst possible time to ask him for a favor,* Crowfeather thought worriedly.

The Clan leader listened without comment as Crowfeather repeated his story of what Kestrelflight had discovered at the Moonpool, and his intention to go with Breezepelt to search for Nightcloud.

"Do you have bees in your brain, Crowfeather?" Onestar asked when he had finished. "You really think this is the right time to go trespassing on ThunderClan territory?"

"Yes—if it's the only way to find Nightcloud—" Breezepelt began desperately, before Crowfeather could respond.

Onestar lashed his tail dismissively. "I care about Nightcloud too," he meowed. "But she's been missing for a long time, and you don't really know where to look."

"We'll start with the last place I found her scent," Crowfeather mewed, his expression grim. Breezepelt stood beside him, eyeing Onestar expectantly. For that moment, at least, they were a united front. Onestar looked back and forth between the two of them and finally sighed in surrender.

"Okay, I won't stop you trying, but it will have to wait. Today we have more urgent matters to deal with." He glared at Crowfeather. "As usual, you have to be *reminded* to put your Clan's needs above your own."

"What urgent matters?" Crowfeather asked, ignoring Onestar's jibe. He had accepted that Onestar would be angry with him for a long time to come, but that didn't mean that Clan business would come to a halt.

"Have you forgotten the stoats?" Onestar asked, a sarcastic edge to his voice. "Or the conversation with Bramblestar yesterday?"

No, how could I? Crowfeather reflected bitterly. *I thought I was the only one who worried about them. That's why I went to ThunderClan in the first place.*

"We have to get rid of the stoats before they cause Thunder-Clan to meddle even more," his Clan leader went on. "That might be what Kestrelflight's vision meant. After all, the dark water emerged from our end of the tunnels, which meant it could have come *from* ThunderClan, right? What if the vision was warning us to be suspicious of our closest neighbors? Maybe their new leader, Bramblestar, is the biggest threat to us. Maybe the engulfing water means that ThunderClan will take over our territory and drive us out."

And maybe our Clan leader can't see beyond the end of his own whiskers, Crowfeather thought sourly. *I know ThunderClan is annoying, but would they really attack us now, so soon after the Great Battle? Sure, they might—and hedgehogs might fly!*

Once again, Crowfeather felt himself being tugged apart. As a loyal warrior, should he follow his leader unquestioningly, or speak his mind if he thought the leader was wrong? Mindful that he wasn't Onestar's favorite cat right now, he struggled to listen in silence as Onestar continued.

"This is our plan: We're going to block up the tunnel entrances with twigs, rocks, and brush—anything we can find."

Crowfeather cringed. *That wouldn't even make sense if the stoats were our only problem.*

"It'll be a tough project, and we'll need *every* warrior to help," Onestar added with a hard glare at Crowfeather and Breezepelt, "but it's the best way to deal with the stoats—*and* it will stop ThunderClan using the tunnels to spy on us."

"That's the most mouse-brained plan I've ever heard!" some cat exclaimed, and Crowfeather realized with horror that it had been him. His disgust at what he had just heard must have driven out all thoughts of being tactful, or of not getting deeper into trouble with Onestar. *Well, it's too late to take it back now.* He took in a breath and went on, "Haven't you thought it through at all?"

"Thought it through?" Onestar repeated, his voice dangerously quiet. "Maybe I haven't. Give us the benefit of your wisdom, Crowfeather."

Crowfeather flicked his ear, uncomfortable. It seemed clear that calling Onestar's plan mouse-brained hadn't been exactly . . . *sensible*. Breezepelt was staring at him, wide-eyed with shock, and one or two other cats were drifting toward them, drawn by the sudden tension and the way Onestar's fur was lifting all along his spine.

But I can't stop now. I have to tell him what I think!

"Blocking the entrances probably won't stop the stoats," Crowfeather continued. "They'll just push the blockages away from the inside. Or, if they don't, they'll be driven out to hunt on ThunderClan's side—and how do you think Bramblestar will react to that?"

Onestar swiped his tongue over his jaws as if he had just swallowed a succulent bit of prey. "That's the *best* part of the plan," he purred. "I'm just in the mood to send Bramblestar a little present. Let's see how *he* likes stoats marauding all over his territory."

"Then you're even more mouse-brained than I thought," Crowfeather meowed roughly. "And if no other cat is prepared to tell you that, I will. Trouble with ThunderClan is the last thing we want right now. I don't think StarClan wants any of the Clans to treat each other as enemies."

"So you're a medicine cat all of a sudden?" Onestar asked, his voice still deceptively calm, contrasted with his bristling fur and glaring eyes. "How lucky I am to have you to advise me!"

"I don't need to be a medicine cat to know that you're leading our Clan into danger," Crowfeather snapped. "Bramblestar came to offer ThunderClan's help—and StarClan knows we need it—but instead you turned him down and insulted him, and now you're looking for ways to antagonize them. We should be making ThunderClan our ally!"

Onestar drew his lips back into a snarl. Faced with his fury, it was all Crowfeather could do not to take a step backward.

"Very well, Crowfeather," he growled. "I've warned you, over and over, and I'm not warning you again. If you like ThunderClan so much, you can go and look for Nightcloud on their territory. In fact, go wherever you want—just *not here*. I don't want to see you in WindClan!"

"What?" For a moment Crowfeather felt unsteady on his paws, as if some creature had hurled a rock at him. "Am I . . ." He couldn't bring himself to complete the question out loud. *Am I being banished?*

"Do I have to repeat myself?" Onestar hissed. "I think you need some time alone to think about what makes a loyal warrior, Crowfeather. And until you do, I don't want you in our camp and on our territory. For the next quarter moon . . . you are not a WindClan cat! Take some time and think about your actions. When you think you've figured out where you went wrong, you may request my permission to return."

So I am being banished? Crowfeather swallowed hard, barely able to believe this was happening. *But not really banished. Only for a few days . . .* He looked around and found himself in the middle of a crowd of bewildered, staring cats. *But to come back, I'll have to grovel,* he realized. *Onestar wants to make me swallow my pride.*

He noticed that Breezepelt, at the front of the group, looked shocked out of his fur, his eyes wide and his pelt bristling.

Some cat speak up for me, Crowfeather begged silently. *You know I'm loyal . . . I'm WindClan through and through! I've given up so much for this Clan! Tell him! Tell him he's being unreasonable!*

But no cat spoke. It seemed that no cat was willing to risk Onestar's ire . . . not for Crowfeather.

Not even Breezepelt, Crowfeather thought ruefully. *And just as I thought we might be getting closer. He's probably glad to get a break from me.*

As his shock faded, anger settled over Crowfeather. *Well, nice try, Onestar! If this is a battle of wills, I'm sure mine is stronger. I'm not going to apologize when I'm right. . . .*

He braced himself, meeting Onestar's furious gaze with his head held high.

"Permission to return!" he snapped. "Ha! If WindClan doesn't need me, then I don't need WindClan."

He turned, thrust his way through the crowd, and stalked up the slope toward the edge of the camp.

No cat called him back.

CHAPTER 19

❦

Walking without thinking, Crowfeather headed across the moor toward the border stream that divided WindClan territory from ThunderClan. The early morning sun had vanished; clouds were massing above the hills, gray and heavy, and so low they almost seemed to skim the top of the pile of memorial stones.

As he drew closer to the stream, Crowfeather tried to recover from his shock and think this through. *Where should I go?* He stopped. *Where does a cat with no Clan go? If I ever wanted to try my luck with another Clan, I suppose this would be my chance. . . .*

For a moment he imagined himself crossing into Thunder-Clan territory, heading for their camp, and offering himself to Bramblestar as a ThunderClan warrior.

Leafpool will be there. . . .

But it took only a few moments for Crowfeather to realize how stupid that would be. Leafpool hadn't loved him for seasons, and if he was honest, his love for her had faded, too. If anything, he missed the way he had felt when he loved her—how young and foolish and hopeful they had been. Besides, asking the ThunderClan medicine cat to be his mate would be the quickest way to get himself banished from yet another

Clan. *Bramblestar won't take kindly to my showing up, announcing my sudden loyalty to ThunderClan, and then taking one of their medicine cats.*

It would never work. Besides, in ThunderClan he would have to deal with Lionblaze and Jayfeather, and StarClan alone knew how *that* relationship could be anything but a disaster.

Bramblestar probably wouldn't want me . . . and I'm not a ThunderClan cat, he added, struggling not to feel sorry for himself. A hollow place seemed to open up inside him. *I've been WindClan all my life. If I'm not a WindClan cat anymore, what am I?*

Crowfeather reached the border stream and stood on the bank for a moment, unsure what to do. He bent his head and lapped the icy water, delaying for a few heartbeats the time he would have to move on. Then he turned and headed upward, away from the lake, away from ThunderClan, making for the open moor. He couldn't stifle the memory of setting out from here with Leafpool, once, long ago, when he had believed that they could leave their Clans behind them and make a new life together.

I was so happy then.

But now all that was left to Crowfeather was bitterness. Leafpool had abandoned him to return to her Clan and her duty as a medicine cat. He had taken another mate, a cat of his own Clan, but he had never really loved Nightcloud, and his relationship with Breezepelt was clearly a mess. All that had remained to him was his Clan, and now that was gone, too.

I gave up so much for WindClan, he thought, *and this is the way it ends. I spoke the truth to Onestar, and he banished me for it.*

Crowfeather knew he was right: It *was* a mouse-brained idea to block up the tunnels and antagonize ThunderClan. But no cat had listened to him, or spoken up for him. Not even Breezepelt.

Some son he turned out to be! I must have had bees in my brain to think I could ever mean as much to him as Nightcloud did.

WindClan scent drifted into Crowfeather's nose, and he realized he was approaching the border with the moorland. Beyond that was unknown territory. He halted on the border, but before he could take the final step that would cut him off from his Clan forever, he heard some cat calling his name.

Crowfeather turned to see Heathertail bounding across the moor toward him, with Breezepelt a few paw steps behind. His muscles tensed and he dug his claws into the ground as he stood waiting for them.

"What do you want?" he asked harshly as the two cats skidded to a halt and stood panting in front of him.

"Onestar led the Clan down to the tunnels to start blocking the entrances," Heathertail explained, her chest heaving as she fought for breath. "We slipped away and picked up your scent trail."

The bitter pain in Crowfeather's heart eased a little, to think that Heathertail and Breezepelt had come looking for him, but he found it hard to respond. Breezepelt was standing a pace or two behind Heathertail, his gaze fixed on his paws, the familiar awkward, sullen expression on his face. He looked as if he didn't want to be there, and at the sight of him Crowfeather's heart hardened again.

"Why would you do that?" he snapped. "You care enough to chase me, but not enough to speak up for me in front of Onestar? Well, thanks but no thanks." He turned and began to continue on his way.

"Wait!" he heard Breezepelt call behind him—a brief, desperate cry. When he paused and turned around, Breezepelt was looking at the ground—but Heathertail spoke.

"We're sorry we didn't speak up for you, Crowfeather, but you made it pretty difficult. You may have been right—but a loyal warrior still respects his leader."

Crowfeather let out a derisive snort, but didn't move. *All right,* he thought, *I'll hear them out.*

"After you left, we talked to Onestar," Heathertail went on, casting a faintly exasperated glance over her shoulder at Breezepelt. "We wanted to give him time to cool down. He was hard on you, Crowfeather, but you gave it right back—telling him you don't need WindClan. Did you really mean that?"

Now it was Crowfeather's turn to stare at the ground, clawing at an imaginary bug as though he were fascinated. *At the time I did,* he thought. *But perhaps it was a flea-brained thing to say.*

Heathertail shook her head, seeming frustrated, and went on. "You're not always the easiest cat to talk to, Crowfeather. Anyway, I think he's sorry that he lost his temper with you. If you came back to camp tomorrow with some prey and apologized to him, I'm pretty sure he'd let you back into the Clan."

"Really?" In his relief, Crowfeather looked at Breezepelt, who still wouldn't meet his eye. *What, does he not want me to come back? Maybe he thought he was free of me. . . .* "What do you think,

Breezepelt?" he challenged his son. "Is Heathertail right?"

Breezepelt scuffled his forepaws like an apprentice caught misbehaving. "Uh . . . I guess," he muttered.

"*I guess*"? The worst of Crowfeather's suspicions confirmed, his fury exploded. "It's obvious to see who *doesn't* want me back!" he exclaimed. "You've barely said a thing this whole time. You're just following the cat you love, trying to impress her with your loyalty to your foolish father!"

Breezepelt looked up at him, a stung expression in his eyes. *He's embarrassed I caught on,* Crowfeather thought. "And there's no way I'm apologizing. I was *right*! And you both know it."

"Yes, sure, you were right." Heathertail's voice was soothing. "As I said. Most of the Clan thinks it's a mouse-brained idea to block up the tunnels. But you still disrespected your Clan leader, in front of the rest of the Clan."

"Onestar deserved it!" Crowfeather snarled. Glaring at Breezepelt, he added, "It's better this way. I can have the freedom I've always wanted, and you can be free of me. I'm leaving, and WindClan will never have to worry about me again!"

The two younger cats stared at him in silence for a moment. At last Heathertail mewed quietly, "What about looking for Nightcloud?"

"You can look for Nightcloud," Crowfeather retorted, trying to ignore the guilt that settled over him like a cloud of dust. "She won't want to see me anyway." *That's probably true, at least.*

"Of all the mouse-brained—" Breezepelt began angrily.

Heathertail shook her head at him and silenced him with a touch of her tail-tip on his shoulder. "It's no use, Breezepelt," she murmured. "Not right now." Fixing Crowfeather with a sorrowful blue gaze, she added, "I'm sure there'll be a way back for you, Crowfeather, if you want to take it. I hope that you do."

For a moment the young she-cat's sympathy almost made Crowfeather give in. Then he pictured himself creeping back into the camp and groveling in front of Onestar. *No way will I ever do that!*

"You'd better go," he meowed curtly. "You don't want Onestar to find out you're missing. He's in a lousy mood."

"Okay," Heathertail sighed. "Come on, Breezepelt."

For a couple of heartbeats Breezepelt gazed at Crowfeather hesitantly, as if there was something he wanted to say. Crowfeather guessed that a word would have encouraged him, but he felt as though his throat were stopped up by a tough bit of prey, and no words would come. Finally Breezepelt ducked his head awkwardly; then the two young cats turned away and headed across the moor, back to the rest of the Clan. Crowfeather watched them go.

Everything I said to them is true, he thought. *I don't need WindClan. I don't even need my mouse-hearted son, Breezepelt, and I certainly don't need that mange-pelt Onestar. I'll show him! I can get along fine by myself.*

But the hollowness, the pain of loss inside him, wouldn't go away.

The shapes of Breezepelt and Heathertail dwindled and finally were lost to Crowfeather's sight. At last he took a deep breath and stepped across the border, heading into unexplored territory. *I suppose I'm a loner right now.*

As he traveled up a long moorland slope, the sky grew darker still, and he thought he could see tiny specks of white floating in front of his eyes. He blinked to clear his vision, but the white specks didn't go away, and as one landed on his nose, the cold shock told him that they were the first tiny flakes of snow.

"Mouse dung!" he grumbled aloud. "That's all I need!"

Crowfeather realized that if he wanted to hunt, he had better do so soon, before the snow drove every piece of prey into their holes. Aware of hunger for the first time since he left the camp, he padded on, setting down his paws even more lightly, his ears pricked and his jaws parted to taste the air.

For a long time he found nothing. The flakes thickened, swirling around him, settling on the ground until he was plodding through snow a mouse-length deep. His paws were so cold he couldn't feel them anymore. Snowflakes clotted in his dark gray pelt and clung to his whiskers.

Crowfeather was thinking that he had better give up and start looking for a place to shelter when a hare started up almost underneath his paws. It fled up the hill, and Crowfeather hurled himself after it, his muscles bunching and stretching. His gaze fixed on the bobbing black tips of the hare's ears, which were all that he could see clearly; the rest of its white pelt was almost invisible in the snow.

The hare disappeared over the brow of the hill and Crowfeather followed. But as he raced downward, his hind legs skidded out from under him and he lost his balance. Letting out a yowl of shock, he rolled over and over down the slope, his legs flailing as he struggled to stop himself.

Then Crowfeather felt a sharp pain in his head as his body slammed into something solid. The white world exploded into blackness, and he knew nothing more.

Crowfeather found himself crouching in utter darkness. The pain in his head was overwhelming, and for a few moments he could do nothing but keep still, clenching his teeth to keep back moans of pain.

At last he opened his eyes, but the darkness didn't lift. Sheer panic pulsed through Crowfeather. *Have I gone blind?*

He couldn't smell or feel anything, but he sensed that a number of cats were gathered around him. *Are they my Clanmates?* he wondered wildly. *Have they come to find me?*

At first the cats were still, but after a little while they began to move, weaving around him in a circle, so close that now and again he could feel their pelts brushing against his.

At last one of them spoke, its voice low and gentle but somehow ominous. "Greetings, Crowfeather."

Now Crowfeather was sure that these were not WindClan cats. He struggled to rise to his paws and face them in the darkness, but his legs wouldn't support him, and he slumped back to the ground. "Who are you?" he asked hoarsely.

"You know who we are, Crowfeather," a second voice murmured. "You have met us before."

"No, I haven't!" Crowfeather protested. "Stop playing

games and tell me what's going on."

As he spoke, a dim light began to grow around him, pale and unhealthy like the shine of rotting wood. It was only enough to show him the outlines of the cats, still weaving around him, with here and there the gleam of predatory eyes.

"Is this . . . is this the Dark Forest?" he stammered.

"*Clever* Crowfeather," a third voice purred. "We're so glad you've come to join us."

"What? No!" Crowfeather lurched upward and this time managed to scramble to his paws. "I'm not going to join you. I'm not even dead!"

"Not quite . . . ," another voice breathed out. "But soon."

Crowfeather couldn't remember ever having been so terrified, not even when he'd been trying to squeeze into the cleft, away from the cruel talons of Sharptooth. *I know Onestar banished me,* he thought frantically. *But surely what I did wasn't so bad that I would end up here? If I have to die, I should be in StarClan!*

He was growing dizzy as he tried to watch the circling cats and work out where the voices were coming from.

"Come with us, Crowfeather."

"You're welcome *here*."

Crowfeather wanted to barrel his way through the circle and flee, but he knew that he didn't have the strength. Besides, he had no idea where he could flee to. A medicine cat might know the paths that would lead him out of this dreadful place and into the sunlit territory of StarClan, but he wasn't a medicine cat.

Soft pelts brushed more firmly against his sides as the circle of cats grew tighter, closing in. Crowfeather forced back a screech of terror. "Leave me alone," he gasped. "I'm not going with you!"

But he knew that his bravado was pointless. There was nothing he could do.

Now the light was strengthening, but this time it came from behind Crowfeather, casting his shadow out in front of him. With a sudden tingling of hope, he realized that this light was different, clear and silvery like the radiance of the full moon.

The Dark Forest cats froze, staring with wide, horrified eyes at something beyond Crowfeather. Then, letting out a chorus of eerie caterwauls, they turned tail and fled.

"Great StarClan, Crowfeather!" A familiar voice spoke behind him. "What have you gotten yourself into now?"

Crowfeather whirled around. "Ashfoot!" he exclaimed.

CHAPTER 20

Crowfeather's mother stepped delicately over to him and sat down beside him with her tail wrapped neatly around her paws. With a grunt of relief Crowfeather slumped to the ground beside her.

"What in StarClan's name do you think you're doing, Crowfeather?" his mother asked him. Her voice was exasperated, but her eyes were warm. "You should be helping your Clan, not wandering about on the moor in the snow."

"You do know that I was banished, right?" Crowfeather retorted. "I was banished for following your advice, and Feathertail's. You told me to go behind Onestar's back and ask Bramblestar for help."

Ashfoot gave her whiskers a twitch, seeming briefly embarrassed. "I'm sorry. I'd hoped that Onestar wouldn't refuse to let ThunderClan help, or insult Bramblestar. But, Crowfeather," she added more briskly, "you know you could have been more tactful in dealing with Onestar. A good deputy needs to judge his leader's mood."

"But I'm *not* deputy," Crowfeather reminded her sourly. "Right now I'm not even a WindClan cat."

"That can be put right," Ashfoot assured him, with a dismissive flick of her tail. "The most important thing is for you to convince Onestar to take Kestrelflight's vision seriously. Don't you remember the second wave of water, the one that engulfed all the Clans? Don't you understand what it means? The stoats are threatening WindClan now, but they're only the forerunner of a much greater threat."

"That's what I thought! What threat?" Crowfeather asked, suppressing a shiver.

"I don't know," Ashfoot admitted. "I'm not sure that even the warriors of StarClan can see so far ahead. But I know this—when trouble strikes, WindClan will need you."

Crowfeather let out a snort of disbelief. "I wish you would tell Onestar that! He doesn't seem to need me at all right now."

"Then you have to make him see sense," Ashfoot pointed out. "You need to stop worrying about yourself and start worrying about your Clan and the cats who love you."

"'Love'?" Crowfeather tried to put all his contempt into the single word. "If any cats 'love' me, why didn't they speak up to defend me?"

"Don't be such a daft furball!" Ashfoot scolded him. "Of course Breezepelt loves you! And there are many more cats who respect you—Heathertail, for one. Didn't they come after you and try to persuade you to go back?"

Crowfeather wasn't sure that he believed his mother, but he wasn't about to argue with her anymore. "But how can I put things right?" he asked her. "Those . . . those other cats—they

said I was dying." He shuddered, remembering the soft voices
that had tempted him to go with them.

"You won't die." Ashfoot touched her nose to his ear. "It is
not your time to journey to StarClan."

"Then . . . then I won't end up in the Dark Forest?"

Ashfoot's tail curled up in amusement. "Crowfeather, you
may be the most annoying furball in all four Clans, but not
even your worst enemy could call you evil. Those cats were
trying to trick you." The light around her began to fade, and
her pale shape began to blur in front of Crowfeather's eyes.

"Don't go!" he begged.

"You'll see me again," Ashfoot mewed, her voice seeming
to come from an immense distance. "For now, wake up and
get on with it."

Crowfeather struggled to open his eyes; snow was crusting
his lids, and a sharp pain stabbed through his head as if some
cat were pounding it with a spike of rock. He was lying on his
side; above him the broad head and muscular shoulders of a
cat were outlined against the sky.

With a hiss of defiance, Crowfeather tried to spring to his
paws, but the explosion of pain in his head made him stagger
and he sank to the ground again. He could feel a smooth wall
of rock at his back.

"Keep still, flea-brain," the cat grunted. "I'm trying to fix
your head."

Crowfeather became aware of some kind of sticky juice
trickling into his head fur, and picked up the clean tang of

some kind of herb. "Are you a medicine cat?" he asked, confused.

"Why do cats keep asking me that? I'm a cat who helps other cats."

Crowfeather felt even more bewildered as the pain in his head eased and his vision cleared. The cat tending to him was a huge tabby tom, with white chest and paws, and amber eyes fixed in concentration as he squeezed out the healing juices from a mouthful of leaves. Crowfeather had never set eyes on him before.

"Who are you?" he asked. "You're not a Clan cat."

The strange cat spat out the leaves and began to massage the juices into Crowfeather's fur with one forepaw. "Oh, you're one of those lunatics who live in the forest," he meowed. "No, I'm not one of them. I like to keep myself to myself. My name's Yew."

"You?" Crowfeather decided he was still in some weird dream. "Like 'Hey, you'?"

"No, flea-brain," the tabby tom responded, with an exasperated twitch of his whiskers. "*Yew*, like the tree."

"Oh, sorry," Crowfeather mewed, then added after a moment, "I'm Crowfeather. Thanks for helping me."

"You're welcome. I've learned a bit about patching up injured cats in my time, and I like to help out when I can." Yew finished his massage and stood back, rubbing his paw in the snow to clean off the juices. "Try sitting up."

Crowfeather obeyed; his head swam, and every one of his muscles shrieked in protest, but he managed to stay upright.

He found himself in the lee of a large, jutting outcrop of rocks, with only a thin powdering of snow covering the tough moorland grass. Beyond the shelter, all the hills were hidden in a thick layer of snow, the white expanse stretching in all directions as far as Crowfeather could see. More flakes were slowly drifting down. Though clouds hid the sun, he guessed that sunhigh would be long past.

"How did you find me, in all this?" he asked.

Yew looked thoughtful. "That was strange," he replied. "I was hunting, down there on the edge of the forest. Then I saw a gray she-cat—the prettiest cat I ever laid eyes on. She beckoned me to follow her, and she brought me up here. But when we got here, I couldn't find her . . . only you, half buried in the snow and looking just about dead." For a moment his bold amber gaze softened. "Her fur glittered like stars. . . ."

Feathertail! Warmth spread through Crowfeather from ears to tail-tip, as if he were basking in the sun of greenleaf. *She saved me!* Injured and unconscious in the snow, he would have frozen to death if no cat had found him.

"Thank you," he repeated. "I guess I would be dead if it weren't for you."

Yew let out another grunt, looking faintly embarrassed. "I don't know about that," he muttered. "I guess you'll be fine once you have some prey inside you. Rest for a bit and I'll see what I can find."

He rose and loped off, vanishing around the other side of the rock.

Crowfeather curled up in the shelter of the overhang. He was half afraid to sleep, remembering his dreadful vision of the Dark Forest cats. But he was too exhausted to fight off unconsciousness, and he was drowsing when the warm, delicious scent of rabbit drifted into his nose. He opened his eyes to see Yew dropping the limp body in front of him.

"Come on, there's enough for both of us," he mewed.

Crowfeather didn't need telling twice. Hungrily he tore at the fresh-kill, savoring the juices and the rich taste of the flesh. *This is the best prey I've ever eaten!* he thought. "Thank you, StarClan, for this prey," he mumbled around a huge mouthful. "And thank you, too, Yew."

"My pleasure." Yew gulped down a few mouthfuls of the rabbit and continued, "You know, I came across another cat with the same scent as yours, a half-moon or so ago."

"You did?" Crowfeather felt his heart begin beating faster. "Where? What was she like?"

Yew gave him a long look through narrowed eyes. "It sounds like you might know her," he remarked. "She was a black she-cat—a pretty tough one, too."

Nightcloud! Crowfeather's chest felt like it would burst. *Could she really be alive?* "Was she okay?" he asked eagerly.

"No, she had a bad wound down one side," Yew told him. "But she wasn't letting it slow her down. She was quite ready to claw my fur off before I finally convinced her I meant her no harm." He paused, then added, "She's a friend of yours?"

"She's one of my Clan," Crowfeather replied, not wanting to launch into an explanation of his complicated relationship with Nightcloud. "We were afraid she was dead. Where did you meet her?"

"On the edge of the Twolegplace."

That reply made no sense to Crowfeather. The only Two-legplace he knew was the one between ShadowClan and RiverClan. He couldn't imagine why Nightcloud would have gone there. "Across the lake?" he asked.

Yew shook his head, giving Crowfeather the sort of look that Crowfeather himself might have given to a dim apprentice. "No, the one on the other side of the forest."

Crowfeather blinked, bewildered. "I don't know that one."

"I'll show you." Yew lumbered to his paws. "Can you climb the rock?"

Crowfeather wasn't at all sure. His head was still spinning as he rose, but Yew was already climbing upward, nimble for all his bulk. Crowfeather gritted his teeth and followed. To his relief, there were plenty of crevices in the rock where he could wedge his paws, and he managed to haul himself to the top. Yew bent his head and fastened his teeth in his scruff to drag him up the last tail-length.

"Over there," Yew meowed, pointing with his tail.

Crowfeather looked out across the snow-covered land-scape. The forest was a dark mass far below, and beyond it he could make out a stretch of uneven ground, which he realized was the Twolegplace Yew had spoken of, snow covering the pointed roofs of the Twoleg dens until they looked like small, steep hills. It was bigger than the one Crowfeather knew, beside the lake. A Thunderpath curved around it like a black snake, with monsters like tiny bright beetles moving to and fro along it.

"I'd been down there visiting my housefolk," Yew began. "I—"

"You're a *kittypet*?" Crowfeather interrupted. *This tough, competent cat is a* kittypet? "I don't believe it!"

A purr of amusement rumbled in Yew's chest. "Well, I drop in on my housefolk now and again," he responded. "When I feel like it. It's warm and comfortable there, but it's pretty boring, and the food is disgusting. So, when I've had enough of it, I leave and go exploring. That's when I met your friend, just outside the Twolegplace."

Crowfeather slid out his claws, scraping on the gritty surface of the rock. "Please tell me what happened," he begged.

Yew crouched down with his paws tucked underneath him, flakes of snow blotching his tabby pelt. "She was on the edge of the forest, right next to the Thunderpath," he meowed. "She was in a pretty bad way, wounded and exhausted. But like I said, she was ready to fight me until I convinced her I was no enemy."

"What happened then?"

"I found her some marigold for her wound," Yew told him, "but it was worse than I could cope with, so I told her to go into the Twolegplace."

Crowfeather gazed at the tabby tom in horror. "You told her *what*?"

Yew twitched his whiskers in amusement. "Most Twolegs are pretty kind to injured cats. Someone would take her in, and they might even take her to the vet." As Crowfeather opened his mouth to ask a question, Yew added quickly, "I guess that's what you would call a Twoleg medicine cat. They'd give her the help she needed."

"And Nightcloud did that?" Crowfeather asked, fascinated

by the idea of his former mate agreeing to set paw inside a Twoleg den.

Yew shrugged. "I think so. She didn't look happy about it, but the whole of the forest there reeked of dogs and foxes, so she couldn't go back that way. She headed for the housefolk dens, and I never saw her again."

"I have to go and find her!" Crowfeather exclaimed. The herbs Yew had given him, and the prey warm in his belly, made him feel full of strength again and ready for anything.

Yet he knew it would be mouse-brained to go into the Twolegplace alone. He had no idea what he would find there, but he was certain that Nightcloud must be trapped somehow, or she would have come home. Crowfeather was worried that it might be hard to get her out. *If she even wants to come with me.*

His first impulse was to ask Yew to go with him. Yet Yew had already told him that he'd been leaving the Twolegplace when he met Nightcloud. He wouldn't want to go back there so soon. Besides, Crowfeather already owed him his life. He couldn't bring himself to demand any more of him.

No, he thought. *I need a different cat for this.* And he knew which cat he wanted by his side.

I need Breezepelt.

CHAPTER 21

❧

Crowfeather plodded across the moor toward the WindClan camp.
The daylight had faded, and the first warriors of StarClan
had appeared through ragged gaps in the cloud, casting a
pale glimmer on the surface of the snow. Crowfeather's head
still throbbed, and he was exhausted from pushing his way
through drifts that reached almost to his shoulders. But at
least no more flakes were falling, and his determination to
find Nightcloud kept him going.

He became more watchful as he approached the camp. He
was acutely aware that he was still not allowed inside, and if
Onestar or any of the warriors spotted him, he could be driven
out before he got the chance to explain why he had returned.

I need to find a way to talk to Breezepelt without any other cat knowing.

Drawing closer still, Crowfeather could see a cat standing
at the top of the hollow, keeping watch. At first he crouched
down in the shelter of a jutting boulder, hoping for a chance
to sneak past without being noticed. Then he recognized the
graceful figure outlined against the gleaming snow.

Thank StarClan! It's Heathertail.

Crowfeather emerged from behind the bush and dropped

into the hunter's crouch. Using the snow for cover, he crept forward, thrusting his way through and wincing as the cold stuff soaked into his fur. He was acutely conscious of how his dark gray pelt would stand out against the snow, and he didn't want to alert Heathertail in case she called out to warn the Clan before he was close enough for her to recognize him.

When he was within a few tail-lengths he rose up and called out in a low voice. "Heathertail!"

Heathertail stiffened as she gazed at him, then bounded lightly through the snow until she reached his side.

"Crowfeather! You came back after all!" she exclaimed.

"Yes, but I don't mean to stay," Crowfeather responded. He felt slightly embarrassed by the warmth in Heathertail's voice, and the glow in her blue eyes. "I'm sorry for the way I behaved before, Heathertail. I'm sure you're figuring out . . . I'm not always the easiest cat."

Heathertail's eyes danced with amusement. "Well, I enjoy a challenge sometimes. Breezepelt isn't always easy, either."

Like father, like son, Crowfeather thought. "Speaking of Breezepelt . . . I need to talk to him, and tell him that I've found out where Nightcloud is."

Heathertail gave a gasp of astonishment. "Really? That's great! How did you do that?"

Quickly Crowfeather explained how he had met Yew, and how the powerful tabby had told him about meeting Nightcloud on the edge of the Twolegplace. "I think she must be trapped there," he finished, "and I want Breezepelt to come with me to get her out."

Heathertail nodded agreement. "I'll go fetch him for you." Heading back to the camp, she glanced over her shoulder. "I'm coming too," she mewed.

While he waited, Crowfeather trudged over to a nearby thornbush and slid underneath the branches. His heart was racing with tension; if any other cat spotted him now, there would be real trouble.

Peering out from his hiding place, Crowfeather thought he spotted a flicker of movement at the edge of the camp. Drawing in a hissing breath, he pressed himself lower to the ground. Everything was still, and for a moment Crowfeather assumed he had been mistaken.

I'm so nervous, I'd run away if a mouse jumped into my paws!

Then a breeze started up, teasing the surface of the snow into little flurries and carrying to Crowfeather a scent that he recognized all too well.

"Okay, Hootpaw," he mewed. "I know you're there somewhere. You can come out now."

Heartbeats later the dark gray tom popped up from behind a rock, scuffled his way through the snow, and skidded into the shelter of the bush beside Crowfeather. His eyes gleamed and his tail was bushed out with excitement.

Oh, StarClan, now what do I do?

"What are you doing out of your den?" Crowfeather asked, fixing the apprentice with a stern glare. *With any luck, he didn't hear anything.*

"I only went to make dirt," Hootpaw excused himself. "But I was so excited to see that you've come back—and you've found Nightcloud!" The apprentice gave a little bounce. "That's so great!"

"So you *were* listening to me and Heathertail!"

For a heartbeat, Hootpaw looked chastened. "I didn't mean to spy," he insisted. "I want to come with you! Please, Crowfeather!"

Crowfeather was briefly tempted. He knew how much Hootpaw cared for his former mentor, just as Featherpaw, surprisingly, cared for him. And Hootpaw had learned his battle moves well; he could be an asset if they ran into trouble.

But then Crowfeather realized that it was quite impossible. And he'd had enough of taking apprentices into danger.

"Absolutely not," he replied. "Take another warrior's apprentice on a dangerous mission?" *It's a secret mission, too,* he reflected. *A banished cat sneaking an apprentice out without his leader's approval!* "You must have bees in your brain," he finished.

Hootpaw's tail drooped and he blinked in disappointment. "*Please*, Crowfeather," he repeated. "I'll do everything you tell me."

"I'm telling you no." Crowfeather slid forward, so close to Hootpaw that his nose almost touched the top of the apprentice's head. *Being tough with him now is the best way to protect him.* "And if you breathe a word of this to Onestar," he continued, "I'll personally make sure that you wish you'd never left the nursery. Got it?"

Hootpaw's eyes were wide and scared. "Got it, Crowfeather." He wriggled out from under the bush and streaked off, back toward the camp.

Crowfeather watched him go, shaking his head a little. *He's got great spirit,* he reflected. *He'll make a fine warrior one day. And I'll do all I can to make sure that Nightcloud is around to help him do it.*

While Crowfeather waited for his Clanmates to return, the sky cleared and the moon shone down on the snowy moor. Crowfeather let out a purr of satisfaction; their journey would be much easier if they could see where they were putting their paws—provided they got away without any cat spotting them.

When Heathertail reappeared with Breezepelt padding in her paw steps, the light was bright enough for Crowfeather to see how battered and exhausted they both looked. Their tails and shoulders were drooping; Heathertail's pelt was matted with twigs, and Breezepelt had a scratch on one foreleg.

He wondered if they were even in any shape to go through with the plan.

"What happened to you?" Crowfeather asked, emerging from his hiding place under the bush. "Has there been trouble?"

Heathertail shook her head. "We spent the whole day lugging stones and brush around to plug up the tunnel entrances," she told Crowfeather. "It's exhausting work."

"And after all that, we didn't have time to do them all," Breezepelt complained. "Onestar insisted on stopping when the sun went down. That means the stoats can still get out, so it was all for nothing. I feel like every scrap of skin has been scraped off my pads."

"It'll be fine." Heathertail gave Breezepelt a friendly nudge. "We can finish tomorrow."

Crowfeather had listened to their news with mounting anxiety. "Are you sure you're fit for this?" he asked. "It's a long way to the Twolegplace."

There was a determined gleam in Breezepelt's eyes as he gazed at his father. "I could do more than this for Nightcloud," he meowed. "We *have* to find her."

"It's the least we can do," Heathertail agreed.

A trickle of pride in the two young cats began to flow through Crowfeather, like a frozen stream beginning to melt. The determined look on Heathertail's face filled him with confidence. She would definitely be a useful cat to have around on this journey. *But what about the camp?* he wondered. *She's supposed to be keeping watch.*

He tilted his head, thinking hard, when the sound of paw steps swishing through the snow behind him made him start. He swung around to see Hootpaw and his mentor, Gorsetail, looming up out of the darkness.

Crowfeather felt every hair on his pelt beginning to rise. "What in StarClan's name are you doing here?" he demanded in a low voice. "Hootpaw, I told you not to tell any cat."

"You told me not to tell *Onestar*," Hootpaw reminded him, as bright and confident as ever. "But I told Gorsetail. I reckoned you'd have to let me come if I had my mentor's permission."

"And has she given it?" Crowfeather angled his ears toward Gorsetail. "Are you as bee-brained as he is?"

"Bee-brained yourself," Gorsetail retorted coolly. "*I'm* not the cat who's showing his face here after being banished from the Clan. And yes, Hootpaw has my permission—on one condition."

"And what's that?" Breezepelt growled, taking a pace toward the gray-and-white she-cat.

"That I get to come with you too," Gorsetail replied.

Crowfeather's eyes widened in shock. *Gorsetail wants to help?*

"Don't look so surprised," the she-cat mewed. "I respected Nightcloud as much as any cat."

Crowfeather stared at his Clanmate, hardly knowing what to say. He hadn't forgotten that Gorsetail had once said that the Clan would be better off if Breezepelt were killed by a badger. Though lately her attitude seemed to have relaxed, she still wasn't a cat Crowfeather wanted with him on a dangerous expedition.

It was Heathertail who broke the silence, giving Crowfeather an irritated nudge. "For StarClan's sake, let them come! If we stand here arguing, some cat will hear us, and we won't be able to go at all."

Crowfeather could see the sense in that. "Okay, you can come," he meowed. Privately he still wasn't sure that it was a good idea to take so many cats, especially when they had to cross a rival Clan's territory. And if Onestar found out, it would surely cause problems. Not to mention, the camp would be unguarded for a little while. *But then,* he told himself, *the more noses, the more chance of finding Nightcloud. We have to take the risk.*

Hootpaw leaped right off the ground in his excitement. "If we meet any stoats, I know what to do," he boasted, landing on his hind paws and striking out with both forepaws against an imaginary stoat.

"If we meet any stoats, you'll stay beside me and do as you're told," Gorsetail responded, with a severe look at her apprentice.

"Sure, Gorsetail!" Hootpaw's enthusiasm wasn't dampened in the slightest.

Let's hope we don't find any stoats, Crowfeather thought as he took the lead away from the camp. *But we will find something. I just hope that something is Nightcloud.*

Surprising himself, he couldn't stifle a pulse of excitement at the thought of seeing her again.

CHAPTER 22

❦

Crowfeather led the way across the moor, guiding his patrol in a wide half circle to avoid the tunnels. "I don't want to risk meeting the stoats," he murmured. "They'll be even more angry with WindClan after you blocked up the entrances."

Even so, he couldn't help feeling a prickling of tension in his pads as they passed by, remembering once again Kestrel-flight's vision. He saw dark water rush out, swelling and tossing until it could engulf all the Clans.

It's so clear. It's almost as though the vision were mine.

He shook his head to clear it of the fake memories.

But I still want to know what it means.

When they reached the stream that formed the border with ThunderClan, Crowfeather halted. "We could trek all the way around the forest," he meowed, "and get to the Two-legplace that way. But it's much farther than cutting across ThunderClan territory; we'd never do it, find Nightcloud, and get back to camp again before dawn."

"*If* we find Nightcloud," Gorsetail put in.

Breezepelt gave her a savage look and opened his jaws to speak, but Heathertail interrupted him with a touch of her tail on his shoulder. "We don't want the Clan to miss us if we can possibly avoid it," she pointed out. "If we don't find Nightcloud, they never need to know we were gone, and if we do—well, Onestar will be so pleased that he won't mind what we did."

Gorsetail shrugged. "ThunderClan it is, then."

Crowfeather gazed into the trees on the opposite side of the stream. "From now on, absolute silence," he told the others. "We'll be on another Clan's territory, and it's possible that some ThunderClan cats will be out and about. We *really* don't want trouble with them right now." He hesitated, then added, "Hootpaw, have you got that?"

Serious for once, the apprentice nodded vigorously.

"I've got an idea," Heathertail meowed before Crowfeather could start looking for the best place to cross the stream. "Why don't we roll ourselves in the ThunderClan scent markers? That way, if we do meet a ThunderClan patrol, we can hide and our scent won't give us away."

"That's a brilliant plan!" Breezepelt exclaimed.

But Hootpaw let out an outraged squeak. "I don't want that ThunderClan stink on my fur!"

Gorsetail gave her apprentice a cuff around the ear, her claws sheathed. "You'll do as you're told. We could still go back to camp."

Hootpaw hunched his shoulders. "Sorry, Gorsetail."

Crowfeather located a narrow part of the stream where it was easy for the cats to leap across. As he and his Clanmates rolled in the ThunderClan scent, he couldn't help feeling some sympathy for Hootpaw. The markers were strong and fresh—clearly they had been renewed at sunset—and he winced as the stench sank into his pelt.

I don't think I'll ever smell like WindClan again! Instead the scent reminded him of Leafpool, and he gave his ears an irritated twitch, as if he were trying to get rid of a fly buzzing around him. *I have to stop thinking about her!*

When every cat was ready, Crowfeather headed into the trees with his Clanmates padding softly beside him. Beneath the trees the snow was not so thick, and they were able to pick up their pace. The forest floor was dappled with black and silver, a pattern that shifted as the branches moved gently overhead, rustling in the breeze. The prey-scents were muted; Crowfeather guessed that most creatures would be safe in their holes, though he thought it worthwhile to glance over his shoulder and whisper, "We take no prey, remember? This isn't our hunting ground."

"What do we do when we get to the Twolegplace?" Heathertail asked as the sound of the stream died away behind them. "It must be huge. How will we ever find Nightcloud?"

"How about we worry about that when we get there?" Gorsetail responded, an edge to her voice.

"I've been thinking about that." Crowfeather ignored the gray-and-white she-cat. "I'm going to start from the pool where I thought Nightcloud died. We might be able to pick up her scent there, and if we can, it will make our job a lot easier."

"Good idea."

The grunted response came from Breezepelt. Crowfeather could barely prevent his tail from sticking straight up in astonishment. *Finally, I've done something right!*

The WindClan cats slipped like shadows through the forest as Crowfeather led them toward the hollow where he had found Nightcloud's blood and the fox scent. Now and again he picked up the faintest trace of his own stale scent, but his anxiety grew when he couldn't find any of Nightcloud's.

Maybe Breezepelt was right, and it has faded. That would make it much harder to find her, if her scent trail has disappeared.

But before the patrol reached the hollow, Crowfeather spotted movement in the undergrowth over to one side, and a flicker of pale light that vanished almost immediately. He halted, signaling with his tail for his Clanmates to do the same.

The pale flicker came a second time, and for a moment Crowfeather wondered if his mother, Ashfoot, was showing herself to him again. Then he dismissed the thought. Ashfoot only came to him in dreams. He must have caught a glimpse of a living animal. *It has to be a cat with a white or pale gray pelt,* he thought. A strong, fresh scent drifted into his nostrils. *Fox dung! It's ThunderClan!*

He beckoned his patrol into the shadow of a bramble thicket, where they crouched in silence, hardly daring to breathe. Rustling came from the undergrowth, followed by a cat's voice raised, half amused and half annoyed.

"Great StarClan, Lilypaw! Do you have to stomp around like an overweight badger?"

"That's Poppyfrost," Crowfeather whispered. "I wonder how many more of them there are."

A heartbeat later the ThunderClan patrol emerged into the open. Ivypool was in the lead, with Poppyfrost and Bumblestripe. Following them were their apprentices, Lilypaw and her littermate, Seedpaw. Moonlight reflected off Ivypool's silver-and-white pelt.

Crowfeather hoped that if they kept still, the darkness still might hide them, or their ThunderClan scent would deceive the patrol, but it was a vain hope. Ivypool stalked straight up to him and stood looking down at him and the rest of the WindClan cats.

"Greetings," she meowed. "I suppose you have a good reason for lurking there on *our* territory?"

Crowfeather remembered that Ivypool had trained in the Dark Forest, spying for ThunderClan, and there wasn't much she didn't know about tracking in the dark. Or fighting, if it came to that. *How long did she know that we were here?*

"Well?" Ivypool asked.

Rising to his paws, Crowfeather gave his pelt a shake, trying to recover a little dignity. "Let me explain . . . ," he began.

But at that moment, Bumblestripe padded forward and pushed his muzzle into Breezepelt's shoulder fur. "They're carrying our scent!" he exclaimed. "That proves they're up to no good!"

Breezepelt started backward, his pelt beginning to bristle, and slapped Bumblestripe away with a lash of his tail. A growl came from deep in Bumblestripe's throat, while Breezepelt slid out his claws. Their backs arched, as if they would leap into a fight at any moment.

"No!" Crowfeather ordered. He pushed Breezepelt back and stepped between him and the ThunderClan tom.

At the same moment, Ivypool snapped, "Stop that, Bumblestripe." She stood beside Crowfeather, separating the two hostile toms.

Reluctantly, Bumblestripe took a step back, though he and Breezepelt were still glaring at each other. Ivypool stood waiting with her head tilted to one side, while Poppyfrost had withdrawn a few paces with the two apprentices. Crowfeather heard her say to them, "If a fight breaks out, *run!*"

"Look, Ivypool . . ." Crowfeather addressed the silver-and-white she-cat, hoping she would be reasonable. "We're here on an important mission. We're looking for Nightcloud."

"But Nightcloud is dead," Ivypool objected. "Onestar announced it at the Gathering."

Crowfeather began to explain how he had followed Nightcloud's scent from one of the tunnel entrances, until he had found her blood and scent beside a pool, mixed with the reek of fox.

"Of course we thought that a fox got her," he mewed.

"So you've been trespassing here before!" Bumblestripe broke in accusingly.

Ivypool twitched her ears in annoyance. "Bumblestripe, will you for StarClan's sake *shut up!*" She nodded to Crowfeather. "Go on."

Crowfeather told her how Kestrelflight had failed to find

Nightcloud in StarClan, and how that made her Clanmates hope that she was still alive, and then how he had met Yew, who'd told him of meeting her on the edge of a Twolegplace beyond the forest. "But our best hope of finding her is to go back to that pool and see if we can find her scent leading away from it."

"Good luck with that, after all this time," Ivypool murmured. "But I can understand that you have to try. Yes, they can, Bumblestripe," she added, glaring at her Clanmate, who had opened his jaws to protest. "Nightcloud is a noble warrior, and she deserves the help of any cat."

Bumblestripe stared down at his paws, a sullen expression on his face, though he didn't argue anymore.

Ivypool turned back to Crowfeather. "Bumblestripe and I will escort you," she told Crowfeather. "We can't have Wind-Clan cats wandering around alone in our territory."

"We don't need—" Gorsetail began, looking outraged, but Crowfeather interrupted her with a lash of his tail.

"That's fine by us," he meowed, and his Clanmates, even Gorsetail, murmured agreement.

It's so easy to work with ThunderClan when we agree on a goal, Crowfeather reflected. *If only Onestar had seen that, we might be done with the stoats by now.*

"Then I'll take the apprentices back to camp," Poppyfrost announced.

"Not fair," Lilypaw muttered. "You said you'd take us night hunting. And we haven't caught anything yet."

"Yeah, trust WindClan to spoil our fun," Seedpaw added.

"Never mind." Poppyfrost gathered the apprentices together with a sweep of her tail. "We'll see what we can pick up on our way back." She dipped her head to Ivypool and padded off in the direction of the ThunderClan camp, with the two apprentices trailing after her, glaring over their shoulders at the WindClan cats.

"Okay, Crowfeather," Ivypool meowed briskly. "Show us this pool."

She padded beside him as they set out again, with Bumblestripe bringing up the rear. Crowfeather could see that Breezepelt was still bristling with anger, glaring over his shoulder at Bumblestripe, flexing his claws. Crowfeather shot him a warning glance and hoped that he had sense enough not to start any more trouble with the ThunderClan tom.

When they finally reached the pool with its fringe of ferns, Crowfeather's heart sank as he tasted the scent of fox in the air, stronger and more recent than when he had been here before. *They must come here regularly. Can't ThunderClan keep the mange-pelts off their territory?*

Examining the ground around the pool, Crowfeather found the spot where he could still see that Nightcloud's blood had sunk into the grass, but there was not the slightest trace of her scent.

"Work outward from the pool," he instructed his Clanmates. "That way we might pick up her trail and find out which way she went."

Ivypool and Bumblestripe stood to one side of the pool while Crowfeather and the other WindClan cats searched for Nightcloud's scent. Crowfeather felt his hope sinking away like rain into dry ground as the moments passed and they found nothing. He was wondering how much longer they could go on searching when Breezepelt let out an excited yowl.

"I've found it!"

Crowfeather looked up. Breezepelt was standing several fox-lengths away from the pool, in the opposite direction from WindClan and toward the Twolegplace that Yew had pointed out to him. Swiftly he skirted the pool and bounded over to join his son, hoping that Breezepelt hadn't imagined finding the scent out of sheer desperation.

Breezepelt pointed with his muzzle to a clump of chervil, the leaves wilting and frostbitten. Crowfeather bent his head to sniff, parted his jaws to taste the air. The fox reek was swamping everything; he was sure there were at least two of them, and possibly three. Beneath the fox scent there was a trace of something else. Crowfeather wanted to believe that Breezepelt was right, but he wondered if he was just smelling what he wanted to smell. He shook his head slowly. "I'm not sure," he murmured.

"It *is* Nightcloud's scent!" Breezepelt insisted.

Hootpaw pushed his way forward. "Let me try!"

Gorsetail hooked his tail around her apprentice's neck and drew him back. "Stay out of the way," he ordered. "We don't want your scent confusing everything."

Crowfeather could see that Breezepelt's eyes looked hopeful and yet uncertain, as if he wasn't quite sure that he had really found his mother's scent after so long. Crowfeather guessed that he too was desperately trying to convince himself.

"If she went this way, she wasn't heading for WindClan," Crowfeather murmured thoughtfully. "And there's only one reason for that."

"The foxes were chasing her!" Heathertail meowed excitedly. "So if we follow the foxes . . ."

Crowfeather nodded. "We stand a good chance of finding Nightcloud."

"But what if . . . ?" There was panic now in Breezepelt's eyes, and his fur began to prickle in alarm. "What if they caught her?"

Heathertail wrapped her tail over his shoulders. "Calm down," she mewed. "We know she isn't dead, right? That other cat saw her. So somehow, she must have shaken off the foxes and ended up in the Twolegplace."

Crowfeather said nothing. The young she-cat was right that Nightcloud wasn't in StarClan, and they had a good idea that she had gone to the Twolegplace, however unlikely that seemed. *That's why we're here,* he told himself determinedly, *and we're not going home until we know for sure what happened to her, one way or the other.*

"Come on," he urged his Clanmates. "We won't find her standing around. Let's follow the foxes."

Ivypool and Bumblestripe padded over to join them as they turned in the direction of the fox trail, Ivypool taking the lead again while Bumblestripe tagged along at the end of the group. Crowfeather felt uncomfortable, almost as if he and his Clanmates were prisoners, but he had to admit they were lucky not to have ended up in a fight, or being chased off ThunderClan territory.

With so many cats involved in their mission, Crowfeather thought to himself, it was growing more and more likely that Onestar would discover what they had done. *We'd better find Nightcloud, and then he can't be too angry. There's not much more he can do to me, but there might be trouble for the others.*

The fox trail led in an almost straight line through the forest. Breezepelt kept his nose close to the ground as they followed it, here and there exclaiming that he had picked up Nightcloud's scent. Crowfeather too thought that he could catch a trace of it, but as they padded onward, he felt his chest tighten with worry. Now and again he spotted the paw print of a desperately running cat, and he wondered how Nightcloud had managed to keep going, wounded as she had been by the stoats. Could she really have had the strength and speed to stay ahead of the foxes for so long?

Crowfeather could imagine the foxes encircling her, catching her and pulling her down, tearing her flesh. He couldn't push away the thought that perhaps Yew hadn't seen Nightcloud, but only another cat who looked like her. He had to halt and close his eyes, repeating inside his head, *Yew said she smelled like me. . . . She smelled like me. . . .*

Breezepelt's voice came from close by. "Crowfeather, are you okay?"

Crowfeather shook his head as if he could drive out the images. "I'm fine," he rasped, and padded on.

But the horrible visions still attacked Crowfeather's mind, fierce as the warriors of the Dark Forest. He had to keep reminding himself that if the foxes had gotten Nightcloud, there would be blood and maybe even a body.

Or parts of a body. Please, StarClan, not that.

He shivered, but the chill had nothing to do with the frosty air of the snow-covered forest.

Eventually, Crowfeather could pick up the familiar tang of the ThunderClan scent markers; they had reached the border of ThunderClan territory. The fox trail led straight across it.

"Are you going any farther?" Ivypool asked.

"Of course!" It was Breezepelt who replied. "We're not giving up until we find Nightcloud."

Ivypool dipped her head; Crowfeather thought he could see a trace of approval in her eyes. "Then we'll leave you here," she continued. "And I give you permission to cross our territory again on your way back—but *not* to take prey. Of course, we will have to report this to Bramblestar."

More trouble to come. Surely Bramblestar will discuss all this with Onestar. And Onestar will think even worse of me—if that's possible. Aloud Crowfeather mewed, "Of course. And you might report the foxes, as well."

"We know about the foxes," Ivypool retorted. "We're keeping an eye on them."

Not a close-enough eye, Crowfeather thought, though he wasn't about to start an argument. "Then thank you for your help," he responded with a polite nod.

"May StarClan light your path," Ivypool meowed. "I hope you find Nightcloud."

As she spoke, there was genuine concern in her eyes and her voice. Crowfeather felt even more worried, guessing that Ivypool didn't really believe that they had much chance of tracking Nightcloud down.

Ivypool turned, jerking her head for Bumblestripe to follow her. The ThunderClan tom gave the WindClan cats a last suspicious look as he turned away, and both cats disappeared into the undergrowth. Crowfeather let out a sigh of relief to see them go.

"Okay," he meowed. "Let's get going."

His head held high, he crossed the ThunderClan border markings, and his Clanmates followed him into unknown territory.

For some time, the fox trail led on in a straight line as before, until the trees thinned out and Crowfeather began to pick up a new, acrid scent. "Monsters!" he exclaimed. "Of course . . . There's a Thunderpath up ahead."

"Fox dung!" Breezepelt hissed.

Crowfeather shared his anger. Picking out Nightcloud's scent was hard enough; it would become even harder when the scent of monsters was added to the mix. And the Thunderpath was one more hazard that Nightcloud had faced. Crowfeather shuddered, wondering if she could have been killed by a monster.

One of them might have caught her after *she met Yew.*

Still, the scent of the Thunderpath meant that they were

drawing close to the Twolegplace. And the fact that Night-cloud seemed to have made it this far made Crowfeather more certain that Yew had been right. He was determined not to give up.

Soon the acrid tang grew stronger, and now and again Crowfeather could hear the roar of a monster prowling along the Thunderpath. The fox scent was growing stronger too, and for a moment Crowfeather wondered if more foxes had joined the ones they had tracked from the pool.

Then he realized that he was wrong. *The fox scent isn't just strong—it's fresh! There are foxes here right now!*

CHAPTER 23

Crowfeather spun around at a flicker in the undergrowth and found himself face to face with a fox as it emerged from behind a bramble thicket: an old dog fox with a graying muzzle and a malignant look in its berry-bright eyes. Crowfeather slid out his claws and let out a growl from deep in his throat.

"Back off, mange-pelt!" he snarled.

But before he had finished speaking, two more foxes leaped out from behind the thicket; they were young and strong, with parted jaws and pointed fangs.

"Run!" Gorsetail yowled.

She took the lead as the cats pelted away through the trees. Crowfeather pounded along, shoulder to shoulder with Breezepelt, aware of Heathertail hard on their paws. The sound of the Thunderpath ahead grew even louder.

Crowfeather's pelt prickled with fear. Which was worse—to die from the bite of a fox, or crushed by the huge round paws of a monster?

Then Crowfeather heard a terrified wail from behind him. "Help me!"

Glancing back, he saw that Hootpaw was falling behind,

almost in the teeth of the leading fox. The fox kept snapping its jaws, getting closer and closer to Hootpaw's tail.

"Hootpaw, I—" Crowfeather began, only to break off as he slammed into something hard. All the breath was driven out of him.

Struggling to his paws, Crowfeather realized that he had run straight into a tree. "Fox dung!" he hissed. He began racing back to help Hootpaw, claws extended, ready to fight the fox.

But before he reached the terrified apprentice, Crowfeather realized something else. "Climb the trees!" he screeched.

He reached Hootpaw as he spoke and barreled into him, boosting him up into the nearest tree. Hootpaw dug his claws into the bark and scrambled up higher. Crowfeather followed him, feeling the hot breath of a fox on his hindquarters as he swung himself up onto the lowest branch. Hootpaw crouched, trembling beside him.

"Thanks, Crowfeather!" he panted.

Looking around, Crowfeather spotted Gorsetail in a nearby beech tree, her fur fluffed up as she spat defiance at the foxes below. *And where were you when your apprentice was in danger?* Crowfeather wondered.

Heathertail and Breezepelt had found refuge in an oak tree a little farther off.

"We're WindClan cats. We don't do trees," Breezepelt complained loudly.

Crowfeather gazed down from his branch to see the other two foxes catching up and skidding to a halt. All three of them began prowling around the trees, glaring up at the cats and letting out vicious snarls between gleaming bared teeth.

"Neither do foxes," Crowfeather responded to his son. "At least, not usually." He had heard now and again of foxes that climbed trees, but they mostly stayed on the ground. If any of these foxes tried it, he'd just slash his claws across their muzzles as they drew close.

That would make them think twice!

Hootpaw shuddered. "What are we going to do?"

"We'll be fine," Crowfeather reassured him. "Look—if you walk along this branch, you can cross into the beech tree where Gorsetail is."

Hootpaw crept forward hesitantly, but as soon as he moved, the branch gave a lurch, and he halted, trembling even harder.

"I don't think I can." He gave Crowfeather a scared look. "I might fall."

"No, you won't. I'll be right behind you. I won't let you fall."

Hootpaw took a deep breath and rose to his paws, once again digging his claws into the bark. Paw step by careful paw step he crept along the branch, then briefly froze again as the branch grew thinner toward the end and began to bounce gently under the cats' weight.

"Go on. You're doing fine," Crowfeather encouraged him. "Don't look down."

The reek of foxes was wafting up to Crowfeather from underneath the tree. He risked a quick glance down and saw that all three foxes had gathered below them, obviously hoping that one or more of them would lose their balance. But Hootpaw carried on steadily, then half leaped, half scrambled into Gorsetail's tree. Gorsetail was waiting to grab him by the scruff and set his paws firmly on a thicker branch.

"Thanks!" Hootpaw gasped. "I've never been up a tree before." Recovering his usual spirit, he added, "It's kind of fun!"

"Tell that to Breezepelt," Crowfeather mewed wryly; his son was right that living on the open moor, WindClan cats didn't have much opportunity for tree climbing. But these trees had just saved them from a fox ambush.

Slowly and cautiously the three cats ventured out onto a branch on the opposite side of the beech tree and managed to jump across to the oak where Breezepelt and Heathertail had taken refuge. The foxes followed, anger and frustration clear in their glaring eyes. The old dog fox sprang up, slamming his forepaws against the tree trunk and tearing at the bark with his claws.

"We're lucky these things don't climb," Breezepelt commented.

"Yes—I hope they give up and go away soon," Heathertail mewed.

"Stupid flea-pelts!" Crowfeather hissed down at the furious creatures. "Go and find yourselves some crow-food!"

"Yeah," Breezepelt added. "Cat isn't on the fresh-kill pile today. Eat your own tails instead!"

Crowfeather turned to exchange an amused glance with his son. But almost at once, Breezepelt's amusement faded.

His head drooped and his ears flattened.

"We will find Nightcloud, right?" he asked, his voice not quite steady.

"Of course we will." Crowfeather's response came before he had given himself time to think. He remembered the monsters and the Thunderpath, and the way that Nightcloud had been wounded by the stoats. *But Yew saw her alive,* he added to himself. *We will find her.*

The cats kept going, moving from tree to tree, but the foxes still followed them on the ground. Crowfeather began to be afraid that they were tenacious enough to keep it up until some cat fell.

We can't go on like this all night. We're already tired; sooner or later one of us will slip, or some cat will leap a little short. . . . He tried to hide his misgivings from the others, but he could tell from their uneasy expressions that they knew the danger as well as he did.

And the trees were thinning out even more; soon they were bound to reach a place where the next tree was too far away for them to jump the gap. When a monster roared down the Thunderpath ahead, he caught glimpses of its glaring eyes. There were other lights, too, scattered and distant, but enough to tell him that they must be coming to the Twolegplace.

Foxes, monsters . . . is there anything else that can go wrong?

But the foxes didn't like being so close to the Thunderpath, either. When a monster roared past, they would back up, half withdrawing into the undergrowth, only to creep back as the sound died away. Then, before the cats could be forced down to the ground again, an even bigger monster swept by, its bellowing seeming to fill the whole forest. The foxes halted; then, with a last flurry of furious snarls, they turned tail and disappeared back into the trees.

"Thank StarClan for that!" Gorsetail exclaimed.

She bunched her muscles to jump down from the tree, but Crowfeather stretched out his tail to stop her. "Wait," he meowed. "They might be hiding in the undergrowth, trying to trick us."

"Like they've got the brains for that," Gorsetail grumbled, but she stayed where she was.

Crowfeather waited, his ears pricked for any sounds that would tell him the foxes were nearby. But he heard nothing, and the fox scent was beginning to fade. Finally he nodded. "Okay."

All five cats scrambled down the tree—Hootpaw complaining that climbing down was much harder than climbing up—and padded past the few remaining trees until they reached a stretch of snow-covered grass leading up to the Thunderpath. In the moonlight it looked like a gleaming black river, edged on either side by filthy slush where the snow was beginning to melt. On the opposite side, more grass separated the Thunderpath from fences around Twoleg dens made of red stone.

"That's a Thunderpath?" Hootpaw asked, his eyes stretched wide.

"That's right," Gorsetail told him. "I don't suppose you've seen one before."

"No, Nightcloud never took me that far from camp,"

Hootpaw responded. He stretched out a paw to touch the surface, then jumped back with a surprised squeak. "It's hard! And cold!"

Gorsetail gently pushed her apprentice away from the edge. "We don't go near Thunderpaths unless we have to," she meowed. "They're dangerous."

Hootpaw blinked in surprise. "Why? They don't *look* dangerous."

"Remember the cute stoats that didn't look dangerous?" Crowfeather nudged Hootpaw's shoulder. "They—"

He broke off at the sound of roaring, faint at first, but soon growing louder. Glaring yellow eyes cast their beams across the surface of the Thunderpath, and the cats crouched at the edge as the monster growled past on its round black paws. Their fur was buffeted by the wind of its passing as they backed away from it, almost choking on the acrid air.

"That's a monster?" Hootpaw asked, watching the huge creature as it disappeared into the distance.

"Yes," Gorsetail told him. "And that's why Thunderpaths are dangerous. Monsters like that have killed cats."

Crowfeather thought Hootpaw looked too excited to be taking his mentor's words seriously. His eyes were wide and sparkling, and he was bouncing up and down on all four paws.

"I've seen a monster!" he exclaimed. "Cool! Wait till I tell Featherpaw and the others."

Crowfeather shot the 'paw a withering glance, and Hootpaw ceased bouncing, abruptly sitting down and casting a nervous lick over his chest fur.

Crowfeather rolled his eyes. "If you're *quite* finished . . . Okay, let's assume that Nightcloud made it this far. We need to pick up her scent trail again. Let's work along the edge of the Thunderpath in both directions. And *you*," he added to Hootpaw, "will not put one paw off the grass, or I'll see to it that you do all the elders' ticks for the next three moons."

"Right," Gorsetail added. "And no hunting patrols."

The apprentice's eyes stretched wide again, this time with horror at the thought. He looked even more scared of the threats than he had been of the monster. Checking on him, Crowfeather noticed that he kept well away from the Thunderpath, his nose busily probing into the grass.

It was Hootpaw who found the trace they were looking for. "Here! Over here!" he squealed.

Breezepelt was the first to reach him, sniffing eagerly at the place where Hootpaw pointed. "He's right. That's Nightcloud's scent." His amber eyes glowed with happiness and relief. "The foxes didn't get her."

Crowfeather bounded along the edge of the Thunderpath and tasted the scent for himself. Relief flowed over him as he recognized not only Nightcloud's scent, but a trace of Yew's, too.

"Yew's scent is here!" he announced triumphantly. "He *did* meet Nightcloud!"

"So where did she go from here?" Heathertail asked.

Although the cats searched for a long time, they couldn't find any more traces of Nightcloud's scent. Breezepelt was getting more and more nervous, tearing up the grass with his claws. Crowfeather's frustration was peaking when he suddenly realized what the problem was.

"Yew said that Nightcloud went into the Twolegplace," he meowed. "We're searching on the wrong side of the Thunderpath."

"Into the Twolegplace?" Breezepelt's tone was abrasive. "She would never have done that!"

Crowfeather flicked his ear irritably. "Normally, no," he agreed, "but she was injured, too severely for Yew to help her. He said he told her to go into the Twolegplace for help."

Breezepelt looked dubious. "She'd never trust a Twoleg to make her better," he insisted.

"She might have," Crowfeather countered, "if it was her only chance. Remember, she was far from home, separated by foxes from *any* medicine cat—never mind Kestrelflight."

Breezepelt turned and stared at the lights beyond the Thunderpath.

"I know it seems weird," Heathertail responded, resting her tail-tip on Breezepelt's shoulder, "but why would Yew lie to Crowfeather? Besides, Nightcloud might have at least wanted to cross the Thunderpath to escape from the foxes. Let's go and look."

After a moment, Breezepelt turned back and nodded his assent.

Relieved, Crowfeather led the cats back to the place where Hootpaw had found Nightcloud's scent. Lining them up along the edge of the Thunderpath, he mewed, "This shouldn't be too difficult. Most monsters don't come out at night. But we still need to be careful. Wait for my order, and when I say run, *run!*"

"Hootpaw, stay beside me," Gorsetail added.

The apprentice was quivering with excitement as he waited with his Clanmates. Crowfeather looked carefully in both directions, but there was no sign of a monster, not even a distant roaring. "Okay," he meowed. "Run!"

He bounded forward, so fast that his paws hardly touched the hard, black surface. Breezepelt and Heathertail were beside him, Gorsetail and Hootpaw a paw step behind. But before they reached the far side, a raucous screeching split the silence of the night. Glaring light swept over them and wind ruffled their fur as the monster swept past, barely a tail-length from their flying paws.

Every cat collapsed, panting, on the other side of the Thunderpath. "Mouse dung!" Gorsetail exclaimed. "I thought we were crow-food for sure."

Breezepelt sprang to his paws. "Well, we're fine," he mewed impatiently. "Let's carry on looking."

Crowfeather cast a glance at his son, half proud and half incredulous. *My paws are still shaking,* he reflected, *but if Breezepelt's are, too, he couldn't care less. This search for Nightcloud is really bringing out the best in him.*

This time Heathertail took the lead, weaving this way and that along the edge of the Thunderpath as she padded along. After a few heartbeats she halted, her tail rising straight into the air as she lowered her head for a good sniff at the grass. A moment later she raised her head. "Here," she mewed.

Crowfeather bounded over to her, his heart pounding with hope. Breezepelt was hard on his paws, and the two toms bent their heads beside Heathertail. The trace was faint, but as Crowfeather tasted the familiar scent, he felt hope swelling up inside him. *Now we know that Yew was right,* he thought. *She escaped the foxes and went into the Twolegplace. If I can only find her, I still have a chance to make peace with her.*

He let Breezepelt take the lead as they padded alongside the Twoleg dens, following the last vestiges of Nightcloud's scent trail. It was hard to distinguish it among so many competing scents of Twolegs, dogs, other cats, and monsters. But Breezepelt in particular seemed to have a knack for following where his mother had gone.

By now moonhigh was past, and most of the Twoleg dens were dark and silent. A few more monsters passed them, but they didn't seem to notice the cats in their headlong rush along the Thunderpath.

The black surface seemed to stretch on forever, with the long row of Twoleg nests on one side of it. Crowfeather's legs ached with weariness, but hope helped him to keep putting one paw in front of another.

Then they came to a point where the scent trail seemed to stop, swamped by the mingled scents of several Twolegs. *What happened to her here?* Crowfeather asked himself. *Could some Twoleg really have taken her away? And if they did, how will we ever find her?*

Glancing at Breezepelt, Crowfeather guessed from his son's desolate expression that similar thoughts were running through his mind.

"Have we lost her?" Breezepelt choked out. "Have we come as far as this, to lose her to a Twoleg?"

Crowfeather had a vision of some dark, faceless Twoleg stooping down and grabbing Nightcloud in its huge clumsy paws. *I can't bear to think what the Twoleg would do to her.* Though he knew the loner meant well, Crowfeather had no faith in Yew's assertion that most Twolegs were kind.

"No—look!" Heathertail drove away Crowfeather's despairing thoughts as she pointed with her tail at the bottom of the Twoleg fence. It was made of flat wooden strips, and at one point the strip had broken away, leaving a jagged hole. "I'll bet a moon of dawn patrols she went through here!"

Crowfeather thought it was quite likely. *If I were here, wounded, I'd want to get away from that Thunderpath.*

"Do you want me to check?" Heathertail asked him.

Crowfeather hesitated, then nodded. "Okay. But be careful."

Heathertail wriggled her way through the gap in the fence, the spiky bits of wood scraping through her fur. A moment later her face reappeared in the hole, her eyes shining with excitement. "Yes! Her scent is here."

The rest of the patrol followed Heathertail and found themselves in a Twoleg garden. Thick bushes surrounded a patch of grass that led up to the walls of the den.

"No stupid behavior now," Gorsetail warned Hootpaw. "There can be all kinds of trouble near Twolegs."

Hootpaw didn't reply, just nodded fervently, his eyes wide and gleaming. He obviously believed it was the best patrol ever. *He'll be boasting about it for moons,* Crowfeather thought, hiding his amusement. Then, reflecting that they weren't out of danger yet, he added to himself, *I hope.*

The scent trail led across several Twoleg gardens. Crowfeather felt his paws prickling with apprehension, wondering what would happen if they were still following it when the sun came up and the Twolegs began to emerge from their dens.

And what is Onestar going to say when we get back to camp? he asked himself. *I never thought we would be away so long.*

His thoughts were interrupted by the sound of high-pitched yapping.

"Dogs!" Gorsetail exclaimed.

Crowfeather spun around to see dogs pouring out of a hole in the entrance to the Twoleg den. At first sight, there seemed to be a whole Clan of them, but he quickly realized there were only five. Before any of the cats could react, they were surrounded and herded into a corner between the den and the fence.

Bushing out his fur to make himself as big as possible, Crowfeather arched his back and hissed at the dogs. "Back off, flea-pelts!"

The dogs were bounding around, their ears flopping and their tongues lolling. They kept making little rushes at the cats, trying to chew their necks and legs, and swatting at them with their huge paws.

"I think they're playing," Heathertail meowed. "They're only kits—dog kits!"

"Kits?" Breezepelt echoed, disbelieving. "Look at the size of them!"

"I don't care if they *are* kits," Gorsetail snapped, pressing herself back against the fence to avoid a huge tongue swiping across her muzzle. "I'll claw their ears off if they don't stop!"

"No, don't hurt them," Heathertail protested. "Climb the fence. I'll hold them off."

Breezepelt instantly stepped forward to stand shoulder to shoulder with her. "I'm not leaving you."

Heathertail gave him a shove. "Go on, mouse-brain. I'll be fine."

Crowfeather could see that Breezepelt was determined not to move. "I think she's right," he meowed. "Come on. We can jump down again if she gets into trouble."

Muttering something under his breath, Breezepelt obeyed. Gorsetail and Hootpaw had already scrambled up the fence and were balancing precariously on the top. Breezepelt joined them, and Crowfeather followed.

Meanwhile Heathertail was bounding to and fro, weaving in front of the dog kits and dodging their pummeling paws. As soon as she saw that her Clanmates were safe, she lashed out with one forepaw, swatting the leading dog kit on the nose.

The dog kit sprang backward; its yapping changed to a high-pitched squeal. The other dog kits' playful yaps became angry, and they advanced, growling, on Heathertail.

But Heathertail was too quick for them. She scrambled up the fence to join the others before any of the dog kits could reach her. At the same moment, the entrance to the den flew open. A Twoleg stood in the gap, yowling furiously.

Crowfeather didn't wait to see what happened next. "Come on," he urged the others, leading the way along the top of the fence until they had put a couple of gardens between them and the pack of dog kits.

"Now what do we do?" Gorsetail asked. "We've lost Nightcloud's trail, and I'm not going back there again."

Breezepelt opened his jaws for a sharp retort, then clearly thought better of it and closed them again, looking miserable.

"Let's check in this garden," Crowfeather suggested, reluctant to give up hope. "This is the direction Nightcloud was going. We might pick up her trail again."

He jumped down from the fence and the rest of the cats followed him. But though they searched the garden from one side to the other, there was no sign of Nightcloud's scent.

We'll have to go back, Crowfeather thought. *Maybe the Twoleg will have taken the dog kits inside.*

But before he could make the suggestion, Heathertail padded up to him and tapped him on the shoulder with one paw. "Look," she mewed, pointing upward with her tail.

Crowfeather raised his head to look where she was pointing. On a ledge a few tail-lengths up the den wall, two kittypets were sleeping. One was a plump tortoiseshell with a rumpled pelt, while the other was a black tom with a white front and paws.

"Kittypets," he muttered. "So?"

"They might have seen Nightcloud!"

Crowfeather realized that Heathertail was right. *I'm so tired, I'm getting stupid!* Without hesitating he leaped up onto the ledge and prodded the plump tortoiseshell in her side. "Hey, kittypet! Wake up."

The tortoiseshell's eyes blinked open, and she fixed an unfriendly gaze on Crowfeather. "Whoever you are, shove off. I'm sleeping," she responded. Her nose wrinkled as if she didn't like Crowfeather's unfamiliar scent.

Crowfeather prodded again, harder. "Not anymore. We need to talk."

By now the black tom was awake too. "Who are you, and what do you want?" he asked irritably. "Don't you know it's very rude to wake up a sleeping cat?"

Before Crowfeather could reply, Heathertail called up from the garden. "Sorry for disturbing you, but we need your help." To Crowfeather she added, "Politeness costs nothing," and then in a lower voice, just loud enough for him to hear, "You daft furball!" *What about politeness to your former mentor?* he thought.

While he waited for the kittypets to reply, Crowfeather tasted the air and thought that he could pick up Nightcloud's scent, stronger than the traces in the forest and beside the Thunderpath. His paws tingled with anticipation. *She must be somewhere around here! Or am I just imagining things?*

The tortoiseshell kittypet looked from Crowfeather to Heathertail and back again. "Okay, what can we do for you?" she muttered ungraciously.

"We're looking for one of our friends," Heathertail explained, while her other Clanmates, who were still searching the garden, padded up to join her and listen.

"A cat called Yew said she came this way," Crowfeather added. "Do you know him?"

"You?" The tortoiseshell stretched her jaws in an enormous yawn. "Like 'Hey, You'?"

"Like the *tree*," Crowfeather responded, stifling a *mrrow* of amusement.

"Weird name," the tortoiseshell sniffed. "No, we don't know him."

"Our friend is black, and quite thin," Crowfeather continued, looking at the tortoiseshell's rounded figure. "And she was probably bleeding from a wound."

"Have you seen her?" Breezepelt asked eagerly.

"Oh, yeah, we've seen *her*," the black-and-white tom mewed, with a glance at the tortoiseshell, who gave a brief nod.

Crowfeather felt a surge of relief, and could see it was shared by his Clanmates in the garden below. Hootpaw leaped into the air and let out a triumphant caterwaul. "Yes! We found her!" For once, no cat told him to keep quiet.

"She turned up quite some time ago, in the garden next door." The tom angled his ears in the direction from which the Clan cats had come. "She was weird. . . . She kept meowing on about returning to her 'Clan.' She said her 'Clanmates' would be looking for her."

"And she wouldn't play stalking with us," the she-cat added. "She said she was a 'warrior,' and that was a game for kits."

"What's weird about that?" Breezepelt asked, bristling. "*We're* her Clanmates, and we're looking for her. We've come to take her home."

The two kittypets exchanged a surprised glance; Crowfeather thought they were impressed to hear that Nightcloud had been telling the truth.

"We thought she must have hit her head," the tortoiseshell admitted. "She was talking about all sorts of crazy things, like cats made of *stars*! And fighting against cats who were already dead! Who would believe that?"

Crowfeather sighed. *How stupid are these two? They have no idea about StarClan—living with Twolegs must make them blind.* "So where is she now?" he asked brusquely.

"The housefolk next door took her in," the tom replied. "And they'll probably be glad to be rid of her. She's so prickly, no gratitude at all—always trying to scratch them and escape."

She's still next door? For a moment Crowfeather found it hard to get his breath. He could hardly believe that they were so close to Nightcloud, after so long and coming so far. *But I knew it! I did scent her!*

"Thank you," he mewed to the kittypets. "We'll leave you to sleep."

"Thank goodness for that," the tortoiseshell responded, wrapping her tail over her nose and closing her eyes.

"Good luck," the tom meowed.

Crowfeather leaped down from the ledge to join his Clanmates. The fence that divided this garden from the one beside it had gaps between the flat wooden strips, and it was easy for the WindClan cats to slip through.

As soon as they emerged into the next garden, they picked up Nightcloud's scent again, but there was no sign of her.

"The kittypets said she's always trying to escape,"

Heathertail pointed out. "That means the Twolegs must be keeping her in their den."

Hootpaw let out a gasp. "You mean we have to go . . . *in* there?" Looking at his wide eyes and bristling pelt, Crowfeather couldn't decide whether the apprentice was delighted or terrified.

"Maybe," he replied. "We have to find Nightcloud first."

Scanning the Twoleg den, Crowfeather spotted a huge gap in the wall, starting at ground level and rising up several tail-lengths above his head. It was blocked by the shiny, transparent stuff that Twolegs used to plug holes in their walls, but he had never seen a hole so big.

Cautiously Crowfeather padded up to the gap, beckoning with his tail for his Clanmates to follow him.

Peering through the transparent stuff, Crowfeather was confused at first; he needed a moment to make sense of what he was seeing. But then he ignored the strange Twoleg material and focused on something that was more familiar: a nest, though instead of moss and bracken, this one seemed to be made of interlaced twigs and lined with soft white bedding.

Inside the nest was Nightcloud. She was curled up asleep. Crowfeather could see her sleek black body rising and falling as she breathed: strong, steady breaths that showed she must have recovered from her injuries. A weird, white object, like a curled, hard leaf, surrounded her head.

"Thank StarClan!" he breathed out, so relieved to see a familiar form that he had thought he would never see again. *Nightcloud!*

"Oh, she's safe!" Breezepelt's voice shook as he pressed

himself up against the shiny barrier.

Then Nightcloud shifted in her sleep, the leaf-object bumping against her soft bedding. Crowfeather gaped in astonishment as he picked up the scent of a second cat, and saw that what he'd thought was bedding, like some sort of Twoleg moss, was another cat curled up in the nest with her—a fluffy white kittypet.

A kittypet *tom*!

CHAPTER 24

For a moment Crowfeather stood frozen, thrown seriously off balance by the appearance of the kittypet tom. Surprise flashed through him, along with a twinge of jealousy that he didn't want to admit to. The excited murmuring of his Clanmates made him pull himself together. At least they were too focused on Nightcloud to have seen his reaction.

His companions crowded up to the barrier, banging against it with their forepaws. At last Nightcloud stirred, raised her head, then sprang out of the nest and bounded over to join them, her expression filled with the shock of recognition. The strange white leaf still clung to her neck, surrounding her face. Crowfeather supposed it was some Twoleg trickery that Nightcloud couldn't take off.

The barrier was divided into two parts with a shiny strip running down the middle. There was a tiny gap between the two sections, and Nightcloud stretched her neck out of the white leaf and thrust her nose into the gap so that she could speak to her Clanmates.

"Well, you certainly took your time finding me," she mewed, though Crowfeather could see from her shining eyes that she was happy and excited to see them.

Disturbed by Nightcloud's movement and the noise of their meows, the white tom woke up and left the nest to pad up behind her. The grumpy look on his squashed-in face showed that he didn't share Nightcloud's happiness.

"Hello there," he mewed. "What's all this?"

Every cat ignored his question. Crowfeather didn't spare him more than a disdainful glance, taking in his plump body and his long, perfectly groomed white fur. "How can we get you out of here?" he asked Nightcloud.

"This door slides open," Nightcloud explained, waving her tail at the transparent barrier. "Maybe if we push . . ."

"It's worth a try," Breezepelt agreed, with an eager twitch of his whiskers.

"Hey, be careful," the white tom warned them. "You mustn't break our housefolk's things. And who did you say you were, again?"

Nightcloud gave him a dismissive flick of her tail. "Not now," she meowed. "I'll explain in a moment."

Crowfeather and the others pushed from outside, and Nightcloud from inside, but there was nowhere to get a grip with their paws, and the barrier didn't move.

"This is no use," Breezepelt mewed at last, huffing out a breath as he stood back. Crowfeather thought that his enthusiasm was waning, as if he was beginning to doubt that he would be reunited with his mother after all. "We need a different plan."

"We need to get the Twolegs to open it," Crowfeather responded.

"But the Twolegs will be asleep," Heathertail pointed out.

"That's right," the white tom put in. "And they *really* don't like it if we wake them."

Crowfeather bared his teeth. "Fox dung to that. If we need to wake them, we wake them."

"I know how!" Hootpaw squealed, bouncing excitedly. "I can yowl *really* loud!"

"Okay, then—" Crowfeather began.

He was interrupted by the white tom, who paced forward to stand beside Nightcloud. "Is all this really *necessary*?" he asked her. "Couldn't you just stay with me? You know how dangerous it is out there. Just look at it! There's *snow* on the ground!"

"Well spotted," Crowfeather muttered.

"And look how long it took these cats to come get you," the white tom went on. "Days and days! How much do they really care about you?"

Nightcloud turned slowly to face the kittypet and paused for a long moment. Crowfeather half expected her to give the interfering creature a swat on the nose, but her voice was actually friendly as she replied.

"I'm sorry, Pickle, but I always told you I'm a Clan cat. I belong on the moor."

Pickle? Crowfeather thought. *What sort of name is that for a cat?*

The tom narrowed his eyes and let out a growl; Crowfeather glared at him through the barrier. *Does he think Nightcloud belongs to him?*

For a moment, Nightcloud stood still, giving him a

thoughtful look. "Would you like to join me out there?" she asked eventually.

Join her in WindClan? Crowfeather was outraged, and he saw Breezepelt giving his mother a look of blank astonishment. *What is she thinking of? He's a kittypet! All that silly white fur would get tangled and matted with burrs.*

Crowfeather had to admit he rather enjoyed imagining that.

To his relief, the tom turned his head away awkwardly. "I can't do that," he told Nightcloud. "It's my job to guard the housefolk. That's very important. I can't just up and *leave*."

"I can see that," Nightcloud sighed, sounding as if she was genuinely regretful. "I'm sorry, then, but we'll have to part ways."

Crowfeather shook his head helplessly. *I can't believe I'm listening to this.* "Right," he mewed briskly, turning to his Clanmates. "Heathertail and Hootpaw, you make the loudest noise you can. We have to wake the Twolegs and make them open the door."

"What about me?" Breezepelt asked. He still sounded doubtful that the plan would work.

"You and I are going to watch the Twolegs when they come down, and make sure that once the door is open, they don't stop Nightcloud from coming out."

Breezepelt bared his teeth and flexed his claws, determination driving out his uncertainty. "I can do that."

"Yes, but don't attack them unless you have to," Crowfeather told him. "We don't want to start more trouble than we can handle."

Breezepelt stared at him for a moment, as if he felt like challenging his orders. He opened his jaws, then glanced at Nightcloud and clearly decided that protest wasn't worth it; the most important thing was to get his mother back. He gave Crowfeather a curt nod.

"And me?" Gorsetail mewed.

"You can just keep a general watch, and pile in when you're needed," Crowfeather replied. "Are you ready, Nightcloud?"

"Ready as I'll ever be."

"Okay." Crowfeather's gaze swept around the little group of his Clanmates. "Let's do it."

At once, Heathertail and Hootpaw threw back their heads and let out the most earsplitting caterwauls Crowfeather had ever heard. *I wouldn't be surprised if our Clanmates heard that all the way back in the camp!*

Meanwhile, he and Breezepelt crouched one on either side of the transparent barrier, ready for when the Twolegs would appear. Gorsetail retreated into the shadows of a bush.

The horrible yowling had gone on for several heartbeats before light appeared in one of the gaps in the wall near the top of the Twoleg den. *The Twolegs must have heard us,* Crowfeather thought, his heart beating faster with anticipation.

A moment later, he heard the thump of heavy paw steps, and the space behind the barrier was lit by what looked like a tiny sun, up near the roof. A male Twoleg came into view, wearing some kind of long, loose pelt. A smaller female followed him, and stooped down, reaching inside the white leaf to give Nightcloud's head a stroke. Crowfeather saw her stiffen under the touch, and guessed she was holding herself back from scratching.

"Come on . . . ," Breezepelt muttered. "Open up."

The male Twoleg did something to the shiny strip that separated the two parts of the barrier, then slid one of them back. He stepped out into the garden, yowling something and gazing around to see where the noise was coming from.

Nightcloud sprang to her paws and was about to slip out when the white tom suddenly shifted, sitting back on his haunches and craning his neck upward. Crowfeather felt his neck fur rising as he guessed—too late—what the kittypet was about to do.

A heartbeat later, Pickle let out a caterwaul of his own, almost drowning out the racket from the garden. Immediately the female Twoleg turned toward him, scooping up Nightcloud as she went. Nightcloud struggled in her grip, but couldn't free herself.

"That mange-pelt!" Breezepelt snarled. "He's trying to mess up our plan so Nightcloud has to stay. I'll *slaughter* him!"

Crowfeather blocked him in time to stop him from charging into the den to attack the kittypet. "No—if you go in there you might get trapped," he meowed. "Then we'd have two of you to rescue. Right now, we have to get Nightcloud out."

Breezepelt hesitated for a moment, then dodged around Crowfeather and darted into the den. Instead of attacking Pickle, he veered aside, leaping at the female Twoleg. She let out a screech, stumbling a pace backward. At the same moment Nightcloud wriggled, sliding out of her grasp and landing on the floor with a thump.

"Out! Breezepelt, out!" Crowfeather yowled.

He raced away from the den and the light that spilled out of it, into the shadows at the edge of the garden. Glancing back, he saw that Nightcloud and Breezepelt were following. The male Twoleg made a grab for Nightcloud, but she dodged him and pelted on, while Gorsetail ran between his hind paws, almost tripping him.

Heathertail and Hootpaw gave up their caterwauling and joined them as they fled, with Gorsetail bringing up the rear.

"This is fun!" Hootpaw exclaimed, his eyes shining.

Crowfeather felt a flash of irritation at the way the apprentice was enjoying all this. But then he reflected that at least Hootpaw was getting through a dangerous situation, and playing a useful part, without losing his nerve. *What's the point of scolding him?*

As they reached the fence, Nightcloud turned back for a moment. "I'm sorry, Pickle!" she called back to the white tom.

The cats didn't stop running until they had crossed the Thunderpath again and reached the outskirts of the forest. Then Crowfeather felt it was safe to slow to a walk, though he kept his ears pricked and his nose alert for any sign of the foxes.

Breezepelt was padding along close to his mother, their pelts brushing, hardly watching where he was putting his paws because his gaze was fixed on her. His eyes were full of concern for her, and relief at having her back. Crowfeather thought that they almost looked like a family, although he still

felt apart from the two of them. Breezepelt had never looked
at him that way. And Nightcloud had certainly never looked
at Crowfeather with the love she felt for Breezepelt.

"What happened to you?" he asked Nightcloud. "How did
you end up in that Twoleg den?"

"It's a long story," the black she-cat replied, scratching at
the white leaf thing. "Before we go any farther, get this off me,
will you? I can't do it myself."

Breezepelt and Heathertail teamed up, clawing and biting
at the white thing until they finally tore it off. Crowfeather
padded up to it and gave it a curious sniff. It carried Twoleg
scent, and Nightcloud's, but that didn't tell him very much.
"What was that for?" he asked.

"Pickle told me it was supposed to stop me from messing
with my wound," Nightcloud explained with a disdainful flick
of her tail. "Like I'd be so stupid!"

Crowfeather twitched his whiskers with amusement. "Flea-
brained Twolegs! They think we have the sense of a sparrow."

Nightcloud sighed. "It's maddening. Anyway, I was hurt
fighting the stoats in the tunnels, and I got completely lost in
there. When I finally came out, I realized I was on Thunder-
Clan territory. I was trying to get back to WindClan, but when
I stopped by a pool to have a drink, three foxes surprised me."

"I found that place," Crowfeather told her. "I smelled your
blood and your fear. I thought you must be dead."

"I thought I was headed for StarClan," Nightcloud admitted. "I tried to run away from the stupid mange-pelts, but I
was so hurt and tired they could have caught me easily." She

gave her tail an angry lash. "If the stoats hadn't wounded me, no *way* would those foxes have gotten anywhere near."

"But they didn't hurt you?" Breezepelt looked completely horrified by his mother's story.

Nightcloud gave him a comforting nuzzle. "No. They just made me go the way they wanted. I think they were playing with me. Or maybe if they can get their prey to their den on its own paws, they don't have to carry it, right? I wanted to climb a tree, but I didn't have the strength even to do that."

Heathertail brushed her tail along Nightcloud's side. "That sounds dreadful. How did you get away?"

Nightcloud gave her chest fur an embarrassed lick. "I hate to say this, but it was a Twoleg and his dogs that saved me. They were walking in the forest, and the dogs—two big, stinky things—frightened the foxes away."

"Was that the Twoleg who took you back to his den?" Breezepelt asked.

"No, I ran away, too," Nightcloud told him. "I met a cat called Yew at the edge of the forest, and—"

"I met him, too," Crowfeather interrupted. "That's how we knew to come and search for you in the Twolegplace."

Nightcloud nodded. "Yew is a weird cat, but decent," she mewed. "He's the one who gave me the idea to go ask for help from the Twolegs. 'Just wail pitifully,' he told me, 'and they'll do anything for you.'"

"So what did you do then?" Heathertail asked.

"I took Yew's advice and crossed the Thunderpath into the Twolegplace," Nightcloud replied. "I reckoned the foxes wouldn't dare follow me there. I ended up in the garden of that den where you found me.

"Those Twolegs took me to a den full of disgusting smells. The Twoleg that lived there gave me some kind of round white seed that made me go to sleep. When I woke up, she'd fixed my wound—look."

Nightcloud turned to one side. Looking at her more closely, Crowfeather could see a patch on her side where the fur had been scraped away and was just starting to grow back. In the middle of the bare patch was a long wound, the edges fastened together with tiny scraps of tendril.

"Weird . . . ," he murmured, giving the wound a sniff. "I wonder if Kestrelflight could fix wounds like that?"

Nightcloud shook her head. "Maybe. It seemed terribly complicated. Anyway, then the Twoleg medicine cat put that stupid white thing around my neck," she went on, gesturing at the leaf with her tail.

"And then what happened?" Breezepelt asked. He was gazing at his mother with awe, perhaps at the story she was telling, perhaps still unable to believe that they really had her back at last.

Nightcloud shrugged. "Not much. The Twolegs took me back to their den, and I figured I'd stay there until I felt well enough to escape and come back to camp."

Crowfeather hesitated. He couldn't quite put his paw on what he was feeling, but he knew that he didn't like thinking about the white kittypet, and he wasn't sure he wanted to know the answer to the question he was about to ask. "What about that tom?" he meowed at last.

"Pickle?" Nightcloud let out a small *mrrow* of laughter. "He was my friend. He was nice, for a kittypet."

Nice? A kittypet? Crowfeather stared hard at his former mate. *How badly were you hurt? Or has the Twoleg medicine done something to your mind?*

Clearly Nightcloud wasn't prepared to say any more, and at last Crowfeather let his gaze soften. "I'm impressed you survived all that," he declared.

"Of course I did. I'm a WindClan warrior, aren't I?"

A slightly awkward silence fell as the cats padded wearily through the trees. Looking up, Crowfeather could see the tracery of leafless branches outlined more clearly against the sky, and realized that dawn was not far off.

How will Onestar react when I return to camp? He won't be happy that I went after Nightcloud without telling him, and brought these cats with me. . . . I can only hope he won't be too angry with me when he sees we've brought Nightcloud home.

It was Nightcloud who broke the silence at last. "I'm surprised you came for me."

Crowfeather's heart clenched and he felt his pelt grow hot. Slightly stung, he repeated her own words. "Of course I did."

"We never would have given up on you," Breezepelt put in.

"I know *you* never would," Nightcloud meowed, giving his ear a quick nuzzle.

A pang of jealousy and guilt shook Crowfeather as he watched his former mate and his son. He envied both of them, and their easy affection with each other. And Nightcloud was right . . . he *had* given up on her. He had been right when he'd thought that they weren't really a family. *I don't belong with them. I wish . . . but it's no use wishing.*

The sky was glowing with the approach of sunrise by the time the WindClan cats crossed the ThunderClan border. Crowfeather explained how they had met Ivypool and her patrol on their way out, and had permission to cross on the way back.

Nightcloud looked unimpressed. "So that's why you all stink of ThunderClan!" She gave a disdainful sniff. "I'm not sure I trust ThunderClan to keep their promises," she added. "It's best if we don't meet any of their cats."

Crowfeather agreed, and the patrol slunk cautiously across the rival Clan's territory, making use of every scrap of cover. When they came in sight of the border stream, Hootpaw started forward, ready to dash up to the bank and leap across, but Gorsetail sprang in front of him and blocked him.

"Wait, mouse-brain!" the gray-and-white she-cat hissed.

Crowfeather halted and tasted the air. "The ThunderClan scent markers are stale," he reported. "That means the dawn patrol hasn't been along yet. I think it would be safer to wait until they've passed."

Nightcloud nodded. "Good idea. And we could all do with a rest."

Crowfeather led the way into the shelter of a bank of ferns, where he and his Clanmates crouched with ears pricked for the approach of the ThunderClan cats. Breezepelt and Heather-tail settled down on either side of Nightcloud, masking her scent with the smell of ThunderClan that still clung to their fur.

"Where are they?" Breezepelt muttered. "All snoring in their nests?"

At last Crowfeather heard the sound of voices and felt the ground quiver from approaching paw steps. Peering cautiously out from underneath the ferns, he spotted the Thunder-Clan patrol padding by, with Dustpelt in the lead. Every cat paused, a tail-length from the WindClan cats' hiding place, while Poppyfrost set a scent marker at the edge of the stream. Crowfeather hardly dared to breathe.

Finally the patrol moved on; Crowfeather waited, limp with relief, until he had given them time enough to get well away. He emerged from the clump of ferns, signaling with his tail for the others to follow him. Swiftly they headed for the bank, then leaped across the stream, pelted through the trees, and burst out onto the moor.

"Thank StarClan! We're home!" Heathertail gasped.

Home, Crowfeather thought. *But is it mine? Will Onestar have me back?*

He had little time to muse on this, because the rest of the journey back to camp was a long and arduous trudge through the snow. By now the sun had risen, and every cat was exhausted; Crowfeather felt as if his paws were going to fall off. He couldn't remember the last time he had slept, and he began to feel a squirming like worms in his belly when he wondered how Onestar would react to his return. *I'd like to find the fattest rabbit on the fresh-kill pile, then curl up in my den and sleep for a moon!* he told himself. *But I'll probably find myself wandering about on the moor again.*

But as he and his Clanmates drew closer to the camp, Crowfeather began to feel even more uneasy. He thought he could hear the voices of cats raised in distress. And as the wind veered around to blow straight at them from the camp, it brought a foul odor along with it.

Crowfeather had to stop himself from retching. "What *is* that?" he demanded.

CHAPTER 25

No cat responded to Crowfeather's question. For a heartbeat they gazed at one another with a terrible realization, then turned as one and raced over the last swell of the moor, until they reached the top of the hollow.

"Oh, StarClan, no!" Heathertail exclaimed.

Looking down into the camp, Crowfeather saw a scene of complete devastation. Bedding from the nests was scattered everywhere, and the gorse bushes that sheltered the nursery and the elders' den were half torn away. Worst of all, the center of the camp seemed to be covered with the bodies of injured cats; Crowfeather couldn't tell how many of them might have been dead. The reek of blood filled the air, along with a lingering, horrible, familiar smell.

Crowfeather's belly clenched in panic. *The stoats have attacked!*

He led the way down into the camp, flinching at the heavy scent of fear and blood. The first cat they came to was Emberfoot, who was lying on his side and bleeding from a deep scratch down his flank.

As Crowfeather and the patrol approached him, Emberfoot raised his head and fixed them with an angry glare.

"Onestar!" he yowled. "They're back!"

The WindClan leader emerged from his den and stalked across the camp, weaving his way through the bodies of his Clanmates. Crowfeather noticed a large, angry-looking wound on his neck and shoulder, and for a moment he couldn't focus on anything else. *What happened here?*

Then he saw that Onestar's eyes were narrowed in fury as he halted in front of Crowfeather and the others.

"How *dare* you leave camp without telling me?" he snarled. Crowfeather realized that the Clan leader wasn't looking at him; his anger was directed toward Breezepelt, Heathertail, and Gorsetail. "You may have noticed," he continued, waving his tail to indicate the wrecked camp, "that the stoats attacked us during the night. They were able to do this because"—he glared at Heathertail—"our border was not being watched."

The she-cat's blue eyes shimmered with shame, as she dipped her head. But Crowfeather could tell, she didn't dare speak.

"It was a terrible battle!" Onestar went on. "It took a long time to drive them away, and many, many cats were injured."

Crowfeather gazed around the camp and at the bodies of his Clanmates strewn on the ground. Some had only minor wounds, though others were barely able to move. Onestar wasn't exaggerating. This was a serious attack.

"It was my idea to—" he began, but the Clan leader ignored him, as if he hadn't spoken, or even as if he weren't there.

"If you had been here, as you were *supposed* to be," One-star went on, "you could have helped fight back. Three more warriors would have made a difference."

Guilt flooded over Crowfeather as he realized that his Clan leader was right. He was glad that his companions, especially Hootpaw, had avoided being injured in the battle, but he knew that they should have been there, doing their duty as warriors. "I'm sorry," he meowed, letting his tail droop. "It's my fault. I took them away from camp. But I had a good reason for it." He stepped aside and Nightcloud came forward.

Onestar gazed wide-eyed at the black she-cat, who dipped her head in greeting. "It's good to see you again, Onestar."

"It's even better to see you," the Clan leader mewed, his voice still heavy with tension, like a storm cloud before it breaks. "Are you well?"

"I am now," Nightcloud replied. "Thanks to them." She waved her tail at the others.

"I'm glad to hear it," Onestar responded. "I thought we'd lost you for good. Later you can tell me the whole story, but just now there's far too much to do." He then turned back to the others. His voice rose to a menacing growl. "I am Clan leader, and you had no right to sneak off. You—"

Onestar broke off as his gaze fell on Heathertail, who was standing at the back of the group, looking down at her paws. "Heathertail, when I couldn't find you after the battle, I thought the stoats had gotten you. How do you think I felt then?"

At that, Heathertail jerked up her head. "I'm sorry," she meowed. "But I *had* to go. I wanted to help."

"That's very noble," Onestar responded, sounding as if he

wasn't sure whether to be furious with her or just glad that she was home safe. "But it doesn't excuse any of you from breaking the warrior code. You could have cost cats' *lives* by not being here. You *did* cost one cat's life. Mine."

"What?" Gorsetail asked, her fur suddenly bushing up with alarm.

"Look at this," Onestar meowed, pointing to his own wound with his tail. "The stoats did that, and robbed me of a life."

Crowfeather closed his eyes briefly, feeling as if he were being drenched in icy water. His Clanmates' absence had been responsible for his leader's losing a life. *Could this get any worse?* When a cat became Clan leader, they received nine lives from StarClan, but when they had to lead their Clan into the worst of every danger, they couldn't afford to throw any of those lives away. *I don't know how many lives Onestar has left, but it can't be many.*

Crowfeather wanted to defend himself and his Clanmates, to point out they'd had no idea the stoats would attack, but looking at the fury in Onestar's face, he knew that would be a very bad idea.

But Breezepelt wasn't so tactful. "It's not our fault!" he retorted. "If you had let us finish blocking the tunnels, like Harespring wanted, instead of traipsing back to camp once it got dark, the stoats couldn't have gotten out—at least not on our side."

Crowfeather stared at his leader, feeling oddly left out. *Harespring wanted to finish blocking the tunnels, but Onestar said no?*

All the things Breezepelt described had happened while he was gone. And he felt an unexpected sadness at the realization that Clan life had gone on without him.

It was clear, too, that Onestar had made the wrong decision. He shivered at the thought of what might have happened. *In a way, we're lucky that the stoats didn't attack ThunderClan,* he thought. *Bramblestar would have been just as furious as Onestar, and we don't need any more trouble from him.*

Onestar fixed his gaze on Breezepelt. "The last time I looked, you weren't Clan leader, or even deputy," he snarled. "I thought you had learned your lesson after the Great Battle, but now I'm not so sure. Are you a loyal WindClan cat?" he demanded.

"Of course I am," Breezepelt replied without hesitation.

"Then you'd better start *acting* like it," Onestar snapped. "I'll be keeping my eye on you!"

Breezepelt opened his jaws to defend himself, but Heathertail slapped her tail across his mouth and gave him a warning shake of the head. Breezepelt subsided, the familiar sullen look settling over his face.

Gazing at his son, Crowfeather felt as small and miserable as a wet kit. *I just wanted to save Nightcloud. I never meant to get Breezepelt into trouble again. Especially now, when he's been doing so well.*

Onestar sighed, clearly trying to control himself. "I don't have time to stand here and yowl at you," he mewed.

Could have fooled me, Crowfeather thought.

"We have to rebuild the camp and help the injured cats," the Clan leader went on. "Heathertail, you can help Kestrelflight in the medicine-cat den. He's completely overwhelmed. Breezepelt, Gorsetail—you can help rebuild the camp. Furzepelt and Leaftail are in charge, so report to them."

As the three warriors moved away obediently, Onestar paused for a moment, gazing down at Hootpaw, who gazed back at him; Crowfeather guessed he was bravely trying not to flinch, or shrink away. "I'm not going to punish an apprentice for following his mentor," Onestar growled. "But you'd better think about what you did, going behind your leader's back, and show *better judgment* in future."

Hootpaw gave a nervous nod, then scurried off to join the other apprentices, who were gathering up the scattered bedding. Crowfeather watched him go, and heard his excited squeak as he joined his denmates.

"We found Nightcloud and rescued her from Twolegs! And we climbed trees and fought foxes and crossed a Thunderpath. It was *amazing*!"

Crowfeather stifled a *mrrow* of amusement. *I hope Onestar didn't hear that.*

Onestar, meanwhile, had turned to Nightcloud.

"I'm truly glad to see you back with us," he meowed. "You've always been a loyal WindClan warrior. Later there'll be time for us to talk about what happened to you, but for now you should go and rest while we clear up the camp."

"Thank you," Nightcloud responded with a respectful dip of her head. "But I don't need to rest. For the last quarter moon, I've been living the life of a kittypet—*not* my choice, I'm sure you understand—with nothing to do except lie around all day and stuff myself with kittypet food."

Onestar gave her a curious look, as if he would have liked to ask her more, but said nothing.

"I'd like to do my part," Nightcloud continued. "You said Kestrelflight is overwhelmed—perhaps he could use my help, too."

Onestar gave her an approving nod and stepped back a few paces. Crowfeather stared at him, dreading what his Clan leader might say to him, but also desperately needing to hear it. *Am I allowed back or not?* Onestar's expression was unreadable.

Crowfeather turned nervously to Nightcloud. Now that their adventure was over, he wasn't sure what to say to her. He had shared so much with this cat, and yet he still felt uncomfortable around her. *If I'm still banished from the Clan, this might be the last time I ever speak to her.*

While Crowfeather was trying to gather his thoughts, Nightcloud gave an angry flick of her tail. "Don't worry," she mewed. "It's not like you have to *talk* to me or anything."

Without waiting for a reply, she strode off toward the medicine-cat den.

Crowfeather felt as if he were sinking down into the ground. *I blew that. Here I've been doing so well with Breezepelt, but I still don't know what to say to Nightcloud.* As his gaze followed her across the camp, he wondered, *Have I learned anything at all?* Crowfeather's sense of guilt loomed over him like a storm cloud as he reflected on all the things he had never realized about his former mate: how brave and industrious she was, how well she had trained Hootpaw, how she had found the patience to be kind to a *kittypet*. He didn't understand how he could ever have been mates with a cat he felt like he barely knew.

As Nightcloud disappeared into Kestrelflight's den, Crowfeather realized that Onestar was standing at his shoulder. "Well, Crowfeather," he sighed. "What am I going to do with you?"

Crowfeather turned to face his Clan leader, once again not knowing what to say. Every hair in his pelt started to rise at the thought of apologizing, when he knew he had been right to ask for ThunderClan's help, right to challenge Onestar about blocking up the tunnels. But at the same time his heart quailed when he imagined himself walking out of the camp again, a cat without a Clan.

"I never intended—" he began.

At the same moment, Onestar spoke. "Crowfeather, you're the worst cat I've ever known for getting under my fur. But I have to admit that this time, you might have had a point. I shouldn't have tried to block the tunnels."

Crowfeather stared at him, scarcely able to believe what he had just heard. *Is he apologizing to me?*

Onestar looked down at his paws, digging his claws into the ground. "Do you want to come back?" he asked, not meeting Crowfeather's gaze.

Crowfeather wanted to yowl, "Yes!" but he made himself appear calm, and dipped his head respectfully to his Clan leader. "Yes, I'd like that, Onestar," he mewed.

"Then you are a WindClan cat again." Onestar raised his head, and his voice dropped into a menacing growl. "I'm welcoming you back because you rescued Nightcloud, and because the Clan needs every able-bodied warrior. But there's a border, Crowfeather, between being difficult and being disloyal. Make sure that your paws stay on the right side of that border."

Crowfeather tried to sound humble. "I will, Onestar."

"Then get yourself over to Kestrelflight and ask him what you can do. And Crowfeather—see that I don't have to remind you about this conversation. Ever."

Crowfeather was crouching outside Kestrelflight's den, chewing a mouthful of marigold for a poultice to put on Sedge-whisker's wound. Sunhigh was just past, and he felt exhausted in his mind and body. The work was hard, and pain tore at his heart to see the injuries among his Clanmates. The air was filled with the scents of blood and fear, almost overwhelming Crowfeather, and his ears ached from the continual yowling of injured cats. There were too many wounds, and not enough herbs, and Kestrelflight had to make tough choices about which cats needed treatment most urgently.

"I still can't believe those stoats are pure white," Crouch-foot muttered; he was sitting nearby, licking one forepaw where a claw had been torn away. "Except for the black tips to their tails. Whoever saw an animal like that before?"

"Maybe they *are* ghosts after all," Whiskernose suggested, twitching his whiskers as blood trickled down from a wound in his ear. "Its almost like they have something personal against WindClan."

"Nonsense!" Kestrelflight, who had been out on the moor collecting more herbs, halted beside the two toms and mumbled around the bunch of chervil in his jaws. "They're not ghosts. They're just stinky, aggressive invaders."

Crouchfoot and Whiskernose looked at each other but didn't respond.

All around the medicine-cat den, cats were moaning in pain. Crowfeather felt even more guilty that there was so little he could do to help. *I should have gone to the Twolegplace by myself,* he thought. *I'm glad we found Nightcloud, but Breezepelt and the others would have been more use here. Maybe with more warriors, there wouldn't have been so many cats wounded.* Then he admitted to himself that he would never have managed the hazardous journey through the forest and the Twolegplace if he had been alone. *This must be the way it was meant to happen.*

Kestrelflight stumbled as he approached the den, letting his bundle of chervil fall. His eyes were dull with weariness.

"Sit down," Crowfeather meowed. "For StarClan's sake, you need to rest. You've been up all night."

Kestrelflight let his gaze travel over the camp and the mass of injured cats, then shook his head. "I can't. There's far too much to do."

"We'll be in even more trouble if you pass out," Crowfeather told him. *"Sit down."*

Letting out a long sigh, Kestrelflight obeyed. His eyes were full of despair as he looked at the injured cats who were still waiting for his help. "I'm not sure I can do this alone," he whispered. "Well—not alone," he corrected himself at once, ducking his head apologetically at Heathertail and Nightcloud, who appeared at that moment with mouthfuls of dripping moss. "But I'm the only medicine cat. . . ."

"We need help," Crowfeather declared, suddenly realizing how true that was. "There are too many injured warriors, and not enough medicine cats or herbs. We need help from another Clan."

"You're right." Kestrelflight rose to his paws again with another heartfelt sigh. "But Onestar will never agree to it."

Crowfeather glanced across the camp to where Onestar was supervising the work on the warriors' den. He remembered the last time he had gone to ThunderClan for help, and how badly that had turned out. Crowfeather's instinct was to blame Onestar for being unreasonable, but he had to admit to himself that he had been to blame, too. He shouldn't have brought in ThunderClan without knowing how Onestar would react.

Now, when WindClan really needed ThunderClan, Crowfeather knew that his earlier rashness had made everything harder. But he knew too that he had no alternative: He had to convince Onestar to send for Leafpool or Jayfeather.

It'll be hard to convince him, he thought, *and it's going to be even harder to convince Bramblestar, after he was insulted when he came here to talk to Onestar—not to mention hearing from Ivypool that WindClan trespassed on his territory. But ThunderClan is the obvious choice to ask. They're closest.*

Crowfeather rose to his paws. "Leave this to me," he meowed.

His paws prickling with apprehension, Crowfeather padded over to his Clan leader. He couldn't forget that he had only just been allowed back into the Clan, and part of the reason he'd been banished was because he had asked for help from ThunderClan. And now he was about to ask permission to do the same.

I'll have to tread really carefully. . . .

"Well?" Onestar asked, turning toward him as Crowfeather approached. His voice and his expression were as icy as a frost-bound stream. "What is it now?"

"I'm sorry for persuading Breezepelt and the others to leave camp," Crowfeather began, hoping that he could bring Onestar into a better mood. "I only did it because I was so worried about Nightcloud. Once I was sure she was alive, I just couldn't leave her to fend for herself, or let my son go on suffering, wondering if she was out there somewhere, in pain. But now I see that what we did left the Clan vulnerable."

A growl rose from deep in Onestar's throat; clearly the Clan leader was unimpressed by Crowfeather's apology. But Crowfeather was relieved to see that at least he seemed to be listening.

"I've been thinking about what we ought to do now," Crowfeather continued. "We only have one medicine cat, and he's overstretched. If we're not careful, he's going to collapse. We need to ask medicine cats from other Clans to help us."

Onestar's tail shot straight up in the air, and he bristled until each hair on his pelt looked like a hedgehog's spike. "Do you have bees in your brain?" he demanded. "Haven't you learned anything? How bad will it look, to ask for ThunderClan's help after I sent them away? Do you want WindClan to seem weak?"

"WindClan *is* weak at the moment," Crowfeather retorted. "We need more skilled cats and more herbs. Okay, we might have to ask ThunderClan's forgiveness, but surely it's worth a bit of groveling? *Please*, Onestar. Cats' lives are at stake."

Onestar was silent, but he let his tail relax and flexed his claws indecisively.

"Isn't protecting WindClan the most important thing?" Crowfeather prompted him. "Emberfoot has a serious wound and needs poppy seed for the pain, but Kestrelflight just used the last of it. Whiskernose and Sedgewhisker need poultices, but there's no cobweb left to hold them in place. Kestrelflight can't go looking for supplies *and* treat the wounded."

While he was speaking, Crowfeather saw Onestar's hostile expression gradually change, and his fur lie flat again. For a few heartbeats he still said nothing, gazing thoughtfully at his paws. Aware of the moments slipping by, Crowfeather wanted to press him for an answer, but he realized that the most sensible thing he could do just then was to keep his mouth shut.

At last Onestar gave a slow, reluctant nod. "Very well," he mewed. "I'll send cats to RiverClan to ask for Mothwing's help."

"And ThunderClan," Crowfeather added. Though he wasn't surprised that Onestar wanted to avoid apologizing to Bramblestar, he knew that one Clan's help might not be enough. "They are close too, and we need all the help we can get."

Onestar sighed, his gaze probing deep into Crowfeather's

eyes. "That's true enough. All right," he agreed. "If you think you can convince them . . . very well. You may go."

Crowfeather dipped his head in thanks to Onestar. As he turned away, he couldn't help feeling pleased: That had been a difficult conversation, but he'd gotten through it successfully.

And it's a good thing, he thought, *because this next conversation is going to be even harder. . . .*

CHAPTER 26

❧

Crowfeather bounded across the moor with Harespring at his side, wondering what he could say to Bramblestar. Hope of finding help for his Clan had given him fresh energy, and he felt that he could face ThunderClan whatever happened. Knowing that Breezepelt and Gorsetail were on their way to River-Clan strengthened him, too. Mistystar had no reason to be hostile to WindClan, so they could at least count on her to send Mothwing or Willowshine. *No WindClan cats will die today.*

Reaching the border stream, Crowfeather and Hare-spring halted. "We'd better wait for a patrol," Crowfeather meowed, peering into the trees at the opposite side. "We don't want to start off by trespassing. That would really get under their fur."

Harespring didn't reply, though Crowfeather became aware that the deputy was gazing at him. He turned toward him and saw that Harespring was shaking his head slightly. "What?" he asked.

"You're more optimistic than I am, if you think you can convince ThunderClan to help us after the way Bramblestar and Onestar confronted each other," Harespring responded.

"What were you *thinking*, going to ThunderClan without Onestar's permission?"

"I was thinking that I wanted to do what was right for WindClan," Crowfeather replied. "Even if that wasn't what Onestar wanted. Isn't the whole Clan more important than any one cat—even if that cat is the Clan leader?"

"Of course it is." Harespring sat down at the edge of the stream, flicking his ears thoughtfully. "But Onestar *is* our leader. We might disagree with him, but in the end we must listen to him."

Crowfeather blinked at Harespring, realizing he had nothing to say to that. "I suppose going to ThunderClan wasn't my smartest move," he meowed. He hesitated before he went on, knowing there was something he had to say to Harespring, however much he might not like admitting it. "Onestar was right to make you his deputy, Harespring. I know now that I still have more to learn."

Harespring's whiskers arched in surprise. "I've always felt it should have been you, Crowfeather. I'm glad you feel you can accept me."

Crowfeather dipped his head in acknowledgment. "Anyway," he added, trying to lighten the mood, "you must have bees in your brain if you think that ThunderClan would *turn down* the chance to get tangled up in another Clan's affairs."

Harespring's tail curled up in amusement. "You could be right," he agreed.

"Leafpool will help, if I can only meet with her," Crowfeather mewed, hoping that he would be able to speak to

Leafpool this time. *Jayfeather will be even more hostile now, if we have to plead with him.*

Harespring hesitated before replying, and Crowfeather thought he was looking slightly awkward. His paws shifted uncomfortably, and when he spoke, his voice was a low murmur. "Is it strange," he asked eventually, "talking to Leafpool after all this time? I know that you two used to be close."

"Close"? That's putting it mildly! Crowfeather thought. *Do I still have feelings for Leafpool?* But then he thought of all that had happened in the seasons they'd been apart. They led separate lives now, and the idea of being together seemed even more impossible than it had seasons ago, when they'd tried to run away. He no longer felt an ache when he imagined Leafpool without him. Now he felt only admiration, and hope that she was happy.

He shrugged. "All that is in the past," he replied. "But I still respect Leafpool, and I think she'll want to help a Clan in need."

Deep in conversation with Harespring, Crowfeather was startled a moment later when a ThunderClan patrol emerged from the other side of a nettle patch. Poppyfrost was in the lead, with her apprentice, Lilypaw, while Birchfall brought up the rear. Crowfeather realized that while he and the deputy had been talking, he had forgotten to keep watch on the far bank of the stream. *Mouse-brain!* he scolded himself.

Harespring rose to his paws; both he and Crowfeather dipped their heads respectfully to the ThunderClan cats.

"Greetings," Harespring meowed. "May we come across?

We need to speak to Bramblestar."

Poppyfrost regarded them with narrowed eyes. "You again, Crowfeather? You're spending more time in ThunderClan territory than in your own."

"I was very grateful for permission to cross," Crowfeather responded, biting back a sarcastic retort. "We found Nightcloud. She's fine, and she's home now."

The ThunderClan cats looked surprised, and a little pleased, relaxing from their first suspicious demeanor. Crowfeather realized that no Clan cat would like to think of another lost and injured, even though she belonged to a different Clan. Ivypool had been concerned, too, and all the Clans had joined together to help one another against the Dark Forest.

We're Clan cats. It's what we do.

"Good," Poppyfrost mewed. "So why are you here now?"

"We have a request to make of Bramblestar," Harespring replied.

Poppyfrost stared at him until she seemingly realized that Harespring wasn't going to reveal the request.

"Let them come," Birchfall prompted her. "It might be important."

Poppyfrost hesitated a moment longer, then nodded. "I suppose two cats aren't an invasion," she decided. "Okay, come over."

The stream here was too wide to leap, but shallow enough to wade through. Crowfeather padded forward cautiously, flinching at the cold feeling of water on his belly fur, though he was grateful for the refreshing touch on his tired paws. *It feels like moons since I've been able to rest.*

On the other side both cats shook their pelts, being careful not to splatter the ThunderClan patrol, and at Poppyfrost's command followed them through the trees in the direction of the ThunderClan camp.

When they arrived in the stone hollow, the whole Clan seemed to be out in the open. Purdy was stretched out in front of the elders' den, telling a story to Seedpaw while the apprentice searched him for ticks. Several warriors, including the deputy, Squirrelflight, were gossiping by the fresh-kill pile. Brightheart and Daisy were enjoying the pale leaf-bare sun beside the entrance to the nursery, while Brightheart's three kits wrestled and rolled about nearby.

It seemed to Crowfeather that as soon as he and Harespring had emerged from the thorn tunnel and advanced a few paces into the camp, the gaze of every cat was trained on them. *They don't look friendly, either. Every cat must know what Onestar said to Bramblestar.*

"Wait here," Poppyfrost ordered them curtly.

She raced across the camp and bounded up the tumbled rocks that led to Bramblestar's den halfway up the camp wall. Crowfeather exchanged a glance with Harespring.

"Let me do the talking," the deputy meowed. "And for StarClan's sake, don't say anything to annoy Bramblestar."

"I'm not stupid," Crowfeather muttered.

A moment later, Bramblestar appeared from his den and picked his way down the rocks to the camp floor. As he approached, Crowfeather could see that he seemed surprised and wary; his amber eyes were cold as he looked the two WindClan cats up and down.

"Why are you here?" he asked.

Harespring dipped his head respectfully. "Greetings, Bramblestar. We've come to ask for ThunderClan's help. We need a medicine cat."

Bramblestar was silent for a moment, his gaze flicking from Harespring to Crowfeather and back again. "You need a medicine cat," he repeated. "You're asking for our help, after Onestar insulted me when I came to *offer* my help with the stoats?"

"We've had more trouble with them," Harespring responded. "Many of our cats are injured."

Bramblestar hesitated for a heartbeat, then turned to Squirrelflight, who had padded up to stand at her leader's shoulder. "I don't want any cat to suffer," he meowed. "Fetch Leafpool and Jayfeather, please."

As Squirrelflight left, Bramblestar faced the WindClan cats again, giving his whiskers a disdainful twitch. "Tell me exactly what happened."

Harespring hesitated, casting an uncertain glance at Crowfeather, who could share his tension, knowing what Bramblestar's reaction was likely to be. "We came up with a plan to deal with the stoats," Harespring admitted at last. "We blocked up the tunnel entrances on our side, but that only made them angry. They attacked our camp last night. We—"

"So you *haven't* dealt with the stoats?" Bramblestar's voice was a hiss of fury, and the fur on his muscular shoulders began to rise. "I suppose it didn't occur to you that if you blocked up the tunnels at your end, that would drive the stoats out into ThunderClan territory? Or did you realize that, but you just didn't care? It never crossed your mind that you might warn us?" He let out an angry snort. "I thought Onestar was an *experienced* leader. He said he had this under control!"

Harespring couldn't find words to reply, merely flexing his claws in the earth floor of the camp. Crowfeather thought that the silence would stretch out forever. *I'm glad Harespring is doing the talking. I wouldn't know what to say to that, either.*

He was aware that the rest of the Clan was gathering around, their ears pricked eagerly to listen to this confrontation. *The whole of ThunderClan will know how badly we've handled this!*

Squirrelflight returned with Leafpool and Jayfeather, and the three cats thrust their way through the crowd to join the group at its center.

Bramblestar was the first to break the silence. "Tell me if I have this straight," he began; his voice was soft, but every word bit as hard as a fox's fangs. "I went to Onestar to offer ThunderClan's help in driving out the stoats. Onestar insulted me and my whole Clan, and insisted he would take care of the problem himself. His plan was a disaster, because he did *not* have the problem under control, and now he's sending you to ask for ThunderClan's help. Is that correct?"

Harespring was obviously finding it difficult to meet the ThunderClan leader's gaze. "Yes," he mumbled at last.

"I want to hear you say it," Bramblestar growled. "I want to hear you say that Onestar's decisions got his Clan into trouble and he needs ThunderClan's help."

Harespring's only response was to cast a helpless glance at Crowfeather. *You wanted to do the talking,* Crowfeather thought. *So talk now. Can't you see that we don't have any choice?*

"Well?" Bramblestar asked, the tip of his tail twitching irritably.

"We got ourselves into trouble and we need ThunderClan's help," Crowfeather replied instantly. "I'm sorry for what happened," he added, "but we need help right now, not anger. Cats could *die.*"

Bramblestar paused for a moment; Crowfeather felt as though his belly were full of squabbling stoats as he waited for the ThunderClan leader's decision. *What kind of leader will he turn out to be?* he asked himself.

Eventually Bramblestar nodded. "Very well. Leafpool may go with you."

Leafpool's expression was full of relief as she took a pace forward to stand beside Crowfeather. Crowfeather knew very well she hated to think of cats in need, whatever their Clan might be. All the warmth and affection he had once felt for her threatened to well up again inside him, and he ruthlessly pushed it down again.

All that was over a long time ago. But even while he admitted that, Crowfeather asked himself whether he had ever felt as strongly as that about Nightcloud. *No, I never did. Is that a bad thing?*

He forced himself out of his musing to hear Harespring thank Bramblestar. "We should leave right away," he meowed.

"Every moment might count for the injured cats."

Bramblestar dipped his head and turned away, heading back to his den. The rest of the cats began to disperse, back to their duties.

Leafpool touched Crowfeather on the shoulder with the tip of her tail. "Wait for me a moment," she mewed. "I need to fetch some herbs."

She bounded away toward the medicine-cat den, with Jayfeather beside her. He was telling her something, his tail twitching as he spoke. *I can't imagine that's anything good,* Crowfeather thought. *He's probably warning her to beware of the vicious, treacherous WindClan cats.*

Leafpool reappeared from the den a few moments later, a leaf wrap of herbs in her jaws, and with Harespring in the lead the three cats headed out of the camp. Crowfeather relaxed as they emerged at the far end of the thorn tunnel, away from all those curious ThunderClan eyes.

Once they were out in the forest, Harespring drew a little way ahead; Crowfeather guessed he wanted to give him and Leafpool the chance to talk.

I'm not sure that's a good idea. There's not much we have to say to each other anymore.

But Leafpool seemed quite unembarrassed to be alone with the warrior she had once valued more than both her Clan and her calling as a medicine cat. "Ivypool told me you went looking for Nightcloud," she began, managing to talk around the leaf wrap. Her gaze was friendly and sympathetic. "Did you find her?"

"Yes," Crowfeather replied. "Some Twolegs were looking after her, and we had to rescue her from their den. She's fine now."

"I'm so glad!" Leafpool hesitated, then went on more diffidently, "Now you and Nightcloud will have the chance to work things out. After all, having kits ties you together forever, no matter what happens after that. . . ."

Her voice trailed off, and she cast Crowfeather an awkward, flickering glance before padding on with her gaze fixed firmly on her paws.

Like we did . . . Crowfeather too looked at the ground to hide his discomfort. What Leafpool had just said applied to them, too, of course, but neither of them dared say it aloud.

After a few moments, Crowfeather summoned the courage to continue. "It's true what you say. And I *would* like to be friends with Nightcloud, if I ever manage to tell her so."

He remembered how he and Nightcloud had been allies during her rescue and on the journey home, but that closeness hadn't survived their return to camp. He still didn't really know what to say to her.

By the time Crowfeather and Leafpool crossed the border stream and left the trees behind to climb up onto the moor, Harespring was out of sight. Crowfeather wondered whether he had gone on ahead to tell WindClan that help was on its way.

Then Crowfeather spotted movement behind an outcrop of rock, and thought that the deputy must be waiting there for them. But the creature that emerged into the open wasn't

Harespring. Instead of the deputy's bright eyes and brown-and-white pelt, Crowfeather saw blinding white fur and sharp teeth.

It's one of those StarClan-cursed stoats!

The small white animal tottered toward them; its legs looked weak, and Crowfeather guessed that it must be ill, or maybe had been wounded in the battle.

"So that's a stoat!" Leafpool exclaimed, her voice sounding intrigued. "I've never seen one before. It looks . . . disgusting."

"They are," Crowfeather told her, remembering how the WindClan apprentices had underestimated the creatures. "They don't look that threatening, but they're vicious fighters. We need to—"

He broke off as the stoat, drawing nearer to them, suddenly made a dart at Leafpool, who started back, scattering the herbs she had been carrying. With a yowl of outrage, Crowfeather dashed in and intercepted it. Even though the stoat had looked sick, it was still a wild, ferocious fighter, rearing up and slashing its small claws at Crowfeather's face.

Crowfeather was terrified that the stoat would tear at his eyes and blind him. Squeezing his eyes shut, he managed to grip the sleek creature with his forepaws and drag it to the ground with him, battering at his opponent with his hind paws.

But the stoat was wiry and sinuous, and Crowfeather couldn't hang on to it. He felt it slip out of his claws, followed by an intense, sharp pain in his hind leg. Opening his eyes, Crowfeather saw the stoat with its teeth fastened in his leg just above his paw. Leafpool had bounded up and was slashing at the stoat's hindquarters.

"No! Get back!" Crowfeather yowled, terrified that the vicious creature would turn on her.

Swiping a forepaw at the stoat's head, Crowfeather knocked it clear. It scrambled to its paws and looked around, its malignant gaze fastening on Leafpool, who was still within a fox-length of it.

As the stoat leaped for her, Crowfeather found a sudden burst of energy. *No way will I let Leafpool die on WindClan territory!* Intercepting the stoat before it could reach Leafpool, he gripped its shoulder with his teeth and dragged it away. He raised one paw, claws extended, to slash at the creature's throat, but before he could strike, the stoat twisted its body, thrust its hind paws at Crowfeather, and managed to wrench itself free. Scrambling out of range, it fled for the tunnels.

I guess it doesn't want to fight anymore, Crowfeather thought. *Well, I won't give it the choice.*

Crowfeather was about to follow the stoat when Leafpool darted in front of him. "Don't!" she meowed anxiously. "You're injured."

Blinking in confusion, Crowfeather looked down at his hind leg. Blood was gushing from the place where the stoat had bitten him.

"Look at that! Now we have *another* injured WindClan cat. The bleeding's bad, Crowfeather," she added. "Try not to go to sleep."

Crowfeather wondered vaguely why he would want to sleep

out here, away from his den. But now that the fight was over, his energy ebbing, the pain in his leg grew until it seemed to take over his whole body. His ears were filled with a sound like rushing water.

Rushing dark water . . . ? As he stumbled on toward the camp, Crowfeather thought once more about Kestrelflight's dream, wondering whether the stoats were what the dark water, gushing from the caves, was pointing to.

Am I going to die? The first death in a series that will end in . . . what? The fall of the Clans? His vision of the second wave, the one that engulfed everything, was somehow mingled with the sight of his Clanmates that morning, lying wounded in the middle of the camp. And somewhere in all the confusion he could hear the amused purring of a long-haired white kittypet.

Harespring's voice seemed to come to him from a great distance. "I heard yowling. What happened?"

Leafpool's voice sounded far away, too, and faded in and out so that Crowfeather could hardly make sense of her words. ". . . fighting a stoat . . . bleeding is so bad . . . Harespring, find me some cobweb."

Crowfeather sensed movement around him, and a firm touch on his leg, followed by Leafpool's distant voice again. "Harespring, help me lift him . . . get him to your camp."

When did I fall to the ground? Crowfeather wondered. He felt strong paws begin to raise him, the movement sending a stab of pain through him that took his breath away. With a sigh of relief, he gave himself up to swirling darkness.

CHAPTER 27

Dark clouds whirled around Crowfeather, shot through with flashes of lurid red light, as if the sun were setting through a storm. Now and again he caught glimpses of familiar faces: Nightcloud, Feathertail, Leafpool, and their kits, but as he imagined they had been in the nursery: innocent young cats with no idea of the pain they would have to suffer. Crowfeather tried to reach out to them, but they were swept away from him into a roaring darkness. At last a great wave surged up around him, closing over his head and leaving him to float in starless night.

Gradually, Crowfeather became aware of quiet movement around him and the sharp tang of herbs in his nose. He opened his eyes to find himself in Kestrelflight's den, with a blurred tabby shape sorting herbs a tail-length away from him.

"Leafpool?" he murmured, managing to focus his eyes. For a moment he wondered why a ThunderClan medicine cat would be working in the WindClan camp. It was seasons since he and Leafpool had been alone together, and Crowfeather half believed she was still part of his hectic dream.

Leafpool turned to him, her eyes wide and welcoming. "Oh, you're awake!" she purred. "Thank StarClan!"

"What am I doing here?" Crowfeather asked, confused and trying to shake off sleep. "Why are you in Kestrelflight's den? What happened?"

"Don't you remember coming to ThunderClan? And then the fight with the stoat?" Leafpool asked. "It gave you a bad bite on your leg, and you lost a lot of blood, but you're going to be fine."

"The stoats . . ." Crowfeather blinked in confusion, then suddenly remembered everything: Kestrelflight's vision, the attack on the camp, and his journey to ThunderClan to fetch Leafpool.

"I'd better be fine," he muttered, struggling to sit up and shaking scraps of bedding from his pelt. A twinge of pain on his leg reminded him of where he had been bitten. "Onestar needs every warrior—"

"Onestar will have to get along without *this* warrior for the time being," Leafpool interrupted tartly. "You're weak, and you'll need time to recover." As Crowfeather was about to protest, she raised her tail to silence him. "Don't you dare argue."

She moved to the back of the den and returned a moment later with a mouthful of wet moss. "There," she mewed, setting it down beside Crowfeather. "Drink. I'll go and find some cat to fetch you fresh-kill."

Crowfeather watched her as she slipped out of the den, then lowered his head to lap water from the moss. It was cool and reviving, and he let out a sigh of resignation.

Being injured isn't bad, he reflected. *It's kind of a relief to* have to *let some other cat take care of me.*

Crowfeather was drowsing in his nest again when Kestrel-flight came into the den and stood over him, giving the wound on his leg a good sniff. "That's coming along okay," he commented. "No sign of infection."

"How is the rest of the Clan?" Crowfeather asked.

"Also coming along okay," Kestrelflight replied with a purr of satisfaction. "Thank you so much for convincing Onestar to ask for help from other Clans. Mistystar sent Mothwing, and she's helping to tend to the injured cats. We have enough herbs for every cat, and all the wounded are being looked after."

"That's really good news," Crowfeather meowed. "I wonder what we'll do about the stoats now."

"Nothing, for the time being," Kestrelflight replied. "We must get all our cats healthy first, and then we can decide."

At that moment, Leafpool reappeared at the entrance to the den with a spray of leaves in her jaws. "Thyme leaves," she mewed, dropping the spray in front of Crowfeather. "Eat them. They're good for shock."

"I don't need—" Crowfeather began, then broke off as Leafpool pushed the leaves closer to him.

"Do as you're told, you daft furball."

Crowfeather rolled his eyes but licked up the thyme leaves without further protest.

Kestrelflight glanced from Crowfeather to Leafpool and back again. There was a wary look in his eyes. "Crowfeather, I'll leave you in Leafpool's capable paws," he meowed. "I'll be back to check on you later."

"I thought you said something about fresh-kill," Crowfeather complained when the medicine cat was gone. "My belly thinks my throat's torn out."

"It'll be along in a few moments," Leafpool responded in an amused tone. Settling down beside him, she added, "How do you feel?"

Crowfeather shifted experimentally. "My leg hurts as if a badger is trying to gnaw it off, but otherwise I'm fine."

Leafpool fixed a steady gaze on him from warm amber eyes. "Are you really, Crowfeather?" she asked. "Tell me the truth."

How can I answer that? Crowfeather asked himself. *How can I tell Leafpool about my problems with Breezepelt and Nightcloud, and how Onestar nearly banished me from the Clan for good?* He shifted uncomfortably in his nest; his chest clenched, and the pain in his leg almost made him forget his hunger pangs. "Things have been better," he admitted. Hoping to distract Leafpool, he added, "How are you doing in ThunderClan?"

Leafpool twitched her ears at him, showing she knew very well why he was changing the subject. "I'm okay," she replied. "StarClan has accepted me again, so I can work as a full medicine cat."

"I'm glad." Crowfeather paused, then went on. "And Lionblaze and Jayfeather—do they . . . ?"

"They've accepted me, too," Leafpool responded. "I think they'll always feel that Squirrelflight is their true mother, but . . . well, we get along. Hollyleaf was the cat who could never accept that she was half-Clan."

And Hollyleaf is dead, Crowfeather thought bleakly. *Before I ever had the chance to get to know her.*

"Hollyleaf died nobly, protecting her Clan," Leafpool told him, as if she could read his mind. "In spite of all that had gone before. You can be proud of her, Crowfeather. You can be proud of all your kits."

Including Breezepelt?

Crowfeather had a sudden impulse to confide in Leafpool. Once, he had been able to open his heart to her, and although those days were past, he still felt that he could trust her more than any other cat. Besides, Leafpool was a ThunderClan cat, and wouldn't be prejudiced against Breezepelt in the same way as his Clanmates. He could speak frankly to her without worrying what other cats would think.

"I *want* to be proud of Breezepelt," he confessed. "But it's hard. There's so much anger inside him. I know he's a brave and loyal warrior, but it's as if he doesn't know how to show that. To me or to his Clan."

"But things may be getting better," Leafpool responded. "From what I hear, he fought bravely against the stoats. And he did well when he went with you to search for Nightcloud."

Crowfeather nodded, feeling a little encouraged. "He would do anything to help his mother." Then he let out a sigh. "Nightcloud . . . I'd do anything to connect with her *and* Breezepelt. But somehow . . . What do *you* think, Leafpool? Why does it always go wrong?"

Leafpool stifled an amused *mrrow.* "Crowfeather asking another cat for advice!" she exclaimed. "What next?" More seriously, she added, "No matter what, Breezepelt and Nightcloud are your kin. True, you've had a difficult past, but you could have a good future." She leaned closer to Crowfeather, fixing him with her amber gaze. "Admit it, Crowfeather," she mewed gently, "you might have had a paw in your problems with both of them. You're not the easiest cat in the forest to get along with."

"You're saying *I'm* difficult?" Crowfeather was outraged, but a heartbeat later he had to recognize the truth of what Leafpool had said. *I did push Onestar too far,* he admitted to himself. *And I could have been more supportive of Breezepelt.* "I suppose. . . ." he grumbled. "So you think I need to make more of an effort?"

"Exactly," Leafpool agreed. "Try to talk to them about how you really feel."

Had she been talking to his dead mother? That was almost the exact same advice Ashfoot had given him. "I'll try, but—" Crowfeather began.

At that moment, a paw step sounded outside the den and Nightcloud entered, carrying a vole in her jaws. "Fresh-kill," she meowed, dropping it beside Crowfeather's nest and giving Leafpool a long look with narrowed eyes.

Crowfeather's pelt prickled with the awkwardness of being so close to two she-cats who had each been his mate. Leafpool gave him a meaningful gaze, and he was pretty sure of what she was trying to tell him.

"Thank you, Nightcloud," he mewed. "That's kind of you. Do you want to share?"

Nightcloud's eyes widened in surprise, and she glanced across at Leafpool, as if she was wondering whether Crowfeather had offered to share in an attempt to make the ThunderClan she-cat jealous.

"No, I already ate." Nightcloud's tone was abrupt, but she settled down beside Crowfeather, tucking her paws underneath her.

"I'd better be going," Leafpool put in, rising to her paws with a polite nod to Nightcloud. "I have to check on the other wounded cats." Picking up a bunch of chervil in her jaws, she padded out of the den.

Crowfeather, who had taken a bite of the vole, quickly swallowed. Though he was struggling to find the right words, he remembered Leafpool's advice, and realized that he had to try. "Nightcloud, I'm sorry if I offended you yesterday," he meowed. "I wasn't sure what to say to you, now that you're back."

Nightcloud gave him a hard stare, and for a moment Crowfeather was afraid that once again he had said the wrong thing. Then the black she-cat seemed to soften.

"The truth is, I was badly hurt in the tunnels," she began after a heartbeat's hesitation. "And as much as I told those kittypets that I was a Clan cat, and I belonged with my Clan . . . honestly, after the Twolegs rescued me, I wasn't sure that I wanted to come back to WindClan."

"Not come back?" Every hair on Crowfeather's pelt prickled with shock. He couldn't believe he was hearing this from Nightcloud. *She's the most loyal WindClan warrior I know!*

"At least, not right away," Nightcloud continued. "I felt so weak and tired. . . . I never seriously thought that I would stay away forever, but for the time being it was good to be a kittypet—to have food and warmth and safety without having to chase prey, or risk my life fighting foxes. And I was . . . well, I was adored just for who I was. I had never felt that before, and it was sort of nice. Even when I was prickly, my Twolegs and Pickle never stopped trying to make me happy and comfortable. Pickle may have been a kittypet, but he was kind to me. He let me share his nest, and gave up his best napping spots for me. He shared his favorite toys with me, even when I told him I didn't play with toys. He acted like I was the most important cat in the world."

Pickle? Stupid name! Stupid cat!

But despising Pickle couldn't keep Crowfeather from hearing Nightcloud's words . . . or from feeling the guilt they brought out. *I never treated her that way,* he realized. *I never thought of her as being important.* There had been warmth in Nightcloud's voice as she described her life with Pickle. Kittypet or not, he'd tried to make her happy.

I was her mate. . . . I should have made her feel happy and valued like that, but I didn't. I failed.

His pelt grew hot with shame as he remembered that he had never paid much attention to Nightcloud's nest or what she was eating, even when she was pregnant with their kits. He had always assumed she could take care of herself. And that, he realized, was because he had never loved her as he had loved Feathertail or Leafpool. Pain stabbed through his heart as he recognized how that must have felt for Nightcloud.

"Mind you," Nightcloud went on, "if you tell any other cat I said that, I'll claw your fur off and use it to line my nest."

Crowfeather let out a *mrrow* of laughter. "You would, too!"

Suddenly the tension between them seemed to have vanished. Hungrily Crowfeather gulped down a few more mouthfuls of the vole, then dared to meow quietly, "I'm sorry, Nightcloud. I never treated you like your feelings were important. I'm sorry you had to wait to get that from a kittypet."

Nightcloud said nothing, but when she looked down at him, her eyes were warmer than he had ever seen them.

"Should we . . . should we be mates again?" Crowfeather suggested hesitantly. *Is that what I'm supposed to say?*

Nightcloud shook her head, but when she spoke, her voice was gentle. "No, and if you're honest with yourself, Crowfeather, you don't want that either. Admit it: We don't love each other, and maybe we never did."

Reluctantly, Crowfeather had to recognize the wisdom in the she-cat's words, though a pang of regret pierced him as he responded. "I think you're right. But . . . I do admire you, Nightcloud. You're an amazing warrior."

Nightcloud let out a tiny snort. "You're not so bad yourself. And remember," she added, "Breezepelt will always be our kit. We owe it to him to try to get along."

"True," Crowfeather sighed. "Nightcloud, I'm sorry that I've treated you badly. Can we be friends . . . if only for Breezepelt's sake?"

"I'd like that," Nightcloud purred. Rising to her paws, she

stooped over Crowfeather and rubbed her cheek against his. "You need to rest, Crowfeather. Maybe we'll talk later."

Crowfeather watched her as she padded out of the den. She was right that he needed rest: Their conversation had taken as much out of him as a patrol around the whole of the territory. He finished the last mouthful of vole, curled up, and closed his eyes.

Oh, StarClan, please don't send me back into that terrible dream. . . .

As soon as Crowfeather slipped into sleep, he saw the pale shape of his mother, Ashfoot, in front of him. This time he wasn't chasing her through the tunnels: She was sitting beside a pool in a lush forest clearing where ferns arched over the water and a tiny spring trickled down from the rocks above.

"Greetings, Crowfeather," Ashfoot meowed. This time her tone was approving. "Finally, you've taken the lessons of your dreams to heart."

"Lessons?" Crowfeather asked, stifling an incredulous *mrrow* of laughter. "What were the lessons? I've nearly worn my brain out trying to understand why I'm even having these dreams!"

"I've told you the most important lesson." Ashfoot's voice was a gentle murmur. "To love. You must open yourself to love again. And I sent you the dream of Hawkfrost and Hollyleaf to show you how much you care about all your kits, whatever happens to them. You must reopen your heart to Breezepelt and be a father to him."

Guilt weighed heavily on Crowfeather's shoulders as he

replied. "I see that now," he admitted. "I only hope I can be as good a father to Breezepelt as you were a mother to me."

Ashfoot's gaze was warm and brilliant. "I'm proud of you, Crowfeather," she purred. "At last, you're beginning to change."

Crowfeather stared at his mother. All at once, he felt a terrible ache in his heart as he realized that their private chats were over. His love for her was simple and overwhelming—the love of a kit for his mother.

Maybe that's how Breezepelt feels about me, he realized, *even though I haven't always deserved it. But I will,* he promised himself, watching the image of his mother weaken.

As the dream faded and Crowfeather blinked awake, back in the medicine-cat den, he decided once and for all that things would be different.

I will make sure Breezepelt knows I love him, just like Ashfoot loved me, he vowed to himself. *Changing is hard . . . but if it saves Breezepelt, it will be worth it.*

CHAPTER 28

❧

The full moon floated over the lake as Crowfeather pushed his way through the bushes that surrounded the clearing on the Gathering island. WindClan was the last to arrive; the other three Clans were already mingling on the moonwashed grass, their heads together as they exchanged news and gossip. Onestar picked his way through the crowd and leaped up to join the other leaders in the Great Oak.

Many days had passed since the stoats had attacked the WindClan camp. Most of the injured cats had recovered, though Crowfeather still felt a twinge of pain when he put his weight on his wounded hind leg. Leafpool and Mothwing had returned to their own Clans and now sat close to the Great Oak with their fellow medicine cats.

As soon as Onestar had settled himself on a branch, Blackstar lifted his head to get every cat's attention: "Before we begin, let us remember the fallen . . ."

As he had done at the last gathering, Blackstar spoke the names of the warriors lost in the Great Battle.

As soon as he'd finished, Bramblestar stepped forward and started the real meeting. The chatter in the clearing died away as the ThunderClan leader reported that his patrols were keeping an eye on foxes visiting their territory, and that they had chased away a Twoleg's stray dog.

"Yes, you chased it onto *our* territory," Blackstar complained, rising to his paws. "Thank you very much. Its Twolegs came looking for it, stomping all over the forest with their huge paws. But it's gone now, so no more problem."

Bramblestar dipped his head politely, then waved his tail at Mistystar for her to begin her report.

"RiverClan is doing fine," Mistystar reported. "The prey is running well, considering it's leaf-bare, and the lake is full of fish. Onestar," she continued, turning to the WindClan leader, "how are your injured warriors?"

"I hope they're recovering," Bramblestar added.

Onestar dipped his head politely to the two leaders. "They are all doing well," he responded. "Thank you for your help. And I think you have all heard that Nightcloud isn't dead after all. We welcome her back to her Clan."

"Nightcloud! Nightcloud!" the cats in the clearing yowled, echoing Onestar's welcome.

The black she-cat, who was sitting a tail-length away from Crowfeather, dipped her head in thanks, her eyes gleaming with pleasure that cats from other Clans were happy to see her again.

You wouldn't get that living with Pickle and the Twolegs, Crowfeather thought.

"And what about the stoats in the tunnels?" Mistystar asked. "Have you been able to deal with them?"

Crowfeather forced himself not to wince. That was a question that Onestar would find hard to answer.

"We haven't forgotten, but our Clan has been concentrating on healing," the WindClan leader replied.

"So you haven't done anything?" Bramblestar's tone was respectful, but he was obviously determined to get at the truth. "The stoats are still a problem—still a threat to more than one Clan?"

"We haven't dealt with them yet," Onestar told him reluctantly. "The stoats have broken through some of the entrances that we stopped up, so that plan won't work."

"And do you have another plan?" Bramblestar asked.

"I've discussed the problem with my senior warriors," Onestar told him. "But so far we haven't come up with an alternative."

Crowfeather remembered that meeting, a few days after the attack on the camp. No cat had come up with a solution, except to ask ThunderClan for help again, and they were all reluctant to test Bramblestar's good nature any further.

Crowfeather was aware of cats stirring around him, exchanging glances and muttering under their breath. His fur began to rise all along his spine as he realized they were blaming WindClan for not dealing with the invaders. He was tempted to agree, but he knew that problems always seemed easier to solve when you weren't the cat trying to solve them.

"Huh! I'd like to see them trying to fight with the vicious little mange-pelts," Nightcloud hissed.

Crowfeather gave her an approving nod. "Yeah, they don't

know what we're up against," he agreed.

Bramblestar raised his voice to be heard over the rising noise in the clearing. "Cats of all Clans!" he announced. "This is not just WindClan's problem. Already in ThunderClan we've had to deal with some of these creatures coming onto our territory. If they aren't stopped, they could easily spread to ShadowClan and RiverClan."

"What?" Blackstar started up, as if he had been half dozing. His eyes were wide with alarm.

He's starting to look old, Crowfeather thought. *How much use will he be to deal with a crisis like this?*

"Onestar," Bramblestar continued, "I'll make you the same offer that I made before. ThunderClan is ready to help. We must work together; it's the only hope we have of driving out the stoats."

"Great StarClan!" Nightcloud whispered in Crowfeather's ear, "Let's not have another argument like the one in our camp. Breezepelt told me all about it, and I couldn't believe what Onestar said!"

"Onestar wouldn't say the same now—not at a Gathering," Crowfeather responded, though he wasn't at all sure that it was true.

Onestar hesitated for a long moment, staring at the ThunderClan leader. Then, slowly, he dipped his head. "Very well. WindClan thanks you, Bramblestar."

"RiverClan will help too, if we're needed," Mistystar meowed. "And ShadowClan too, Blackstar?"

Blackstar gave his pelt a shake. "I suppose so," he grunted.

The decision made, the cats in the clearing were settling

down again when Crowfeather noticed that his son Lion-blaze was looking uncomfortable, shifting impatiently as if he wanted to speak. *What's biting him?* he wondered.

Lionblaze suddenly leaped to his paws. "Bramblestar, I want to say something!"

His Clan leader looked down at him, a slight look of disapproval in his eyes. "Very well. Go on," he mewed.

Crowfeather saw Lionblaze's glance swivel around the clearing until it lighted on Breezepelt. For a couple of heartbeats the two half brothers glared at each other. Dread bubbled up inside Crowfeather as he realized where this was going.

"I don't want to fight beside Breezepelt," Lionblaze growled, with an angry glare at the WindClan warrior, who was sitting beside Heathertail in the shadow of the bushes. "He tried to kill me in the battle with the Dark Forest."

I thought all that was over. Crowfeather's heart sank as he had to accept that he was wrong. It was many days since he had heard a WindClan cat speak out against Breezepelt, but he had forgotten how Lionblaze might still be bearing a grudge.

"And I still think WindClan was spying on us when we caught Crowfeather and Breezepelt in the tunnels," Berry-nose added, coming to stand beside Lionblaze.

Crowfeather could hear other ThunderClan warriors murmuring agreement, and was bracing himself to stand up. He didn't want to make a scene at a Gathering, and he had the horrible feeling that whatever he did, he was going to upset one of his sons. But he couldn't let the chance pass of showing support for Breezepelt.

However, before Crowfeather had decided what to say,

Bramblestar waved his tail for silence once again.

"The trouble with the Dark Forest is over," the Thunder-Clan leader meowed decisively. He turned a cold gaze on Lionblaze and Berrynose. "Raking up old quarrels will do no cat any good. We must all learn to trust one another. We must move forward and not think about the past."

Lionblaze, though he was obviously unhappy about his leader's rebuke, dipped his head and sat down again. Berrynose sat beside him and muttered something into Lionblaze's ear.

Crowfeather could hear more grumbling remarks from the cats around him. Though most of them were too low-pitched for him to make out the words, he had a good idea of what was being said.

"ThunderClan *would* feel that way." That was Weaselfur; he was sitting so close to Crowfeather that he had no trouble hearing him. "They had cats who trained with the Dark Forest, but no *real* traitors." His eyes narrowed with hostility as he turned his head to gaze at Breezepelt.

Crowfeather saw from Breezepelt's hostile glare at the gray-and-white she-cat that he had noticed, and that he understood Weaselfur's implication that he was a real traitor, since he had fought on the side of the Dark Forest.

His Clanmates still don't trust him, Crowfeather thought sadly. *Even after all he's done, battling the stoats and helping to bring Nightcloud home.*

For the first time, instead of becoming angry and uncomfortable himself, Crowfeather imagined how his son must be feeling. He rose to speak, but before he could, Breezepelt leaped to his paws and spoke in a voice so confident, his words rang out across all the clearing.

"No cat has to trust me, or the other Dark Forest warriors. We will prove ourselves, and then no other cat will dare to doubt our loyalty."

"Yes! You'll see!" Whiskernose yowled.

"We're just as loyal as the rest of you!" Larkwing added.

Harespring backed up his Clanmates sturdily. "We trained in the Dark Forest to *help* our Clans!"

The yowls of support for Breezepelt rose up everywhere in the clearing from the other cats who had been deceived by the Dark Forest. *They must all be feeling that they have something to prove,* Crowfeather realized, *not just Breezepelt.* Onestar had made a Dark Forest warrior his deputy, Crowfeather knew, but not all the Clan leaders had made such public displays of acceptance and support. *I wonder how the Dark Forest cats in other Clans are getting along.*

The rest of the cats fell silent; glancing around, Crowfeather could tell that some cats had at least had been convinced by Breezepelt's bold declaration.

Mistystar spoke from her branch of the Great Oak, her blue eyes gleaming and the moonlight turning her blue-gray fur to silver. "Then it's agreed," she meowed. "WindClan and ThunderClan will cooperate to tackle the stoats, and will call on RiverClan and ShadowClan if the need arises."

No cat raised a voice in protest, though Crowfeather noticed that Lionblaze and Berrynose, who had started the argument, still looked unhappy.

"The Gathering is at an end," Bramblestar announced.

The four leaders leaped down from the Great Oak. While Mistystar and Blackstar gathered their warriors together for the journey home, Onestar and Bramblestar held back, deep in conversation, and signaled to their cats to go ahead without them.

Jumping down from the tree-bridge, Crowfeather spotted Breezepelt and Heathertail just ahead of him, padding along the shore of the lake. He picked up his pace and caught up with them, inwardly flinching a little at the wary look Breezepelt turned on him. But if Crowfeather had learned anything, it was that he couldn't let moments like this stop him from being a father to Breezepelt.

"Breezepelt," he began, "I was really impressed by what you said back there."

For a moment, Breezepelt looked surprised. "Well," he said. "I wouldn't have said it if I didn't mean it."

"I don't doubt you," Crowfeather continued, realizing with a jolt of surprise that what he said was true. "Whatever you need . . . you have my support."

Breezepelt hesitated for a moment, and Crowfeather realized that Heathertail had dropped back, leaving him alone with his son. He felt suddenly as exposed and vulnerable as if an eagle were hovering over him on the open moor.

Breezepelt looked awkwardly down at his paws. *He looks just as uncomfortable as I am,* Crowfeather thought.

"I trained with the Dark Forest to become a stronger warrior," Breezepelt explained at last. "I needed some cat to believe in me, and the Dark Forest cats did—or at least they seemed to. But I wasn't fighting against the Clans. I'll always be a WindClan cat first. This battle with the stoats is my chance to prove myself," he finished resolutely.

Listening to him, Crowfeather remembered the terrible moment in the battle when Breezepelt had attacked Lionblaze. That hadn't been the action of a traitor, he realized now, but of a cat driven to desperation by his sense of failure and isolation.

Now, looking at Breezepelt's determined face, Crowfeather felt a wave of tenderness wash over him. He could see in his son something of the innocent kit—so eager for new challenges and adventures—that Nightcloud had first presented to him, before it had all gone wrong.

"Like I said, I'll do whatever I can to help," he assured Breezepelt. His voice was hoarse with the strangeness of the words and his anxiety that his son wouldn't accept what he was offering. "I know I haven't always been the father you deserve," he added, "but now I want to change that."

Breezepelt said nothing. He only ducked his head awkwardly, but the warmth in his eyes told Crowfeather all he needed to know.

As he padded along beside his son, their pelts brushing, Crowfeather felt an answering warmth welling up inside him.

This is what it must feel like to be a real father, he thought.

CHAPTER 29

The day after the Gathering dawned damp and cloudy, and there was a tang of rain in the wind that blew from the top of the moor. By now most of the snow had disappeared, except for drifts in sheltered hollows, but frost furred the tough moorland grass, and every pool was rimmed with ice.

My paws are cold enough to fall off, Crowfeather thought.

He shivered as he headed toward the ThunderClan border along with Onestar and a chosen group of WindClan warriors. Harespring padded along at his leader's shoulder, while Nightcloud and Breezepelt followed closely behind. Heathertail was bringing up the rear.

After the Gathering had ended, Onestar and Bramblestar had remained behind and talked. They'd decided that they would meet at the border to discuss how their Clans would work together to defeat the stoats. Crowfeather could only hope that this time they would come up with a plan that would succeed.

As they left the moor behind and entered the strip of woodland beside the stream, Crowfeather became aware of a strong ThunderClan scent just ahead. Drawing closer to the border, he spotted a large group of the ThunderClan cats assembled on the opposite bank; Bramblestar and Squirrelflight stood in the center, with Jayfeather on one side of them and Lionblaze on the other.

Crowfeather couldn't help noticing how many of the ThunderClan warriors looked wary and distrustful, muttering to one another as the WindClan cats padded up. His pelt prickled with apprehension at the sight of them.

How will we unite to fight the stoats if we can't get along among ourselves?

In particular, Crowfeather noticed that Lionblaze and Breezepelt were glaring at each other.

However, Bramblestar dipped his head politely to Onestar as the two leaders faced each other across the stream. "Greetings, Onestar," he meowed.

Equally polite, Onestar returned the greeting, and Crowfeather breathed a sigh of relief. Clearly, no cat was going to mention Bramblestar's lack of experience or Onestar's failure to control the stoats on his own.

"So," Bramblestar began, "what do you suggest, Onestar?"

"We've tried going down the tunnels to fight the stoats," Onestar replied, "and it was a disaster. The stoats know the tunnels better than we do, and there are too many places for them to hide. There are more of them, and they're smaller than us, so they fight better in tight corners. Somehow we have to get them out into the open."

Bramblestar looked thoughtful. "Of course, Thunder-Clan has some experience with underground fighting . . . ," he mused.

Crowfeather slid out his claws. Seasons ago, when Firestar was still ThunderClan leader, WindClan had attacked Thunder-Clan in the tunnels and been soundly defeated. Later he had learned that Hollyleaf, who had once lived down there, had trained her Clan in special fighting techniques.

Is Bramblestar genuinely offering to use their special skills, he wondered, *or is he finding another, more subtle way to insult Onestar? Not that Onestar doesn't have it coming,* he added wryly to himself, remembering Onestar's scathing attack on Bramblestar in the WindClan camp.

But Onestar seemed unaware of any possible insult, or perhaps he'd realized he couldn't afford to be insulted. "I still think we need to get them out," he mewed. "But whatever we decide, we will have to kill a good number to have any real chance of getting rid of them."

Crowfeather saw Rosepetal and Mousewhisker of ThunderClan exchanging a scornful look. "I can't imagine how the WindClan warriors were defeated by animals that are so much smaller than them," Rosepetal murmured.

"Yeah, they're *tiny,*" Mousewhisker agreed.

Squirrelflight's head swiveled around to glare at her Clanmates. "Hold your tongues!" she snapped.

"You've obviously never fought with them," Furzepelt mewed disdainfully. "They're fierce, their teeth are sharp, and they attack when you're not expecting them."

"And you should see them leaping and twisting in the air," Larkwing added. "Does ThunderClan have any better battle moves? I don't think so."

Crowfeather saw several of the younger ThunderClan

warriors glancing at one another, their eyes stretched wide with alarm, though the more experienced warriors looked disbelieving.

"I'm sure they must have *felt* like a pack of ravenous beasts," Thornclaw meowed with a lofty air.

"Our warriors are right," Harespring told him. "Of course I've seen stoats before—we all have—but not in a large pack like this. These snow-white ones are ferocious. We need to take them seriously."

"Of course we do." Bramblestar took control again. "So, let's hear some ideas of how to fight the stoats without attacking in the tunnels and putting ourselves at a disadvantage."

"I think we should block up the tunnels as we did before," Crowfeather suggested, giving voice to an idea he'd been mulling over since the Gathering, "and then send in a force of cats to drive the stoats out to one place, where the rest of us will be waiting."

"That could work," Heathertail agreed. "We'll have to be sure we cover all the tunnels."

"Yes," Lionblaze put in, "and make sure the stoats don't retreat the other way and come out on ThunderClan territory. It'll work best if we can keep them on the WindClan side of the underground river."

Standing beside Lionblaze, his mate, Cinderheart, twitched her ears in amusement, but Crowfeather saw the golden tabby tom look suddenly sheepish, while Heathertail briefly averted her gaze. He knew Heathertail was familiar with the tunnels between the territories—he'd always wondered if she'd explored them alone, or with the ThunderClan cat.

Beside him, Crowfeather sensed Breezepelt bristling. Obviously, he had drawn the same conclusion.

Why can't he let it go? Crowfeather wondered. *Heathertail's heart is clearly with Breezepelt now, but he still holds on to every scrap of his hostility to Lionblaze.*

"I've got a better idea." Breezepelt spoke loudly, and Crowfeather suspected he wanted to distract Heathertail's attention from the golden ThunderClan warrior. He didn't even look at Lionblaze, as if his half brother weren't there at all. "Instead of endangering several cats by trying to drive the stoats out of the tunnels—and maybe driving them over to ThunderClan—why not send in one cat to attack a stoat and draw the others out?"

Lionblaze huffed out his breath. "Are you suggesting we put a lone cat into danger?" he meowed to Breezepelt. "Or are you volunteering to go confront the stoats yourself?"

Breezepelt turned his head to stare at him. "Of course I'm volunteering," he responded instantly. "Mouse-brain," he added under his breath, only loud enough for Crowfeather and perhaps Nightcloud to hear.

Crowfeather clamped his jaws shut, not allowing himself to intervene. He felt intensely proud of Breezepelt, but the thought of his son venturing alone into the stoat-infested tunnels made every hair on his pelt bristle with fear.

Then he remembered how he had once thought that a breeze was a kind of wind, driving back the engulfing water in Kestrelflight's vision. Perhaps Breezepelt was the cat destined to take this risk and save his Clan.

"Are you sure?" Onestar asked Breezepelt.

Breezepelt nodded. "I promised at the Gathering that I would prove myself a loyal warrior," he declared. "Now I'm fulfilling that promise."

Crowfeather's gaze swept over the assembled cats as Breezepelt made his courageous offer, noticing a glint of approval in Onestar's eyes. Most of the others seemed impressed, too. But when he glanced hopefully at Lionblaze, he saw that his ThunderClan son's face was set in cold dislike. Crowfeather felt that look like a claw slicing through his heart. Clearly, the offer wasn't enough for Lionblaze to forgive Breezepelt for trying to kill him.

The need to show his support for Breezepelt flooded over Crowfeather. He wanted to be the father to him that he always should have been. And now he knew how to do it, and at the same time show that he put his Clan's needs above his own.

It will be dangerous, but if Breezepelt can take the risk, then so can I.

"I'll go as well," he meowed, padding up to his son's side.

A murmur of surprise came from his Clanmates. "It's not necessary," Harespring told him.

"I want to support my son," Crowfeather responded, catching a look of surprise on Lionblaze's face, and Jayfeather's. *Did I choose the right words there?* he asked himself, briefly anxious. *Will they think I don't accept them as my sons?* Then he dismissed the worry. This wasn't the right time. Glancing at Onestar, he added, "I suppose I need to prove my loyalty to WindClan, too."

Onestar clearly shared his Clan's surprise, but something in his gaze told Crowfeather that he was impressed, too. "I think we should combine the plans," he suggested to Bramblestar. "We'll block every tunnel that we can, and leave just one entrance open, on the WindClan side."

Bramblestar nodded agreement. "Then Breezepelt and Crowfeather will try to infuriate the stoats—"

"They should find that really easy," Jayfeather put in.

His Clan leader gave him a stare from narrowed eyes. "Thank you, Jayfeather," he mewed, an irritated edge to his voice. "As I was saying," he continued, "Crowfeather and Breezepelt will infuriate the stoats enough to draw them out of the tunnels, where the warriors will be waiting for them."

"It should work well." Harespring, who had been sitting at the very edge of the stream near his Clan leader, sprang to his paws. "I'll lead the patrol to find the tunnels and block them off, if Lionblaze and Heathertail will help."

"Of course," Heathertail mewed, and Larkwing added quickly, "I'd like to help, too."

Birchfall stepped forward from the ThunderClan group across the stream, with Mousewhisker at his side. "We'll organize the fighters to be ready to spring out and attack the stoats."

"We'll be waiting for them," Blossomfall meowed, pushing forward with Thornclaw hard on her paws.

"And me!" Whiskernose called from the WindClan side. Onestar shook his head at the light brown elder, but Whiskernose ignored him.

Crowfeather noticed that all the volunteers had trained with the Dark Forest cats; they were all cats who had been doubted and feared and distrusted by their Clanmates, yet here they were, eager to prove themselves loyal warriors of their Clans at last.

Glancing around, he saw that other cats had realized it too: Murmurs of praise rose from them, and they exchanged glances of approval.

Let's hope their lives will be easier from now on, Crowfeather thought.

CHAPTER 30

❧

Crowfeather stood at the tunnel entrance where—moons ago, it seemed—Hootpaw had first glimpsed the white stoat. The sky was scarlet over the moor, the cats' long shadows stretching out behind them as the sun went down. It was the day after the meeting with Bramblestar and the ThunderClan warriors at the stream, and everything was ready for the final attack on the stoats.

The creatures seemed to be more active at night, and so during the day, while they slept, the cats had filled in as many unblocked tunnels as they could find. Now only this one entrance remained. Crowfeather raised one paw to lick his pad where it still stung from maneuvering stones and brush. His fur itched with dust, but he felt warm with satisfaction from ears to tail-tip.

The stoats should be waking up by now. I hope they're ready to be lured out.

Breezepelt padded up while Crowfeather was still licking his sore pads. "Ready?" he asked.

Crowfeather nodded, glancing up at his son. He was surprised to see that Breezepelt wore an expression of determination and held his head high. *I know he's afraid of the tunnels,* Crowfeather thought, *but he's not showing the slightest sign of fear now.*

Breezepelt returned Crowfeather's nod, his gaze softening a little.

"We can do this," Crowfeather mewed. "For WindClan."

"We can," Breezepelt agreed. "I'm ready."

His voice was steady and resolute. Crowfeather couldn't help thinking of the danger ahead. It didn't matter so much for him, but Breezepelt had his whole future to lose if he was killed or injured: his place in the Clan; the opportunity to take a mate, have kits, and raise them as warriors. *He's willing to risk all that to prove his loyalty,* Crowfeather reflected, even more impressed by his son's courage. *I may have been lacking as a father, but Breezepelt still turned out to be a worthy warrior.*

Crowfeather glanced around at the moorland landscape that surrounded him. He knew that behind the rocks and underneath the gorse bushes, warriors of ThunderClan and WindClan were hiding, waiting to leap out into battle. There was a strong scent of cat, but he couldn't see any of them, not even a single whisker or the tip of a tail.

The stoats will get the shock of their lives!

But with that realization Crowfeather accepted that he had to contain himself. He couldn't let his longing for revenge get the better of him. Excitement and confidence were bubbling up inside him like a spring of fresh water, but he knew that he needed intelligence, too, and a cool head.

Then Heathertail emerged from behind a boulder halfway

up the slope and padded down to join Crowfeather and Breezepelt. "You're sure you know what to do?" she asked.

Like we haven't gone over it so many times! Crowfeather thought, but he didn't speak the thought aloud. He was well aware that Heathertail wasn't really asking that question; what she wanted to know was whether Breezepelt was sure he wanted to go through with this.

She knows he's a capable warrior, but she wants to be his mate. Of course she's worried.

"Yes, we'll be fine," Breezepelt replied.

"You've been in there before, so you should remember what it's like," Heathertail continued. "There's a clear path in a huge circle to take you deep into the tunnels and back out here. For StarClan's sake, don't head off down any side passages."

"We'll be careful," Breezepelt promised her.

Crowfeather wasn't sure that "careful" was the word he would have chosen. He and Breezepelt would be running the path as fast as they could, swiping and yowling at stoats to attract their attention and make them give chase.

I hope we don't get caught and find ourselves surrounded by stoats. It would be easy enough to get the creatures' attention, and easier still to get trapped in the tunnels, outnumbered in the dark. *I know how that feels, and I don't want to feel it again—but that's in the paws of StarClan.*

Breezepelt and Heathertail had leaned closer together, speaking softly to each other, when Onestar padded up. Crowfeather suppressed a *mrrow* of amusement when he saw the two young cats guiltily jump apart.

"It's time," Onestar declared; if he had noticed anything, he made no comment. "Are you ready?"

Crowfeather nodded; Breezepelt stood up a little straighter.

"Then may StarClan light your path," the Clan leader meowed. "Go!"

Crowfeather let Breezepelt take the lead as the two toms raced into the tunnels. Light from the entrance quickly died away behind them, though the passage was dimly lit through chinks in the roof.

At first the only sign of the stoats was the smell. Crowfeather's nose wrinkled at their scent and the reek of their rotting prey. Then a stronger, fresher scent flooded over him, and he realized that the passage opened up at one side into a den. He could make out several white bodies crowded together.

Without hesitation Breezepelt darted in among them and slashed his claws across the nearest stoat's face before darting out again and running on. "Take that, mange-pelt!" he yowled. The injured stoat let out a screech of pain, and a furious chittering rose from its denmates.

As Crowfeather ran past the den, hard on Breezepelt's paws, he heard the stoats scrambling after him, their tiny claws scratching on the floor of the passage, their scent like a foggy cloud around him. Alarmed by how close they were, he bunched and stretched his muscles in an effort to run even faster.

We must have had bees in our brains to volunteer for this!

As he and Breezepelt raced onward, attacking stoats in every den they passed, Crowfeather realized that more and more of the stoats were following them. A hasty glance over his shoulder showed them pouring down the passage like a vast white wave ready to engulf them.

How much farther? he asked himself desperately. *We must be close to the way out by now!*

Reaching what Crowfeather thought must be the last den, Breezepelt once more leaped into the attack. But this time the stoats in the den seemed more alert, maybe warned by the sound and scent of their approaching denmates. The leading stoat sprang forward beneath Breezepelt's outstretched paws and fastened its fangs into his throat.

Breezepelt let out a yowl of shock and fear. A heartbeat later the white creatures were swarming around him; he almost looked as if he were sinking into a snowdrift, except this wasn't snow: It was a heap of squirming bodies, with claws and teeth bared to tear and bite.

Crowfeather didn't take time to think. He waded into the swarm of stoats, lashing out with his claws to thrust the creatures aside on his way to his son. When he reached Breezepelt, he swiped with all his strength at the stoat that still clung to him, breaking its grip and knocking it back against the den wall.

"Run—*now!*" he screeched to Breezepelt.

Breezepelt turned and fled down the passage; Crowfeather barreled after him, hearing the whole crowd of stoats on his hind paws. Moments later the dim light of the tunnel grew brighter, and Crowfeather spotted the ragged circle of the tunnel entrance a few fox-lengths ahead.

Breezepelt broke out into the open, his voice raised in a triumphant yowl, and Crowfeather followed him. The stoats poured out behind them, an unstoppable wave.

Ahead of them, cats rose up from the seemingly empty hillside. WindClan and ThunderClan together charged down the slope into the attack. Their eyes gleamed in the last of the daylight, and their voices were raised as one in a challenging caterwaul.

Crowfeather kept on running until he and Breezepelt were well away from the tunnel, then gave his son a hard shove with one shoulder into the shelter of a jutting rock.

"Catch your breath," he panted.

Breezepelt nodded, his breath coming in harsh gasps as if he couldn't manage to speak. "Thanks, Crowfeather," he rasped eventually. "I can't believe how strong you were, attacking that last stoat!"

Crowfeather let out a snort. "Nor can I. I have no idea where that came from. Maybe it was just seeing my kit attacked!"

Breezepelt's tail curled up with amusement, but there was unexpected warmth in his gaze. "If you hadn't been there," he mewed, "I'm not sure what would have happened. But I doubt I'd be here to tell the story."

"Are you okay?" Crowfeather asked. Breezepelt's throat was bleeding, but not too badly; it looked as if the stoat's fangs hadn't sunk in very deep.

"Fine," Breezepelt replied. "You?"

Crowfeather nodded. "Let's go and kill some stoats!"

Breezepelt instantly leaped into the battle, but Crowfeather paused a moment to take in what was happening. The open ground between the gorse-covered hillside and the tunnel entrances in the steep bank was covered by writhing bodies: cats and stoats locked together in combat. Harespring and Thornclaw had taken up their position in front of the only open entrance to make sure that the stoats couldn't flee back into safety. Yowls and shrieks split the air, and the scents of cats and stoats were already mingling with the tang of blood.

Our blood as well as the stoats', he realized, fury welling up inside him.

For a heartbeat his anger blinded him, so he didn't notice that one stoat had broken away from the main battle and charged at him, until it was almost on top of him. As it sprang, he lashed out at it, scoring his claws down its side. The stoat scrabbled away, whimpering. Then fighting surged all around him, and it was all he could do to stay on his paws.

The cats were much larger than the stoats, but even the two Clans together were still vastly outnumbered. The stoats were sharp-toothed, and very fast-moving; Crowfeather saw many of them leap into the air unexpectedly, to land on their enemies' backs and tear at their spines and shoulders. He spotted Furzepelt with a stoat clinging to her shoulders; she rolled over in a desperate attempt to get rid of it, smothering it under her weight. Next to her Mousewhisker slashed his claws down the side of a stoat that had pushed Emberfoot down; the gray tom scrambled to his paws, and the two cats together drove the stoat back into the press of its denmates.

Heading for where the fighting was thickest, Crowfeather

raked his claws across the faces of stoats that got in his way. Already it was hard to move because of the bodies of stoats lying underpaw, yet he could see that many of the cats had serious injuries. He spotted Birchfall, who had blood running down his muzzle from a wounded ear, and Larkwing had a long gash down one side. Even though they were so badly injured, they were still standing, still moving forward, not letting their wounds slow them down.

It's the cats who trained with the Dark Forest who are fighting hardest, Crowfeather realized. *They're throwing themselves into the worst of the battle.*

As he looked around, Crowfeather's heart swelled with pride as he saw his Clanmates, who had suffered so much suspicion after the mistake they'd made, showing their loyalty by risking their lives for their Clan. At the same time, rage against the stoats gave him new strength and energy.

A stoat rushed at him, rearing up to attack him with both forepaws. Crowfeather ducked underneath its forelegs, and as the stoat landed, he spun around to fasten his teeth in its throat. He pinned it to the ground, his paws gripping it determinedly until he felt a warm rush of blood; the stoat went limp and he tossed it aside. Looking up, he found himself staring into the face of Nightcloud.

"Neat kill," she commented. "Leave some for the rest of us, won't you?"

As she spoke, a stoat dived for her, leaping up to land on her back. But before it could get a firm grip on her, Crowfeather lashed out with one forepaw, knocking it to the ground.

Nightcloud sank her claws into its throat; the stoat twitched and lay still. She gave Crowfeather a nod of gratitude before turning back to the battle.

Crowfeather and Nightcloud fought together, standing tail to tail as they turned in a circle, paws striking out at the endless surge of stoats. As soon as they killed or injured one, another would take its place. The white bodies, the small, malignant eyes and snarling fangs, seemed to Crowfeather like something out of a nightmare. He could only go on struggling, grateful for Nightcloud's steady presence beside him.

Then pain exploded in Crowfeather's shoulder. He turned his head to see a stoat gripping him with its claws, while a splash of drool on his muzzle warned him it was going for his throat. Crowfeather couldn't shake it off; he dropped to the ground, buying time, but the pressing weight of the frenzied creature made him feel there was no escape. The angle of their bodies meant that he couldn't batter at it with his hind legs. *StarClan, help me!* he prayed.

The stoat abruptly vanished. Crowfeather looked up to see Nightcloud holding it by the scruff, shaking it vigorously, then tossing it away into the crowd.

"Thanks," Crowfeather gasped, scrambling to his paws.

"Anytime," Nightcloud responded.

They turned as one to attack two other stoats that dived in from opposite directions. Even while his body remembered his battle moves, Crowfeather could reflect on how well he and Nightcloud fought together, how well they knew each other.

We may not be in love, but we make a fierce team on the battlefield. I know she'll fight ferociously for me, and for all her Clanmates.

Crowfeather's reflections were interrupted by a screech of pain. Glancing over his shoulder he saw Lionblaze fall, the golden tabby warrior overwhelmed beneath a swarm of stoats. Crowfeather leaped toward him, only to run into what felt like a solid wall of wiry white bodies. He tried to fight his way through, but too many of them surrounded him. A throb of terror for his ThunderClan son pulsed through Crowfeather; he couldn't reach Lionblaze to help.

He was thrusting vainly against the tide, knowing he would be too late, when Breezepelt leaped into the battle, seeming to come from nowhere. Crowfeather could see that he was bleeding from several wounds, but they hadn't sapped his energy. He grabbed two of the stoats on top of Lionblaze, shaking them and ripping out their throats.

Lionblaze managed to stumble to his paws. He and Breezepelt stared at each other uncomfortably for a moment, then turned away, back to the battle.

Crowfeather couldn't believe what had just happened. "Did you see our son?" he breathed out.

Nightcloud's response was a rough shove. "Don't stand there gaping, mouse-brain!" But Crowfeather could see that her eyes were warm with pride.

Looking around for his next opponent, Crowfeather realized that the war was all but over by now. The stretch of ground between the gorse bushes and the tunnels was strewn with the bodies of stoats. The last few were fleeing, bleeding and whimpering with fear.

In the middle of the devastation, Onestar and Bramblestar

padded up to each other, each of them dipping his head in gratitude and respect to the other.

"Cats of ThunderClan and WindClan!" Onestar called out. "You have fought well today. The battle is won."

"And the stoats are gone for good, I hope," Bramblestar added.

Meanwhile Kestrelflight, Leafpool, and Jayfeather, who had waited out the battle among the gorse bushes, began to move among the injured cats, examining their wounds and applying treatment with the herbs they had brought.

Crowfeather looked around for Breezepelt and spotted him standing a couple of fox-lengths away, licking a wound on his shoulder. Before Crowfeather could join him, he saw Lionblaze limping toward him. Crowfeather held back while his two sons confronted each other.

"Thank you for helping me," Lionblaze began, halting a pace or two in front of Breezepelt. His gaze and his tone were wary. "But why did you? You said I should never have been born. You wanted me dead."

Breezepelt looked up at him, equally awkward. His eyes were guilty as he replied. "I should never have listened to the Dark Forest cats," he mewed stiffly. "You're a Clan cat, and my loyalty should be to the Clans."

Crowfeather realized that this was as close as Breezepelt was ever going to get to an apology for attacking Lionblaze during the Great Battle. He felt his muscles tense as he waited for Lionblaze's response, aware for the first time of how much he wanted his two sons to get along. *Come on,* he urged Lionblaze silently. *Accept his apology!*

Clearly, Lionblaze knew how hard it was for Breezepelt to say even so much. "You fought well," he meowed reluctantly. "I'm glad we were on the same side this time."

The two toms stared at each other and exchanged an awkward, jerky nod before each of them quickly turned back to his own Clan.

Crowfeather felt an unexpected surge of affection for Breezepelt. He was such a surly, difficult furball sometimes, but he was trying so hard to redeem himself. If Breezepelt could do it, so could he. *I can tell my son how I feel about him.*

Crowfeather headed toward his son, who turned to gaze at him. Breezepelt opened his jaws, clearly about to speak, but before he could utter a word, his legs folded under him and he collapsed limply to the ground.

Crowfeather darted to Breezepelt's side. He saw blood pooling beneath him, and, gently turning him over, saw a nasty bite on his belly, as if the stoat had torn his flesh away. The wound had been concealed when Breezepelt was standing upright. Blood trickled through his matted fur. Crowfeather lost his breath as he realized how serious this could be.

"Help!" Crowfeather forced air into his lungs again and yowled. "Kestrelflight, over here!"

But it was Nightcloud who arrived first, crouching beside her son's body and calling his name while she frantically licked his ears. Breezepelt didn't respond.

Crowfeather stared down at his son, digging his claws into the ground. *You can't die now,* he thought helplessly. *Oh, StarClan, no—not when we're starting to understand each other at last!*

CHAPTER 31

Night had fallen by the time Crowfeather and Nightcloud reached the WindClan camp, carrying Breezepelt's unconscious body between them. Crowfeather might almost have thought that his son was dead, except for the faint rise and fall of his chest and the blood that was still trickling from his belly wound and many others.

Kestrelflight had already made a nest for Breezepelt in the medicine-cat den, and prepared a thick wad of cobwebs to begin staunching the flow of blood. Crowfeather and Nightcloud hovered anxiously at the entrance to the den.

Several of the other WindClan warriors were resting close by; some of them licked their wounds, while others lay stretched out with their eyes closed. None of them looked as badly injured as Breezepelt.

As Kestrelflight began to lick the dirt from Breezepelt's lacerated body, the unconscious cat let out a whine of pain. Crowfeather and Nightcloud exchanged an anxious glance, then crowded into the den to get closer to their son's nest.

Kestrelflight looked up, a harassed expression in his eyes. "You'll have to wait outside," he mewed. "I can't treat

Breezepelt if I'm continually tripping over the two of you."

Crowfeather began to retreat, but for a moment Nightcloud stood frozen, staring at her unconscious son. Crowfeather nudged her gently. "Come on," he murmured. "Let Kestrelflight do his job." After a heartbeat Nightcloud followed him out, though they both still watched from the entrance to the den.

Kestrelflight's not usually so snappy, Crowfeather thought. *That must mean he's really worried about Breezepelt.* He felt as if a heavy, rotting lump of crow-food had lodged in his belly. *What if I've made peace with Breezepelt just in time to lose him?*

Crowfeather remembered a time when Breezepelt was still in the nursery. There had been an outbreak of whitecough in the WindClan camp, and Breezekit's had turned into the deadly greencough. Crowfeather had spent each night barely sleeping, wrapped around the tiny kit as though his love and attention could cure his son. When Breezekit woke up one morning with the cough almost gone, Crowfeather's relief had been so intense that he couldn't remember having felt anything like it since.

I shouldn't have forgotten that, he thought. *I was a good father to him once. I shouldn't have doubted myself so much.*

While Crowfeather and Nightcloud waited, Heathertail limped up to stand beside them. "How is Breezepelt?" she asked, fixing Crowfeather with a worried gaze.

Crowfeather simply shook his head, while Nightcloud replied, "Not good."

Heathertail's claws worked for a moment in the ground,

her head and tail drooping. Crowfeather caught a questioning look from Nightcloud, and responded with a nod. *Yes, this will be the mother of our son's kits.* Breezepelt was lucky, he reflected, to have such a strong warrior in his life, so loyal to him and to their Clan.

Nightcloud brushed her tail down Heathertail's side. "Kestrelflight is doing everything he can," she mewed. "Now it's in the paws of StarClan."

Heathertail nodded, then took a deep breath and stood quietly waiting beside her Clanmates.

Just as Crowfeather was beginning to feel that he couldn't hold on to his patience for another heartbeat, Kestrelflight rose and came out of the den. "Breezepelt is seriously injured," he began.

Tell us something we don't know, Crowfeather thought irritably.

"But will he be all right?" Nightcloud asked.

After a long moment, Kestrelflight nodded. "Provided he gets plenty of rest, he should get better."

Nightcloud let out a long sigh of relief. "Thank StarClan!"

"If you want," the medicine cat continued, "*one* of you can spend the night with him so you'll be there when he regains consciousness. That way I can see to treating the other injured cats."

Crowfeather glanced at Nightcloud; he would be happy to stay with their son, but Breezepelt would probably rather see Nightcloud when he woke.

But before either of them could speak, Heathertail stepped forward eagerly. "I'll stay." Then she too glanced at Nightcloud, ducking her head in embarrassment. "If that's okay with you, of course," she added.

Crowfeather expected Nightcloud to object, knowing how possessive and protective of Breezepelt she had always been. At first she was clearly fighting with the urge to admonish Heathertail, her whiskers twitching irritably, but then she stepped back a pace with a glance at Crowfeather. He gave her a nod of approval, knowing how hard it would be for her to release her hold on Breezepelt.

Finally, Nightcloud let out a pleased purr and gestured with her tail for Heathertail to enter the den. While Heathertail padded inside, the black she-cat and Crowfeather waited for Kestrelflight to check their wounds and treat them with chervil to prevent infection.

"You should be fine," the medicine cat meowed. "Go get some rest, and I'll examine you again in the morning."

Crowfeather was so exhausted that he didn't put up any kind of fight. He went directly to the warriors' den, and not even the pain of his injuries or his worry about Breezepelt could keep him awake. He fell asleep before his eyes even closed.

It felt as if only moments had passed before a paw prodded him on his shoulder, rousing him at last. He opened his eyes to see the sun rising above the moor and Nightcloud standing over him.

"What are you, a dormouse?" she asked. "Come see how Breezepelt is getting along."

Crowfeather willingly followed her to the medicine-cat

den, trying to ignore the uncomfortable fluttering in his belly when he wondered what he would find there. He felt shaky with relief when he heard Breezepelt's mew as they approached the den, sounding strong and free from pain.

Stepping inside the den at Nightcloud's side, Crowfeather saw that Kestrelflight wasn't there. Breezepelt was sitting up in his nest, with Heathertail crouched beside him. The two young cats were gazing into each other's eyes; Crowfeather could sense the love between them.

He cleared his throat, and at the sound Breezepelt's head swiveled toward the entrance, while Heathertail eased back a little so she wasn't so close to him.

"Greetings," Nightcloud meowed. "How are you feeling, Breezepelt?"

"Like every stoat on the territory has taken a bite out of me," Breezepelt replied wryly. "But I'm going to be fine."

"A group of WindClan and ThunderClan cats are going to go through the tunnels and make sure the stoats are really gone," Nightcloud went on. "If you want to go, Heathertail, I'll stay with Breezepelt."

"Oh, I'm happy to stay if Harespring wants you to go," Heathertail responded eagerly.

I'm sure you are, Crowfeather thought, exchanging an amused glance with Nightcloud. The two young cats were gazing into each other's eyes again, and Nightcloud leaned over to murmur into Crowfeather's ear.

"I think the Clan will be welcoming new kits before long."

* * *

The next morning, Crowfeather padded through the dim tunnels, part of a patrol that included Nightcloud, Lionblaze, and Cloudtail, with Harespring in the lead. His nose wrinkled at the smell of stoat.

I'm going to vomit if I can't get away from that stink, he thought. *It's sinking into my fur . . . I'll be tasting it for moons! If I never see another stoat, it will be too soon.*

The patrols found plenty of evidence that the stoats had been there: holes filled with rotting prey and dens where nests had been scratched together from scraps of grass and bracken. But there was no sign that any of the stoats had returned.

All the while he was patrolling, Crowfeather was acutely conscious that Lionblaze was part of the group. He kept an eye on him, and started forward a couple of times before he eventually braced himself and managed to maneuver to walk beside him.

"There's something I want to say to you," he told the ThunderClan cat.

Lionblaze tilted his head to one side, giving Crowfeather a slightly suspicious look. His golden fur was torn to reveal scratches underneath, and he was limping slightly on one forepaw, but he was still the magnificent ThunderClan warrior who Crowfeather could hardly believe was his son.

"Okay," Lionblaze mewed at last. He slowed his pace so that he and Crowfeather gradually dropped behind the rest of the patrol. "How is Breezepelt?" he asked hesitantly.

"He'll be fine," Crowfeather replied. When Lionblaze acknowledged his news with a nod, he continued awkwardly, the words he had been waiting to say bursting out of him.

"I'm sorry I didn't accept you and your littermates when I found out about you. I'm sorry that I said I had only one kit, and that anything else was a lie. If I'd known . . ." He stumbled over his words and had to begin again, while Lionblaze listened, expressionless. "If I'd only known when you were kits, when you needed me, surely things would have been different. I have no excuses, but . . . I hope you can forgive me for the way I acted."

Lionblaze paused for a moment before replying, his amber eyes gleaming with disbelief in the dim light of the tunnel, as if he was questioning why Crowfeather was even bothering to talk to him. "It doesn't matter," he responded at last. "I was a full-grown warrior by the time I found out that you and Leafpool were my parents. I don't need to be your kit. Bramblestar was the only father we knew, and he was a great one. He'll always be my father, no matter what."

Crowfeather nodded, feeling the pain of rejection. He was glad that he had spoken, but he accepted that he could not control how his son responded. *I guess Lionblaze and Jayfeather will always resent me.*

"I'm not angry with you," Lionblaze added. "I accept your apology, and I'm grateful for the way it all turned out."

A little reassured, Crowfeather dipped his head again in acceptance. He began reaching out his tail to touch Lionblaze on the shoulder, then hastily drew it back again as he realized that would never be their relationship. This cordial agreement, with the air cleared between them, was the best he could hope for. *And I have to learn to be okay with that.*

Part of Crowfeather was sad at the thought of what might have been, but mostly he was filled with relief that he and Lionblaze had reached an understanding. It felt like a cool shower of rain in a dry season.

For a brief moment, Crowfeather wondered what his life would have been like if he and Leafpool had never returned to their Clans. They would have found a place to live happily, with Lionblaze and Jayfeather and Hollyleaf, and maybe many other kits. But then Crowfeather pushed the vision away. All three of their kits would have been different if he and Leafpool had raised them together, and he guessed that in the end Leafpool's love of her Clan would have drawn her back to her calling as a medicine cat. The knowledge hurt, but everything had happened as it was meant to. And Crowfeather felt humbled that Lionblaze had forgiven him.

Crowfeather and Lionblaze caught up to the rest of the patrol as they emerged from the tunnels, blinking in the sunlight that seemed dazzling after so long in the dark. Harespring, who had been leading the patrol, bounded up to Onestar.

"The tunnels are clear of stoats," he reported.

"And it's time we were leaving," Squirrelflight added, gathering the ThunderClan cats together with a wave of her bushy tail. "Let us know if you have any more trouble."

"I'm sure we won't," Onestar meowed, with a respectful dip of his head. "The stoats are gone, and we couldn't have achieved that without your help. Please take the thanks of WindClan to Bramblestar."

Squirrelflight nodded, equally respectful. "I will. And may StarClan light your path."

"And yours," Onestar responded.

Crowfeather watched as Squirrelflight led the Thunder-Clan cats away toward the border. Warm satisfaction filled him at the thought that their two Clans had worked together, along with hope that they could rely on each other in the future. As they went, he caught Nightcloud's eye and saw that she was looking calm and approving.

In the past she had always been angry and contemptuous of ThunderClan, never losing a chance to quarrel with them or accuse them of overstepping. For the first time, Crowfeather realized that so much of that had been because of him.

It must have been hard for her, he thought as he and the rest of the WindClan cats headed for their camp, *knowing that for so long my heart lay across that border. Maybe now she won't be so angry. And maybe in future the Clans can finally learn to get along in peace.*

CHAPTER 32

An icy wind swept across the moor, buffeting Crowfeather's fur as he stood watching his apprentice. Featherpaw had picked up the scent of a rabbit where it crouched in a clump of long grass, and now she chased it up the hill, her muscles bunching and stretching as she gradually gained on her quarry. His heart warmed to see her speed and strength, as if she had never been injured.

The rabbit doubled back, and without a heartbeat's hesitation Featherpaw changed direction, not chasing the rabbit anymore, but seeming to know instinctively where it would run. She leaped on it with outstretched paws; Crowfeather heard the rabbit's squeal of terror, abruptly cut off as Featherpaw killed it by biting its throat.

He waited for his apprentice as she trotted back to him, her prey dangling from her jaws. "Was that okay?" she asked, her eyes shining as she dropped the rabbit in front of him.

"No, it wasn't okay," Crowfeather meowed, then added quickly before Featherpaw had time to look disappointed, "It was magnificent. Well done!"

Featherpaw blinked up at him happily. "It's your catch

really," she purred. "You're such a great mentor!"

Crowfeather felt a tingle of satisfaction in his paws, reflecting that even though he hadn't been the best father when his kits were growing up, he was at least a good mentor now. *Maybe that can make up for my other failings. . . .*

"We'd better head back," he meowed, picking up the rook he had caught earlier and leading the way down the hill and into the camp.

"What shall we do now?" Featherpaw asked, dropping her rabbit on the fresh-kill pile.

Glancing around the camp, Crowfeather spotted the other three apprentices dragging soiled bedding out of the elders' den. "Go and help them," he mewed, angling his ears in that direction.

Featherpaw's tail drooped. "Do I have to?"

"Yes, you do. Life isn't all rabbit-chasing, you know." Crowfeather let out a little purr of satisfaction. "Tell them I said you made the best catch this season."

"Yes!" Energized again, Featherpaw dashed across the camp to join her denmates.

I'll miss her when it's time for her to become a warrior, Crowfeather thought as he watched her go. *But she's shaping up to be a really fine one.*

He turned toward Kestrelflight's den to visit his son. Several days had passed since the final battle against the stoats, and Breezepelt was the only one of the injured warriors who hadn't returned to his duties. His recovery hadn't gone as quickly as Crowfeather had hoped. He spent much of the time in a troubled, unhealthy sleep, and when he was awake, he was dull and listless. The day before, he had looked up at Crowfeather and called him Lionblaze before shaking his head and seeming to come to his senses.

Maybe he'll be better today, Crowfeather told himself, but it was hard to make himself believe it.

As Crowfeather approached the medicine-cat den, Heathertail emerged and hurried over to him. "Where's Nightcloud?" she asked.

Crowfeather pointed with his tail to where the black she-cat was crouched near the fresh-kill pile, sharing a pigeon with Sedgewhisker. Immediately, Heathertail bounded over to her, and Crowfeather followed.

"I want you both to come to Kestrelflight's den," Heathertail meowed when she reached Nightcloud.

Alarm in her eyes, Nightcloud immediately sprang to her paws, gulping down her mouthful of prey. "What happened?" she demanded.

"I went to visit Breezepelt this morning," Heathertail explained as she led the way back to the den, "and he's taken a turn for the worse. You need to see him."

Crowfeather and Nightcloud exchanged a look of alarm as they followed Heathertail. Inside the den, Crowfeather saw that Breezepelt was awake, but his eyes were glazed, and when Crowfeather touched his shoulder, he could feel heat radiating from his pelt. He didn't seem to recognize any of them, but he was muttering to himself. "Stupid stoats . . . kill you all . . ." His head kept sagging to one side, as if he was half-asleep.

Kestrelflight appeared from the back of the den, carrying a mouthful of borage leaves in his jaws.

"Eat those," he meowed, setting the leaves down in front of Breezepelt. "They'll help bring down your fever."

"What's the matter with him?" Nightcloud asked anxiously.

"Most of his wounds are healing nicely," Kestrelflight told her, while Heathertail coaxed Breezepelt to eat the herbs. "But there's one very bad bite, the one on his belly, and it's infected. If it gets any worse, I'm afraid he won't make it."

Crowfeather stared at the medicine cat in horror. *Won't make it? What about his future with Heathertail? What about my chance to be a real father to him?* "There must be something you can do," he meowed.

"I have plenty of herbs for the pain and the fever, but the remedy for infected bites is burdock root," Kestrelflight explained. "And I'm all out of it. I used up the last of my supply on Breezepelt and the other injured warriors after the battle."

Crowfeather raised his head, his expression grim with determination. "It's settled, then. We'll go and search for burdock root if you tell us what to look for and where we might find it."

"This is leaf-bare," Kestrelflight replied. "The leaves die back, and without the leaves it's hard to know where the roots are. But I can send cats to the other Clans to ask the medicine cats if they have any to spare. I'd go myself, but I need to keep a close eye on Breezepelt."

Nightcloud spun around to gaze at Crowfeather. "You should go to ThunderClan and ask Leafpool," she meowed. "She won't say no to you."

Kestrelflight glanced away and gave his shoulder an embarrassed lick, clearly uncomfortable at being reminded of Crowfeather's history with the ThunderClan cat.

Feeling awkward, Crowfeather hesitated. *Is Nightcloud really asking me to go visit Leafpool?*

A hint of her old rage glimmered in Nightcloud's eyes, but it wasn't jealousy that Crowfeather saw there. "You must!" she insisted fiercely. "Leafpool won't let your son die if she can stop it. Crowfeather, you owe it to me and to Breezepelt to ask her. You *have* to do everything you can."

Crowfeather realized that she was right. *This is no time to start raking over old troubles.* "Of course I'll go," he mewed.

Crowfeather stood on the bank of the border stream, his shoulders hunched against a thin drizzle that had started as he crossed the moor. He was waiting for a ThunderClan patrol. His claws tore impatiently at the grass as he wondered how long it would be before any cats appeared.

If they're waiting for the rain to stop, it could be too late for Breezepelt.

Crowfeather's paws itched to leap across and hurry toward the camp on his own, but he knew it would be a bad idea to trespass when he had come to ask a favor.

I wish I'd thought to bring another cat with me, he thought. *Featherpaw, for example . . . We could have done some training, and then I wouldn't have the time to worry about Breezepelt.*

But when Crowfeather had asked Onestar's permission to visit Leafpool, his Clan leader had told him to go alone. "You won't have any trouble," Onestar had assured him. "Not since you're on medicine-cat business."

Finally, Crowfeather picked up a fresher ThunderClan scent and heard the sound of a patrol brushing through the undergrowth on the far side of the stream. He stepped forward to the very edge as Sandstorm, Berrynose, and Ivypool emerged into the open.

"Great StarClan, it's you again!" Berrynose exclaimed.

And it's you again, you rude furball. Crowfeather didn't speak the thought aloud. "Greetings," he meowed politely, addressing Sandstorm. "Please, may I come across? I'm on medicine-cat business from Kestrelflight, and I need to speak to Leafpool."

"This *is* a border," Berrynose pointed out, before Sandstorm could reply. "Smell the scent marks? You can't come in here when you feel like it, as if you were a kittypet going in and out of its Twolegs' den."

Crowfeather felt the fur on his spine beginning to rise at being compared to a kittypet, but he forced it to lie flat again. He needed to stay on good terms with these cats and get the help he needed quickly, however much he might want to claw the smug expression off Berrynose's face.

"That's enough, Berrynose," Sandstorm snapped, and Crowfeather caught Ivypool rolling her eyes.

I guess ThunderClan cats find Berrynose just as much of a pain in the tail as we do, Crowfeather thought.

"You can come over, Crowfeather," Sandstorm went on. "We're ready to go back to camp, so we can escort you."

Sandstorm led the way through the woods with Crowfeather behind her and Berrynose bringing up the rear with Ivypool. Crowfeather winced at the cold touch of wet grass and fern against his pelt, and the drops of rain from the trees that plopped down on his back. *Somehow the forest seems so much wetter than the moor,* he thought as he trudged along with his head down.

When they reached the stone hollow, Sandstorm took Crowfeather as far as the entrance to the medicine-cat den and left him there. "Go right in," she instructed him. "I'll tell Bramblestar you're here."

Crowfeather brushed past the brambles that screened the entrance to the den, calling out Leafpool's name as he entered. But once he was inside the den, he saw that Leafpool wasn't there, only Jayfeather and Briarlight curled up asleep in her nest. He halted, freezing.

Now what do I do?

Jayfeather turned from where he was sorting herbs toward the back of the den. "That's WindClan scent," he muttered, tasting the air. A moment later he added, "Oh, it's you, Crowfeather." He didn't sound happy about it. "What do you want?"

"I was looking for Leafpool," Crowfeather explained, realizing that he would have to make the best of the awkward situation.

"She's out gathering herbs," Jayfeather told him curtly. "But if you're here on medicine-cat business, I can help with that just as well as Leafpool can. She certainly doesn't need you taking up any more of her time. You've already done enough of that."

Crowfeather flinched, glad that Jayfeather couldn't see him. "Kestrelflight sent me to ask if you could spare any burdock root," he mewed.

Jayfeather flicked his tail. "Lionblaze told me Breezepelt was injured in the battle," he responded dryly. "Is that who the burdock root is for? Is that why Kestrelflight sent *you*?"

The tight lines of Jayfeather's shoulders, the tilted back, the furious angle of his ears, even the clipped, sullen tone of his voice all seemed so familiar to Crowfeather. He looked and sounded like Breezepelt at his angriest.

In fact, Crowfeather realized with a weird little lurch in his belly, *they both look and sound like* me, *at my worst.*

For the first time—and Crowfeather knew that it was pretty useless to see it now—he felt a flush of recognition for Jayfeather. Even though Bramblestar had raised him, there could be no doubt: The blind medicine cat really was his kit.

"Yes, the burdock root is for Breezepelt," he admitted, allowing a bit of impatience into his own voice. *Jayfeather needs to know I'm serious.* "He's badly hurt. Kestrelflight says he has an infected stoat bite. He's feverish and he doesn't recognize any cat, and Kestrelflight told me he needs burdock root. He—"

"I'm sorry." Jayfeather cut him off with barely concealed contempt. "I don't have any to spare."

The disappointment struck Crowfeather like a blow. For a moment he'd thought he understood the cranky, blind medicine cat. . . . *But I was wrong. And why shouldn't I be? I barely know him.*

Crowfeather felt a sinking feeling deep in his chest and was about to take his leave when he realized something: Jayfeather had said he couldn't spare any burdock root, not that he didn't have any at all.

"If you can lend me some, just for a little while," he pleaded, "I'll find more for you. I—"

Jayfeather interrupted again, every word spat out as if it were rotting crow-food. "Breezepelt tried to kill my brother. He said he was glad that Hollyleaf was dead, and that none of us should ever have been born. Lionblaze might have forgiven Breezepelt, but Lionblaze is a nicer cat than I am. Or a more stupid one." His blind eyes glared at Crowfeather, the pelt on his scrawny figure bushing out. "I can't forgive Breezepelt. I can't forgive you. And I don't have any burdock root to spare."

Crowfeather stood still, his shoulders sagging as he took his son's hostile expression. The thought crossed his mind that he could fight his way past Jayfeather and take the burdock root, but he knew how bee-brained that would be. *I'd never make it out of the camp.* But it was hard to know that the root to save Breezepelt was only a few tail-lengths away, at the back of the den.

"I'm sorry I treated you badly when I found out you were my kit," Crowfeather meowed at last, breaking the long silence. "And I know that Breezepelt is sorry for what he did in the battle against the Dark Forest."

If he had hoped for a sympathetic response from Jayfeather, he was disappointed. The medicine cat said nothing, only flicked his tail dismissively.

Crowfeather dipped his head in acceptance. "Good-bye," he murmured. "I should have known that you would say no."

Then he turned and left the den.

I'll go on around the lake and stop off in ShadowClan, and if that's no good, I'll visit RiverClan on my way home. Mothwing won't refuse if she has the burdock root. But even so, every extra paw step takes time Breezepelt may not have. . . .

The rain was still falling, depressing Crowfeather's spirits even more. He headed for the thorn tunnel, but before he reached it, he heard Jayfeather calling out behind him. "Crowfeather, wait!"

Crowfeather halted and turned. Jayfeather was approaching him, carrying something in his mouth. In spite of everything, Crowfeather was impressed by the way the blind cat found his way across the camp, even skirting neatly around a puddle that lay in his way.

When Jayfeather reached him, Crowfeather saw that what he was carrying was burdock root; he dropped it on the ground at Crowfeather's paws.

"I still don't forgive you," Jayfeather mewed. "Everything I said is still true. But I'm a medicine cat, and I can't just let a cat die when I could save him. Not even Breezepelt. So here is the burdock root."

Crowfeather could hardly catch his breath. "Th-thank you!" he stammered.

Jayfeather didn't respond. Turning away, he padded back to his den and disappeared behind the bramble screen. Crowfeather picked up the burdock root from the muddy ground and bounded back toward WindClan territory.

Hang on, Breezepelt, he thought. *I'm on my way.*

CHAPTER 33

❦

Nightcloud and Heathertail leaped to their paws as Crowfeather entered the medicine-cat den. Breezepelt was curled up beside them, shifting in an uneasy sleep.

"Well? Did Leafpool have burdock root?" Nightcloud demanded.

"I saw Jayfeather, not Leafpool," Crowfeather replied, dropping the root in front of Kestrelflight. "He gave me the root." *No need to tell them* how *he gave it to me.*

Instantly Kestrelflight seized the burdock root and began chewing it into a pulp. Once he had some ready, he spread it on the swollen stoat bite and bound it in place with a cobweb.

"That should help with the pain and deal with the infection," he explained.

As sunhigh came and went, Crowfeather, Nightcloud, and Heathertail all remained in the medicine-cat den, anxiously watching over Breezepelt. At first Crowfeather couldn't see much change in his son's condition, but after a long while Breezepelt seemed to fall into a deeper, quieter sleep.

"That's a good sign," Kestrelflight meowed. "A real sleep— not the restless kind he's had up to now—is healing."

All three warriors looked at each other, and Crowfeather saw his own relief reflected in the she-cats' faces. He noticed too that they both looked exhausted after their long vigil.

"You should go and get some prey, and then rest," he told them. "You've been here in the den, worrying, all day." Nightcloud opened her jaws to protest, but Crowfeather forestalled her. "I'll stay right here beside Breezepelt," he promised, "and I'll call you if anything changes."

"Crowfeather's right," Kestrelflight agreed. "You should go. It won't help Breezepelt if you make yourselves ill."

Nightcloud and Heathertail exchanged a glance, then, still clearly reluctant, padded out of the den. Crowfeather settled down beside Breezepelt's nest, his gaze fixed on his son's sleeping face. Kestrelflight came and went silently, busy with his medicine-cat duties.

Crowfeather's mind flew back to the day when Breezepelt was born. Even then he hadn't loved Nightcloud in the way he had loved Feathertail, and later Leafpool, but he'd admired her for her strength and her loyalty to WindClan. He was proud that she was having his kits, but he wasn't prepared for the sharp pang of love he felt for Breezepelt when the kit was finally born.

The birth had been a difficult one. There were two other kits in the litter—one had been born dead, and the other lived for only a few moments. But Breezepelt had been perfect and strong.

How did I get so far from that feeling?

Crowfeather became aware of scarlet light from the sunset

seeping into the den, and then the remaining daylight fading into night. Kestrelflight was asleep in his nest and Crowfeather was dozing when Breezepelt finally stirred.

Crowfeather looked up to see that his son's eyes were open, and they weren't glossy and unfocused as they had been earlier—they were now sharp and alert.

"How do you feel?" Crowfeather asked him. "You've been really ill. We were all worried about you."

"I'm fine . . . ," Breezepelt murmured. He raised his head and looked around him, blinking in vague surprise to see the sleeping Kestrelflight and the darkness outside. "You've been here all night?" he asked.

"Yes, well . . ." Crowfeather felt uncomfortable as he realized that Breezepelt was touched to see him there. "Heathertail was watching over you," he went on rapidly, "but she got so exhausted that I talked her into going for a rest. She and Nightcloud will be back at dawn to see how you are."

"That's good," Breezepelt responded. "Heathertail is . . . amazing."

"She certainly is," Crowfeather agreed.

"I can't believe she actually wants to be with me," Breezepelt continued, a bewildered but happy expression on his face.

"Why on earth not?" Crowfeather touched Breezepelt's shoulder with his tail-tip. "You're a loyal WindClan warrior, and one of the bravest."

Breezepelt met his gaze, disbelief in his eyes. "You really believe that?"

"I really do."

Talking softly to his son in the dark, Crowfeather felt like things truly were changing. He was keeping the promise he'd made to Ashfoot, and to himself. *This is good,* he thought. *Why was it so difficult before?*

Soon Breezepelt went back to sleep, and Crowfeather felt reassured enough to do the same. At once he found himself on a hillside, with wind rippling the grass and blowing through his fur, flattening it to his sides. The air was full of wild moorland scents. The sky glittered with stars, and light came from somewhere behind him, so that he cast a long, wavering shadow out in front. Turning, Crowfeather saw Ashfoot.

His mother stood facing him. Her gray fur shone with the pale glow he had seen before in his dreams, but this time her ears shimmered faintly, and there was a frosty sparkle around her paws.

"You made it to StarClan!" he exclaimed, overawed by how beautiful she was.

Ashfoot dipped her head. "It was time," she mewed. "I'm so proud of you, Crowfeather. Proud that you're finally listening. No cat can be a good warrior, or a loyal Clanmate, with a closed heart. Now you have opened yours . . . and WindClan is better for it."

Deep happiness flowed through Crowfeather at his mother's praise, but apprehension was mixed with it, too. "It scares me a little," he admitted. "Caring, when for so long I tried not to. Any cat you love, you can lose."

"The loss is worth it," Ashfoot purred warmly. "I loved you . . . so much . . . and now it hurts to part. But I'm better for it, and so are you."

"Then I won't see you again?" Crowfeather asked, feeling as if a forest tree had crashed down on top of him.

"Not like this," Ashfoot responded. "But I'll always watch out for you, from StarClan."

Crowfeather heaved a long sigh, forcing himself into acceptance. "Good-bye, then," he meowed. "I'll always love you, and miss you."

"Take care of your kin," his mother meowed. "And remember that I'm always with you. . . ."

Her voice died away on the last few words. Crowfeather saw her shape begin to fade, until it was no more than a frosty glimmer in the air, and then was gone.

CHAPTER 34

❧

The sun was almost touching the top of the moor as Crowfeather and Featherpaw carefully pressed a flat stone against the side of one of the tunnel entrances, shoring up a spill of crumbling earth.

"Good," Crowfeather meowed, stepping back with a purr of satisfaction. "We should get this job finished before nightfall."

More than a half-moon had passed since the battle against the stoats, and so far none of the survivors had returned. Even their scent had well and truly faded. Onestar had ordered the tunnel entrances to be blocked more securely, all except for one, and had decided that WindClan needed to patrol the tunnels to discourage any other animals from settling there in future.

"Imagine if a family of badgers decided to live there!" he had meowed.

As Featherpaw went off to find more stones, Nightcloud and Hootpaw emerged from the entrance and stood beside Crowfeather, shaking dust from their pelts.

"That's done!" Nightcloud exclaimed. "The whole place is

clear of the last of the old prey."

"It was disgusting!" Hootpaw added, passing his tongue over his jaws as if he could taste the crow-food. "I thought we'd never finish."

"Well done," Crowfeather mewed with an approving nod, surprised at how comfortable he felt around Nightcloud now.

"You've done enough!" Heathertail's voice came from farther along the bank; Crowfeather turned to see her with Breezepelt. "Onestar has chosen you to go to the Gathering, so you should rest first."

Breezepelt gave her a friendly shove. "I'm perfectly fine," he mewed.

Crowfeather could hardly believe how carefree Breezepelt sounded, as if more had been healed within him than just the infection from the stoat bite. *It's good to hear him like that.*

He exchanged an amused glance with Nightcloud as they listened to the two young cats' amiable wrangling.

Nightcloud leaned closer to him and whispered into his ear, "I wouldn't be surprised if there are new kits in the nursery soon."

"Really?" Crowfeather asked. "I know you said that before, but—"

"Just look at them, mouse-brain!" Nightcloud's words were harsh, but her eyes were sparkling and her tail curled up playfully.

"Kits . . . ," Crowfeather murmured. "Great StarClan, *this* soon . . . ?" *I'm just figuring out how to be a father. . . .*

Onestar's voice, calling the Clan together, interrupted his

musing. The sun was beginning to set, casting scarlet light across the moor. A chilly breeze had sprung up, but the sky was clear, a good omen for the night's Gathering.

"Duties are over for the day," the Clan leader announced as his cats padded up to him. "We'll head back to the camp, and the cats I've chosen for the Gathering should go to their dens and rest."

At least, Crowfeather thought as he began to climb the hill behind his Clan leader, *this time we have good news to report.*

Crowfeather slipped into the shifting mass of cats in the clearing beneath the branches of the Great Oak. Once again WindClan was the last to arrive, but the Clan leaders seemed to be in no hurry to start the meeting. The WindClan cats had time to mingle with the earlier arrivals, greeting their friends from other Clans.

Crowfeather found a space for himself not far from the roots of the Great Oak, where Harespring had taken his place with the other deputies. Not far away, he spotted Leafpool and Jayfeather with their fellow medicine cats.

For a long time before the battle against the Dark Forest, Crowfeather had been barely able to look at either of them, but now all he could feel toward them was gratitude.

Leafpool had helped him heal his heart after Feathertail died, even though in the end they couldn't be together, and Jayfeather might still hate Breezepelt, but he'd done what was right to save his life.

Finally, Blackstar lifted his head to get every cat's attention:

"Before we begin, let us remember the fallen . . ."

This again, Crowfeather thought, although it did feel important to not forget the fallen warriors.

As soon as he'd finished, Blackstar then declared that prey was running well in ShadowClan territory. "My patrols picked up fox scent near the Twoleg greenleafplace," he continued, "but it faded quickly and hasn't returned. We think that the fox was only passing through."

He stepped back, waving his tail for Mistystar to speak for RiverClan. The blue-gray she-cat dipped her head in acknowledgement before she began.

"All is well in RiverClan," she announced. "This last moon we had several cases of whitecough, but Mothwing and Willowshine were able to treat it before it turned to greencough, and the sick cats are recovering well. Mothwing, Willowshine, your Clan thanks you."

The RiverClan cats joined in chanting the names of their two medicine cats, as Bramblestar stepped forward to begin his report.

"Life is good in ThunderClan," he meowed. "Two of our apprentices, Cherrypaw and Molepaw, have completed their training, after Whitewing took over and worked with Cherrypaw. We welcome them as warriors, Cherryfall and Molewhisker."

"Cherryfall! Molewhisker!" Yowling erupted from the assembled cats, while the two new warriors ducked their heads, looking happily embarrassed.

Crowfeather half expected Bramblestar to mention the

battle against the stoats, but the ThunderClan leader gave his place to Blackstar without saying any more.

He must be leaving that piece of news to Onestar, Crowfeather thought, as Bramblestar sat on his branch again with a nod to Onestar to give his report.

Crowfeather thought that his Clan leader looked proud as he rose to his paws and let his gaze travel over the assembled cats on the ground below him. *And no wonder, after all the problems at the last Gathering. So much has changed since then.*

"WindClan fought a battle with the stoats in the tunnels," Onestar began. "Many of the stoats were killed, and the survivors fled. The tunnels are now clear again. But WindClan did not fight alone. ThunderClan came to our aid, and without their bravery and the generous help they gave us, we could never have won this victory. Bramblestar, WindClan thanks you and your Clan from the bottom of our hearts."

Onestar paused, dipping his head deeply toward Bramblestar; Crowfeather could see how much he now respected the young ThunderClan leader. Bramblestar's amber eyes glowed in response, as if praise from the older and more experienced leader meant a lot to him.

"I also want to mention another cat," Onestar went on. "A warrior from my own Clan, with whom I've had my differences, but who never gave up on his determination that the stoats must be driven out. Crowfeather, while we've butted heads, I appreciate your devotion to WindClan."

Crowfeather felt a warming beneath his pelt as Onestar nodded in his direction. *Don't go softhearted on me,* he thought, but in his embarrassment he managed to nod his head to show his appreciation. Onestar nodded back, then went on.

"I must also mention the cats who fought with special bravery and deserve our collective thanks," Onestar went on. "From ThunderClan, Mousewhisker, Birchfall, Thornclaw, and Blossomfall; from WindClan, Harespring, Larkwing, Whiskernose, and Breezepelt."

As Onestar spoke the names, a murmur arose from the gathered cats, as they realized that these were the cats who had trained with the Dark Forest behind their Clanmates' backs.

As soon as Onestar had finished speaking, Rowanclaw, the ShadowClan deputy, sprang to his paws from where he sat on the roots of the Great Oak. Crowfeather felt dread rise in his belly, knowing very well that Rowanclaw was about to disrupt the spirit of friendship that was growing among the Clans.

"So they should fight bravely!" he snapped. "They've got a lot to make up for before any cat trusts them again."

Bramblestar rose, glaring down at Rowanclaw, but before he could speak, Lionblaze leaped up and faced the Shadow-Clan deputy.

"Shame on you, Rowanclaw!" he meowed. "Every cat knows that those cats were tricked. They thought they were becoming stronger warriors to protect their Clans. They've taken an oath of loyalty, and have proved themselves since then. Breezepelt saved my life when the stoats swarmed over me. If I can forgive Breezepelt for his part in the Great Battle, then you, Rowanclaw, have no excuse." The golden tabby tom turned his head until his cool amber gaze rested on Breeze-pelt. "I, for one, think the past should be left in the past," he finished.

Rowanclaw subsided onto his root with a glowering look, but he said no more. While Bramblestar briefly thanked One-star and brought the meeting to an end, Crowfeather kept his gaze fixed on Lionblaze.

What a straightforward, generous, candid cat Lionblaze is, he thought. *He's a strong warrior, and any cat should be proud to call him kin.* A little wryly he admitted to himself that being raised by Bramblestar probably had a good deal to do with his having turned out to be that kind of cat. *Maybe one day I'll thank Bramblestar for that.*

Crowfeather padded between Onestar and Harespring as they crossed the moor on their way back to the WindClan camp. Thin clouds scudded across the sky, driven by a stiff breeze, but the moon floated serenely above them all, and the warriors of StarClan glittered from horizon to horizon.

"That was a great Gathering," Harespring remarked, blinking in satisfaction. "It's good that there's peace among all the Clans."

"Yes," Crowfeather agreed. "Now there's time for the Clans to grow strong, unthreatened by one another."

For several heartbeats Onestar was silent; his eyes were dark and inward-looking. "Are you okay?" Harespring asked him.

Onestar glanced at Harespring, then at Crowfeather, and then at his own paws, padding steadily uphill. "I don't know how long there will be peace in the Clans," he mewed softly. "I can't shake off the feeling that something bad is coming."

"Do you know *what*?" Harespring asked his Clan leader.

Onestar shook his head. "No," he responded, shivering. "But sometimes I have bad dreams."

Crowfeather remembered Kestrelflight's vision of water gushing from the tunnels, strong enough to overwhelm and drown all the Clans. *I've thought all along that the stoats weren't enough to explain such a terrible sign,* he thought with a sudden quaking in his belly. *What if I'm right? What if there is a second wave that will engulf us all?*

They returned to the camp, and Crowfeather curled up in his nest. In spite of Onestar's misgivings, he felt at peace. WindClan had learned a lesson: We must trust the other Clans.

Sinking into sleep, Crowfeather dreamed that he was lying in a sunny hollow on the moor, with the scents of fresh growth filling the air. Healthy, boisterous kits were swarming all over him, batting at him with their soft paws and letting out excited squeaks as they tumbled about. One of them, he noticed, had Heathertail's wide blue eyes, while two of the others were as black as Breezepelt.

"Oof! Get off!" Crowfeather exclaimed, batting gently at them with claws sheathed.

"You're a badger!" one of the kits squealed. "And we're warriors coming to get you!"

"Yeah, get off our territory, stinky badger!" Another of

them dug his paws deep into Crowfeather's fur.

One of the kits, more adventurous than the rest, was heading off across the moor. Nightcloud intercepted her and guided her back toward her littermates. Breezepelt and Heathertail, their tails twined together, looked on with laughter in their eyes.

Crowfeather had never known such feelings of deep happiness and peace. Looking up, he saw a cloud above him suddenly shift into a familiar shape. Ashfoot's face was looking down at him, and Crowfeather basked in the pride and love in her expression.

Thank you, Ashfoot, he thought. *You taught me what I needed to learn. Everything I endured brought me to this, to give me something to fight for in WindClan.*

And if trouble does come, he added to himself, *then WindClan will deal with it. After the Great Battle, and the fight against the stoats, there's surely no threat that our Clan can't face.*

READ ON FOR AN

EXCLUSIVE MANGA ADVENTURE . . .

CREATED BY
ERIN HUNTER

WRITTEN BY
DAN JOLLEY

ART BY
JAMES L. BARRY

I GUESS YOU'RE RIGHT. I HOPE YOU'RE RIGHT. IT'S JUST...

SO MANY CATS TRUSTED HIM. SO MANY WERE READY TO TRUST HIM. AND LOOK WHAT HE DID.

OPENING UP ALL THESE OLD WOUNDS. MORE BETRAYALS.

WILL THIS KEEP THE CLANS FROM EVER TRUSTING THE DARK FOREST WARRIORS?

I WISH I KNEW THE ANSWER TO THAT QUESTION.

BUT BEFORE I CAN COME UP WITH ONE--

AHEAD OF US.

THUNDERCLAN PATROL.

WHICH CATS? GOT A SCENT YET?

I KNOW HE'S ON EDGE.

SURROUNDED BY SO MANY CATS WHO WANTED NOTHING TO DO WITH HIM FOR SO LONG..

IF HE THINKS OUR CLANMATES DON'T TRUST HIM, WILL HE START DRIVING THEM AWAY?

WILL HE MAKE THEM THINK HE DOESN'T BELONG HERE AFTER ALL?

I CAN'T LET THAT HAPPEN AGAIN.

I WON'T.

LOOK AT THIS...EVERY SINGLE CAT HERE IS STARING AT US.

GREAT.

ARE THEY GOING TO REJECT BREEZEPELT?

HAS EVERYTHING WE'VE DONE BEEN FOR NOTHING?

NO...WAIT...

BREEZEPELT, IS IT MY IMAGINATION?

OR DOES EVERY CAT LOOK...HAPPY?

I DON'T THINK YOU'RE IMAGINING IT...

CROWFEATHER, IF YOU CAN SPARE A MOMENT...?

I--OF COURSE, WHAT DO YOU--

WINDCLAN! I HAVE AN ANNOUNCEMENT TO MAKE!

MY SONS...MY FAMILY... MY WHOLE CLAN, AT PEACE.

I DON'T KNOW IF I DESERVE ALL THIS.

BUT I'LL TAKE IT.

LET ALL CATS OLD ENOUGH TO CATCH THEIR OWN PREY JOIN HERE BENEATH THE TALLROCK FOR A CLAN MEETING!

I SAY THESE WORDS BEFORE STARCLAN...

AND I SWEAR...

I'LL BE THE BEST DEPUTY I CAN POSSIBLY BE.

CHAPTER ONE

Swiftcub pounced after the vulture's shadow, but it flitted away too quickly to follow. Breathing hard, he pranced back to his pride. *I saw that bird off our territory,* he thought, delighted. *No rot-eater's going to come near Gallantpride while I'm around!*

The pride needed him to defend it, Swiftcub thought, picking up his paws and strutting around his family. Why, right now they were all half asleep, dozing and basking in the shade of the acacia trees. The most energetic thing the other lions were doing was lifting their heads to groom their nearest neighbors, or their own paws. They had no *idea* of the threat Swiftcub had just banished.

I might be only a few moons old, but my father is the strongest, bravest lion in Bravelands. And I'm going to be just like him!

"Swiftcub!"

The gentle but commanding voice snapped him out of his

dreams of glory. He came to a halt, turning and flicking his ears at the regal lioness who stood over him.

"Mother," he said, shifting on his paws.

"Why are you shouting at vultures?" Swift scolded him fondly, licking at his ears. "They're nothing but scavengers. Come on, you and your sister can play later. Right now you're supposed to be practicing hunting. And if you're going to catch anything, you'll need to keep your eyes on the prey, not on the sky!"

"Sorry, Mother." Guiltily he padded after her as she led him through the dry grass, her tail swishing. The ground rose gently, and Swiftcub had to trot to keep up. The grasses tickled his nose, and he was so focused on trying not to sneeze, he almost bumped into his mother's haunches as she crouched.

"Oops," he growled.

Valor shot him a glare. His older sister was hunched a little to the left of their mother, fully focused on their hunting practice. Valor's sleek body was low to the ground, her muscles tense; as she moved one paw forward with the utmost caution, Swiftcub tried to copy her, though it was hard to keep up on his much shorter legs. One creeping pace, then two. Then another.

I'm being very quiet, just like Valor. I'm going to be a great hunter. He slunk up alongside his mother, who remained quite still.

"There, Swiftcub," she murmured. "Do you see the burrows?"

He did, now. Ahead of the three lions, the ground rose up even higher, into a bare, sandy mound dotted with small shadowy holes. As Swiftcub watched, a small nose and whiskers poked out, testing the air. The meerkat emerged completely, stood up on its hind legs, and stared around. Satisfied, it stuck out a pink tongue and began to groom its chest, as more meerkats appeared beyond it. Growing in confidence, they scurried farther away from their burrows.

"Careful now," rumbled Swift. "They're very quick. Go!"

Swiftcub sprang forward, his little paws bounding over the ground. Still, he wasn't fast enough to outpace Valor, who was far ahead of him already. A stab of disappointment spoiled his excitement, and suddenly it was even harder to run fast, but he ran grimly after his sister.

The startled meerkats were already doubling back into their holes. Stubby tails flicked and vanished; the bigger leader, his round dark eyes glaring at the oncoming lions, was last to twist and dash underground. Valor's jaws snapped at his tail, just missing.

"Sky and stone!" the bigger cub swore, coming to a halt in a cloud of dust. She shook her head furiously and licked her jaws. "I nearly had it!"

A rumble of laughter made Swiftcub turn. His father, Gallant, stood watching them. Swiftcub couldn't help but feel the usual twinge of awe mixed in with his delight. Black-maned and huge, his sleek fur glowing golden in the sun, Gallant would have been intimidating if Swiftcub hadn't known and loved him so well. Swift rose to her paws and greeted the great lion affectionately, rubbing his maned neck with her head.

"It was a good attempt, Valor," Gallant reassured his

daughter. "What Swift said is true: meerkats are *very* hard to catch. You were so close—one day you'll be as fine a hunter as your mother." He nuzzled Swift and licked her neck.

"*I* wasn't anywhere near it," grumbled Swiftcub. "I'll never be as fast as Valor."

"Oh, you will," said Gallant. "Don't forget, Valor's a whole year older than you, my son. You're getting bigger and faster every day. Be patient!" He stepped closer, leaning in so his great tawny muzzle brushed Swiftcub's own. "That's the secret to stalking, too. Learn patience, and one day you too will be a *very* fine hunter."

"I hope so," said Swiftcub meekly.

Gallant nuzzled him. "Don't doubt yourself, my cub. You're going to be a great lion and the best kind of leader: one who keeps his own pride safe and content, but puts fear into the heart of his strongest enemy!"

That does sound good! Feeling much better, Swiftcub nodded. Gallant nipped affectionately at the tufty fur on top of his head and padded toward Valor.

Swiftcub watched him proudly. *He's right, of course. Father knows everything! And I will be a great hunter, I will. And a brave, strong leader—*

A tiny movement caught his eye, a scuttling shadow in his father's path.

A scorpion!

Barely pausing to think, Swiftcub sprang, bowling between his father's paws and almost tripping him. He skidded to a halt right in front of Gallant, snarling at the small sand-yellow scorpion. It paused, curling up its barbed tail and raising its pincers in threat.

"No, Swiftcub!" cried his father.

Swiftcub swiped his paw sideways at the creature, catching its plated shell and sending it flying into the long grass.

All four lions watched the grass, holding their breath, waiting for a furious scorpion to reemerge. But there was no stir of movement. It must have fled. Swiftcub sat back, his heart suddenly banging against his ribs.

"Skies above!" Gallant laughed. Valor gaped, and Swift dragged her cub into her paws and began to lick him roughly.

"Mother . . ." he protested.

"Honestly, Swiftcub!" she scolded him as her tongue swept across his face. "Your father might have gotten a nasty sting from that creature—but *you* could have been killed!"

"You're such an idiot, little brother," sighed Valor, but there was admiration in her eyes.

Gallant and Swift exchanged proud looks. "Swift," growled Gallant, "I do believe the time has come to give our cub his true name."

Swift nodded, her eyes shining. "Now that we know what kind of lion he is, I think you're right."

Gallant turned toward the acacia trees, his tail lashing, and gave a resounding roar.

It always amazed Swiftcub that the pride could be lying half asleep one moment and alert the very next. Almost before Gallant had finished roaring his summons, there was a rustle of grass, a crunch of paws on dry earth, and the rest of Gallantpride appeared, ears pricked and eyes bright with curiosity. Gallant huffed in greeting, and the twenty lionesses and young lions of his pride spread out in a circle around him, watching and listening intently.

Gallant looked down again at Swiftcub, who blinked and glanced away, suddenly rather shy. "Crouch down," murmured the great lion.

When he obeyed, Swiftcub felt his father's huge paw rest on his head.

"Henceforth," declared Gallant, "this cub of mine will no longer be known as Swiftcub. He faced a dangerous foe without hesitation and protected his pride. His name, now and forever, is Fearless Gallantpride."

It was done so quickly, Swiftcub felt dizzy with astonishment. *I have my name! I'm Fearless. Fearless Gallantpride!*

All around him, his whole family echoed his name, roaring their approval. Their deep cries resonated across the grasslands.

"Fearless Gallantpride!"

"Welcome, Fearless, son of Gallant!"

His heart swelled inside him. Suddenly, he knew what it was to be a full member of the pride. He had to half close his eyes and flatten his ears, he felt so buffeted by their roars of approval.

"I'll—I promise I'll live up to my name!" he managed to growl. It came out a little squeakier than he'd intended, but no lion laughed at him. They bellowed their delight even more.

"Of course you will," murmured Swift. Both she and his

father nuzzled and butted his head. "You already have, after all!"

"You certainly—" Gallant fell suddenly silent. Fearless glanced up at his father, expecting him to finish, but the great lion was standing still, his head turned toward the west. A light breeze rippled his dark mane. His nostrils flared.

The pride continued to roar, but with a new strange undertone. Fearless wrinkled his muzzle and tried to work out what was different. He began to hear it: there were new voices. In the distance, other lions were roaring.

One by one, the Gallantpride lions fell silent, looking toward the sound. Gallant paced through them, sniffing at the wind, and his pride turned to accompany him. Swift walked closest to his flank.

Overcome with curiosity, Fearless sprang toward the meerkat hill, running to its top and staring out across the plain. His view was blurred by the haze of afternoon heat, but he could see three lions approaching.

They're not from our pride, thought Fearless with a thrill of nerves. He could not take his eyes off the strangers, but he was aware that other lions had joined him at the top of the slope: Gallant, Swift, and Valor. The rest of the pride was behind them, all quite still and alert. Swift's hackles rose. Gallant's whole body looked taut, his muscles coiled.

"Who are they?" asked Fearless, gaping at the three strange lions.

"That is Titan," replied his mother. "The biggest one, there, in the center. Do you see him? He's the cub of a lion your father once drove away, and he's always hated Gallant for that. Titan's grown a fine mane, I see." Her voice became a low, savage growl. "But he was always a brute."

The three lions drew closer; they paced on, relaxed but steady, toward Gallantpride. Fearless could make out the leader clearly now: he was a huge, powerful lion, his black mane magnificent. As he came nearer, Fearless found himself shuddering. His mother was right—there was a cold light of cruelty in Titan's dark eyes. His companions looked mighty and aggressive, too; the first had shoulders as broad as a wildebeest's, while the other had a ragged ear, half of it torn away.

"Why are they in our territory?" asked Fearless in a trembling voice. He didn't yet know whether to be furious or very afraid.

Gallant spoke at last. "There's only one reason Titan would show his face here," he rumbled. "He wants to challenge me for leadership of this pride."

Don't miss these other Erin Hunter series!

SURVIVORS

Survivors
- ◯ #1: The Empty City
- ◯ #2: A Hidden Enemy
- ◯ #3: Darkness Falls
- ◯ #4: The Broken Path
- ◯ #5: The Endless Lake
- ◯ #6: Storm of Dogs

Survivors:
The Gathering Darkness
- ◯ #1: A Pack Divided
- ◯ #2: Dead of Night
- ◯ #3: Into the Shadows
- ◯ #4: Red Moon Rising
- ◯ #5: The Exile's Journey
- ◯ #6: The Final Battle

SEEKERS

Seekers
- ◯ #1: The Quest Begins
- ◯ #2: Great Bear Lake
- ◯ #3: Smoke Mountain
- ◯ #4: The Last Wilderness
- ◯ #5: Fire in the Sky
- ◯ #6: Spirits in the Stars

Seekers: Return to the Wild
- ◯ #1: Island of Shadows
- ◯ #2: The Melting Sea
- ◯ #3: River of Lost Bears
- ◯ #4: Forest of Wolves
- ◯ #5: The Burning Horizon
- ◯ #6: The Longest Day

HARPER
An Imprint of HarperCollinsPublishers

www.shelfstuff.com

www.warriorcats.com/survivors • www.warriorcats.com/seekers

ERIN HUNTER

is inspired by a fascination with the ferocity of the natural world. As well as having great respect for nature in all its forms, Erin enjoys creating rich, mythical explanations for animal behavior. She is also the author of the Survivors, Seekers, and Bravelands series.

Visit Warriors online at
www.warriorcats.com.

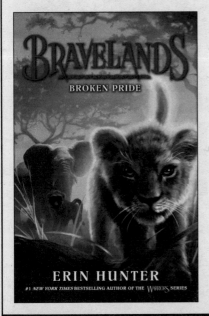

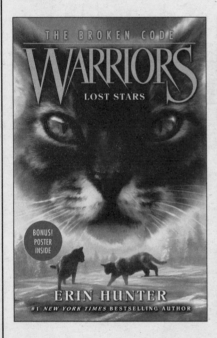
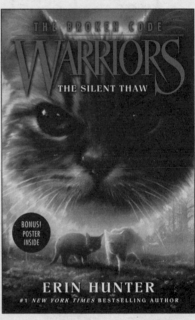

SUPER EDITIONS

- ◯ Firestar's Quest
- ◯ Bluestar's Prophecy
- ◯ SkyClan's Destiny
- ◯ Crookedstar's Promise
- ◯ Yellowfang's Secret
- ◯ Tallstar's Revenge

- ◯ Bramblestar's Storm
- ◯ Moth Flight's Vision
- ◯ Hawkwing's Journey
- ◯ Tigerheart's Shadow
- ◯ Crowfeather's Trial
- ◯ Squirrelflight's Hope

GUIDES FULL-COLOR MANGA

- ◯ Secrets of the Clans
- ◯ Cats of the Clans
- ◯ Code of the Clans
- ◯ Battles of the Clans
- ◯ Enter the Clans
- ◯ The Ultimate Guide

- ◯ Graystripe's Adventure
- ◯ Ravenpaw's Path
- ◯ SkyClan and the Stranger

EBOOKS AND NOVELLAS

The Untold Stories
- ◯ Hollyleaf's Story
- ◯ Mistystar's Omen
- ◯ Cloudstar's Journey

Tales from the Clans
- ◯ Tigerclaw's Fury
- ◯ Leafpool's Wish
- ◯ Dovewing's Silence

Shadows of the Clans
- ◯ Mapleshade's Vengeance
- ◯ Goosefeather's Curse
- ◯ Ravenpaw's Farewell

Legends of the Clans
- ◯ Spottedleaf's Heart
- ◯ Pinestar's Choice
- ◯ Thunderstar's Echo

Path of a Warrior
- ◯ Redtail's Debt
- ◯ Tawnypelt's Clan
- ◯ Shadowstar's Life

HARPER
An Imprint of HarperCollinsPublishers

www.warriorcats.com • www.shelfstuff.com